Edgar stroked his mustache thoughtfully as he studied Emilie. She was obviously furious at his manner of proposing marriage.

"Perhaps I should sweeten the affair," he continued boldly. "If you'll give me your consent, I'll promise not to consummate the marriage until you're ready."

"Sir, I don't *want* to marry you—under *any* circumstances!"

"Oh, but you *do*, Emilie," he corrected. Slowly, he moved closer, passion sparking in the brown depths of his eyes.

Emilie backed away, struggling to think of a retort, when the grandfather clock began to chime, distracting her.

Seeing her hesitation, Edgar reached out, pulling her into his arms. "Say yes, sweetheart, before the clock ceases its strokes, or I'll withdraw my offer— and take you to my bed, married or not!"

Emilie glared up into dark, laughing eyes. "Why you—"

But Edgar kissed her, silencing her protests.

At first, Emilie flailed out at him. But his kiss was breathtaking, and she was swept by an inexplicable magic—his warm chest, his hard lips mastering hers, his masculine scent making her senses swim.

And the clock chimed remorselessly, drawing her inexorably into his web!

His mouth moved to her ear. "Say yes!"

EXCITING BESTSELLERS FROM ZEBRA

PLEASURE DOME (1134, $3.75)
by Judith Liederman
Though she posed as the perfect society wife, Laina Eastman was harboring a clandestine love. And within an empire of boundless opulence, throughout the decades following World War II, Laina's love would meet the challenges of fate . . .

HERITAGE (1100, $3.75)
by Lewis Orde
Beautiful innocent Leah and her two brothers were forced by the holocaust to flee their parents' home. A courageous immigrant family, each battled for love, power and their very lifeline—their HERITAGE.

FOUR SISTERS (1048, $3.75)
by James Fritzhand
From the ghettos of Moscow to the glamor and glitter of the Winter Palace, four elegant beauties are torn between love and sorrow, danger and desire—but will forever be bound together as FOUR SISTERS.

BYGONES (1030, $3.75)
by Frank Wilkinson
Once the extraordinary Gwyneth set eyes on the handsome aristocrat Benjamin Whisten, she was determined to foster the illicit love affair that would shape three generations—and win a remarkable woman an unforgettable dynasty!

THE LION'S WAY (900, $3.75)
by Lewis Orde
An all-consuming saga that spans four generations in the life of troubled and talented David, who struggles to rise above his immigrant heritage and rise to a world of glamour, fame and success!

Available wherever paperbacks are sold, or order direct from the Publisher. Send cover price plus 50¢ per copy for mailing and handling to Zebra Books, 475 Park Avenue South, New York, N.Y. 10016. DO NOT SEND CASH.

BY
EUGENIA
RILEY

ZEBRA BOOKS
KENSINGTON PUBLISHING CORP.

ZEBRA BOOKS

are published by

KENSINGTON PUBLISHING CORP.
475 Park Avenue South
New York, N.Y. 10016

Printed in the United States of America

To Sterling—and to passion

Love
I walked through flames for you,
Shed
My heavy cloak of pride
Turned
To find it forever in the ashes.

Even then
When I came to you
Your touch
Seared me to the core—

But love
How good it hurt.

Prologue

March 13, 1836

On a rise overlooking the eastern bank of the Guadalupe River, a young girl knelt shivering in the March rain as she clutched a cross hewn from sycamore limbs. Beneath the cross, in a hastily dug grave, lay Emilie Barrett's mother and small, stillborn brother. Oblivious to the chaos of the burning village of Gonzales and the retreating Texan army, Emilie clung to her mother's grave marker. Strange, she thought numbly, that a breaking heart makes no sound. . . .

Nearby, a frail, silver-haired woman sat in a crude ox cart. Glancing about worriedly, Rosanna Barrett noted in the distance two soldiers stacking crates of gunpowder inside the doorway of the farmhouse she and Emilie had just abandoned. With a curious detachment, Rosanna watched as the two Texans set torch to the structure and it exploded into flames. The entire town was a blazing inferno—black smoke hung acridly in the wet air, obliterating the usual sweet-rot smell of river trees.

Rosanna turned from the hysteria surrounding her

and again pleaded to Emilie, "Please, child, hasten—most everyone else has gone. Just heard tell Deaf Smith spied General Sesma approaching from San Antón. Hurry, now, or we'll be butchered like your brave daddy at the Alamo!"

But Rosanna Barrett's words fell upon her granddaughter's seemingly deaf ears. Only the word "daddy" penetrated Emilie's cottony brain. "Too much . . ." she whispered, to no one.

The news of Matthew Barrett's death had been too much for sixteen-year-old Emilie and her mother. As the cold, quiet rain drenched Emilie, she once again relived the horror of the afternoon several days past when Susannah Dickerson had come to the village with Sam Houston's scouts, confirming reports of the fall of the Alamo. Herself widowed by the slaughter, Mrs. Dickerson had informed two dozen of the townswomen of the fate of their men. Emilie remembered the piteous wails of grief. Her own mother, so silent, simply slipped to the ground in a faint. But that was only the beginning of the nightmare, for Emilie then watched in horror as her mother went into labor with the tiny brother she had carried almost to term, after so many miscarriages. After the babe was delivered dead, Emilie cowered nearby in deepening shock as her mother, now beyond all caring, bled to death in the cold, miserable farmhouse. The grim vignette ended, in an effusion of blood, everywhere blood. . . .

"Madam, General Houston has ordered all citizens evacuated! Get this cart rolling!" someone shouted.

At the sound of this commanding voice, Emilie glanced up through the steady rain to see a soldier clad in black approaching on a magnificent black Arabian. He halted his mount close to Rosanna

Barrett's wagon, and, as the majestic beast whinnied and tapped the muddy ground impatiently, he again urged the old woman to be off. "Do you wish to be murdered by the Santannistas where you sit, madam?"

"Oh, no, sir!" Rosanna protested in a thin, near-hysterical voice, as she viewed the hatless young man dressed in muddied boots, tight breeches, and a soaked broadcloth jacket. "It's my granddaughter, sir. She's taken leave of her senses and won't leave her dead mother."

Sweeping rain from his brow, the soldier turned to look at Emilie, who by this time had again forgotten her surroundings as she moaned and clutched the cross like a drowning woman clinging to a bit of flotsam. Grimacing, the tall, powerfully-built Texan dismounted and drew near the grandmother. "I'm Captain Edgar Ashland, madam. What is the girl's name?" he inquired gently.

"Emilie, sir."

Taking Rosanna's hand, the soldier whispered, "Be along your way, then, old woman. I'll see that Emilie joins you shortly."

Rosanna opened her mouth to protest, but the soldier said simply, "I promise," and squeezed her hand.

The old woman sighed heavily. "Her life's in your hands, then, sir. God bless you!" she cried, giving rein to the oxen.

The soldier watched the Barrett wagon, with its store of pitiful, precious possessions, lumber off to join the band of fleeing soldiers and citizens. Then he tied his horse Apollyon to a nearby cottonwood, and approached the small, drenched form of Emilie Barrett.

In his twenty-eight years, Edgar Ashland could not

remember seeing a sight more piteous than the young girl shivering in the black mud. Kneeling, he laid a hand on her shoulder, then addressed her gently. "Emilie?"

When she did not reply, he shook her slightly and repeated her name. The girl turned. As she peered up at him with sad eyes that were a bright crystal blue, Edgar sharply drew in his breath, feeling astonished, awed. Despite the girl's gold-blonde hair, the eyes were shaded by long, black lashes, causing them to dominate her beautifully-proportioned face.

A normally gruff man, Edgar found the young girl moved him to great gentleness. His eyes moved down her trembling figure, stopped at the firm young breasts outlined by the soaked, thin cloth of her dress. Protectively, he reached out, pulled the edges of her wool shawl tightly about her.

"Emilie, dear," he spoke a bit raggedly, spellbound by her eyes, "we must leave, now. The Santannistas will soon be upon us."

Vaguely, Emilie heard him. She shivered as thunder clapped overhead. "Sa-tan," she murmured brokenly, keenly regarding the swarthy Texan. Was this man, with the dark hair and eyes and fiercely handsome face, the devil, here to tempt her away from the land of the living? Or was she already dead? Was this hell?

"No, little one," Edgar replied patiently, "not Satan. The Mexicans."

The Mexicans! The war! Emilie gasped as she remembered, and fresh waves of pain assaulted her. Seeing her distress, Edgar pulled her into his arms. She clung to him, now sobbing.

"Poor darling, poor babe," he soothed, stroking her long, golden hair.

Damn all wars, Edgar thought bitterly, holding

Emilie close. Orders had been given by General Houston—to evacuate citizens, destroy stockpiled munitions, burn structures that might provide shelter for the enemy. But those simple directives involved real people, their homes and lives . . . as real as the pathetic young girl in his arms now.

Hearing a distant explosion, Edgar stood, picked up Emilie and sloshed toward Apollyon. The girl lay meekly in his arms until he got to the horse, then suddenly, something snapped in her cloudy mind. My God, she thought hysterically, this madman is taking me away from my mother! She began kicking and screaming, then bit the Texan on the arm so savagely that he dropped her into the mud and bellowed in pain.

"What the hell!" he yelled, his dark features twisting in rage, all his sympathy for the girl vanishing.

Edgar Ashland was not a man to be crossed.

But Emilie had already scrambled off toward her mother's grave. Furious, Edgar pursued her, grabbing the back of her gray, homespun dress, which gave with a rending tear.

Emilie spun about to face Edgar, her eyes flashing blue fire. Crazed with grief, she showed no fear of the towering Texan who wore a Bowie knife sheathed to his hip, a pistol tucked in his belt. "How dare you touch me!" she ranted. "Be gone, you—you loathsome beast! Leave me to my grief!"

Edgar let out a low whistle. "So the kitten has a scathing tongue as well as sharp teeth," he remarked, his voice dangerously calm as he rubbed his wounded arm.

Then, in one swift movement, he grabbed Emilie's mane of blonde hair, making her cry out at the pain. Dragging her roughly into his arms, he pulled her head back, his hands twisting her hair as he forced her to look up into his rage-blackened eyes.

"If I left you, you ungrateful chit," he began, his harsh words splintering the air, "it would not be to your grief but to the tender mercies of the Mexicans. Do you know what they would do to you, Emilie? Were it not for your delicate age and general uncomeliness, I would at this moment show you in detail!"

Suddenly, the soldier again yelled in pain, as Emilie kicked him forcefully in the shin. He grabbed his calf, cursing as she ran off. He quickly hobbled after her, caught her under a sycamore tree, pinned her squirming body against the smooth trunk.

For a moment, Edgar glared down at her, his face hard, a slight quiver in his jaw betraying the fury buried beneath his features. Emilie struggled against him, horrified to have a man's muscular body pressed against hers so intimately.

Her movements, though guileless, sent a spark of desire through Edgar Ashland, and he quickly decided how he would vent his anger. "Put your mark on me, will you? Then I'll have mine on you, sweetheart!"

Emilie opened her mouth in astonishment, just as Edgar's lips landed squarely on her own. She fought like a cornered wildcat, but her struggles seemed meaningless to the strong soldier.

Indeed, Edgar hardly noticed the fingernails clawing at his chest—he was not even conscious that the rain had stopped—for he found himself lost in the sweetness of the girl's mouth, wanting to explore thoroughly her innocent young body. His hands moved to her breasts; his senses swam. He wanted to take this girl—here, now! Hell—he might be dead tomorrow! Why not pull her to the ground, know a

12

bit of heaven while he could?

Then he tasted her tears in his mouth and came to, her muffled sobs shaking him deeply. He backed off. Jesus, what had he done? She was practically a child!

He warily eyed her tear-streaked, furious face, her heaving bosom. "Girl, you mustn't vex me so," he chided. "I lost control—"

"You monster!" Emilie shrieked, stumbling forward and slapping him full across the face.

For a moment, Edgar stood motionless, stunned. Then, eyes wild, he jumped backwards. "Oh, no you don't!" he cried, dodging Emilie's well-aimed foot.

Emilie dived for Edgar.

Edgar grabbd her. "Enough!" he roared. Features grim, he dragged the struggling girl to Apollyon. Mounting, he hoisted her upon the horse. When Emilie refused to abandon her kicking and screaming, he growled, "Be damned!" and threw her face-down across the saddle.

Emilie screamed in impotent fury as Edgar snapped the riding crop, stinging both the horse and her thigh. Apollyon lurched forward, and soon Emilie fell limply acquiescent, exhausted by the painful position and the rush of blood to her face.

As Apollyon raced across the desolate, muddy prairie, silent tears flew from Emilie's eyes at the pain and indignity of her position, with her face forced against the Texan's muscular thigh, her skirts flying in the wind, the saddle horn grinding relentlessly into her belly. The journey by horseback was mercifully brief, for Edgar soon caught up with the Barrett wagon and literally threw the girl into a pile of bedding at the rear of the cart. Humiliated, Emilie crawled under a blanket, as Rosanna Barrett joyously thanked the Texan for her return.

"You're welcome to her," Edgar replied dryly.

13

"A more ungrateful child I've never seen! I trust she'll recover her senses in a day or two."

"The girl is strong—her mind will mend," Rosanna agreed, taking the reins in hand. "God's blessings to you, sir. Lord knows, I'd never have moved her myself. Bad spoilt she was by her mother. An only child, she is, and mighty stubborn."

"Indeed, madam," Edgar agreed. "If she tries to bolt on you, send word to me, and I'll have her tied to the wagon!"

Upon hearing these callous words, Emilie sprang up from the back of the cart, glaring at the Texan. "God damn you for taking me from my mother!" she hissed convulsively. "If it takes my last breath, I'll see you in hell for what you did to me, sir!"

The handsome soldier smiled broadly. "And the top of the morning of you, too, miss," he mocked. He winked at Rosanna. "I see she's recovered already."

Edgar Ashland laid crop to his horse, grinning to himself as Apollyon raced down the trail. What a hellcat the girl was! Someday, it might be interesting to catch up with her, he mused. Once grown, would she cry if he kissed her? He thought not.

If she ever grew up. If, indeed, they ever got the damn Mexicans off their backs!

Edgar frowned, pushing the girl from his thoughts, turning his mind to his forthcoming meeting with Sam Houston to discuss his next scouting assignment. . . .

Framed by the crimson afterglow of the burning village, the Barrett wagon followed the other shivering settlers across the dreary Texas landscape. In the back of the cart, Emilie wept bitterly, her young mind focusing all her hatred and hurt upon the Texan who had torn her from oblivion and thrown her back into the anguished arms of the living. . . .

Back in Gonzales, a small detachment of Houston's ragtag Texas Revolutionary Army remained, grunting and groaning as they shoved the twin cannon too heavy for transport into the Guadalupe River. Then, they gathered their torches, loaded their wagons and left, satisfied that the Santannistas would find no succor in Gonzales. As one of the carts ascended the rise overlooking the eastern bank of the river, it ripped past a freshly-filled grave, felling the sycamore cross, grinding it into the bottomless mud.

Book One

Chapter One

Sunshine sifted through the dusty window on silken strands, bathing the bed where Emilie Barrett lay sleeping. Half-wakening, the twenty-one-year-old girl drew her hand across her face, as if to brush the brightness away. But March's radiance refused to fade, and soon the girl stretched and yawned, greeting the crisp, cool day. A languid smile curved her pink mouth at the sound of a nearby rooster's crowing.

With a sudden, jolting burst of memory, Emilie sat up in bed. In her lethargic state, she had forgotten her anguish, and now it cut her again with razor sureness. Granny Rose . . . dead. Had it been only a week since her grandmother had been laid in a grave at the end of Main Street? Had it been just eight days since she last wiped the burning brow of the old woman? Poor Grandmother—the season's first victim of the hated Yellow Jack. Fresh tears stung Emilie's eyes at the memory, and she hastily got out of bed, straightening the quilted coverlet.

Emilie drew her wrapper around her eyelet gown and went to the window. Fingering the lace-edged gingham curtain, she looked out upon the muddy

16

streets of Houston. Ramshackle shacks squatted in heaps upon the black mud, interrupted only by a few elegant grogshops. Vendors, with their fruits and wares, were already clamoring about.

Emilie realized she felt well-rested, for once. The night had been quiet—no drunken cowboys shooting up the town. Was order finally coming to this dissolute community?

Perhaps the coming of permanent churches had stimulated the decline of lawlessness. Emilie glanced at the new John Calvin Presbyterian church down the street, the city's first permanent edifice. A white frame stanchion of respectability in a sea of debauchery, it stood with doors firmly ajar, as if in supplication to the heathen masses. Only three days past, the structure had opened its doors for the first time. "Oh, Grandmother, could you have seen that day," Emilie murmured wistfully.

Emilie turned from the window and went to the dresser to begin her toilette. She sighed as she drew the brush through her bright gold tresses. "What am I to do?" she asked the empty room.

Grandmother had provided for them through her skills as a seamstress, even buying this small but elegant house. She had trained her granddaughter faithfully, and Emilie had learned to sew simple garments. But she lacked the old woman's genius with a needle and thread. She did have three years of training at Houston Women's Seminary, qualifying her to teach school, but schools were few and far between on the rugged frontier. Of course, girls were always needed in the saloons and brothels . . . she shuddered at the thought.

At least she was safe and had a roof over her head. Houston seemed a haven of respite compared with the experiences she and Granny suffered five years

17

earlier during the War for Independence. Drawing a pink satin ribbon through the curls at the nape of her neck, Emilie remembered their harrowing escape from Gonzales and the soldier who had treated her so callously. What was his name? Grandmother had mentioned it several times, but she had forgotten. Whoever he was, he was probably rotting in hell, she reasoned with satisfaction. Many had been killed in the war. But she was secure now, unlike those months in '36 when they and the other settlers had fled the Santannistas like hunted animals, hiding, foraging for food where they could. Now she lived in the proud Republic of Texas, freed from the treachery of the Mexicans.

A sharp knock at the front door interrupted Emilie's reverie. Who would be calling this early? she wondered. Perhaps they would leave if ignored.

"Miss Emilie, open up, please!" a voice shouted from the porch.

Emilie recognized the voice of Padraic O'Brien, president of the Bank of the Republic. What would he be wanting of her at this hour? It seemed she had no choice but to let him in, for he was now banging upon the door. Frowning, Emilie hurriedly donned a pink muslin dress, struggling with the buttons as she rushed into the parlor. Her foot caught a splinter from the rough puncheon floor, and she cursed as she pulled out the fragment.

Throwing open the door, she snapped, "What is the meaning of this intrusion, sir?"

Portly and balding, Paddy O'Brien stepped into the parlor. Tossing his beaver hat upon the settee, he said, "Forgive me for banging, lass. I thought you were still abed." Turning to the door, he called out, "Come along, David, me boy!"

Emilie turned to the porch to notice a slim young

18

man dressed in black frock coat and trousers. For a moment, the gentleman stared at her, a flush heating his face. Then he cleared his throat nervously and entreated, "By your leave, miss."

Emilie found herself staring into the vivid blue eyes of a young man who appeared to be in his early twenties. "You may as well enter," she conceded.

The tall gentleman ducked his blonde head through the doorway. Emilie spun about to confront the banker. "Well, sir? State your business."

The bulky man had the grace to look embarrassed as he jammed his thumbs into the pockets of his overstuffed vest. "Lass," he chided softly, "you know my business."

"I—know nothing of the kind!"

The banker shifted his weight uncomfortably. "Miss Emilie, I told your granny three weeks ago that I can't be giving you more time—"

"My grandmother—is dead," Emilie interrupted, glowering at him with diamond-hard eyes.

"Aye, and I'm sorry, lass," the banker replied sincerely. "But that doesn't change things. I'm just a simple businessman, lass, and I can't be giving you more time—"

"Time!" Emilie hissed in exasperation. "Time for *what?*"

A sticky silence followed. Then O'Brien's young companion protested, "See, here, man, you gave me no indication the place was occupied."

"It shan't be for long, sir," the banker replied. Then, more gently, he said to Emilie, "Lass, didn't you know your granny was indebted to me?"

"No! What on earth are you talking about?"

The banker sighed, stroking his handlebar mustache thoughtfully. "Very well, Miss Emilie. I'll show you."

Emilie's eyes narrowed as O'Brien drew a rolled parchment from the pocket of his frock coat. "Tis not a pleasant task I'm about today," he continued, handing Emilie the coiled document. "But this note has been due for well over a month, lass, and if you haven't the coin to buy it, I'm afraid you must leave."

"Leave?" Emilie asked, her eyes wide with disbelief as she took the document.

Emilie sank upon the settee, uncoiling the parchment with trembling hands. Her future halted abruptly as she read the inscribed words, "Due this first day of February, 1841 . . . the sum of three hundred dollars." She shuddered as she read the description listing the house as collateral. At the bottom of the page was her grandmother's familiar, scratchy signature.

Emilie's heart thudded. Three hundred dollars—and well over a month overdue! It might as well be three thousand! The few United States gold coins she possessed could not begin to repay the debt, and their collection of Texas-issue Redbacks was virtually worthless. Oh, why hadn't Grandmother told her of the debt, prepared her for this? She had assumed their financial situation sound, yet evidently Rosanna had mortgaged their home heavily in order for them to survive.

Emilie looked up in despair, handing O'Brien the parchment. "It seems the house is yours, sir," she said woodenly.

The banker cleared his throat, replacing the document in his pocket. "Aye, lass, and I'm sorry." Turning to his companion, he announced, "This is Mr. David Ashland, the possible future owner of this cottage. Mr. Ashland makes frequent trips to Houston in supplying his plantation, and he finds the accommodations at the Capitol Hotel rather—er—lacking.''

Emilie, ignoring both men, did not see the sympathy in David Ashland's eyes. "Come along, David, me boy," O'Brien continued nervously. "Let's have a look at the place."

"Is that agreeable to you, miss?" David Ashland inquired shyly.

"It doesn't matter," Emilie muttered.

As the two men left the room, Emilie felt tears stinging her eyes. Yet her mind was curiously blank as snatches of conversation drifted past her ears from the other room. "Real feather bed . . . windows of glass, a rarity in this town."

The two men returned to the parlor. "There be a kitchen across the dog run which we'll see directly," O'Brien said. "Fine furniture in the parlor, here, too. Nice old rocker, this," he concluded, pushing Granny's Windsor rocker into motion.

Emilie sprang up from the settee, the full impact of her situation dawning upon her. "You'll not have my grandmother's rocker!" she exclaimed. As she firmly grasped the spindle back of the chair, a sudden memory of cold, wet sycamore limbs assaulted her senses. Grandmother's cherished rocker, lovingly brought with the family from Georgia, preciously guarded through the nightmare flight from Gonzales, creaking with memories of happier years . . . Emilie regarded the two men coldly—no, she would not let them take it from her!

Seeing Emilie's outrage, O'Brien threw his arms wide in exasperation. "Very well, lass, take the rocker," he conceded, then added pointedly, "take anything you can carry. But mark my words, Miss Emilie. You must leave."

Breaking his long silence, David Ashland asked

21

O'Brien, "But what is the girl to do, man? You can't simply throw her out!"

The banker shrugged. Then, weakening under David Ashland's glare, he turned, eyeing Emilie speculatively. He grinned. "Aye, she's too pretty a piece to throw out."

O'Brien went to Emilie, laying a bulky arm across her shoulders. She shrank from his heavy grasp and the rank odor of his flesh, but he held her tightly. "Never fear, mavournin," he whispered confidentially, "Paddy O'Brien will take care of you. I'm in tight with Nell Dooley at the Mansion Hotel, and she's always needing fetching gals like you."

With a startled cry, Emilie threw off O'Brien's grasp. Meanwhile, David Ashland strode angrily toward the banker, snapping, "Guard your tongue, man, before I cut it out!"

O'Brien grinned slyly, turning to his young companion. "Come, now, Mr. Ashland, the lass could suffer a much worse fate than becoming one of Nellie's girls. Why the outrage, me boy? Would you be preferring she offer herself with the house?"

It happened so suddenly that Emilie's head spun. David Ashland grabbed the banker by his frock coat collar, both hands twisting the brown fabric, causing the bulky man to sputter and choke in fear. "Get out, you blackguard!" David stormed, his eyes sparkling with cold anger. "The house—is sold! You'll have the money in your grasping hands by day's end! Now—may I suggest you leave, sir, while you still have the ability!"

David released O'Brien suddenly, and the older man tottered, struggling to keep his balance. Then the banker hastily grabbed his hat and hurried toward the door. But as he turned the knob, he looked back, glaring at both of them. "Jesus, Mr.

Ashland! I gave the wench over a month! I'm just a simple business—"

David took a quick step toward O'Brien, and the older man scurried out, slamming the door.

Once the two of them were alone, David Ashland shifted uncomfortably from foot to foot. "I—I—" he faltered. "Forgive me, miss. I've been told I've inherited my uncle's temper. I hope I didn't frighten you, but that man—was not a gentleman!"

Emilie stood firmly clasping a spindle of Rosanna's rocker, her eyes downcast. "Thank you for—uh, seeing Mr. O'Brien out," she said, smiling weakly.

Slowly, David approached Rosanna's rocker, then gingerly, he fingered the polished mahogany. He was perilously close to Emilie now, so close that she caught the fresh scent of his shaving soap. But she felt no alarm. She looked up at him. For a moment bright cerulean eyes met those of crystal blue, then David hastily glanced off.

"You're not to worry, miss," he assured her. "No one shall take this rocker, or throw you out of your home. You're to have all the time you need to settle your affairs."

Emilie, lowering dark eyelashes, whispered, "Thank you, sir." How could she tell him there was nothing to settle, nowhere to go?

David looked about nervously. "I'll see to the matter of the house, then, before that vulture bothers you again."

Emilie nodded, smiling wanly. After all, it wasn't Mr. Ashland's fault. He simply wished to purchase a home to use during business trips to Houston.

David approached the door. Before leaving, he turned and regarded Emilie's downcast face. For a moment, she felt he was going to speak, but instead, quietly, he left.

Emilie sat down in her grandmother's rocker, the harsh reality of the banker's visit splintering her brain. The house was no longer hers. She had nothing. True, the future owner was a kind young man, but he owed her naught. Was she to be cast upon the streets, then, forced to seek her livelihood in the saloons and gaming houses of the city? She shivered, remembering the visits to their home of several notorious prostitutes. Although a practicing Christian, Rosanna had sewn for some of the city's most famous courtesans. "Money's all the same to me," the old woman had quipped practically. Emilie remembered the tawdry satin gowns, the painted faces, the cheap perfumes. . . . Was such to be her lot?

"Oh, Grandmother!" she whispered to the empty room. "What is to become of me?"

David Ashland strode into the front hall of the Capitol Hotel. Shivering, he hurried to the iron stove. The bright spring day had turned cold, with a norther blowing in.

"Howdy, mister," said the cowboy sharing the stove with him.

David narrowly regarded the grizzly, blanket-coated man next to him. "Good afternoon, sir," he replied stiffly, backing off a bit from the manure smell exuding from his filthy companion.

The cowboy grinned, displaying brown-stained, gapped teeth. "Ain't nothin' like a mean Texas wind to freeze a man's ass to granite, eh, mister? I'm gittin' me a feisty piece to heat the sheets tonight. How 'bout you, mister?" The jaundice-eyed cowboy expectorated a generous portion of tobacco juice, narrowly missing David's foot.

24

David hastily stepped back. "Good day, sir," he returned coldly.

David entered the parlor, relieved to find it deserted. He sat in a wing chair near the crackling fire, holding his hands out. Lord, he would be glad to leave Houston! Although the Capitol boasted a separate parlor and dining room for the gentry, he was sick of running into riffraff like the cowboy in the front hall. He missed Brazos Bend—the elegance, the simplicity. And his uncle needed him.

Yet someone else needed him—Emilie Barrett. David leaned back in his chair, pulled the coiled deed to the Barrett house from the pocket of his frock coat. He had bought the house, but now, what was he going to do about the girl?

He could, of course, give her the deed. The money was meaningless—there was plenty in the accounts. But would giving her the house solve anything? The girl would still be alone in Houston, subject to the whims of ruffians like the odious creature in the hallway.

Frowning, David returned the deed to his pocket. How could he leave the girl here? Strong, yet vulnerable, she had struck a responsive chord deep inside him.

How lovely she was! he thought wistfully. Her face was that of an angel—delicate nose, high cheekbones, diamond blue eyes framed by black lashes. She was a bit taller than most women he knew, and carried herself with great grace.

Yes, she was a lady—with pride, dignity, beauty. And the gentleman in him could not abandon a lady in trouble.

Suddenly, David snapped his fingers. He could take Emilie to Brazos Bend! Then, he frowned. How did one go about asking a refined young woman to

25

live with two men on an isolated cotton plantation?

More specifically, how could he ask her to live in the same house with Uncle Edgar? David shook his head grimly. His uncle could be very intimidating!

Though things might not be so bad, he mused. Lately he had seen hope—he had recognized signs that his uncle was coming out of his retreat from the world. The man was talking more—he now laughed on occasion, and David saw traces of the old self-assured cynicism. If Emilie could be persuaded to come to the plantation, her bright presence might really cheer up Uncle Edgar. David hoped she could help, for it killed him to see his uncle confine himself at home, neglecting old friends, even Sam Houston. Perhaps Emilie might reestablish social activities at Brazos Bend.

At least he could assure the girl that she would not be unchaperoned at the plantation. After all, there was the housekeeper, and soon Maria would return.

"Maria!" David whispered aloud, his eyes alive and eager as he gazed into the flames.

Maria! Of course, why hadn't he thought of the girl? She might be the key to it all!

Chapter Two

The next day, Emilie answered the door to find Mr. David Ashland on her porch. In cheerful defiance of the muddy streets, the young man was dressed in a fawn frock coat, his cream-colored trousers tucked into shiny brown boots.

"Good morning, Miss Emilie. Might I have a word with you?"

"Of course," Emilie rejoined wearily. Although the sight of the handsome man was pleasing to Emilie's senses, she was exhausted after a sleepless night, and couldn't resist adding, rather bitterly, "I take it the house is yours, now, anyway."

David Ashland flushed uncomfortably as he entered the parlor. "You're not to fret yourself about that, miss."

Emilie gestured to the settee. "Please sit, sir," she said, herself taking seat in Rosanna's rocker and smoothing her blue gingham skirts about her.

David spoke awkwardly from his perch across the room. "You look uncommonly pretty today, my dea—I mean, Miss Emilie."

27

Emilie flashed him a quick, guileless smile. "Please state your business, sir."

A bit nervously, David rose and walked to the front window. "It has occurred to me, Miss Emilie, that I might have a solution to your—er—situation."

"Indeed, sir?"

David's fingers tapped the window sill. "Now that I have purchased your home, it occurs to me that you are in need of a protector." He turned to her, blurted, "What I mean is—Emilie, how would you like to come live with us at Brazos Bend?"

"I beg your pardon, sir?" came the stiff reply.

David hastily continued, "At Brazos Bend, where I live with my uncle, we've a young woman of seventeen who could use your companionship and guidance."

Emilie's features softened at David's statement, but she was silent, considering his words carefully.

David cleared his throat and rushed on. "Actually, Maria is away at the moment, but soon she'll be home to stay. The girl is an orphan who has lived in our home for the past six years. I've been gone much of that time and my uncle—well, my uncle prefers his own company. What I'm trying to say is that Maria has been sadly neglected—in fact, she still speaks Spanish much of the time."

"I see," Emilie murmured, her brow puckered. "You say the girl's away right now?"

Nodding, David bit his lip. "I've become most concerned about the girl—how isolated, how withdrawn she is. So a few months ago, I made arrangements to enroll Maria in an excellent girls' boarding school in Nacogdoches. In early January, I took the girl there. However—" David shifted his weight uncomfortably, "right before I left for Houston, I received a letter from the school's

28

headmistress. It seems Maria has been—dismissed."

Emilie strained forward in her chair. "Dismissed? But why?"

David's expression grew guarded, and he replied enigmatically, "Emilie, I do need your help with the girl."

There was an undercurrent of desperation in David's voice which was both compelling and distressing to Emilie. Leaning back, she asked carefully, "Then, sir, if I understand you correctly, you are offering me a position as companion to this young lady?"

David Ashland strode forward, pulled a ladder-back chair up close to Emilie, and sat down. "No, Emilie, I am not offering you a post as companion," he corrected gently. "I am offering you a place in our family."

Emilie's finely-arched brows shot up. "But why, sir?"

David swept a blonde curl from his forehead. "I really can't explain it, Emilie. Suffice it to say that as a gentleman I feel responsible towards you." As if to prove his point, David pulled the deed from the pocket of his coat. "You may have the house back, Emilie, if you so desire. But think it over carefully, my dear. Houston's a wild, dangerous town. Don't you think you'd be better off living with a family, in a proper, elegant environment?"

Staring at the deed in David Ashland's hand, Emilie Barrett blinked back a tear. The young man was so dear, so kind. "You mean you would give me back the house?" she whispered incredulously. "But surely, sir, if you bought it, you must have need of it yourself."

"Aye, I do visit Houston on business," David admitted. "But that is a minor problem, Emilie.

What we are discussing here is *your* future, in what direction *you* should best proceed. And I think you're better off at Brazos Bend."

Emilie bit her lip. "But sir, this arrangement could hardly be permanent—"

"And why not?" David countered. "Our home is certainly permanent. Besides, you may later decide to marry, have a family of your own."

Emilie smiled tremulously. "Your arguments are well-taken, sir, and I am touched by your kindness. But—"

"Yes?" David asked, leaning forward eagerly.

"Are you sure I'll be welcomed at this—Brazos Bend? The young girl you spoke of may not want a companion. And you say your uncle prefers his own company—"

"Bosh!" David retorted, waving her off. "Brazos Bend needs a woman's touch, Emilie."

Emilie looked at David admiringly. How tempting his proposal was! Yet she had her pride. "I don't want your charity, sir," she said, staring at her lap.

David shook his head firmly. "Not so, Emilie. It is *you* who will favor us, by being a friend to Maria, by adding something very special and lovely to all our lives." Studying the mixture of emotion on Emilie's downcast face, he added, "But there's no rush, dear. I'll be in Houston for another week, so do think it over."

Emilie looked up with relief. "Aye, sir, I shall. Your offer is quite generous, but it is rather sudden. May I give you my answer in a few days?"

"Of course."

Emilie stood, escorted David Ashland to the door. After she thanked him for his visit, he asked, rather awkwardly, "Would it be acceptable to you if I check on your welfare frequently while I'm in town, Emilie?"

Emilie smiled, a warm smile which lit her bright blue eyes. "Sir, it would be my pleasure."

Chapter Three

March 12, 1841

The shiny black open carriage glided effortlessly across the wildflower-carpeted Texas prairie. Overhead, the sun hung brightly at midday. Emilie, sitting next to David, drank in the beauty of the cool spring day. The clip-clop of horse hooves upon the blossom-scented air soothed her as she thought of the events of the past week.

Emilie had decided to accompany David Ashland to Brazos Bend. Her decision had been hastened by a couple of drunken cowboys—four nights previous, Emilie awakened to hear much clatter out on the porch. Listening in deepening dread, she heard two men stumbling about and cursing as they fought over which one would "git the Barrett gal." Emilie's heart had pounded frantically, as she realized the two must have heard she was living alone.

Luckily for Emilie, a third companion—obviously more sober—had come up and urged the two to accompany him to Nell Dooley's place. The three sauntered off amicably, but Emilie shook in fear all through the night.

The next day, Emilie told David of the incident. He alerted the sheriff, and insisted upon sleeping on a cot in the kitchen, across the dog-run porch from the rest of the house. Emilie had felt sorry for him—having to sleep in the cramped quarters of the kitchen for three nights in a row—but she knew it would hardly be proper for her to offer him Granny's old room.

Of course, after the cowboy incident, David had found it unthinkable that Emilie remain in Houston alone, and Emilie reluctantly conceded that he was right. Poor David—he must be exhausted! she now thought. Things had been so rushed the past three days, with the gathering of supplies, the finding of a caretaker for the Houston house, the frantic packing, that Emilie had scarcely gotten better acquainted with the young man sitting beside her. She studied him now, and found he looked handsome, even earthy, in his white broadcloth shirt and dark brown trousers. She admired his collar-length wheat-blonde hair, the thin but handsome face, the lean brown hands firmly grasping the reins. All Emilie's hopes—indeed, her life—lay in those hands now.

Putting her thoughts aside, Emilie glanced back at the oxen-drawn wagon that trailed behind them. In the cart lay supplies for the plantation where David lived with his uncle. A black lad drove the oxen relentlessly, shouting foreign commands which the yoke of oxen seemed readily to understand. Also in the wagon was Emilie's trunk, filled with household linens, the eyelet and lace-trimmed lingerie and satin wedding dress Granny Rose had sewn for her three years past. "A young lady needs to be prepared," Grandmother had pronounced solemnly. Emilie again glanced at David, remembered his words, "You may later decide to marry. . . ." Would she ever wear the dress?

Emilie had never had a serious beau, and, at twenty one, was often teased by her girlfriends about being "an old maid." She remembered the few young men from their church who had come to call upon her. Usually, they came once and did not return. Grandmother had scolded, "You put them off with your manner, child." But Emilie could not help it—she had felt coldly toward men since her experience with the soldier at Gonzales.

But David was beginning to restore her faith. Ever since meeting him, she had expected the spell to end—for David to vanish, or, worse yet, to take possession of the house and throw her out. But he did nothing of the kind. In every way, he personified the solicitous hero of a young girl's dreams.

Things could not have turned out better. She had gained a true friend, indeed, a saviour, in David Ashland, and soon she would have a new home, a new family.

Emilie's entire life had assumed a dreamlike quality. Before leaving Houston, David had insisted upon buying her precious lengths of silk, gingham, calico and dimity. He had smothered her protests ("You're a member of the family, now, Emilie!") and bought her satin slippers and matching reticules, kid walking shoes, sunbonnets and poke bonnets. He had even apologized that suitable ready-made dresses were not available. She had laughed, assuring him that she was competent with a needle and thread. As if to prove just that, she had hastily sewn the red and yellow calico traveling frock she now wore, along with bright saffron sunbonnet. She felt a bit guilty purchasing such finery and traipsing off with David so soon after her grandmother's funeral, but she knew the practical Granny Rose would not wish her to mourn, and had firmly detested black.

Fortunately, the heavens seemed to approve their journey, Emilie noted to herself. Usually in March, the rain was ceaseless along the coastal prairie, causing all the bayous to overflow and flood the roads. But spring had come earlier and milder than usual—it had not rained for over a week, and their trip since leaving Houston several hours before had been uneventful, aside from having to dodge an occasional pothole or tree stump.

Hearing a curse from the wagon behind them, Emilie broke the long silence between her and David. "Are there many slaves at Brazos Bend?"

"About fifty," David replied, clucking to the horses. "We have over two thousand acres planted in cotton. Uncle runs the plantation quite efficiently. But I wish something could be done to help him—"

"Oh?" Emilie prompted, her curiosity piqued.

For a moment, David was awkwardly silent, then he shrugged, as if to get on with an unpleasant task. "I might as well warn you, Emilie, that Uncle Edgar is not—well, not like us. For the past five years, he has stayed at Brazos Bend, showing no interest in the outside world."

"Indeed?" Emilie questioned. She bit her lip. "He's not—well, not demented, is he?"

"No, of course not, Emilie," David quickly replied. "To all appearances, he's normal. But he's given up a promising political career and all his friends. It's quite sad."

"Oh, dear," Emilie said, as if to herself. Then, looking up quickly, she asked David, "Are you *sure* I'll be welcome?"

David nodded. "You must not concern yourself with that, my dear. The estate is half mine. My uncle is hardly going to throw you out."

Despite David's words of reassurance, Emilie felt

threatened by his odd relative. "What is the reason for your uncle's—behavior?"

David sighed. "Of that, I can tell you little. Only that Uncle has suffered the deepest torment. A few years after our family came over from England, he found my mother and father slaughtered by the Cherokees. My mother was killed—rather slowly. Uncle and I were out fishing when it happened, you see—" David finished lamely.

Emilie touched his arm. "Oh, David, I'm so sorry!" she soothed, her own concerns vanishing as she saw David's anguish.

David clenched his jaw and continued, "But Uncle and I got on fine. That was in '33, when I was a boy of thirteen. Uncle became a father to me and took charge of the estate, making it the most successful cotton plantation on the upper Brazos. Things would be fine, even now, were it not for Olivia, and the babes. . . ." David's voice drifted off, his countenance grim.

"Olivia? The babes?" Emilie echoed in confusion.

"Uncle married Olivia Rice in '34. When he came home after the Battle of San Jacinto in '36, he and Olivia quarrelled. She fled with their twin infant sons. Uncle gave chase, and Olivia lost control of the carriage, which—which careened into the Brazos." David paused, then whispered grimly, "The Brazos was raging at flood stage—it was—was hopeless."

David turned away, his hands vigorously working the reins. Emilie's sympathies were fully engaged now. No wonder David's uncle was a recluse—surely there was no describing the man's pain. She thought she had suffered, but to lose a beloved wife, two precious babes, all in one fell blow. . . . And poor, dear David. Olivia must have been like a mother to him during his adolescent years.

"Do you know why they quarrelled—your uncle and Olivia?"

David's eyes darted sharply to Emilie. "No!" he retorted, snapping the reins.

Emilie felt slapped. Never had David been short with her. From now on, she must mind his temper—inherited from his uncle, he had told her in Houston. Oh, dear—she began to dread meeting this peculiar Uncle Edgar.

Moments later, they heard muffled curses from the ox cart behind them. David halted the carriage and descended to the crusty ground. While he trekked off, Emilie calmed herself by studying a distant stand of pine, and a field in the foreground, awash with wildflowers.

A few minutes later, David returned. "Jacob's rig is stuck in a bog back there, my dear. I must help him unload the supplies so that we can pull the wagon out. Otherwise, we'll never make Piney Point tonight."

For a moment, David studied Emilie uncertainly, then suddenly, shyly, he grinned. "For you, m'lady," he announced, pulling from behind his back a bouquet of flowers. Bowing deeply, he presented Emilie with a huge gathering of bluebonnets, Indian paintbrushes, and black-eyed Susans.

It was the perfect offering of peace.

Chapter Four

March 15, 1841

Emilie Barrett stood alone on the hurricane deck of the *Belle of the Republic*, studying the swirling chocolate waters of the Brazos River. Scatterings of cool morning wind tugged at her blue silk skirts as she listened to a distant whippoorwill calling soulfully to its mate. Feeling warmth upon her head, she looked up to find the sun breaking through the steamy morning fog, dancing a shimmering havoc upon the barren, dew-bejewelled branches of pecan trees at shoreside.

Emilie and David had been on the small steamboat *Belle* for over a day now, as the side-wheeler made plodding, tortuous progress against the current toward Washington-on-the-Brazos, their destination upstream. The landscape possessed a comfortable sameness as they journeyed—yellow clay banks, adorned with budding trees and lush wildflowers, rose twenty feet on either side of the *Belle* as she snaked upriver. The quiet churning of the riverboat's wheels lulled them, its droll, soothing cadence belying the wheeler's struggle against frothy swirls.

The night spent on the steamer had been

comfortable, despite the spartan sleeping quarters. Each room contained a chair, a washstand, and a one-leg-bed—an apparatus nailed to the wall, with rawhide strips holding a prairie grass mattress. But the linens had been clean, and the *Belle's* small dining room boasted appetizing fare, though of the standard frontier variety—venison and bacon, corn dodgers, sweet potatoes and black coffee.

The *Belle's* accommodations were as typically Texan as the ones David and Emilie had encountered on the trail during their two-day journey from Houston. Along the sparsely-populated frontier, any home was considered approachable for lodging. The two travellers spent their first night with a young family in a miserable, mud-floored shack, the only structure near Piney Point. The second night of their journey, they fared better, staying with friends of David's at a plantation near the Brazos River.

The next day, David and Emilie completed their journey to the Brazos, traversing several miles of rich bottom land. They knew they were nearing the river when they entered a dense forest, replete with blooming vines and lush undergrowth. After traversing the moss-hung woodland for about a mile, the travellers found themselves deposited, suddenly, on the edge of a yellow rise. Below them, down a steep bank, was the cold, turbulent Brazos, swirling a muddy winter black in the midst of spring lushness. The river seemed an alien, malevolent force in the quiet nature surrounding it—huge gnarled roots protruded from its slopes, while above, half-dead trees gave evidence of its ravages.

The journey down the banks of the river was a harrowing one. While Emilie watched, David and Jacob took first the carriage then the ox cart down the incline. Both man and beast protested the journey down the treacherously slippery grade. Then David returned and assisted Emilie.

Two boats awaited them at waterside—the small steamboat *Belle of the Republic*, and a ferry to the village San Felipe, a collection of miserable shanties across the river from them. After loading the supplies on the *Belle*, David asked the ferryman to take the carriage and wagon to the livery in San Felipe from which he had rented them while journeying to Houston.

Thus they boarded the *Belle*, and now, almost twenty-four hours later, they would soon be approaching Washington-on-the-Brazos. As the steam whistle announced the morning meal, Emilie failed to hear the footsteps approaching from behind her.

"You're about early, my dear," David greeted her as he stepped from the companionway leading to their rooms.

Emilie turned. She caught herself just in time to suppress a shiver of delight as she viewed David and caught the fresh, familiar scent of his shaving soap. Lord, he looked handsome this morning in his chocolate-brown suit!

David joined Emilie at the railing, peering down to study the churning waters. "You look lovely, today," he remarked, the morning breeze ruffling his blonde hair. "The blue of your gown so complements your eyes. My uncle should find you charming."

Emilie murmured, "I'll hope so."

She did, indeed, hope David's uncle would approve of her, for the more she learned about the man, the more uneasy she felt about meeting him. After all, "Uncle" was supposedly a wild-eyed hermit who had despaired of the society of others.

Wouldn't he find Emilie's presence a galling intrusion, and order her thrown out? If he did, would David protect her, fight for her? Or would he bow to the dictates of his uncle? She shuddered at the thought.

"Are you cold, dear?" David asked. "The air is a bit crisp this morning, so perhaps we'd better fetch you some hot coffee."

Taking David's arm and gathering up her skirts, Emilie strolled with him down the stairway to the main deck. At the bow, two malarial-looking hands were raising the red, white and blue flag of the Republic of Texas. The couple continued down the companionway into the oak-paneled dining room, where the captain and several gentlemen in black frock coats had gathered.

Captain Trey Porter sprang up to greet the handsome young couple, his callused hands sweeping imaginary wrinkles off his brass-buttoned coat. "Miss Emilie, you warm this chilly morn," he announced gallantly, bending his auburn head to plant a kiss on Emilie's outstretched hand. "Sir," he acknowledged, turning to shake hands with David.

Around them, benches were noisily thrust back as the other three gentlemen, all planters from the upper Brazos, hastily got to their feet. Both the captain and David aided Emilie in being seated. Emilie gingerly smoothed her skirts around her, hoping the rough cedar bench would not snag the watered silk. Despite the rustic furniture, the table was set with fine English china. Emilie hastily began drinking the steamy coffee set before her by the black steward. But before David could even unfold his napkin, one of the gentlemen launched into a continuation of the debate the planters had begun the previous evening.

"I still maintain, Mr. Ashland, that the imbecile Adams should be shot as a traitor!" the one called Hollingshead attacked. "The nerve of the man, slandering the noble name of the Republic of Texas from the floor of Congress!"

Far from chagrined, David seemed mildly amused. "A traitor to whom, sir? Adams is a citizen of the United States, not the sovereign Republic of Texas. Besides, the man has a right to his views on slavery."

Hollingshead shook his graying head. "The man has *no* views on slavery, as he would abolish the institution. I suppose the fop would have us free these lizard-brained Africans, then watch them cavort while the cotton rots on the stalk. A fine abolitionist old Johnny Q. would be then, with no cotton crop and naught to cover his naked hide!"

Emilie, all this time listening with her eyes demurely on her plate, now covertly eyed the black man serving those assembled. Hollingshead was insensitive to speak so loosely in the slave's presence. Emilie had always felt insulated from the slavery question—her family had never owned slaves, nor taken a stand on the subject. But now, she buttered her cornbread and considered the African's fate—to be owned, body and soul, by another. The graying, white-garmented servant seemed deafly impassive to Hollingshead's insults as he continued his rounds, serving bacon from a cobalt blue platter. But what of the man's soul, his inner torment? How did it feel to be the prisoner of another?

"Mr. Hollingshead, be mindful of the lady's presence," Captain Porter admonished, entering the fray.

"May I urge you to heed the captain's advice," David agreed brittlely.

But Hollingshead continued, undaunted, "Doesn't

that Yankee idiot realize freeing the darkies would mean anarchy?'' Pounding his fist on the table, he sputtered, "Ain't no controlling the black animal without the chain or the whip!''

A furrowed brow indicating his displeasure, David gritted, "It may interest you to know, sir, that the plantation I share with my uncle is run quite efficiently without any such torture devices.''

His mouth filled with cornbread, Hollingshead answered thickly, "I'm aware of the fact, Mr. Ashland. The way that demented uncle of yours has relinquished all control, I'm surprised the darkies haven't carried the place off!'' Snorting derisively, he added, "Your uncle has no more sense than the negras!''

Reaching for coffee to wash down the grainy bread, the planter failed to notice David bolting to his feet, his eyes filled with ire. But before David could speak, Hollingshead suddenly shrieked, "Aaaagh!''

Emilie hastily buried her face in her napkin to hide her mirth, for the servant, filling Hollingshead's cup, had errantly overturned a full measure of the scalding brew into the planter's lap. Hollingshead flew up, enraged, frantically dabbing himself with his linen napkin. "You black jackass!'' he screamed, his face a full-blooded red, while his arm thrust away the slave's proffered cloth.

The black man's eyes rolled wildly with fear before he humbly lowered his gaze to the floor. "Sorry, suh,'' he crooned meekly. "Us niggars got no sense, suh.''

Hollingshead's bulging eyes scorched the slave. "Are you mocking me, boy?''

"No, suh,'' the black replied, his gaze riveted to the floor.

43

There was a moment of sticky silence, then Hollingshead drew himself up surlily and departed the room.

The company remaining burst into uproarious laughter. "I think we can agree that Mr. Hollingshead has been well-served," the captain quipped. "A fine performance, Lucas," he complimented his servant.

Emilie thought she spotted a half-smile on the African's face as he gathered the emptied plates. "And now, gentlemen," the captain continued, "may I suggest that we broach a subject less sensitive than the slavery question?"

"Aye," a gentleman from Hempstead agreed. "The talk around the Capitol Hotel is Sam Houston will again run for the Presidency. I, for one, shall support him—that fool Lamar has the treasury in a scandalous mess."

"Lamar *is* a scandalous mess," another chimed in, and all present fell into easy laughter.

While the gentlemen relaxed over fresh cups of coffee, Emilie Barrett stared at David Ashland with frank admiration. He had been so courageous and eloquent during the debate moments earlier! Oh, how much longer could she delude herself? She was falling in love with this young man! Never had she known a man as chivalrous, as honorable as David. She studied him thoughtfully as he discussed politics with the other gentlemen. Would it be possible— perhaps someday—that he could return her feelings? Might he already? Surely he felt something towards her, else why should he have rescued her from her predicament?

Oh, could she and David marry, how marvellous that would be! Emilie smiled wistfully, envisioning herself as the bride of a young planter. As mistress of

44

the manor, she could bring a return of graceful society to Brazos Bend. If she and David were married, she would make it clear to old Edgar that she would not follow his misanthropic tendencies! Or, better yet, she would have David build their own home as soon as possible.

Emilie sighed, dreaming of courtly garden parties, elegant dinners, parlor games—with fine gentlemen just like those now present, their wives and children. Yes, she would make a fine wife for David. She could suit his needs.

Needs. The thought of marriage brought a sensitive subject to Emilie's mind—the deep, dark needs of a man for a woman. Emilie felt herself flushing at the very thought of the marriage act, and hoped the gentlemen present did not notice. If she and David married, would he assert his husbandly rights? Could such a reserved young man perform upon her the painful, vulgar act Grandmother had once described? "A wife's Christian duty," Granny Rose had called it. Duty, indeed! How did husbands and wives escape death by embarrassment in the process? But men and women must perform this act every day—otherwise, there would be no children. The act, as Granny had explained, led to pregnancy, and pregnancy led . . . to her mother's miscarriage and death!

Oh, why think of that now? Besides, David was far too courtly to force anything upon her should they marry.

"My dear, you've grown pale!" David fretted.

Emilie looked up to see David standing above her, offering his hand.

"It's getting a trifle close in here. Gentlemen, please excuse us," David concluded.

After they departed the dining room and returned

to the upper deck, David queried gently, "Emilie, you aren't worried about meeting Uncle Edgar, are you?"

Emilie braced herself with a deep breath of crisp spring air, then looked up at David. "I do fear I'll disappoint him," she conceded.

David grinned broadly. "That's impossible! Though, I'll admit, Uncle possesses a formidable temper. But you're so thoughtful and kind, Emilie, I can't conceive of you provoking him. And don't be fooled by his manner—he has a heart of gold!"

Heart of gold, indeed! Emilie suffered to herself. Since David was only making matters worse, she hastily changed the subject. "Tell me more about Brazos Bend."

David mused, "Where shall I begin? With its history, I suppose. Uncle Edgar and my parents, Charles and Amelia Ashland, emigrated from England in 1830. I was a lad of nine at the time. As you know, Texas was still under Mexican control. Uncle and my father secured *empresario* grants along the Brazos totaling six *leguas*—that's about 27,000 acres. Of course, now that my parents are—deceased—Uncle and I share ownership of Brazos Bend. We've spoken of someday dividing the grant."

"How marvelous!" Emilie burst out. Then, noting David's confused countenance, she quickly inquired, "Would such a division be practical?"

"Indeed, yes. Uncle runs the plantation quite well, whereas I—" his face colored with excitement—"I have a dream of my own."

"Yes?" Emilie prompted.

"Only a small portion of the estate—the bottom land—is suitably rich for cotton production. The upper lands comprise less fertile prairie.

46

Longhorns—thousands of them—roam freely with no one to attend them. There's a fortune to be had simply by rounding them up and driving them to New Orleans."

Emilie studied David's animated face with fresh curiosity. She could not imagine the refined David in the colorful garb of the cowboy—she had seen such characters on the streets of Houston, and David seemed far too genteel to join their ranks. But, she reminded herself, this same young man had thrown Paddy O'Brien out of her parlor. Perhaps, at heart, he thirsted for adventure.

"But what happens after you've sold all the longhorns?" she inquired.

David chuckled. "Not *all* of them. We couldn't gather them all, even if we wanted to. I'd plan to continue the herd, maybe invest in new breed stock. I'd also like to farm a bit—that is, once I've built my own house."

"Your own house?" Emilie echoed. "How marvellous! When?"

David shrugged, glancing off at a reed-roofed shack along the shoreline. "It's only a dream," he muttered.

Emilie decided not to press him. "Tell me of the others at Brazos Bend."

"Let's see," David reflected, rubbing his jaw, "there's Avis Gerouard, the housekeeper. And, of course, Maria Ramero—" here David's tone took on a reverence—"Uncle's ward. As I told you, she'll be home from school soon."

Emilie's eyes narrowed as she studied David's rapt face. What manner of young woman was this Maria, that she would cause David's face to light up when he spoke of her? And why did David avoid discussing the reasons Maria had been dismissed

47

from school? "Ah, yes, Maria—the girl I am to befriend," Emilie murmured. "Do tell me all about her. How did your uncle acquire this—ward?"

"Seven years ago, she and her father came to the plantation, seeking work. I remember the day well—Maria was a pathetic thing, dressed in rags and not speaking a word of English. It seems her mother died bearing her, and her father dragged her from town to town afterwards, he being quite a drinker and a hell-raiser."

"What a shame," Emilie said.

"Luckily for Maria and her father, that was when Olivia was still alive. Olivia remembered that the man had once worked for her family in Hempstead, and had quite a talent with animals. She got Edgar to hire Ramero to take charge of the stable. Unfortunately, though, the man vanished a year later, abandoning Maria. Of course, we took her into our home at that time. We soon heard that her father was killed in a knife fight in a brothel in Houston."

"How terrible for Maria! But it was fine of your family to take her in."

"Aye," David nodded. "She might not have been welcomed elsewhere."

Emilie frowned. "What do you mean?"

"I mean other families in the vicinity no doubt would have turned her away. Surely you're aware that the hatred between Texan and Mexicans runs deep."

A pained expression crossed Emilie's features. "The Mexicans did kill my father—though I'd never blame Maria for that. Actually, I haven't thought of such matters much. There aren't many Mexicans living in Houston."

David laughed ruefully. "Haven't you wondered why? The problem began decades ago, when whites began colonizing the state, which had been the unchallenged domain of the Mexicans and the Indians for so long. Since the war, Mexicans have been persecuted, pushed off their land, even killed in cold blood by Texans seeking revenge. But not by my uncle. Not after what he saw at San Jacinto.''

Emilie had heard rumors of the atrocities suffered by the Mexican soldiers at the Battle of San Jacinto, and she had no desire to hear the details. "At least your uncle took in Maria. That speaks well for him. By the way, when is the girl coming home? Will you be going to Nacogdoches to fetch her?''

David shook his head. "Fortunately, the head-mistress, Mrs. Ferguson, arranged transportation for Maria with a parson and his wife who are moving to Houston. The three of them will set out next week, and Maria should be home by the end of the month.'' Smiling as he turned to Emilie, he added, "I know you and Maria will get on famously. You're not that far apart in age, and she's so—beautiful.''

Listening to David, Emilie felt an increasing uneasiness. Was there truly something between him and Maria? He obviously felt devotion towards the young lady. What if he intended to marry *her*?

"I'll look forward to meeting Maria," Emilie murmured. "How soon shall we arrive at the plantation?''

David considered the shoreline, with its profusion of leafing sycamores and naked-branched, still-dormant pecan trees. "Half an hour's time, with luck. We're passing plantation land, even now.''

Biting her lip, Emilie took in this information. A silence fell between them, broken only by scattered birdsong and the soothing cadence of the side-wheeler lapping against the current. Emilie fervently hoped her appearance, her manners, would please

David's uncle and Maria. Mentally, she hung a large mirror in front of them above the water. She saw the *Belle*, with its twin stacks billowing smoke into the March air, while dungaree-clad deck hands scurried about below them. On the upper deck of the white frame steamer, a young couple stood at railside. They seemed a balanced pair, he a head taller than she. He wore a brown suit and shiny black boots. How handsome he was, with the sun dancing fire in his wheat-blonde hair. Beside him stood a young woman, dressed in her best, full-skirted blue dress.

Peering more closely into the mirror in her mind's eye, Emilie scrutinized every detail of her appearance. She had chosen the blue silk frock despite the fact that Rosanna made the dress four years earlier, when her figure was more girlish. The dress fit tightly across her now-riped breasts, making the *décolletage* quite daring for morning. Noting the fact, she pulled her cape, with its double layers of lace-trimmed blue mull, more closely about her. At least her usually troublesome tresses had responded well to the hairbrush this morning, and honey-rich curls cascaded smoothly from her poke bonnet. The bonnet had also been carefully chosen—it was of beige satin, faced with a festive ruching of tulle interspersed with tiny bows of blue satin. David had mentioned that the blue of her outfit brought out her eyes, and that "Uncle" would be charmed. But what of David? Did he find her charming?

Emilie firmly decided it was time to get better acquainted with David Ashland. Turning to face him she urged, "Tell me of your duties at the plantation."

"I don't really have any at the moment," David admitted, returning her gaze. "I have been travelling quite a bit to Houston and Galveston, straightening out the legal and financial affairs of our cotton business. There's only so much Uncle can do, staying at the plantation as he does. Things got in quite a state while I was gone."

"Oh, yes—you mentioned you were gone for several years. But where?"

David grinned. "Forgive me, Emilie. I neglected to mention that I graduated nine months ago from William and Mary University, where I studied the law."

"The law?"

"Yes. Uncle was quite firm about my getting an education, having given up a seat in the House of Lords when we emigrated."

"The House of Lords," Emilie repeated to herself. The prospect of meeting "Lord Ashland" was becoming rather intimidating! Just why did your family emigrate?"

"That's a complicated matter. Mainly because of Prime Minister Wellington's resignation. Both Uncle and my father were closely allied with the Duke. Not agreeing with Grey's reform politics, they decided to try their luck in North America."

Straightening his ruffled linen cuffs, David continued, "Things went well here at first. Then my parents were killed, then the war—and all the rest. It's such a waste, to see my uncle now—"

Suddenly, David's eyes darted to the shoreline. Emilie, following his gaze, caught sight of a rider flying down the trail at bankside. A satiny black Arabian supported a powerful man dressed entirely in black.

Even at a distance, there was no mistaking the wild light in his eyes, the unruly black hair curling in the wind, the swarthy features that lent the face an almost demonic light—

"Uncle!" David yelled joyfully.

The rider turned in his saddle to study the steamboat with a mixture of curiosity and disdain. Spotting the couple on the upper deck of the *Belle*, he gestured a stiff recognition with his riding crop, then returned his gaze to his mount, urging the majestic beast on with pressure from his long, muscular legs. As swiftly as he had appeared, the mounted man vanished under an overhang of moss-draped branches.

David's gaze being occupied, he did not see Emilie's face turning white. The incident was so brief, that for a moment she thought her mind deluded her. But then the truth sank in upon her.

While the steam whistle screeched, Emilie turned away from the railing, grasping her chest as if to block the exit of her palpitating heart, while her breath came forth in short, sharp gasps. It was him! Him! Him! That horrible man from Gonzales! All the time she knew—yet did not know—

"Edgar Ashland!"

Chapter Five

Just beyond a bend in the Brazos River, the *Belle of the Republic* had nosed onto a sandbar. Deckhands, loading wood and unloading cargo, scurried back and forth on the plank leading from the steamer to the shoreline.

Feeling curiously numb, Emilie watched from the hurricane deck as two men below her loaded her brown steamer trunk onto the rear of an ox cart waiting at shoreside. She gripped the rough wooden railing as she looked beyond the cart to the steep embankment, where a narrow road had been carved, leading to the tree-lined terrain above . . . and Brazos Bend!

The panic she had felt upon spotting Edgar Ashland had disintegrated into dull despair. She felt utterly defeated. It wasn't fear of the man recognizing her—she doubted such a recollection would cause him to expel her from the plantation. But how could she hope to live in the same house with that beast of a man? She fought back a violent memory—brown hands twisting her hair, remorseless lips bruising hers, strong hands throwing her across a black horse.

The sound of distant, melodic laughter brought Emilie back to the present. She surveyed the shoreline, noticing several black children chattering as they romped among the trees. The air drifting toward the youngsters was acrid, filled with smoke.

Emilie rubbed her smarting eyes, then looked around for David. She spotted him below, directing unloading activities.

Seeming to feel Emilie's gaze, David threw back his blonde head and shouted up to her, "Please join us, Emilie. We're ready to disembark."

Gathering her rustling silk skirts, Emilie descended the staircase to the lower deck and joined David at the bow. The two crossed the plank onto the sandbar. A buggy, hitched to two dappled grays, awaited them upon the crude yellow road. As David assisted Emilie into the carriage, she stumbled, almost losing her balance. She realized her knees were as weak as a colt's.

"Are you all right, dear?" David asked solicitously as he got in beside her.

"Lovely," Emilie stammered, gripping the edge of the leather seat. "I'm just—lovely."

David snapped the reins; the horses nervously climbed the steep clay road. Trailing behind them was the ox cart occupied by Jacob and the two blacks who had come from the plantation to meet them. At least, Emilie consoled herself, Edgar Ashland had not met them at the steamer. She shuddered at an image of a scowling Uncle Edgar, clothed in black, riding crop in hand.

As the buggy crested the bank, Emilie turned to watch the *Belle* push off the sandbar, its shrill whistle cutting her ties with the past.

The team plodded through a dense wooded area,

its dusky, sweet-rot smell reminding Emilie painfully of earlier years in Gonzales. The horses dodged giant knarled roots and tree stumps protruding from the road. Overhead, a choir of birds sang, while shafts of sunlight sifted through the moss-graced branches, dancing a ghostly light play upon the travellers below.

Soon, they left the river trees and entered a vast, wildflower-carpeted prairie. Emilie glanced behind them, noticing they had been joined by a trio of giggling black children.

"Emilie, look!" David exclaimed from beside her.

Emilie followed David's gaze to the top of a hillside several hundred yards beyond them. She gasped as she caught her first glimpse of a stately pink brick manor house. "That's . . ."

"Brazos Bend," David announced proudly. "Isn't she grand?"

"Grand! Why she's—she's—" But Emilie was too spellbound to continue. Eyes wide, she studied the structure. Mansions this majestic simply did not exist in Texas, yet there it stood, two-storied, with full Greek columns, as if transported from the moss-draped recesses of the deep South, where Emilie was born.

"Let me tell you a bit about her," David chuckled. "Brazos Bend was built in 1832, right before—right before my parents were killed. The brick was brought in from Mexico and laid by Mexican craftsmen. The Greek columns were shipped from England. The house cost a pretty penny, but those were good years for the cotton market, and the estate was flourishing."

Absorbing this information, Emilie scrutinized the plantation house. The two stories were topped by a wood-shingle roof and spanned by a full veranda.

The massive front door, flanked by symmetrical rows of shuttered windows, was canopied by a second-story portico. All of the exterior woodwork looked recently whitewashed, and even at a distance the windowpanes gleamed with reflected light. The grounds blazed with a blanket of wildflowers, dotted with cedar, leading up to the blossom-clad azaleas and oleanders adorning the exterior. On either side of the house, massive pecan trees provided shade, while blooming pyracantha and bougainvillaea crept the chimneyed walls.

Rather than delighting Emilie, the sight of the imposing plantation house served to make the thought of meeting David's uncle more threatening. Lord Ashland—lord of the manor—she mused bitterly. How would he feel about David bringing a strange, penniless young woman to his lofty estate?

The horses plodded up the hillside, drawing Emilie inexorably into Edgar Ashland's life again. Glancing away from the house, Emilie soothed her troubled mind by drinking in the heady smell of wildflowers, the dew-washed sweetness of the morn. Once she felt more relaxed, she analyzed her fear of Edgar Ashland. Her encounter with him in Gonzales had been so brief—perhaps his ruthlessness had been justifiable, considering the danger they were in at the time. Removed from war, the man could hardly yank young girls about by the hair—she even giggled at the thought.

"Happy, Emilie?" David asked.

Emilie touched his arm. "I'm just fine."

But moments later, as they alighted from the buggy and approached the house, Emilie was ready to eat her words. Her stomach knotted violently, while her heart seemed ready to jump out of her mouth. She noted that the trio of children who had followed them home had now scampered into the branches of a large pecan tree, and were prattling away as they watched the young couple. Emilie had an insane urge to follow them up the tree—she giggled a trifle hysterically at the image of herself disappearing into the branches in a flurry of petticoats.

"Something wrong?" David inquired.

"Of course not!" Emilie retorted fretfully, as she fished through her reticule, drawing out a handkerchief to dry her clammy hands.

Emilie shakily stepped onto the porch. David reached for the door, but it opened from within. Emilie's breath caught in her throat, then she sighed with relief as a wizened black man bid them enter.

"Lordy be, Mister David, welcome home!" the old man greeted them. The servant, in butler's garb, threw wide the door, a joyous smile on his face. "Who have you got there?" he asked, ebony eyes coming to rest upon Emilie.

Taking Emilie's arm, David escorted her into the front hall. "Daniel, this is Miss Emilie Barrett, who will be staying with us. Kindly inform my uncle that we've arrived."

The black man beamed at David. "Bless your bones, Mister David! You brought home a gold-haired angel. We'll have some joy in this house agin!" He turned to Emilie, his eyes dancing with delight. "Welcome, child!"

Emilie smiled. "Thank you, Daniel."

David chuckled as the black man, hurrying off, called, "Mister Ashland, come quick! You gotta see this sight, sir!"

Emilie clutched David's arm as she surveyed the magnificent hall in which they stood. It was about ten feet wide and forty feet long, extending to the rear of the house. Oaken floors, heavily sanded and polished, were flanked by smooth wood planked walls, wainscotted and painted white. The Empire style furniture was of dark rosewood, with gilt edging and marble tops. A suspended staircase curved upward on the left, its bannister gleaming with beeswax. Light beams from the myriad window panes surrounding the front door danced playfully upon the polished floor. The hall looked and smelled well cared-for—fresh flowers spilled from several crystal bowls, while the Turkish rugs looked freshly shaken.

"Do you like the house, Emilie?" David asked from her side.

"It's—breathtaking," Emilie murmured reverently, her eyes moving from the double doors on her right leading to the pleasant yellow drawing room to those on the left revealing a book-lined library. For a moment, she drank in the elegance, forgetting her worries.

"I see, nephew, that you've brought home a playmate."

Emilie spun about to see Edgar Ashland standing on the staircase above them. As he casually descended, Emilie stared at him, stupefied.

He was bigger than life—bigger than she remembered. Tall and powerful, shoulders broad and straight, there was a princely quality to his gait. His pleated white linen shirt was partially unbuttoned, revealing a matting of curly black hair on his chest. The dark fabric of his trousers strained against his muscular legs as he moved, while his gleaming black boots clicked authoritatively upon the wooden floor as he neared them.

"Welcome, nephew," he announced in a deep,

58

resonant voice, as he shook hands with David. "Welcome, Miss, er—" he paused, turning to Emilie. His eyes gripped her, something unfathomable flickering in their brown depths.

Emilie met his gaze steadily, but her heart roared in her ears. Had he paled beneath his tan? Did he recognize her?

"Uncle," David said, "may I present Miss Emilie Barrett."

Edgar arched a black brow at David, then returned his gaze to Emilie, scrutinizing her sharply, suspiciously. But a mocking smile pulled down one corner of his mouth as his eyes came to rest upon her creamy young breasts. "Tell me, David, for what purpose did you bring home Miss Barrett?" he asked, his eyes still fastened upon Emilie's bosom.

Coloring hotly under Edgar's rakish gaze, Emilie pulled her cape tightly about her, as David informed his uncle, "I fancy Emilie would be the perfect companion for Maria."

Edgar threw back his head and laughed. "Companion to Maria? The last thing that little prima donna needs is a companion, albeit a spinster governess with a strong switch might do the girl some benefit, seeing she eats German schoolmistresses for breakfast." Again, he looked at Emilie, his eyes glowing with cynical amusement. "Though it might be diverting to watch the two kittens cavort once the girl returns—see which one claws the other's eyes out first, the silky black-haired one, or this golden bit of fluff."

Emilie bit her lip at Edgar Ashland's insufferable arrogance, struggling not to tell the man to go straight to hell. But Edgar boldly walked up to her, taking both her hands in his, causing the cape to fall away against her shoulders. For a moment, his eyes again ravished her breasts, then he chuckled. "I'm forgetting my manners, sweetheart," he said in a silky, soothing tone. He leaned over and kissed her quickly on the mouth. "Welcome, my dear, you're lovely."

Now Emilie was forced to look up into the haunting depths of Edgar Ashland's eyes. She hadn't remembered the eyes, or, perhaps, being an unschooled sixteen at the time, she hadn't noticed their devouring quality. Dark brown, almost black, they were eyes that could penetrate a woman's very soul. She felt trapped. The nerve of the man, kissing her on the mouth! She should slap his face, force him to release her, yet there was something spell-binding about him, a frightening animal magnetism. Her lips could still feel his mustache where it had bristled against her, and her hands were still tightly clasped in his strong brown ones.

She half-wanted to shake loose from him as rudely as possible, but reminded herself that she was standing in *his* house. "I'm pleased to meet you, sir," she said stiffly.

Edgar chuckled. "I'll just bet you are."

Emilie studied his sardonic face, his taunting eyes, wondering if his remark meant he had recognized her. Lord, she hadn't remembered him as this hand-some—the broad face, straight nose, high cheek-bones. His black, wavy hair was touched with gray at the temples. His mouth, sensually full beneath his mustache, curved downward at one corner. He smelled of leather and tobacco.

"Uncle, I think Emilie may be tired," David interrupted, his boots nervously scraping the floor.

Edgar nodded to David and released Emilie's hands. "Avis!" he called.

Almost instantly, a tall, dark-haired woman

appeared. *"Bonjour,* M'sieur David," she said as she joined them.

David nodded to the Creole woman, while Edgar, gesturing towards Emilie, said, "Avis, this is Miss Emilie Barrett, Miss Maria's new companion."

A pair of black eyes scrutinized Emilie dispassionately. Then the woman turned to Edgar. *"Pardon,* M'sieur Ashland?"

"Miss Maria's new companion, Avis," Edgar repeated impatiently. "Kindly deposit Miss Barrett in the Blue Room."

"But M'sieur, that room is right next—"

"God damn it, Avis, must I repeat *everything*?" Edgar snapped.

Emilie almost jumped, her heart thudding at Edgar Ashland's sudden shortness with the housekeeper. So this was Uncle Edgar's formidable "temper."

The Creole woman lowered dark eyes. "As you wish, M'sieur."

Edgar Ashland smiled grimly. "That's much better, Avis." With an air of distraction, he turned to David. "Now, nephew, I wish to hear all the details of your transactions in Houston. You will join me in the office?"

The two men walked off, leaving Emilie alone in the hallway with Avis. "I'm Avis Gerouard, Mam'zelle," the older woman addressed Emilie. "May I show you to your room?"

Emilie sighed. At least she wasn't being thrown out—yet. She turned to the Creole woman. The housekeeper was a handsome woman, a slightly overlong nose being the only flaw in an otherwise perfect face of clear classical proportion. She seemed, like Edgar, to be in her early thirties, although her black hair, neatly drawn into a bun at the nape of her neck, was as yet unstreaked by gray. She was dressed in black, relieved only by a white collar and a white lace housecap. She stared at Emilie with dark, implacable eyes.

"That would be nice, thank you," Emilie replied.

She followed Avis up the stairs to the second floor, where bedrooms were arranged neatly on either side of a wide hallway. Opening the second door on the left, Avis led Emilie into a large, pleasant room, done entirely in shades of cool blue.

"How lovely!" Emilie exclaimed, noting the delicately feminine canopied bed, the silk brocade day bed, the gleaming mahogany Chippendale chest and dressing table.

Avis replied, "I understand Madame Olivia decorated this room. She selected a different color for each room of the house."

Olivia—that would be Edgar's deceased wife, Emilie thought.

"May I get you anything, Mam'zelle?"

Emilie walked to the bed, fingering the pasty blue crocheted counterpane. Suddenly, she was exhausted. "Thanks, no. I believe I'll rest until time for lunch."

"That will be an hour from now, Mam'zelle," the older woman advised, leaving the room.

With a sigh of relief, Emilie removed her bonnet and cape. She crawled under the mosquito netting and sank into the bed. Oh, that horrible, mesmerizing man—whatever was she to do! Had he recognized her? A raw, unguarded emotion had flickered in his eyes when he first saw her. Did he hate her? Surely her days—indeed her hours—in this house were numbered!

But a tiny voice of calm penetrated Emilie's

torment. After all, she did have David, and so far, he had not let her down. But would David stand up to his dictatorial uncle?

Emilie shivered. Whatever she had expected David's uncle to be like, it wasn't this! She had vaguely pictured a wild-eyed, bearded old fanatic who spoke little and stayed to himself. She certainly hadn't expected the handsome but arrogant Edgar Ashland, that dreadful man from Gonzales!

"Uncle Edgar," Emilie muttered sarcastically.

Edgar Ashland seemed too young, too virile, to be anyone's uncle! The way he had gaped at her just now, he certainly didn't seem to be mourning his wife! She didn't trust the man—if he didn't send her packing, he would probably throw her into his bed! For if what David said were correct, Uncle Edgar had been without a woman for five years. What an odd man!

A moody, unpredictable man! Oh, how could she live in the same house with him? If only she had stayed in Houston—

Houston—that was it! She would convince David to take her back! But how? Emilie frowned, lacing her hands behind her head. After the incident with the cowboys, Emilie knew David would not let her live alone at Granny's house. No, if she and David returned, it would have to be as husband and wife.

Husband and wife! Emilie half-laughed at her wild thoughts. But was there any other solution? She loved David Ashland, would like nothing more than to be his bride. Yet, did he return her feelings?

She knew it wasn't proper for a lady to inquire of a gentleman's feelings. But the gleam in dear old Uncle Edgar's eyes was hardly proper, either!

Emilie's jaw tightened. Yes, she would have to risk her pride, tell David she loved him. Besides, there was a good chance he returned her feelings, considering his solicitous treatment of her. Maybe he was just shy and needed a push in the right direction.

Emilie yawned as she plotted her course of action. She would get David alone as soon as possible. She would suggest they go back to Houston once they were married. After all, he had studied law—he could set up practice there!

Emilie frowned. What of Maria, the young girl she was to help? After hearing David explain about Maria's tragic background, Emilie was sure the girl desperately needed her guidance and friendship. Was it fair to leave Maria in Edgar Ashland's clutches?

Sighing, Emilie decided the question was too much for her tired mind. Perhaps later, she could see what she could arrange for the girl's welfare.

Emilie pushed aside her thoughts. She must rest, now, so her eyes would be bright and persuasive when she approached David. She pulled the soft counterpane around her, feeling drowsy, emotionally drained from the ordeal of meeting Edgar Ashland. Perhaps soon she would be home at Granny Rose's house.

Granny Rose! Inexplicably, tears ran down Emilie's tired cheeks at the thought of her dead grandmother. Tears of guilt, she decided—guilt because she hadn't loved Granny enough to mourn her these past weeks. It had taken her years to get over the deaths of her parents, yet she had hardly given the recently-deceased old woman a thought. She remembered Granny's frequent words, "You're my duty, now, Emilie." Love could live beyond the grave, but duty . . . ? There was no duty left.

"I must see to myself, now, Grandmother— there's nothing I can do for you," Emilie whispered, the black veil of sleep closing over her tears.

Chapter Six

March 15, 1841

The face hovered above her. The black, devilish eyes laughing. The arms encircled her, drew her close. The lips brushed hers.

Her arms reached upward, curled around his neck. Her lips yielded. She was lost—

Emilie jumped awake, looked quickly about the room. She drew a ragged breath, relieved that she was alone. Her hand moved to her lips. Funny, she could almost feel the imprint of his mouth—

The nerve of the man—invading her dreams! She shook off the covers, got out of bed. She noted with displeasure that her blue silk dress was damp from sleeping in the stuffy room. She opened the French doors and went out onto the veranda. The midday breeze instantly refreshed her, as the scent of honeysuckle and the buzzing of bees drifted up from the bushes below her. From this height, she commanded a good view of the plantation—the rolling, verdant lawns, outbuildings beyond, neatly planted green fields in the distance.

Noting that the sun was at high noon, Emilie returned to the room to prepare for lunch. To her dismay, she found that her hairbrush was not in her reticule—she ached to repair her tousled coiffure and to change her gown, but her trunk had not been brought up.

Smoothing wrinkles out of her dress and hair as best she could, Emilie descended into the drawing room, where she found David alone.

He stood. "You look rested, Emilie."

"I am," Emilie replied, glancing about the room and into the dining room beyond, relieved to see that they were alone.

"I see you're studying the room," David said. "Olivia called this the Yellow Room."

Distracted, Emilie replied, "That's obvious." Olivia again! How much control could a dead woman have over those she left behind? Obviously no meager amount, since the house had been maintained as she left it. Like the Blue Room, the Yellow Room was a study in monochrome, awash with hues ranging from candlelight to saffron. Yet it seemed somehow without personality.

Enough of this digression, Emilie scolded herself! She must speak with David, or lose her chance! "David, could we sit for a moment?"

"Of course!" he replied. Taking her arm, he led her to a massive Chippendale wing chair. He then sat in the twin chair across from her. They were separated by only a few feet, but the distance seemed insurmountable.

Emilie studied the claw and ball feet of her chair as she said abruptly, "David, I don't think I'm welcome here."

David frowned. "Nonsense, Emilie—of course you're welcome! What makes you say such a thing?"

Emilie looked up at him, biting her lip. "It's your uncle."

David considered this statement in frowning concentration, then said gently, "Emilie, don't let his manner intimidate you. You must get used to him, my dear, since I'll be away frequently." David paused, loosening his cravat nervously. "In fact, I must leave again within two days. Uncle just received a letter from our agent in Galveston, and it seems one of our cotton warehouses has burned. I hadn't intended to leave you this soon, dear, but I must personally settle the matter."

Emilie's jaw dropped. "Oh, no, David, you can't mean—with *him*, alone! No, David! You must take me home!"

"But Emilie," David explained patiently, "this *is* your home now."

"Anyone hungry?" a deep voice demanded. "Or would you prefer eating your lunch in Houston?"

Emilie looked up to see Edgar Ashland leaning indolently against the doorway to the dining room. How much had he heard? Enough, obviously. Now formally dressed in black frock coat and trousers, he stood studying Emilie and David with amused derision. Emilie watched him, a feeling stirring inside her—a primal, forbidden longing she couldn't name. He repelled her, yet he attracted her in a frightening manner which made her feel traitor to her feelings toward David.

David sprang up, said hastily, "Of course, Emilie would not dream of being anywhere else." Offering Emilie his arm, he added, "Shall we eat, dear?"

In the dining room, they were served by a white-aproned negress. Emilie was shocked to find Avis Gerouard seated with the family. She was more astonished by the feast presented her—fresh fruit, followed by a hearty stew David called a duck and sausage gumbo. Hot and spicy and served with mounds of steaming rice, the stew scorched her nostrils before the fork reached her mouth.

During the meal, David chatted with Emilie and complimented Avis on the cooking, while Edgar ignored the others, eating his food slowly and deliberately. As Avis served pecan pie, Edgar abruptly got to his feet, causing a hush to fall upon the room. "Pray continue with your chatter, all of you," he said sarcastically, his expression annoyed as he started for the door.

But he paused by Emilie's chair, reaching out to finger one of the honey-gold curls that cascaded down her back. "Pretty," he murmured idly, tugging playfully on the lock before he tossed it back. "Perhaps we'll keep you."

Insulted by the barb, Emilie spun about to confront thin air—Edgar was gone. How rude and mercurial the man was! she thought irritably. She turned back to the table to seek reassurance from David, but he was telling Avis of the rice he'd brought her from Houston.

Angrily, Emilie got up and went to the window. She saw Edgar Ashland disappearing down the lawn in a flurry of hooves and flying coattails. Black horse. Black-clothed man. Seized by memory, Emilie gritted her teeth and called to David, "Is it the same horse?"

"I beg your pardon. Were you speaking to me, Emilie?" came the confused reply.

Emilie did not bother to turn around—her eyes held coldly on the vanishing man and stallion. "The same horse," she repeated, her voice cracking. "Is it the same horse he took to the war? Ap—Apollyon?"

"Apollyon—the same horse—Emilie, what an odd question! How did you know about Uncle and the war?"

"You told me!" Emilie snapped, her fingernails digging into the smooth velvet draping the window.

"Oh. Well—no, it's not the same horse. That Apollyon was killed at San Jacinto, along with Houston's Saracen."

"*That* Apollyon! What's this one called?"

"Well—also called Apollyon, I believe."

"Which means?"

"Devil, I think."

"Of course."

After lunch, David rode off to join Edgar, and Emilie returned to her room. Spotting her hairbrush and perfume bottle on the dressing table, she realized that her trunk had been unpacked.

Emilie opened the wardrobe to find all her dresses hung in a neat row. The edge of a crimson garment caught her eye, and she giggled as she pulled out a tawdry red satin gown. How did *that* get packed? Oh, well, she had been so rushed leaving Houston, it would not surprise her to find she had thrown in a chamber pot!

Emilie went to the mirror and held the dress in front of her. With red feather trim, deeply plunging neckline and sheer sleeves, the dress could have graced the highest-paid strumpet in Houston. And it probably would have, had word not gotten around to Granny's customers that she had contracted Yellow Jack. Staring at her reflection, Emilie remembered Edgar Ashland's words, "Pretty— perhaps we'll keep you." Damn the man! She must lose no time in persuading David of her plans, else risk being left at his dear uncle's mercy!

Emilie spent the afternoon alternately pacing and reading one of the books she had brought with her from Houston. Towards evening, she was delighted when two of the maids fetched her a bath.

Afterwards, Emilie dressed in her most modest frock—it was white, hand-embroidered linen, high-collared, trimmed with blue ribbon and lace. She donned delicate blue satin slippers and piled her hair high upon her head, resolutely pinning down the springy curls to gain a restrained, matronly effect. Tonight, it was quite important that she impress David with her maturity, her grace—as well as giving his uncle nothing to gawk at!

Emilie opened a dresser drawer and took out her prized possession—Grandmother's gold and sapphire brooch. For a moment, she held it in her hand, studying the heart-shaped pin encircled by tiny blue stones. It felt like a cold, alien lump. Sighing, she put it on.

As a finishing touch, Emilie took her crystal perfume bottle and put a few drops of rosewater on her temples and throat. Replacing the rose-colored bottle on the dresser, she thought of her mother. The bottle was the only thing she had left that had belonged to Camille Barrett. Emilie summoned an image of a tall French woman with high cheekbones and dark hair. She remembered vividly her mother's generous, loving spirit—harder to recall were her mannerisms, the tone of her voice, although the French inflection in Avis Gerouard's speech seemed hauntingly familiar to Emilie now.

Emilie closed her eyes, remembering her father. Diamond blue eyes flashed from a laughing face encircled by a halo of gold hair. Had he really died at the Alamo?

She opened her eyes, sighing. For several years after the war, she had been tormented by dreams of demons and burning villages. But more recently, she had seen the past with a kind of detachment, as if she, her parents and stillborn brother, were all characters in a play.

And Edgar Ashland—was he the hero or the villain of the drama? True, he had rescued her from certain death. She could understand what he did, but could she ever forgive the way in which he did it? His role in the play would always seem brutally real. Would the nightmares return now that he had come back into her life?

Emilie shivered, then put aside her memories, realizing her digression had probably made her late for dinner. She left the room, hurrying down the stairs. She bounded into the parlor, running headlong into Edgar Ashland.

Strong arms closed about her. "Easy, little one," Edgar teased, his sardonic brown eyes dancing with mischief.

For a moment, Emilie stared at his rakishly handsome face, her heart thudding. The feel of his hard chest against her, the smell of him—all man—was alarmingly titillating.

Emilie recovered, stiffening. "Release me!" she ordered in a cracking voice.

Edgar chuckled. "Certainly, sweetheart." He strolled off to the tea table, pouring two glasses of wine. Sauntering back to Emilie, he handed her a glass, coaxing, "Join me, little one."

Emilie's eyes went from the glass of wine to Edgar's face. How handsome he looked, the rogue! He was dressed in a rich brown velvet frock coat and fawn trousers. His shirt was of crisp white linen, with ruffled cuffs and front. A gold satin waistcoat and black cravat topped off the outfit, making him look lordly and very intimidating.

"I—I don't sip spirits, sir," Emilie choked out.

Raising a black brow, Edgar said, "Drink it."

71

Although he spoke casually, there was a restrained timbre of steel in his tone.

Emilie hastily took the goblet, almost choking on her first gulp of wine. She fought back tears as the potent liquid burned all the way from her mouth to her stomach. As a child, she had occasionally taken a sip of wine from her father's glass, but this brew was headier, thick and fiery, surely a port or brandy. She cautioned herself to sip the wine slowly.

"Good evening, Emilie."

Emilie turned to face David, who had quietly entered the room. She noted he looked handsomely sedate this evening, in black frock coat and trousers. His bright blue eyes were serious—his face unusually tense as he studied Emilie.

Emilie felt her heart warming at David's presence. "It's good to see you, David," she murmured. "I missed you all this afternoon."

If David were pleased by Emilie's friendly overture, he did not show it as he solemnly walked to the tea table, pouring himself a glass of wine. "I don't like your hair that way, Emilie," he said slowly, his back to her. "It's just not you."

Astonished, Emilie put a hand to the curls pinned on top of her head. "Why David—"

"David, you're being rude to our guest," Edgar laughed, joining his nephew at the tea table. "Admit it—the girl looks enchanting."

David turned, again staring at Emilie. He shrugged and said stiffly, "Forgive me, Emilie. I spoke out of turn."

Emilie stared at David confusedly, but before she could reply, Edgar took her arm and led her towards the dining room.

The three dined alone—Avis Gerouard was nowhere in sight. They consumed a sumptuous feast—turtle soup and okra gumbo, followed by rice cake with whiskey sauce. A different wine accompanied each course, and despite her earlier resolve, Emilie found herself feeling slightly giddy as the meal progressed. After that first burning gulp, the wine slid down her throat with ease—her mouth seemed inured to its igneous bite.

Throughout dinner, Emilie tried her best to start a conversation with David, but the young man was strangely taciturn. However, Edgar compensated for his nephew's silence—he was unusually charming throughout the meal, asking Emilie all about their journey from Houston. She felt almost as if the two men had exchanged personalities.

After dinner, Emilie drifted with the men back into the drawing room, where the three sipped cups of *cafe brûlot*. Emilie began to wonder if she would ever get a chance to speak with David alone. She certainly must not risk it tonight, since her appearance seemed to put him off. Perhaps tomorrow . . . .

While David and Edgar smoked cheroots and discussed the lack of rainfall that spring, Emilie wandered over to the piano occupying one corner of the room. It was a magnificent cabinet grand, with cabriole legs and a scrollwork music stand. A collection of Chopin waltzes lay open on the stand. Emilie leafed through it, finding a familiar one. Instinctively, her hands silently fingered the smooth ivory keys.

"Play for us, love," a silky voice coaxed.

Emilie turned to find Edgar beside her. "How did you know I play?"

"It shows in your touch."

Now David had also walked up. Staring up at the two of them, Emilie swayed dizzily, then seated herself upon the leather swivel stool.

She giggled. "It's been ages since I've practiced at the seminary."

But with a flamboyant arpeggio, Emilie found herself launching into a *grande valse*. The piano had a deep, rich tone, and she thoroughly enjoyed the opportunity to play after so many months. The waltz filled the room with its poignant, slightly haunting melody. Emilie forgot the presence of the two men as she threw herself into her performance. When she concluded, their applause caused her to blush profusely.

"You have a gift, my dear," Edgar remarked. "But a waltz is meant for dancing, and we can't dance while you are playing."

Edgar boldly strode to Emilie, pulled her up into his arms, calling over his shoulder, "Play for us, David."

Emilie looked from Edgar to David in astonishment.

"Ah," Edgar laughed, "you are not as yet aware of—er—*all* my nephew's talents!" Frowning at David, he urged, "Well, Nephew, don't just stand there—a waltz, if you will!"

Before Emilie knew what was happening, she was whirling about with Edgar to the lilting strains of a *valse brilliante*. David was a gifted pianist, and filled the room with beautiful song. Emilie felt swept into a dream, and found herself laughing gaily as Edgar twirled her about. On one of the slower refrains, he drew her close and whispered in her ear, "How lovely you are, little one. We are fortunate to have you in our home." Emilie was caught in the spell of the wine, floating in Edgar's strong arms. . . .

The music stopped. They stood for a moment transfixed. Then Emilie remembered herself. She pushed Edgar away, stared up at him with bewilderment and fear. But he merely smiled sardonically as he bowed deeply.

Watching him straighten, Emilie felt the room tilting. "David, I—I think I'd best go to bed," she announced shakily.

David stepped forward and took her arm. "Of course, dear—let me help you upstairs," he said gently.

After David left her at her door, Emilie stumbled into her room. She collapsed upon the bed, only to find the room spinning crazily. Fighting nausea, she got up and staggered to the dressing table, splashing water on her face. She scolded herself soundly for getting into such a state, and, taking her book, sat down upon the day bed, determined to go to bed with a clear head.

But as the lamplight flickered and sent ghostly images across the page, the print began to blur and fade. . . .

Downstairs in the library, the Ashland men had been talking over snifters of brandy for the better part of an hour.

"The question remains, Nephew—why did you bring the girl here?" Edgar asked, his long form stretched across the arms of a Jacobean wing chair.

From the settee across the room, David leaned forward and explained, "I told you, Uncle, that she was destitute, and Maria—"

"The *obvious* reason, of course," Edgar interrupted. "Now give me the *real* reason."

David frowned, but was silent as he stared down at the amber liquid in his snifter.

"Did you get no hint tonight?" Edgar pursued, half-scowling. "Tell me—are you romantically involved with the girl?''

David looked up, frowning. "I find that question—unfair, Uncle. Suffice it to say I couldn't leave the girl alone in a wild town like Houston.''

A wry smile tugged at Edgar's lips, as he rubbed his jaw thoughtfully. "We'll keep the girl, of course.''

David's face relaxed. "Good. Let's just hope Maria will welcome Emilie here, too.''

Edgar waved David off. "Don't concern yourself with Maria. I think we can find a *better* way to occupy Miss Barrett.''

David arched an eyebrow. "Just what are you implying, sir?''

Edgar grinned. "If you're not interested in the girl, I'll consider her fair game.''

David's eyes widened. "You'll *what?*''

"I fancy the girl,'' Edgar said simply, draining his snifter.

Watching his uncle return to the sideboard and pour more brandy, David bristled, "But this is so—so sudden!''

"It's not as sudden as you think,'' Edgar chuckled, raising the glass to his lips. "Oh, the things I could do with that girl,'' he mused, his hand tightening around the snifter.

David stared aghast at Edgar's determined face. "Why, Uncle, I never could have dreamed you would be a—a ravisher of young women! Maria has been here all this time—''

"Maria's a child,'' Edgar scoffed, returning to his chair.

"She's not—she's seventeen years old—''

"And I, David, am thirty-three, twice Maria's age. But I find your Miss Barrett a great deal more mature—and desirable.''

76

David shook his head in disbelief. "Uncle, you have sequestered yourself at this plantation for five years! There were months when you hardly spoke to a soul. I thought it obvious you did not wish further companionship."

Sipping his drink, Edgar reflected, "What I have in mind for Miss Barrett does not involve much—conversation."

David choked on his brandy. "Damn it, man!" he sputtered hoarsely. "If you would stoop to such—then I'll not go to Galveston and leave Emilie in your clutches!"

Edgar leaned forward, his eyebrows lifted in puzzlement. "Truly, David? Even with the warehouse in ashes?"

"*Truly*," David replied firmly. "Not unless you assure me that Emilie's virtue will be safe while I'm gone."

Upon hearing this dramatic remark, Edgar laughed so hard that tears sprang to his eyes. "Emilie's virtue, indeed! You say the girl is twenty-one, and has been living in Houston?" He paused, scowled. "Oh, very well, David, don't jump up! I'll not 'ravish' the girl, as you so delicately put it."

David settled back upon the settee, breathing a sigh of relief, as Edgar returned, a trifle unsteadily, to the sideboard.

"You know, I think she fancies *you*, foolish girl that she is," Edgar remarked as he refilled his snifter. "That will change, once you leave—much as I'll miss you, Nephew."

David frowned. "Uncle, are you already contemplating breaking your promise?"

Edgar shook his head. "I've no desire to force myself upon the girl." He smiled pensively. "But there are ways, nephew—there are ways."

77

David stared at Edgar in consternation. "Doesn't it discourage you that she dislikes you, sir?"

Edgar downed the brandy quickly, his eyes darkening perceptibly. "Nay, Nephew. It adds interest to the game."

Upstairs, Emilie jerked awake, her head pounding. She wasn't sure what awakened her, but thought she had heard a door slamming in the next room.

Dizzily, she arose from the day bed. Her damp dress clung to her. She must have dozed for some time, she decided, pouring herself water from the porcelain pitcher. She gulped down a glassful, soothing her cottony throat. Then she doffed her clammy dress and chemise and donned a filmy white nightgown. Still warm, she opened the French doors. The cool, blossom-scented breeze flowed in from the veranda.

Turning, Emilie swayed as she walked toward the lantern—for some odd reason, the water seemed to be making her lightheaded. She was about to extinguish the lamp when a scraping sound drew her attention back to the French doors.

Brandy glass in hand, Edgar Ashland sauntered into the room.

Emilie gasped in shock. She hadn't realized the veranda connected her room with his. "Sir," she rasped, "you forget yourself."

Staggering into a pool of light, Edgar Ashland leered at Emilie. "Impossible," he murmured, his glazed eyes glittering. "Impossible to forget."

The fact that he was fully clothed was no consolation to Emilie as she crossed her arms to cover her thin bodice. She opened her mouth to issue a crisp retort, but Edgar astonished her by throwing his emptied brandy snifter across the room. It smashed against the fireplace, splintering into a thousand tinkling fragments. The violence of the act made Emilie's heart thud.

Grinding glass beneath his boots, Edgar strode to Emilie, grabbing her, pulling her arms from her bosom. "Impossible to forget," he reiterated with brandied eloquence. His black eyes fastened upon her thinly-clad breasts. "Olivia—the witch! Why won't she leave me be? I'd give a king's ransom to get my hands on her again—to grind her refined little fanny through the floor!"

Emilie was horrified, for as Edgar spoke, his eyes grew wild, while his hands pinned her against him with fingers of steel. She pushed against his chest, pleading, "Please—please let me go. You're drunk."

Suddenly, Edgar pushed her away; she stumbled, almost falling. "Me drunk?" he sneered, gesturing wildly. "Edgar Ashland, lord of the realm, drunk? Heed this warning, wench—malign the name of an Ashland and I'll see you flogged!"

Emilie decided to indulge his drunken fantasies, hoping he could be humored into leaving. "Forgive me, m'lord," she cajoled, "I spoke out of turn. But the hour is late, indeed, to be attending a lady in her boudoir."

For a moment, Edgar eyed her suspiciously. Then he grinned amiably. Taking his cue, he bowed. "Truer words—truer words have never been spoken. Miss Barrett, I bid you goodnight."

Drawing himself up with dignity, Edgar turned to leave. But when he got to the archway, he paused, then turned. "But darling," he murmured thickly, "don't I get a goodnight kiss?"

Edgar's taunting grin told Emilie he hadn't been fooled by her charade. She dashed for the door, dodging glass fragments, but strong arms caught her, and a hot mouth closed over her own.

It was a long, thorough kiss—a slow and steady ravishment. Emilie fought him, flailing at his chest with her hands; yet his lips forced hers to yield, while his tongue audaciously explored the sweetness of her mouth.

Then his arms tightened; his kiss intensified. And deep inside Emilie, something inexplicable happened. Was it the wine? For suddenly, she was drowning. Her hands reached up, curling around his neck. His hands reached down, pulling her pelvis against the hardness of his manhood. A new and desperate yearning quickened between her thighs, cutting like an exquisite knife. She hated him and wanted him with all her being. She knew if he took her to the bed now, she would let him take her, anything to ease the tormenting ache within her.

At last the kiss ended. Edgar released her, then regarded her flushed, gasping form with triumph and tender amusement. With a lazy fingertip, he touched the diaphanous fabric of her nightgown, tracing the outline of one tautened nipple, then the other. She stood motionless as the same brown finger caressed her mouth, tracing the path of his kiss, while his eyes held her spellbound.

She ached for him. And *he* knew it!

He leaned over and kissed her quickly, gently. "Patience, love," he admonished.

As he turned and left her, Emilie heard his soft laughter echoing down the veranda.

Chapter Seven

Emilie lay shrouded in a veil of sleep. Muffled sounds filtered in and out of her consciousness—footsteps in the hall, birdsong, whispers in another room. But her eyes remained drowsily shut.

Suddenly, a bell began to clang, its discordant cadence bludgeoning her ears. She sat up in bed, then fell back dizzily, her head swimming.

Memories splintered her throbbing brain. That man! That horrible, arrogant, mesmerizing man! How dare he! How dare she let him do it!

Emilie threw back the crocheted counterpane and sat up, grasping the edge of the bed to keep her balance. She must have still been inebriated when he came to her room, to let him—let him—

"Oh!" she gasped, her hand flying to her mouth. Her lips still bore his mark, the bruise of his passion. His kiss—thorough as a rape. Had he taken her to the bed and concluded the vignette, she could not have felt more humiliated.

She shivered. The man was strange, frightening—his near-violent lust, the way he spoke of his deceased wife. She must leave this house as soon as possible!

81

Emilie got up and staggered to the open French doors. Her head was now exploding with the sound of that asinine bell! "Stop, damn you!" she yelled, slamming the doors.

Miraculously, the bell stopped. Despite herself, Emilie giggled. The hands must have literally danced to the fields amid that interminable clanging, she reflected as she splashed water on her face. She peeled off her clammy nightgown and donned her chemise and blue gingham dress.

Once she completed her toilette, Emilie was about to leave her room, when she heard the sound of horses. Opening the French doors, she went out onto the veranda. Below her, two horsemen galloped off in a cloud of bluebonnets. Edgar and David. "Lovely," she muttered sarcastically. "Now when will I get to talk to David?"

Emilie went downstairs, finding the dining room deserted. Sitting down, she took the china coffee pot and poured herself a large cupful. She took a huge swallow of the strong brew—it scalded her throat going down, causing her eyes to burn. But her head began to clear, and the relief was reassuring.

Avis Gerouard flittered into the room. Did the woman always wear black? Emilie wondered as she eyed her. David had told Emilie that Avis had been a recent widow when she came to them from New Orleans four years earlier. But surely the woman wasn't still in mourning! The color made her look sinister somehow.

Avis uncovered an earthenware crock and scooped out a huge bowful of mush. She handed the bowl to Emilie—it looked like wet, mutilated cornbread. Emilie fought back nausea as she looked at the bits of brown crust floating in the oily yellow paste. She had a strange intuition that Avis was aware of her indisposition, and was taking secret pleasure in tormenting her this morning.

"It's *coush-coush*, Mam'zelle," Avis informed her, picking up the creamer. Emilie watched, distressed, as Avis drowned the *coush-coush* with cream. "Enjoy your breakfast, Mam'zelle," Avis concluded, leaving the room.

Emilie stared at the bowl of yellow and white cereal. Oh, well, her stomach could feel no worse than it now did—she might as well eat.

"Dig in," she groaned.

At mid-morning, feeling much better, Emilie stood on the veranda outside her bedroom, and spotted David riding back from the fields. She rushed downstairs, opening the front door just as he came in.

"Well, good morning, Emilie!" he said cheerfully, sweeping past her, emanating the smell of leather and horseflesh. He hung his riding crop on a wooden peg. "Did you sleep well last night?"

Emilie laughed mirthlessly, but ignored David's question. "David, may we please talk—alone?"

David turned, eyeing Emilie quizzically. "Of course, dear. Let's sit in the parlor."

Emilie shook her head. "No, not here. Couldn't we go for a walk, or take out the buggy?"

David swept tousled hair from his brow. "Well, I suppose," he said, less than enthusiastically. "Get a cape, dear, and I'll have the stable boy see to the team."

Emilie was greatly relieved to have found, at last, her opportunity to speak alone with David. Half an hour later, she rode beside him in the buggy. A light breeze wafted across them as they journeyed beneath a canopy of leafing limbs on River Road. The air was thick with spring, and Emilie took deep breaths of the heady essence, and found herself relaxing.

As they rode along in comfortable silence, Emilie tried to decide what approach to take with David. He was leaving tomorrow, and it was essential that she accompany him—one way or another. Should she tell him what his uncle had done—last night, even previously, in Gonzales? Would he believe her?

That was where the rub came. David thought of Edgar as a father. Perhaps it would be best to tell David of her feelings without mentioning the threat from his uncle, unless absolutely necessary—

The buggy stopped, jerking Emilie out of her thoughts. She glanced about, spotting a large marble monument. She looked at David in confusion.

"Olivia," he explained, getting out of the buggy and offering her a hand. "This is the spot where . . ."

Emilie alighted, peering up at David's emotion-twisted face. "Why did you bring me here?"

"You'd find it, sooner or later."

Emilie went to the large, spear-shaped monument and read the inscription aloud. "Olivia Rice Ashland—Beloved Wife of Edgar—Infant Sons Edgar and Charles. By Drowning, April 26, 1836."

Emilie paused, her eyes travelling to the base of the monument. She silently read the epitaph, felt chilled to the bone.

She looked up at David. "Such sad words," she whispered. " 'A death of dreams.' "

"My uncle's words," David replied woodenly.

Emilie touched the marble—it felt ice-cold. On one side of the marker was the road, on the other, the imperturbable Brazos. Studying the steep yellow clay banks, Emilie had a vision of frothy, hysterical horses flying through the air, dragging a young woman and two infants to their deaths in the raging waters below. She shivered at the thought.

But today the Brazos flowed calmly—a river of many moods, Emilie decided. Then it struck her. "Where are—" she began, looking up at David. "I mean, they're not buried here, are they?"

David turned to her, his eyes glistening. "No, they're not. That's why we have the monument. That's all we have of them. That—and the river."

There was anguish and hatred in David's eyes as he turned to study the tranquil waters below him. "The Brazos—like a woman," he whispered bitterly. "No, a whore. Silky, inviting, murderous."

Emilie gasped. Was this the gentle, shy David speaking? She would expect Edgar Ashland to talk like this, but not David! Deep inside this young man, there was a hard bitterness!

Upon hearing Emilie's gasp, David hastily apologized. "Forgive me, Emilie. I forgot myself. The things I said were—unpardonable."

Seeing David's torment, Emilie felt her heart wrench. "You musn't apologize. Nature can be cruel—brutal."

David took Emilie's arm. "Let's go see the cotton fields," he urged.

Moments later, as they turned back onto River Road, Emilie's heart thudded—Edgar Ashland was galloping towards them! David waved, but, luckily, Edgar merely nodded, sweeping past them towards the house. Emilie sighed with relief.

David turned the team onto a narrow trail which snaked through the fields. Soon, Emilie was distracted from her worries, as she viewed rows of cotton which stretched into infinity. The plants, just a few inches tall, were being thinned and weeded by several dozen cottonade-clothed slaves. The air was filled with the smell of alluvial soil and hardy vegetation.

"I didn't know the estate was this large," Emilie commented.

"Large!" David laughed, urging the grays down the trail. "Why, you've only seen a portion of our holdings—look around you, as far as you can see—Brazos Bend land."

As the grays trotted on, Emilie did as she was bid—her eyes roamed past the cotton fields to the mammoth prairie beyond. A half-dozen longhorns grazed on the bluebonnet-strewn grassland—an incongruous addition to a cotton plantation, Emilie decided. The cattle shared two common features— oversize horns and a black line down the back. But there the similarities ended—their coloring and configuration differed vastly. Some were speckled red and white, others blues or browns or bays. Solid or splotched, the color combinations were endless.

Emilie studied the cattle in fascination. "They're beautiful," she murmured, "in their way."

Taking her cue, David turned the grays from the trail and started out across the prairie. As they passed numerous clusters of the exotic-looking cattle, Emilie realized David hadn't exaggerated when he said there were thousands of them. And to think, she might be able to share all of this with him! She leaned back against the leather seat, mentally rehearsing what she must soon say to him.

They rode along silently for a while, then David stopped the buggy on the crest of a grassy hillside. He alighted, straightened his brown frock coat, then assisted Emilie down.

They stood in the center of the circle of mammoth oaks, as if deposited on a vast stage surrounded by a curtain of greenery. "What a lovely spot," Emilie whispered, reaching down to pick a plum-colored buttercup.

"I come here often," David told her, his eyes sweeping the peaceful setting. "Someday, I'd like to build my own house on this rise."

Emilie quickly looked up at David. Here, at last, was her opportunity. Taking a deep breath, she asked, "And when you have your own home, start your cattle business, won't you be needing a wife, David?"

David flushed to the roots of his blonde hair. "Why, Emilie, I'd hardly even thought—"

"Because if you are," Emilie plunged on, "I want to be that wife."

David shook his head in bewilderment. "Emilie, you can't know what you're saying."

Emilie could feel her face heating, but she moved forward and took David's hand. "Yes, I do!" she whispered, her eyes glowing. "I—I love you, David!"

David dropped Emilie's hand, as if her touch burned him. Strange emotions clouded his deep blue eyes, as he spoke in an intense, shaky tone. "Emilie, if I were—seeking a wife—a young woman of your beauty and grace would be beyond my wildest dreams. While I am honored that you esteem me so highly, I'm afraid I have no intention of marrying—ever."

Emilie could hardly believe her ears. "But why?" she gasped. "With all you've done for me, I thought—I thought that you cared!"

David shifted uncomfortably from foot to foot, staring at the grass at his feet. "I *do* care, dear, but not in the way you think." He looked up, his eyes anguished. "I'll always be your friend, Emilie. But marriage—marriage can mean disaster between two people."

"What do you mean?" Emilie asked confusedly. "Are you talking about your parents? Or your uncle and Olivia?"

David sadly shook his head. "*That* I am not at liberty to discuss, dear." He sighed. "Emilie, please accept the fact that I've no desire for a wife, and do not question me further."

"No!" Emilie retorted, her voice rising. "You must give me a better explanation than that!"

"I cannot," he said doggedly.

"Oh—oh, you're exasperating!" Emilie sputtered in frustration. Clutching at her hopes, she pleaded, "Then at least take me away from here, David. Take me back to Houston tomorrow!"

David's eyes became sympathetic. "I've thought of that possibility, Emilie, but you must be here to welcome Maria home. And besides, it just wouldn't be proper, leaving you in Houston alone."

Emilie's wounded pride exploded into anger. *"Proper?"* she stormed. "Is it *proper* to leave me here alone—with *him?"*

"Him?"

"Your uncle!"

"Emilie, my uncle is a gentleman—"

"Your uncle is a lecherous old reprobate!" Emilie seethed, angry tears burning her eyes.

David reached for her arm, his eyes dazed, hurt. "Emilie, how can you say—"

She threw off his grasp, spinning about so he could not see the tears overflowing her eyes. "Oh, take me back to the house!"

David helped Emilie out of the buggy in front of the house. Then, muttering something about making an inventory of the gear in the stables, he drove off.

Emilie stormed into the house, kicking the door

shut, then wincing as a sharp pain shot through her foot.

"Did you have a nice drive, love?" a man's laughing voice inquired.

Emilie glared down the hallway at Edgar Ashland. Showing no evidence of his carousing the night before, Edgar sauntered towards her, dressed in a white, partially-unbuttoned shirt and dark trousers. His dark eyes were mocking her, and a cynical smile played upon his lips.

"Where's David?" he asked.

"He's off counting harnesses, or some such nonsense," Emilie retorted nastily.

Edgar laughed heartily. "Then may I assume, sweetheart, that you were unable to slip *your* harness around my young nephew?"

Emilie's face burned at Edgar's affront; she spun about and haughtily swept towards the stairs.

But Edgar grabbed her arm. "Just a moment, Emilie. I'll have a word with you," he said smoothly.

"Let me go!" she blustered, trying to yank free.

"No, love," he said firmly, "and if you persist in fighting me, I'll be forced to silence you in the manner I know works best."

Emilie froze at his words, their many implications. "Very well!" she hissed. "I'll listen. But take your filthy hands off me!"

Edgar chuckled, releasing her. "Very well, I'll get right to the point. David's leaving tomorrow—"

"Yes, I know!"

"Leaving you and me here—alone."

Emilie gulped as she met his gaze, but did not comment.

Edgar grinned engagingly. "My point is, Emilie, that I would advise you to marry me immediately, since—after last night—there is very little chance of you staying out of my bed.''

Emilie's eyes widened in amazement. "Why you arrogant, conceited—"

"Steady, Emilie!" Edgar laughed. "After all, I'm doing the honorable thing, marrying you, rather than merely bedding you, which I could easily arrange.''

"Easily!" Emilie shrieked.

Edgar frowned. "Calm down, woman! If you've ever looked at yourself in the mirror, you can't expect to become an old maid. And since David has rejected you—"

"How do *you* know David has rejected me?" Emilie asked, her voice rising with emotion.

"See—you've admitted it!" Edgar chuckled. He moved closer. "You've seen the estate, my dear. All my wealth will be yours, as my wife.''

Emilie shook her head in bewilderment. "But *why* do you want a wife? All these years you've stayed to yourself—"

Edgar laughed shortly. "I'm not a snivelling schoolgirl, Emilie. When you're wanting company, you may go titter with Maria when she returns. What I want is a *wife*, to share my bed, bear my sons. Do you understand precisely what I'm saying, my dear, or is your education lacking?''

"Yes, I understand—*precisely*—and you may go to the devil, sir!" Emilie gritted, hands on hips.

Edgar shook his head, grinning. "Thank God David had the wisdom to turn you down. You'd have cut him into mincemeat in an hour's time!''

Emilie stamped her foot in frustration. "May I go, sir?''

Edgar stroked his mustache thoughtfully as he studied the furious girl. "Perhaps I should sweeten the offer. Very well, if you'll give me your consent,

I'll promise not to consummate the marriage until you're ready."

"Sir, I don't *want* to marry you—under *any* circumstances!"

"Oh, but you *do*, Emilie," he corrected. Slowly, he moved closer, passion sparking in the brown depths of his eyes.

Emilie backed away, struggling to think of a retort, when the grandfather clock began to chime, distracting her.

Seeing her hesitation, Edgar reached out, pulling her into his arms. "Say yes, sweetheart, before the clock ceases its strokes, or I'll withdraw my offer—and take you to my bed, married or not!"

Emilie glared up into dark, laughing eyes. "Why you—"

But Edgar kissed her, silencing her protests.

At first, Emilie flailed out at him. But his kiss was breathtaking, and she was swept by the same, inexplicable magic—his warm chest flattening her breasts, his hard lips mastering hers, his masculine scent making her senses swim.

And the clock chimed remorselessly, drawing her inexorably into his web!

His mouth moved to her ear. "Say yes!" he demanded hoarsely. "Show that scoundrel David! Say it!"

"No! No!" she moaned, only to have her lament again smothered by his lips, as his fingers moved to her breasts, titillating the nipples exquisitely through the cloth of her gown.

"Say it!" he growled. "Or, by God, I'll have you, right here—right now!"

Emilie's eyes grew enormous. "No!" she cried. "You can't mean—"

He kissed her much harder then, his tongue sliding

deep inside her mouth, even as his hands caressed her body at will. Her fists beat against his shoulders, then unclenched, as a sob died inside her throat. . . .

Emilie knew she was sinking fast—the intimacy was shattering, devastating. She could not think or breathe when he held her thus!

"Tell me you'll marry me—say yes!" he repeated, his tone hypnotic.

Suddenly, the clock ceased its chiming. Edgar pulled back, nodding meaningfully.

"Yes!" Emilie found herself gasping, in a voice not her own. "I mean—yes—if you'll promise—promise—"

His eyes lit up. "Of course, sweet. You may come to my bed when you wish."

She eyed him warily, trying to catch her breath and quiet the frantic beating of her heart. She wondered wildly if she had lost her mind. Why should she trust him?

Yet did she have a choice—at the moment?

"Settled, then," Edgar continued, without waiting for her to reply. "I'll send David for the parson this afternoon."

"This—this afternoon!" Emilie sputtered, pushing him away.

"Oh, tomorrow, then," Edgar replied agreeably. "But mind it must be early. David's leaving at noon."

Emilie's jaw dropped.

"M'sieur, lunch is served," a raspy feminine voice announced.

Emilie spun about to face Avis Gerouard, who stood in the archway to the parlor, coldly eyeing them.

"Thank you, Avis," Edgar said, taking Emilie's arm.

Feeling numb, Emilie let Edgar lead her to the dining room table. Once the three were seated, she picked at her food, the full impact of the last few moments dawning upon her.

This time, she couldn't blame the wine! What demon of insanity had possessed her to consent to marry Edgar Ashland? Even if to escape immediate ravishment?

"Avis," Edgar said casually as he cut his meat, "Miss Barrett and I shall marry in the morning, so do show her about the place after lunch."

Oh my God—he's wasting no time! Emilie thought hysterically, her eyes growing like saucers. Gulping, she glanced from Avis's astonished face to Edgar's smiling countenance.

"Also, Avis, there's no bread on the table, and Hannah is nowhere in sight," Edgar commented. "Do be a dear and go fetch some from the kitchen." He winked at Emilie. "Suddenly, I'm ravenous."

Emilie dropped her fork, blinking dazedly at Edgar, as Avis murmured, *"Oui*, M'sieur," and departed the room.

Slowly, Edgar Ashland stood, walked around the table to Emilie's side. She stared down at her food, her heart pounding, but a brown finger lifted her chin, forcing her to gaze up into his determined eyes.

"Having second thoughts, Emilie?"

"I—well—" she stammered.

"Emilie, you have given me your promise," Edgar said sternly. "Let me make one thing clear to you, my dear. I am the last man on earth you would want to cross."

After lunch, Avis Gerouard did as Edgar had bid, showing Emilie the house. Although she did not take Emilie into any of the rooms of the family members, she showed her three guest bedrooms upstairs, as well as the unfamiliar office and library downstairs.

Then Avis led Emilie out the back door across the grassy yard toward the kitchen. Emilie glanced off past the neat rows of slave quarters, desperately hoping to spot David returning. But she saw only chattering black children—some playing under shady trees, other tending family garden plots.

The two entered the kitchen, a frame and shingle building directly behind the house. Emilie was shocked by the size of the pleasant, white-washed room, and the bustle of activity present. A dozen prattling black women were busily at work—some grinding, chopping, and mixing, others carding cotton, spinning, looming and sewing. Avis explained that aside from the preparation of the food, all the ironing was done in the kitchen, as well as the making of homespun "cottonade" clothing for the slaves.

Walking about, Emilie studied the spices strung up to dry about the ceiling, and the stone bake-oven and fireplace occupying one entire wall of the structure. On the hearth, a large iron kettle bubbled hambones into broth, filling the room with a succulent, enticing aroma. Emilie thought ruefully that she felt as if she were floundering about in the soup herself.

Avis pointed out the myriad tin and iron kitchen tools—candle makers, food warmers, kettles, mills and grinders. She showed Emilie the key to the black, funnel-shaped "flour safe" on the wall. "With flour sometimes reaching seventy-five dollars a barrel, we must guard it carefully," the housekeeper told her.

Once they were outside, Avis pointed to a small cedar building on their right. "That's the dairy, Mam'zelle."

Emilie nodded. "I'm impressed, Mrs. Gerouard. The house—everything—is spotless."

"Thank you," Avis replied woodenly. Then, a malevolent smile tugged at the housekeeper's thin lips. "Before we go inside, Mam'zelle, may I offer my congratulations. It seems that rather than being a—governess—you are to become a bride. How very fortunate."

Emilie looked sharply at Avis Gerouard. There was unmistakable sarcasm in the woman's tone. "Thank you for your—fond wishes—Mrs. Gerouard," she returned archly.

The brown eyes studying Emilie flickered strangely. "In all fairness, Mam'zelle, I must warn you that you will find M'sieur Ashland—extremely difficult to please."

That remark rankled. "Are you speaking from *personal* experience, Mrs. Gerouard?" Emilie snapped.

A mask closed over Avis Gerouard's features. "*Pardon*, Mam'zelle, I have duties to attend to."

Avis Gerouard turned and swept into the house, leaving Emilie alone in the yard. What a witch the woman was! Emilie seethed. It would almost be worth marrying Edgar just to secure the woman's dismissal!

Emilie took a ragged breath of spring air, and was about to enter the house herself, when she saw a solitary figure approaching from the stables. "David!"

Spotting Emilie, David seemed to slow his pace. Undaunted, Emilie rushed towards him, her blue gingham skirts billowing in the breeze. This time, she would hold nothing back, tell him *exactly* what his uncle was up to! Then he would *have* to take her home to Houston!

They met under a huge, bare-branched pecan tree. "What is it, Emilie?" David asked, his face puzzled.

She clutched his arm, her blue eyes wide and entreating. "Now he wants me to marry him!" she blurted anxiously.

"He—you mean Uncle?"

"Of course your uncle!" Emilie retorted. "Last night, he came to my room and kissed me, and now he says I must marry him, else face ravishment at his hands!"

A flush spread across David's features at this revelation. Then, frowning, he took Emilie's hand. "Emilie, you simply mustn't let my uncle intimidate you," he said firmly. "I happen to know for a fact that he has no intention of forcing you—"

"David, *listen* to me!" Emilie cried desperately. "He just *forced* me to consent to marry him!"

David's features twisted in confusion, then he shook his head. "Emilie, my uncle promised me you'd be safe with him—"

"You don't believe me!" Emilie interrupted, throwing off his hand. "You're going to desert me!"

David flung his arms wide in exasperation. "Emilie, what can I do? I can't leave you alone in Houston! The best I can do, dear, is to think your situation over carefully while I'm away, try to find an alternative for you—"

"Then it will be too late!" Emilie stormed, angrily brushing a windswept curl from her eyes. "Your uncle will have—will have his way with me! As things stand, I have only escaped his bed by promising to marry him!"

David's eyes narrowed. "Emilie, simply tell him to back off, and I'll have a word with him before I go—"

"Oh, the devil with you!" Emilie seethed,

clenching her fists and stamping her foot. "Will you understand *nothing*? I thought you were strong and gallant, but you're not! You're weak and stupid—and—and you disgust me!"

Emilie's voice shook with emotion, and her vision blurred with tears. David reached for her, but she dodged him.

"Get out of my sight!" she choked. "I'll—I'll marry him! It's exactly what you deserve!"

Chapter Eight

March 17, 1841

Emilie stood on the veranda adjoining her room, watching the sun's silken rays slowly illuminate the quiet landscape below her. Even though it was barely morning, she was already dressed in a dove-gray cotton frock, her hair neatly brushed, cascading into golden ringlets about her shoulders.

Her appearance belied the turmoil within. She had tossed and turned all through the night, endlessly trying to plot a way out of her dilemma. She had thought of leaving the house and running—wildly, aimlessly, anywhere—but she had realized only a fool would set out in the dark, across unfamiliar terrain. Yet the approach of morning brought no answers.

What was she to do? she now wondered miserably. Stay and marry Edgar Ashland? Or take her chances, alone and penniless? At least at Brazos Bend, she would have a home. But at what price? She didn't trust Edgar Ashland at all, especially with David leaving.

David! Again her heart wrenched as she thought of his abandoning her. He claimed he did not want her to marry Edgar, yet he wasn't willing to lift a finger to prevent his uncle's ravishing her. As she told the scoundrel yesterday, her marrying Edgar was just what he deserved!

Marrying Edgar! She shuddered at the thought. For Edgar Ashland was another matter entirely. When she had accepted his suit yesterday, she was too confused to fully consider the implications. Yet the night—long and comfortless—had afforded her a leisurely opportunity to envision her future with this brooding, unpredictable man. She turned now, eyeing the dark, curtained French doors at the other end of the veranda, doors she was now sure led to *his* room. Edgar had promised that if she wed him, he would not consummate the marriage until she was ready. Yet could she depend on him to keep his word? She was already painfully aware that he was very strong, exceptionally virile. How long before he tired of the game and took her to bed in that shadowy, frightening room just beyond her?

His wife had borne him twins, she thought, shivering. . . .

The remembrance spurred a horrible surge of panic in the pit of Emilie's stomach. She turned from the veranda and shakily reentered her room, her mind spinning as she recalled her mother's death from miscarriage at Gonzales. For a terrible moment, she feared she was going to be ill. The nausea finally passed, but the panic remained. What on earth was she to do?

Leave! Her mind suddenly seemed to scream the thought. *Leave! Walk out! Just leave!*

And Emilie found herself doing precisely that, propelled by an inner voice of desperation. She left her room and started down the dark upstairs hallway. She had no idea where she was going—only that she was, indeed, going—

She moved down the stairway like one possessed, entering the downstairs hallway without looking back. She was heading for the front door when a hand grabbed her shoulder.

Emilie gasped, whirling about, her hands flying to her heart.

Edgar Ashland chuckled. "Aren't you going the wrong way, love?"

Catching her breath, Emilie stared at Edgar in disbelief and dismay. Yes, it was him! He stood fully dressed next to her, his arms akimbo as he studied her with cynical curiosity.

His lips curled into a smile. "I'm not surprised you're a bit confused this morning, love, this being our wedding day." He extended his arm to her. "The dining room is *this* way, my dear. And we'd best get to our breakfast, since David tells me the parson will be here by mid-morning."

Staring at the determined stranger she was soon to marry, Emilie gulped as she remembered Edgar's words from yesterday: "I am the last man on earth you would want to cross. . . ."

Wordlessly, she took Edgar Ashland's arm, and walked with him towards the dining room.

"Ve shall begin, Herr Ashland?"

Pastor Heinz Fritz stood near the window in the drawing room of Brazos Bend, a beam of morning sunlight pouring a halo upon his bald head as he smiled at those assembled. Dressed in a black robe and clerical collar, the portly man cleared his throat and gazed down at his prayer book through horn-rimmed spectacles.

Emilie stared past the two dozen mother-of-pearl buttons travelling down the bodice of her satin wedding gown to the bouquet of wildflowers in her hands. Moments earlier, Edgar had surprised her with the bluebonnets. Now he stood next to her, looking solemn and devastatingly handsome in his black velvet suit and ruffled linen shirt. Near him stood David—the traitor!—looking appropriately sober. A few feet behind them sat Avis Gerouard, her dark eyes watching the vignette dispassionately.

Edgar took Emilie's hand, nodding to her. "We are ready, Pastor," he gravely told the parson.

Emilie's heart thudded as she stared at Edgar's brown hand tightly holding hers. What in God's name am I doing? her mind screamed as Pastor Fritz began droning the service in broken English.

She was marrying Edgar Ashland! Heedless of the consequences, she was marrying the man! David had finalized her decision after breakfast that morning. He had taken her aside, again urging her not to rush into marriage with his uncle. Yet when she had demanded, "Will you take me back to Houston?", he had merely shaken his head sadly. She had left him to go dress for the service, snapping, "I hate you!"

But did she really hate him? Emilie gazed past Edgar to look at David now—tall, handsome, so serious! Her heart ached at his betrayal, his abandonment—but the mortal blow he had dealt her was refusing her love, throwing her feelings back in her face! He had wounded her pride, and that she could not accept, for she was a proud woman. Now, she gained a certain perverse pleasure from knowing she was doing precisely what David wanted her not to do. She would marry his uncle and get her revenge. But was that what she *really* wanted?

Feeling Edgar's stern gaze piercing the corner of her eye, Emilie turned her attention back to the pastor. How unreal everything seemed! She only half-understood what the parson was saying; in fact, the whole service seemed wrong, held in a parlor instead of a church. But then, Edgar Ashland had refused to leave Brazos Bend for five long years. Why should his wedding day be any different from all the rest?

Suddenly, the pastor was silent, and Emilie realized that all eyes were upon her, waiting for her to speak. Dodging Edgar's scowl, she turned to Pastor Fritz, whispering, "Pardon?" The parson repeated the vow; she mouthed the words woodenly.

Before she knew it, all the vows had been repeated, and she was staring at a gold and sapphire band on her finger—Edgar had told her the ring had belonged to his mother. She was inanely reflecting that she could not imagine *him* as ever having a mother, when he pulled her into his arms, throwing back her gauzy silk veil. To her horror, he kissed her slowly and thoroughly, holding her scandalously close.

Finally, he released her; she stood glowering at him. He smiled, leaned over and whispered in her ear, "I never promised not to kiss you, love."

Then everyone was shaking hands—David's lips brushed her cheek—champagne was served. The German pastor toasted the bride and groom, smiling jovially and apologizing that he had not had time to bring "a present for ze *Braut*."

All too soon, the gathering dispersed—the pastor to the village, David to the steamboat, Avis to her duties. Suddenly, Emilie found herself alone in the parlor with her new husband. He stood across the room from her, gazing at her with frank admiration.

"Congratulations, Mrs. Ashland," he whispered, moving closer. "You're a very beautiful bride."

She stared at him, not answering as he reached her side and took her hand. The sunlight danced jet highlights in his hair, and his eyes glowed with a tender light.

"Unfortunately, I, too, have duties to attend to." He leaned over, kissed her on the forehead. "Later, sweet."

He left her. She stood in the parlor, a deserted bride holding a bouquet of flowers.

So that was it. She was married. Just that simple, that cold.

She left the room, not even noticing that she had dropped the bluebonnets, crushing them with satin slippers as she walked.

The day passed in agonizing slowness for Emilie. She returned to her room, changed her clothes and waited—for what, she knew not.

Edgar was absent at lunch. Emilie picked at her food, as she and Avis sat silently in the dining room. Afterwards, there was nothing for Emilie to do but to return to her room, where she unsuccessfully tried to amuse herself with a book. The stillness became unnerving, exhausting, yet Emilie was too tense to take a nap.

Late in the afternoon, Emilie's boredom was relieved when Avis Gerouard came to her room, bringing with her a young negress. "M'sieur Ashland thought you would need a maid, Madame," the housekeeper informed Emilie.

The girl's name was Hallie. Once Avis left, Emilie and she became acquainted. Hallie was seventeen, sweet-tempered and inclined to giggle. Shorter and stockier than Emilie, she was dressed in blue slave cottonades, a matching turban catching her fuzzy black hair.

Hallie assisted Emilie with her bath, then helped her into her modest white hand-embroidered frock. Afterwards, Emilie sat at the dressing table while Hallie delicately piled shiny gold tresses upon Emilie's head.

"You ain't showin' yer bosom t'night, Missus?" the slave asked, grinning.

Emilie frowned at Hallie as their eyes met in the mirror. "Why should I show my bosom, Hallie?"

The slave giggled, revealing milk-white teeth. "Well, t'night be the night, Missus!" she tittered.

"*What* night?"

"Well, t'day Mistah Ashland marry you, and t'night he have his way with you!"

Emilie's eyebrows flew up. "Hallie, you are speaking of matters that are none of your concern!" she rebuked.

The slave humbly lowered chocolate-brown eyes. "Yes'um."

"And he's *not* going to have his way with me!" Emilie snapped.

But later, as Emilie sat in the dining room alone wth Edgar, she began to doubt her adamant statements to Hallie. Why had she trusted Edgar Ashland? For the man simply would not quit staring at her! Although she had worn the modest gown to cool his attentions, she now realized ruefully that it wouldn't have mattered if she had worn a grain sack—his eyes were utterly burning holes in her flesh!

The silence of the room made things worse, for they spoke only in passing the food. Emilie drank a glass of wine to steady her nerves, but only picked at her chicken fricassee. Her husband's brown eyes—deepset, hypnotizing—would give her no peace.

"Why are you staring at me so?" she finally snapped.

Edgar grinned. "You'll have to get used to your husband's perusal, Mrs. Ashland. It's hardly illegal."

Looking at her husband's broad, handsome face—the high cheekbones, sensual mouth, the black, wavy hair shimmering in the lamplight—Emilie felt a sinking sensation in the pit of her stomach. She steadied herself and retorted, "No, not illegal. Only indecent!"

Edgar laughed deeply.

After dinner, they went into the drawing room, and Emilie shyly asked if she could be excused to go to bed.

"What—this early?" Edgar inquired.

"I couldn't sleep last night," Emilie replied miserably, eyes lowered.

"Don't tell me you were a nervous bride-to-be," Edgar teased. Grinning at her deepening blush, he added, "All the more reason to get you—really exhausted—so you'll sleep soundly tonight."

Emilie glared at Edgar, but he had already turned, seated himself on the settee. "Play something for me on the piano," he told her.

Grudgingly, Emilie decided to indulge him. She sat down, played a nocturne and two waltzes. Afterwards, she again asked if she could go up to bed.

Edgar now sat with a snifter of brandy in his hand, another glass and the decanter in front of him on the tea table. "Ah, what a romantic frame of mind your lovely music has put me in, my dear," he said whimsically. Patting the seat beside him, he coaxed, "Join me for a nightcap."

"Sir, there are limits to my obligations to you!"

Emilie bristled tiredly, holding her ground.

"Indeed there are, Mrs. Ashland," he returned with silky sarcasm. "But unless my eyes deceive me, we are not—at the moment—in the bedroom. So kindly move your derriere over here!"

Emilie scowled and flounced across the room, sitting down next to him.

Edgar leaned forward and poured Emilie a glass of brandy. He handed her the snifter, and she took a sip, glowering at him.

His eyes darkened. "You're lovely when you pout, sweet," he breathed, encircling her waist with his arm.

Emilie's lower lip quivered at the unabashed passion in her husband's gaze. "Edgar—please!" she pleaded, trying to push him away.

"Quit squirming!" he demanded, pulling her closer.

Emilie decided not to risk provoking him further, and let his arm remain about her middle. They sat silently drinking their brandy, as the cool, blossom-scented breeze drifted in from the open window, blowing Edgar's clean male scent across her.

She began to feel drowsy and comfortable, sitting with him thus, the brandy warming her veins. Then suddenly, her cheek brushed the rough wool of his frock coat, and she jerked upright.

Edgar took the near-empty glass from her hand. "You've had enough," he said gently, placing the snifter on the table. "You really are tired, aren't you sweetheart?"

He led her from the parlor towards the stairs. She half-stumbled on the first step, and he swept her up into his arms. She found she was too sleepy to protest.

As he moved up the stairs, his mustache tickled

her ear. "Will you come to my bed tonight, Emilie?" he asked huskily.

She stiffened in his arms. "No!" she whispered adamantly, gazing at him through half-shut eyelids.

He sighed, then took her through the upstairs hallway to her room.

Once they were inside Emilie's bedroom, Hallie nervously jumped up from her chair. Edgar planted Emilie on her feet, then looked longingly from his wife's flushed face to the diaphanous white gown laid out across the bed.

He leaned over, kissing Emilie's mouth quickly, firmly. Then he nodded to Hallie. "Get her to bed," he groaned.

Chapter Nine

March 17, 1841

Emilie jerked awake in the darkness to find herself being lifted from bed, into strong arms.

"What are you doing?" she gasped, as she saw her husband's hard features outlined against the moonlight.

He held her tightly as he walked out onto the silvery veranda. "What does it look like I'm doing, sweetheart?" he asked silkily. "I'm taking you to my bed, so that I may undress you and make love to you."

Emilie blinked dazedly, her heart thudding as they entered Edgar's bedroom. He strode through a pool of light to the bed, then deposited her upon the cool sheet.

Though Emilie was still foggy from sleep and the brandy, she managed to protest, "But you p-promised! Not until I'm ready!"

Her husband did not smile as he untied his black velvet dressing gown. "I've just decided you're ready."

"No!" she cried, struggling to get up, her eyes growing wild at the overwhelming sight of Edgar, now naked, standing next to the bed.

Before she could throw her legs over the side of the bed, his hands grabbed her shoulders. "Lie still!" he ordered hoarsely, lowering his hard body on top of hers.

Despite her anger, chills shot through her at the feel of his warm, naked strength pressed against her flesh through the thin batiste of her gown. "You—you promised!" she repeated weakly.

Edgar frowned as he gazed down at her, his eyes darkly determined, his strong limbs making her struggles meaningless. "Your naïveté astonishes me, love," he uttered evenly. "Surely you did not expect me to play the celibate monk. Besides, our little bargain was null and void from the beginning, since you did not give me your consent until *after* the clock ceased its chiming."

"But that's not fair!" she protested.

"Neither is it fair—or legal—for a wife to withhold her services from her husband," he countered smoothly.

He buried his face against her throat. Emilie tried to push him away, but he ignored her, murmuring, "How did you think I would resist you, love? You're adorable—so sweet."

Deftly, he began unbuttoning the front of her gown.

"No! No!" she protested, beating on his chest with her hands.

Above her, his dark eyes flickered with irritation. "Hush!" he commanded.

His mouth descended upon hers; his hands pinned hers to the mattress. He kissed her slowly, deeply, and she fought for control, as the brandy and his overpowering maleness tugged at her senses. Wrenching her mouth from his, she cried desperately, "No, let me go!"

"Never!" he growled.

He pulled her onto her side. Emilie struggled frantically as he began raising the hem of her gown. He seemed mindless of her distress as his hands slid boldly over her bare buttocks, pulling the gown upward about her neck. Within seconds, she was stripped naked, helpless beside him. His hard fingers gripped her wrists, as his dark eyes slowly savored her nude form; tears welled in her eyes at the indignity of her position.

But as he rolled her onto her back once more, and pressed his flesh upon hers, she groaned from an entirely different emotion—his naked body on hers was electrifying! For a moment, she forgot to fight him, as she was swept up by traitorous, riotous, ecstatic sensations. He felt strong, warm against her, his coarse hairs rubbing into her softness, his muscular chest melding into her breasts. Yet most provocative of all was his hard, enlarged manhood, imprinting her pelvis, making her innermost parts treacherously twinge to be filled.

"I have dreamed of this moment since the instant I first laid eyes on you, Emilie," he whispered, his eyes blazing with passion above her. "You know I'll have you this night! Must you turn a beautiful experience into something ugly?"

"Blast you!" she hissed back, again struggling beneath him, torn asunder by conflicting desires. She hated this man, yet her carnal body knew complete surrender was inevitable!

He must have seen the anguished yearning in her eyes, for he smiled with tender triumph, then kissed her; his tongue parted her lips and boldly assaulted her mouth, making her moan deep in her throat.

He was relentless. He made no move to penetrate

her, but kissed her repeatedly, thoroughly, until at last she began to melt, clinging to him as she half-sobbed from the sweet torment.

"Let it happen, love," he urged.

It was already happening! His kisses were deep, dizzying, and, unwittingly, she began kissing him back. She was too transported to protest when his mouth moved to her breasts, his tongue exciting her in ways she had never dreamed possible. She writhed in ecstasy beneath him as his heavenly lips sucked hard on a taut nipple. Running her hands through his thick, soft hair, she hardly noticed when he rolled off her, and his fingers slid down her belly. But when his hand teased between her legs, she closed against him instinctively.

"No, love," he admonished.

He did not force her, instead propping himself on his elbow beside her, while his fingertips traced concentric circles on her smooth, bare thighs, moving inexorably towards the forbidden space between. She breathed in gasps at the unbearable titillation of his touch. All the while his eyes, now near-black with yearning, devoured every inch of her nakedness in the silky light—and she, too, could not tear her gaze from his muscular, golden form beside her! When at last his hand slid between her legs, she sobbed, "Oh God!" and let him have his way. . . .

She shuddered as his hand invaded her trembling thighs, teasing the bud of her passion. His tongue tickled her breasts as his skillful fingers grew bolder, probing her tender flesh. Her need for him now cut between her thighs, a palpable, exquisitely painful ache. She flinched slightly as his finger slid deeply inside her—it hurt, but hurt so good! She moaned his name.

He took her hand and guided it to his manhood.

But she pulled back, unsure of herself.

"Don't be afraid, darling," he coaxed. "There, sweet, feel how much I want you."

His words made her entire body quiver in a spasm of need. She boldly reached out—he groaned at her touch, kissing her violently.

The shaft, smooth and hard, seemed huge in her hand. She felt a final moment of fear, realizing the throbbing organ would soon invade the tiny crevice his fingers now explored so painfully.

He mounted her. Involuntarily, she tensed, holding out that last bit. "No, please—"

"Relax!" he ordered hoarsely, his hands firmly spreading her thighs.

For a moment, he hung above her, large, satan-like, his dark features etched in the lamplight. Oh, God! she thought. Why aren't I fighting him? Why can't I?

But her thoughts became jumbled as he started to push vigorously against her delicate flesh, seeking to pierce her maidenhead. "Stop it, you're hurting me!" she gasped.

"Just this once, love." His eyes grew tender as he drew her knees upward and outward, all the while probing harder against her. "I am the first," he whispered reverently.

His words were lost upon Emilie, as he tried to arch away from his invasion, unwittingly arousing him further. He lost control, then—his hands slipped beneath her, holding her still as he shattered her resistance, penetrating quickly and deeply until her body was no longer her own. Tears sprang to her eyes, as his mouth smothered her cry of pain.

"Forgive me, love, forgive me," he breathed, planting kisses all over her face.

He began to move inside her with slow, sure

strokes. There was no escaping the hot probe, so large and unyielding within her, for he held her tightly. At first, Emilie gritted her teeth, feeling rent by his passion, but then she was swept by a curious, primal abandon, a sense that the moment, the pain, was preordained, necessary. Instinctively, she let go and arched against him.

He went wild. "Yes, love, yes!" he urged. His hands locked beneath her and his strokes became deeper, powerful, while his mouth kissed away her tears.

His thrusting reached a violent, consuming crescendo—Emilie knew an instant of fierce, hurtful wonder, then he grew still inside her.

For long moments, they lay quietly, slippery bodies entwined. Then, slowly, sanity began to filter into Emilie's consciousness. Gone was the brandied web of magic that had seduced her senses. Now the heavy weight of her husband's victory pressed down upon her, a blatant reminder of her shameful carnality. She felt hurt, used—coldly, soberly awake.

She pushed against his chest.

"Am I crushing you?" he whispered.

She winced as he withdrew from her flesh. "Did I hurt you, sweetheart?" he asked, gazing at her solicitously.

Emilie sat up, noticing the flecks of blood on the sheet. "You—you wounded me!" she accused.

Edgar sat up beside her, frowning. "Love, I didn't wound you. The blood is the proof of your virginity. Didn't anyone explain—"

"Not about that!" she snapped, coloring hotly. She bit her lip, feeling tears of humiliation flood her eyes. "You—you broke your promise to me and you hurt me and—I hate you!"

Edgar looked stunned. "Love, you seemed willing

enough beneath me,'' he chided.

Emilie cringed inwardly at Edgar's crude reminder of her terrible, fatal vulnerability. Her lower lip trembled as she replied with bravado, ''You—you took advantage of me in a weak moment, plying me with brandy! And—and I hated it! I'm leaving you first thing in the morning!''

Now Edgar was angry, his dark brows knitted thunderously. ''The hell you are! You're my wife, Emilie! I'll never let you go!''

''Oh, leave me alone!'' she choked, grabbing the pillow and burying her tear-stained face in its softness.

Still scowling, Edgar got up from the bed, moved to the lamp and blew it out. ''Emilie, promise me you won't try to run away,'' he demanded as he came back to her.

In the darkness, she felt his weight upon the mattress. ''Of course I'll *promise*!'' she cried sarcastically, throwing the pillow at him. ''And I'll *keep* my promise—just like *you* did!''

He grabbed her arm, but she threw herself away from him, pulling up the sheet.

''Don't turn your back on me, Emilie!'' he ordered.

She ignored him.

The sheet flew back and she was yanked, hard, against his chest. ''I'll not have a cold-blooded little bitch in my bed!'' he growled.

The words hit Emilie like a slap. ''Bitch!'' she sobbed indignantly. ''Is that what I was beneath you just now? Go to the devil, you heartless cad!''

She flailed out at him, but his arms imprisoned her. ''There, love,'' he cajoled. ''Forgive me for wounding your vanity. You were—heaven—beneath me just now.''

114

She froze. His audacious words seared a raw nerve. How dare the great oaf think she cared one whit whether she pleased him! "Spare me your—your reviews!" she choked angrily.

He chuckled softly in the darkness, making Emilie mindless with fury. She fought him like a wildcat, but it was useless. He held her tightly against him, letting her wear herself out struggling and sobbing, until she fell asleep in his strong arms.

As was his custom, Edgar Ashland arose before sunrise. Quietly, he shaved and dressed in the half-light.

Then he stood by the bed, staring at Emilie for a long time. Morning's first amber rays crept across the room, illuminating her lovely face, surrounded by an abundance of honey-gold tresses.

She had pleased him. Oh, how she had pleased him! The feel of her, tight and warm about him, had been heaven. Even now, a fire burned within his loins, and he longed to awaken her, kiss her into submission. . . .

But he didn't. He had hurt her enough this past night. He must go slowly now, woo her, lest she always look upon him with fear and revulsion.

He reached out, caressing her sunswept curls. She frowned in her sleep, and he removed his hand, lest he awaken her.

Perhaps she had always been in his blood, he thought, ever since that first time he kissed her at Gonzales. What a little spitfire she had been then! How he had admired her courage, her stubborn strength. How he had regretted having to manhandle her to get her to safety. Should he tell her he remembered? What if *she* didn't remember him? Ah, that might be a blessing. No,

115

best leave the subject alone, not risk alienating her further.

How very precious she was! And she was his. Entirely his. No man had touched her before, and none other ever would! He would school her, teach her to fill his needs, to give of herself, holding nothing back.

And what would he give her in return? "Ah, there's the rub," he murmured, staring at her beautiful, sleeping form. Part of him was playing a game with her—a cruel game with the past. He knew that, inevitably, he would reach out to her in his torment, and he would hurt her.

Sometimes, when the past closed in upon him, he lost control. Would she grow to hate him?

He leaned over and kissed her forehead. "Poor darling," he whispered. "Hate me if you must, but I must take you—and take you."

As if chilled, Emilie clutched the top of the sheet, her black-lashed eyelids still shut. Edgar gathered up the heavy velvet counterpane and draped it across her.

He went to the dresser, fingered his key ring. She would be furious if he locked her in the room. But did he have a choice, after what she said last night? Could he risk losing her?

"Forgive me, love," he murmured, frowning.

Taking his keys, he quietly left her.

Chapter Ten

March 18, 1841

By the time Emilie awakened, the room was bathed in sunshine. She stretched languorously. But the movement brought a twinge of pain, and a flood of humiliating memories.

Edgar Ashland! She jumped upright, noting with relief that she was alone in the bed. She glanced about the unfamiliar room—red velvet draperies, dark, masculine furniture. *His* room.

Yes, it was done—she hadn't imagined it. The marriage had been consummated. And she had—had—

"Ooooh!" she cried. She had let him make love to her! She had wept—slept in his arms!

Angrily, she threw back the counterpane and grabbed her nightgown, covering her nakedness. Donning her wrapper, she hurried from his room, crossing the veranda to her own.

Once inside, she opened the wardrobe, pulled out a yellow frock and threw it across the bed. She would get dressed, by God, and get the hell out of here!

She pulled off her gown and wrapper and stared

hard at her naked reflection in the dressing table mirror. Had she changed? Yes—blast it!—every inch of her glowed!

So this is what it felt like, looked like, to be bedded, she mused bitterly. Her face, her breasts were rubbed pink by Edgar's beard. Like the devil, he had seared her, put his mark upon her flesh!

Emilie stormed about getting dressed, then sat down at the dressing table, brushing her gold curls vigorously. "Traitor!" she hissed at her reflection. "How could you let him do those things—feeling as you do about David!"

Her hasty toilette completed, Emilie hurried towards the door. Where she was going, she was not sure—perhaps a servant could take her to the village, to see Pastor Fritz. He might be able to help—

She grabbed the doorknob. Locked! She tried it again—it did not budge!

Confusedly, she tore out onto the veranda, then back into his room. She rushed to his door. Also locked.

God in heaven—the monster had locked her in!

Suddenly, the bolt shot back. Emilie backed up, as Avis Gerouard entered the room with a breakfast tray.

Emilie's mind raced as she watched Avis stroll in, nonchalantly place the tray on the tea table. Making a quick decision, Emilie hurried for the door.

"I wouldn't try that if I were you, Madame," Avis said woodenly. "Jacob is waiting in the hallway."

Emilie froze, her hand inches from the doorknob. She turned, glared at Avis incredulously. But Avis swept past her to leave, ignoring her completely.

Emilie grabbed her arm. "Just a moment, Mrs. Gerouard!"

Avis carefully disengaged Emilie's fingers. "Do

you wish something, Madame?"

"Do I wish something!" Emilie mimicked sarcastically. "Indeed, I wish something, Mrs. Gerouard! An explanation!"

"An explanation, Madame?" The brown eyes staring back at Emilie were devoid of the slightest curiosity.

"Yes, an explanation!" Emilie sputtered. "An explanation for this—this imprisonment!"

Avis Gerouard shrugged. "Your husband explained to me that you've taken the fever and are given to dangerous flights of fancy."

"Flights of—of—do I look ill, Mrs. Gerouard?"

"Madame, you're quite flushed."

"Flushed! If anyone's ill, it's that lunatic I married!"

Avis's eyes narrowed slightly. "M'sieur Edgar is quite in control of his senses. It is *you* we are concerned about. I do fear you're becoming hysterical, Madame."

Emilie was so befuddled, she could only stare at Avis agog, her limbs trembling with rage.

"You're shaking, Madame, you should go to bed," Avis muttered. "These seasonal fevers can be quite dangerous."

As Emilie gaped at Avis, the older woman quietly left the room. Emilie heard the key scratching into the lock, and the bolt shooting, sealing her fate.

Ignoring her breakfast, Emilie went out onto the veranda, desperately seeking a means of escape. Standing at the railing, she peered to the bushes below. The ground was a good twelve feet down, and the honeysuckle vine looked too scrawny to support her weight. She could jump—and would probably break a leg! How could she escape lame?

Useless. She was imprisoned by Edgar Ashland,

119

the strange man to whom she was now married. Oh, what manner of demon was he? He had lied to her, taken her virginity. Then he had locked her in, telling the servants she was insane with the fever! The brute! Surely he delighted in tormenting others! Would he not be satisfied until he drove her, like Olivia, to her death?

Emilie returned to the Blue Room, irritably throwing herself across the bed, amusing herself by alternately studying her white satin slippers and the bluebonnets wallpapered on the ceiling.

Presently, Avis Gerouard returned to Emilie's room, along with a grinning Hallie toting a bucket of water. "M'sieur Ashland informed me you wished a bath," Avis informed her.

Rather than seeing the kindness of the act, Emilie was chagrined. Had Edgar informed the entire house he had bedded her?

"Do you think it wise for me to bathe, Mrs. Gerouard?" Emilie hissed at the housekeeper. "Considering my failing health, I might take a deathly chill."

Avis shrugged. "That would be a pity, Madame."

Although Emilie was furious, the bath, moments later, was heaven. She scrubbed vigorously, wishing she could wash away Edgar's memory as easily.

Afterwards, Hallie helped Emilie into a green and white frock, then insisted upon again putting up Emilie's hair. "I love t' touch that angel stuff," the black girl told her.

Emilie grudgingly indulged the slave. She felt closer to the black girl this morning, almost like a prisoner welcoming a cellmate, since they were now *both* locked in the room.

As Hallie worked, she asked, grinning, "Mistah Ashland, he have his way with you, Missus?"

120

Emilie bit back an impulse to rebuke the slave. "He had his way with me," she admitted bitterly.

"Why you fussin', Missus?" Hallie asked, winding a gold strand about black fingers. "You a walkin' around, ain't you? My Jacob was messin' with me that first whole night. I was a soakin' the next mornin' through!"

Emilie jumped up, sending her half-finished curls tumbling about her shoulders. "Hallie!" she gasped, mortified.

But the black girl merely giggled. "You could have it a mess worse, Missus," she advised. "Mistah Ashland is a breakin' you gentle."

Breaking me, Emilie thought. Yes, he's breaking me.

Hallie frowned. "You sit down, Missus, I got to start over," she scolded.

Numbly, Emilie did as bid. She stared into the mirror, studying the black girl arranging her hair—the callused brown hands, the warm, kind face. Emilie desperately needed a friend. "Hallie, are you aware that I was—duped—into marrying Mr. Ashland?"

The black face puckered in confusion. "I wonder why you is locked in this room, Missus. But what that be—duped?"

"Well—Mr. Ashland—promised he would not force his attentions upon me if I married him, then after we wed—well, he took advantage of me."

Hallie dropped a gold lock, throwing a black hand over her giggling mouth. "Oh, that Mistah Ashland, he a case, Missus!"

"But Hallie, it isn't fair!"

Hallie shrugged. "Nothin' in this here life is fair, Missus."

Emilie turned, looked up at the slave imploringly.

121

"Hallie—help me. Let's escape—together!"

The black girl backed off, her eyes white with fear. "Missus, you a scarin' me half dead! 'Scapin'! Why I be whupped senseless, and you—" the girl paused significantly—"Mistah Ashland got a pow'ful temper, Missus!"

Emilie sighed. "Yes, I know."

The day passed in slow torment. Emilie soon felt like a caged animal as she paced her room. Hallie remained, watching her and listening. Emilie ranted and raved about Edgar. That he was unfair, insane. That she hated him.

Her tirade, giving her some relief at first, soon became as tiresome as the four walls of the room. She showed no interest in her lunch, which Avis brought and later removed, untouched.

In the early afternoon, it occurred to Emilie to get out the bolts of cloth David had bought her in Houston. Although the memory of his betrayal made her want to fling his gifts from the balcony, she realized the fabrics would give her something to do.

With Hallie's help, she cut out two dresses, one of green and yellow calico, one of pink dimity. She realized ruefully that Edgar would probably be the only person to see her creations, but it was heavenly to sit down with needle and thread and sew up some seams.

Presently, the door opened and Avis brought in her dinner. Oh, God! she thought desolately. Where had the time gone? Soon, that beast would show up, demanding—demanding—

Despite her fears, Emilie found she was starved, and ate heartily of chicken-stuffed tomatoes, fresh bread and *calas*. Afterwards, Emilie refused to dress for bed, hushing Hallie's protests. She had made up her mind—she would not lift a finger to aid in Edgar Ashland's ravishment of her!

All too soon, Avis returned, taking Hallie out for the night. As the loneliness of the room closed in upon Emilie, she sat down upon the day bed with a book, trying to distract herself.

He would undoubtedly be furious that she wasn't in his room, she thought. But if he thought she would submit like some common whore, he could just go hang himself! Tonight she was coldly sober, perfectly willing to fight him to the death! She set her jaw firmly, then cursed as her nervous fingers ripped the page she was turning.

She did not have long to wait, for, presently, the French doors opened and her husband walked into the room.

He stood with booted feet spread, his tall form outlined by the fading amber light. His face was lined with weariness, making his unsmiling countenance even more forbidding.

"Good evening, Mrs. Ashland," he said quietly. "Time for bed."

Emilie shook her head, her eyes spitting blue fire. "Your arrogance amazes me, *Mr.* Ashland," she scoffed. "You think just because you married me, you can treat me without feeling, locking me up like a kept woman—"

"You're the one who threatened to run away, Emilie!" he cut in, striding towards her. "I wouldn't have to lock you in if you'd promise to be an obedient wife!"

"*Wife!*" she seethed. "You don't want a wife! You just want a bedmate—"

"*Precisely,*" he gritted. "*A wife.*"

She threw down her book. "You have no idea what a wife is! You know nothing of tenderness, of

123

compassion! You're nothing but a rutting boar!''

He reached her side, yanked her to her feet. "If you're through flattering my ego, Mrs. Ashland, come to my bed and I'll show you *exactly* what a wife does!''

She pushed him away, stamping her foot. "I have no intention of submitting to you, sir!''

For a moment, he stood glaring at her, his face twisted with angry emotions. Then he smiled contemptuously. "Indeed, love? Kindly explain last night.''

His remark caught her off-guard. For a moment she stared at him stupidly, her face reddening. Then she recovered, snapping, "Simple! I merely closed my eyes and pretended you were David!''

In an instant he was beside her, grabbing her roughly, shaking her until her teeth chattered. "You're going to regret saying that, you heartless bitch!''

He began dragging her towards the bed. Realizing his intent, she dug her heels into the carpeting, lashing out at him. "It's true!'' she screamed. "I love David! I always will!''

Suddenly, he flung her away from him. She fell against the bed, sank to the floor, momentarily stunned. Gulping, she looked up at his tall frame, saw the clenched fists, the blackened eyes, the vein throbbing in his temple.

"Love,'' he said in a strangely calm voice, "you shouldn't have said that.''

Slowly, he started towards her. She scrambled to her feet, dodging him, grabbing a white and gold leaf vase from the bedside table. He lunged for her; she hurled the vase at him. Eyes wild, he ducked; the urn smashed against the wall.

Emilie dashed into a corner, watching Edgar

warily. But, oddly, he seemed to forget her presence as he stared at the fragments of porcelain on the floor, the violence in his features melting into anguish.

After a moment, he knelt, picked up a hand-painted fragment, examined it sadly. "Chantilly porcelain," he murmured. "My brother Charles brought this over from England. It—was—priceless."

Watching him there, on his knees, holding the precious fragment, Emilie realized she had made a horrible, fatal mistake. "Edgar, please—I'm sorry!" she choked.

He looked up at her. She gasped sharply as she saw the rage now burning in his eyes. In a flash, he was up, diving for her. She screamed as his hard, crushing arms swept the floor from beneath her.

If she had ever doubted her helplessness against his strength, she would no more. He threw her onto the bed, then landed squarely on top of her, grinding her into the mattress with a strength that threatened to crush her ribs.

He took her without preliminaries, without feeling. At first he hurt her; then her flesh defensively yielded. But the wound to her pride was unbearable.

She turned her head to the side, gritting her teeth and thinking of how she hated him, willing herself not to respond. But he slowed his pace, turning her face with a large brown hand.

She glared up at him, saw the bitter determination in his eyes. She tried to yank her head from his grasp, but could not; angrily, she closed her eyes, shutting him out—

He made a quick, hard movement which made her moan as her eyes flew open. He smiled triumphantly.

She jerked forward, unwittingly aiding him as she spat, "I hate—"

But he silenced her with his mouth, ending his assault so quickly and forcefully that for a split second, she quite forgot to hate him.

Edgar stood, buttoning his trousers. "Now, Mrs. Ashland, shall we go to bed?"

Emilie stared at him with abhorrence. She despised him—yet she dared not defy him! Wordlessly, she fixed her clothing, then got up from the bed. She followed him across the veranda and into his room.

He sat down upon the settee, gazed up at her intently. "Come here."

She hesitated.

He shook his head. "You have a stubborn, willful streak, my dear. Must I pain you with another—demonstration?"

She went to him. He took her hand, pulled her down beside him. She glared at him defiantly.

He sighed angrily. "Girl, why do you vex me so? You know you've only yourself to thank for what just happened!"

"Only myself to thank!" she cried. "Did I bludgeon myself into this marriage? Did I lock myself in my room?"

He threw his hands wide in exasperation. "Emilie, I'm responsible for your safety—I can't have you roaming the woods at will! You're my wife now—that you must accept!"

"No, I'll *never* accept it!" she seethed, bolting to her feet, clenching her fists. "You lied to me and—and you broke your promise! As far as I'm concerned, I *never* married you—*never!*"

He reached out, yanked her back down. "Damn it, girl, I did no more than to assert my legal rights!

The marriage has been consummated—your reluctance, at this point, comes a bit late!"

"Oh, you're hateful!" she spat, burying her face in her hands to hide her tears of rage.

He silently watched her struggle to contain the ire welling in her chest. Then, gently, he touched her shoulder. "Emilie, can we not begin anew?" he asked softly. "I don't want to force you this way—or lock you up."

She sat upright, her eyes bright with hatred. "Certainly, sir, we'll start anew! As soon as you return my virginity!"

"Hell!" he groaned. He leaned over; a chill swept down her spine as he grasped one of her slippers, removed it.

She flinched, started to rise. "Don't," he said.

She watched, unnerved, as he removed her other slipper, then drew off her stockings. He stood, pulled her to her feet. "Turn around," he instructed, his eyes determined.

She glowered at him.

His jaw tightened; his firm hands turned her. She felt his deft fingers unbuttoning her dress. Pulling the printed cotton over her head, he tossed the gown upon the settee.

He turned her, catching his breath sharply as he stared at the soft curves of her body veiled by the thin cloth of her chemise. Her eyes seemed to ignite with desire at the sight of her. "Love, your skin is like satin," he murmured wonderingly.

Involuntarily, she shivered. For suddenly, he was very different. The bitter determination had left his features, replaced by naked, searching desire.

Somehow, he was more frightening this way. She could understand and fight his anger. But how could she combat the desperate need now burning in his eyes?

His hands reached out, pulled the pins from her hair one by one. Emilie stared down at the floor, feeling the tension, the slight trembling in his fingers. As the curls tumbled down about her shoulders, she heard him sigh deeply. The pins clattered to the floor, scattering about their feet.

She looked up at him. Abruptly, he groaned, pulling her hard against him, burying his face in her hair. She stood stiffly in his arms, as he whispered fiercely, "This time I'm not going to hurt you, Emilie. This time you're going to beg me to make love to you."

"No! she moaned.

His fingers reached for the ties on her chemise. "Please—" she whispered, pulling away.

He released her. "Get in bed, love."

Shivering, she hurried to the bed, crawled in, pulling the covers up to her neck. She averted her face as he undressed. Oh, God, how she wanted to run away from him! But where could she go?

She heard him blow out the lamp; the room glowed with silvery moonlight. Then his body sank into the mattress next to her.

"Please—no!" she whispered.

He pulled back the covers, drew her unyielding form against him. Part of her wanted to claw his eyes out, but she could not bear the thought of being forced again this night. Thus, she lay corpse-rigid in his embrace, willing herself to think of anything but the hard, warm body pressing into hers.

Seeming to guess her plan of resistance, he began his assault very slowly, stroking her shoulders and back and face, sending involuntary chills through her body. He tickled her ear lobe with his tongue, whispering to her soothingly. Then, he finished undressing her, moving her hands aside when she weakly protested.

As the long moments passed, Emilie found herself unwittingly relaxing in his arms. She was exhausted, wanting to forget everything—the unbearable tension of the day, the violence of his rape. She wanted to close her eyes, surrender to blackness, hope all of this would somehow disappear, like a bad dream—

But then he was kissing her. And his kisses were thorough, melting, devastating. His hands swept her body with consummate skill; his lips followed.

"No—no!" she moaned, even as her small, ragged gasps belied her protests.

But the slow torment continued. Emilie found herself weakening, then wanting him—forgetting who she was, who he was, as her entire being became the exquisite ache deep within her.

He pushed her onto her back, rolled on top of her. But pride rose up, forcing her to deny what she most desired. She stiffened, clenching her thighs.

In the darkness, his passionate eyes burned down into hers. "Emilie, open to me," he demanded hoarsely. "I told you I'll not hurt you, girl."

The lump of pride in her throat burst; she wanted to wound him, just as denying him wounded her. "Yes, you'll hurt me!" she cried. "And I'll scream out to the night that Edgar Ashland could have his wife *only* by rape—because—because you disgust me!"

"Goddammit!" he roared, rolling off her. She heard his fist pound the mattress. "I *should* rape you, you cold-blooded little hypocrite!"

Had Emilie not been in an agony of need herself, she would have laughed at him then, spoken her triumph. But as much as she hated him, not having him now seemed a hollow victory.

They lay tensely silent for long moments. Then he rolled towards her, supporting himself on an elbow as his eyes, glowing like coals in the moonlit room, devoured her.

"What a witch you are!" he muttered. "You torment me, woman, yet I only want to awaken you to the sweetest pleasures imaginable."

He reached out, touched one of her nipples with a fingertip. Instinctively, she groaned.

"Admit you want me, Emilie."

"Never!" she retorted, her voice quavering.

He sighed. "Do you know what you do to me, Emilie?" he asked quietly, his fingers teasing her nipple to unbearable tautness. "Do you know what it feels like, to have you beneath me, to enter you—"

"No! Don't!" she cried out, revolted, ashamed, clapping her hands over her ears.

He yanked her hands away. "By God, you'll listen!" he growled. He perched above her, eyes wild with desire, pinning her hands into the mattress. "Do you know what it's like—to go all these years without a woman, then to have you, beneath me? It's heaven, Emilie. Your skin is like satin, your lips sweet and yielding, and when I take you—"

"No! Stop!"

"When I take you you're warm and tight around me. Last night, when you moved upward to meet me—"

"Stop it! Stop it!" she screamed.

"You know how to stop it!" he growled. "Last night, when your hips arched to meet me," he continued ruthlessly, "you turned hot and melting around me, velvet soft—"

"Oh God!" she groaned, driven beyond pride. "Damn you, take me! Take me!"

For a moment, he stared at her in disbelief. Then he gently rolled on top of her. "Love," he whispered, shuddering.

Emilie opened to him, her entire being aching for fulfillment. But Edgar teased her for long moments, enticing her with the tip of his manhood, then pulling away. She lost control, reaching downward; but his hand grabbed hers.

"Say 'I want you, Edgar,' " he whispered.

"Please—" she pleaded miserably.

"Say it!"

"All right! I want you!" she choked.

"Edgar," he prompted.

"I want you, Edgar!"

"That's better," he breathed, his arms tightening about her, even as he violently surged downward.

She gasped at his suddenness, then his warm mouth stilled the trembling of her lips. There was no pain, only hot, thirsting flesh meeting in shared rapture. Emilie lost all thought of time and space—her whole being became frantic need. She took him deeply inside her, welcoming with joy his hard thrusts, letting him lead her to what she knew was coming—

He drove her to the precipice of a new, glorious sensation, held her there until she softened to him completely, then fell with her into the riotous, primitive chasm of release. . . .

Afterwards, she clung to him for long moments, too shaken to break the spell. But then she remembered. He had won again. She stiffened, pushed him away, tears stinging her eyes.

He grabbed her arm. "No, Emilie, I'll not let you freeze me out! Not after what we've shared tonight!"

Parting her legs, he mounted her, his mouth smothering her sobs.

At daybreak, Edgar Ashland was already dressed for the day, and again stood by the bed, studying his sleeping wife. He put his hand out to touch her gold curls, then drew it, trembling, back.

God, he had nearly lost her! First, she had driven him wild with her taunts about David. Then, when she threw the vase at him, a horrible image of Charles and Amelia, their mutilated bodies, had blinded him. He had become pure, uncontrollable rage. He had raped her—hurt her.

Afterwards, when he came to, he died inside. He felt as if he had taken a small bird and slowly, savagely, crushed its every fragile bone.

But he had gotten her back again, breaking through her defenses with half-pleading, half-bravado. God, she had been sweet!

"Angel," he murmured, his eyes misting over as he gazed at her. Young, innocent, she had given herself to him completely. She had not learned how to hold back, or pretend an emotion she did not feel. She was guileless, giving. Must he destroy her? Must he teach her to deceive him, to loathe him?

What did he want of her? The blinding truth hit him—he wanted her to love him! But could he love in return? Wasn't it too late? And hell—she loved David, anyway!

"What have I done?" he groaned weakly. He had

coerced this beautiful girl into marriage—to satisfy his lusts, to warm his bed in this haven away from the world. He had not for a moment thought of her as a person, considered her hopes or dreams. It had been a game—carnal, ruthless.

A dangerous game. Part of him wanted to punish her, eradicate her womanhood. Part of him could not forgive, or forget.

But the joke was on him. If he could not control the beast within him, he would break her gentle, beautiful spirit.

And he knew it would kill him.

Chapter Eleven

March 19, 1841

Late the next day, Emilie stood in her chemise, staring at her dresses now hanging next to Edgar's garments in his wardrobe. She tapped her foot impatiently. She had awakened that morning to find Avis Gerouard and Hallie moving all her things into Edgar's room. Emilie had protested strenuously, to no avail. "M'sieur Ashland's orders," Avis had informed her.

After Avis left, Emilie found that the French doors to her old room had been bolted shut. Furious at Edgar, she was ranting to Hallie about his cruelty when Avis returned, taking Hallie out for the day, claiming she had chores for the girl in the kitchen.

Thus, Emilie had spent much of the day alone, thinking of what had transpired between her and Edgar, and becoming prideful, enraged. It wasn't enough that the beast had broken through her body's resistance! Now he had taken away her room, drawing her deeper into his web, leaving her completely trapped!

Trapped in his room, his arms. Trapped in the carnal emotions her body betrayed. She hated him—wanted him—and hated herself most of all for giving in to him!

She had spent much of the day plotting a way to get her revenge, with little result. Growing nervous and exhausted, she had tried napping, but found her mind spinning with the thought of Edgar returning to the room that evening. What new torture would she be subjected to?

Now, as the day aged, she held out her dresses one by one. What would most suit his majesty? she mused derisively. Then her eyes caught the crimson garment she had brought from Houston by mistake. With a low, bitter laugh, she drew it out—studied the tawdry red satin, the plunging neckline, feather trim, sheer sleeves. She held the dress against her.

"Oh, well," she quipped. "Better here than on the streets of Houston."

Emilie studied herself in the mirror, satisfied with her handiwork. The dress fit her perfectly, tightly, exposing a generous portion of her ripe, young breasts, making her look lewdly voluptuous. Her face was brightly painted—she had used the rouge stick she once sneaked off to buy in Houston when on a rebellious tear against Granny. To top off the outfit, she had pulled some of the scarlet tassels from Edgar's velvet drapes, lacing them through the curls piled on top of her head.

She giggled, satisfied. He treated her like a strumpet. Let him see how he liked this little surprise!

Hearing the bolt spring back, Emilie swirled about, her face taunting, triumphant.

Avis Gerouard entered the room, almost dropping the tea tray she carried. Emilie struggled not to giggle at the uncharacteristic astonishment on Avis's face.

"I—I brought your tea, Madame," Avis sputtered.

"Thank you, Mrs. Gerouard," Emilie returned haughtily.

Avis hastily set down the tray, then left the room, softly closing the door.

Emilie gasped. Had her ears deceived her? She hadn't heard the bolt shoot back!

She hurried to the door, tried the knob. Yes—it was unlocked! She started to go tearing into the hall, then thought better of the idea, rushing back to the dressing table.

"Oh, fiddlesticks!" she groaned at her strumpet reflection. "I can't leave the house like this!"

Quickly, she wet the corner of a cloth, began scrubbing at the rouge on her cheeks. But the paint was stubborn, and very little rubbed off. "Blast!" she hissed, stamping her foot.

Then she heard the sound of a horse approaching. She rushed out onto the veranda, cautiously peering over the railing. Oh, God—there he was, dismounting from Apollyon! She could only hope he would not come directly upstairs!

She ran back inside, trying in vain to remove the rouge from her cheeks. As the moments passed, no footsteps approached the door, and she realized with relief that Edgar must be in his office. But surely he would come to her soon—she must leave, dressed as she was, or lose her chance!

The choice was no choice. Her heart beating wildly, she opened the door and crept into the hallway. Good—no one about.

She tiptoed down the stairs, breathed a sigh of relief when she found the downstairs hallway was also deserted. She hurried to the door, then rushed outside.

A crisp spring breeze greeted her as she tore down the front steps of Brazos Bend. But once she got to the lawn, she stopped dead in her tracks, spotting a buggy coming up the hillside.

Oh, no! What if it were David? But she braced herself, hurried on. Whoever it was would have to take her away from Brazos Bend, she decided desperately.

Within moments, the buggy stopped before her; a stout man in a black robe stared down at her.

"Why, Pastor Fritz!" Emilie exclaimed, looking up at the red-faced parson.

The portly man's eyes were bulging in his round face as he climbed out of his conveyance. "*Guten Tag*, Frau Ashland." Lamely, he extended a pudgy hand holding a lace fan. "I bring ze present for ze *Braut*. Ze fan belonk to my *Mutter*."

Her eyes darting about wildly, Emilie took the fan. "Thank you, Pastor," she said shrilly. What madness was this? she asked herself. She was dressed like a prostitute, conversing with a parson about wedding presents, and any moment her husband might come storming out—

She whirled to face the parson. "Will you take me to the village?"

Pastor Fritz shook his head in befuddlement. "*Entschuldigen*, Frau Ashland?"

"The village! Washington-on-the-Brazos!" Emilie hissed exasperatedly, pointing towards his rig. "In your buggy!"

For a moment, the parson frowned, pondering Emilie's statement. Then, suddenly, he seemed to comprehend her remarks. He clapped his hands. "Ah, ze village, Frau Ashland. I begin to see! That *ist* why your face *ist heiss*. You have ze *Fieber, ja*? You need ze *Doctor?*"

137

"Yes! Yes!" Emilie cried, grabbing his arm. "I have a desperate case of the fever! Anything you say! Just take me to the village! Now!"

"*Ja, Ja,*" the parson agreed, nodding vigorously.

The bald-headed man helped Emilie into the carriage; then the springs groaned as he climbed in beside her, breathing laboriously. He clucked gently to his team of matched sorrels, and the buggy rattled off down the bluebonnet-strewn hillside.

"Can't you go any faster?" Emilie asked hoarsely.

Pastor Fritz nodded solicitously. "Ah, Frau Ashland, I fear you are quite *unwohl.*" He shook the reins vigorously. "*Sich beeilen,* my beauties!"

As the buggy bounced toward River Road, Emilie spread out the beige lace fan the parson had given her, inanely studying the mother-of-pearl sticks, the satin medallion picturing a man and woman embracing. Finding that the man on the cameo reminded her of Edgar, she shuddered, began fanning herself nervously.

This is insanity! she thought as they clattered along. She hadn't even considered what she would do when they got to the village. What a sight they would be—a man of God escorting a daughter of the devil! Despite her fears, it took great effort on Emilie's part not to burst out laughing.

But when the parson began humming "Amazing Grace," Emilie giggled hysterically, then succumbed to spasmodic laughter.

Pastor Fritz sympathetically squeezed Emilie's hand. "Poor Frau Ashland. Your mind *ist* not vith you. Ve get you to ze village, braf lady."

They had just turned onto River Road when Emilie heard hoofbeats approaching—her heart sank. Within seconds, her worst fears were confirmed, as she heard her husband shout, "Hold up there!"

"No! Please!" Emilie gasped.

But Pastor Fritz had already begun pulling back on the reins. "*Guten Tag*, Herr Ashland!" he called to the grim-faced Edgar.

Edgar dismounted, tied Apollyon to a tree, then approached the buggy on the Pastor's side. He peered into the conveyance, saw Emilie—his face went white. "What the hell is this? A parson taking my wife whoring?"

Thankfully, Edgar's invective seemed lost on the smiling pastor. "You are vorried about your vife, Herr Ashland? She haf *ein streng* case of ze *Fieber*, and needs ze *Doktor, ja?*"

"I think I know *exactly* what my wife needs," Edgar replied, striding to the other side of the buggy.

Ungentle hands pulled Emilie to the ground, into her husband's hard embrace. Their eyes met, held.

"Don't force me to make a scene!" Emilie hissed up at him. "I'm going with Pastor Fritz to the village!"

Edgar's hands were like iron bands on Emilie's squirming spine, as he leaned over and whispered calmly in her ear, "No you aren't, sweet. Surely you won't force that dear old man to defend your—er—rather questionable virtue? He'd lose, you know."

She pushed him away, glaring up at him, her lower lip trembling.

"You will take your vife to ze *Doktor*, Herr Ashland?" the parson inquired of Edgar

Edgar turned, his arm tight about Emilie's waist. "I'll take care of her, Pastor. Good day, sir."

The jovial man nodded, reaching down to hand Emilie the fan she had left on the leather seat. "You forget ze present, Frau Ashland. I hope your health *ist besser.*"

"Thank you, Pastor—goodbye," Emilie muttered, a frozen smile on her face as she grasped the fan.

As the parson's buggy lumbered off, Edgar said smoothly, "Let's go home, Mrs. Ashland."

He led her to Apollyon, untied the horse, then mounted. He extended his hand to her, looking down sternly.

Gulping, she gave him her hand; he pulled her in front of him astride the horse.

Edgar was ominously silent as the horse trotted off. Not able to see his face, Emilie stammered, "W-what are you going to do?"

Edgar laughed mirthlessly. "I'm going to do what I should have done days ago, sweet," he said in a deadly soft voice, his arm tightening about her middle. "I'm going to take you home and beat the willfulness out of your hide. When I'm finished with you, madam, your hussy face will seem pale by comparison!"

"No!" Emilie screamed, kicking and clawing at him, trying to jump off the horse.

"Be still!" Edgar barked, at once trying to control Emilie and calm Apollyon's nervous neighing at these shenanigans.

But Emilie fought like a wildcat. They had reached a fork in the road; Apollyon reared, snorting angrily. Then, ignoring Edgar's commands, the Arabian tore down the river bank onto the sandbar where the *Belle* had landed.

Edgar managed to stop the horse mere feet from the water's edge. Dismounting, he yanked the struggling girl down into his hard arms. "Damn you, woman, calm down!"

She beat against his chest and bit his shoulder, shrieking at the top of her lungs.

"Mother of God!" he hollered. "You defiant little

bitch! Paint your face and play the whore, will you? I'll remedy that!"

He quickly strode to the edge of the sandbar. Then, forcefully, he threw his kicking, screaming wife into the Brazos.

The shock of cold water slapped Emilie, and she fell, grasping at the rushing blackness. Her rage turned to terror as she realized that the sandbar had dropped off, suddenly, into deep, turbulent water. An undercurrent tugged her deeper, making her lose her sense of direction, as her skirt tangled about her legs. She struggled wildly for the surface, her lungs bursting.

Daylight flashed about her. Surfacing, she gasped for air, screaming, "Edgar, I c-can't swim!"

She saw a vision of his face—white with panic—then she was pulled downward again and the blackness engulfed her. . . .

Emilie drifted, finding herself back at Gonzales during the war. The houses were exploding, the air thick with panic. But the sounds became muffled, for she was drowning! Edgar was there, holding her beneath the cold, black waters of the river. . . .

Emilie awakened to the sound of her own, ragged sobs. Slowly, she opened heavy-lidded eyes. Edgar swam before her—a monster with two heads—one white, one black.

She gasped. Her vision cleared. Edgar and Hallie stood before her in a pool of lamplight. It was night.

"W-what happened?" she asked weakly.

Edgar rushed to her side, his face creased with worry. "Darling, darling, you've come to your senses! You've been babbling incoherently for hours. I thought—I feared—you were deprived of air too long and had lost your mind—"

"You have us a mess scared, Missus," Hallie interrupted, "a rantin' and a screamin'!"

Edgar glowered at the slave and Hallie, eyes white, darted out of the room, closing the door.

Edgar sat on the bed and took Emilie's hand. She let her fingers rest limply in his—she was too tired to care. "You tried to drown me," she muttered.

His face was stricken. "Darling—no—I never meant to hurt you!" He lay down next to her, burying his face in her hair. "Forgive me, love, forgive me."

"Forgive you," she repeated with a feeble, bitter laugh. "You don't care whether I forgive you. You—you hate me."

"No, darling, no!" he denied, his face tortured as he pulled back to look at her. "I don't hate you. I hated—what you looked like. I hated your leaving me."

"So you decided to drown me," she mumbled.

"I didn't decide anything!" he insisted. "When I realized you'd run away, I grew wild with anger. Then I saw you in that nauseating costume—and you defied me! All I could think of was making you stop fighting me, and getting that damn paint off your face! The next thing I knew, you were in the water, flailing about. . . ." His voice faded, trembling.

Weakly, she pushed him away. "I wish I had drowned!"

"No!" he choked, yanking back the covers, grabbing her around the waist. With a gasp, she realized she was completely naked, vulnerable.

He pulled her hard against him, the buttons of his shirt digging into her bare breasts. "I will show you that you want to live, Emilie. I will feel your forgiveness. Now."

He gave her an agonized look, then began planting

142

kisses all over her face. She submitted passively, too exhausted to fight him.

Her cheeks were wet. With her tears? His? Did it matter? "Please, Edgar—I'm so tired."

His arms tightened about her as his lips travelled down her body. "Forgive me, love, but I must . . . I must. . . ."

Chapter Twelve

March 20, 1841

Emilie awakened in the half-light to see Edgar standing across the room from her. He was naked, his face lathered. Their eyes met in the mirror. He paused, the razor against his face, his expression tender. "Good morning," he said.

For a moment, she smiled, turning towards him. Then she winced with the pain the movement brought, and remembered. She turned away.

She hurt. She felt shaken-up from her struggles with Edgar the previous day, and her muscles ached from battling the black currents of the Brazos. How could he have done this to her? She trembled as she remembered the moment of terror when he threw her in the river, the darkness engulfing her. . . .

Then her face burned as she remembered a far worse humiliation—she had let him make love to her last night! Tears burned her eyes at the memory of her weakness—

He had taken her with gentle ruthlessness until she responded, sobbing her anguish, clinging to him. . . .

"Are you all right, love?"

Emilie turned to see Edgar standing by the bed; he leaned over, gently took her face in his hands.

Looking at his powerful body perched above her, she stiffened, the place between her thighs twinging with the memory of his ceaseless lovemaking. She felt sore, utterly possessed. Surely he would not, again—

"Please—I feel bruised—after everything," she pleaded breathlessly.

He frowned, then leaned over and kissed her forehead gently. She smelled his shaving soap as his smooth cheek caressed her temple. "Love, could I but undo it." He sighed resignedly, then stood, taking his clothes from the foot of the bed. "You must soak in a tub of hot water."

Oh, yes, a tub of hot water would fix everything! she thought angrily. But she said nothing, fearing his reaction. Lest he change his mind and return to the bed, she got up and donned her wrapper.

Warily, she watched him dress. Why was he so damned handsome? she asked herself irritably, studying his rugged face, his muscular chest. If he were ugly, scar-faced and paunchy, it would be easy to resist him! But the man exuded an electric sensuality. His flesh owned hers, and, damn him, he knew it!

She eyed him cautiously as he buttoned his frock coat. But when he approached the door, keys in hand, her rage overrode her reason. "*Do* lock me in," she taunted. "Is that what you did to Olivia?"

He turned violently, his face white. She knew she had hit a raw nerve, but she couldn't stop herself and continued ruthlessly, "Did you lock her in, too, Edgar? Did she escape the first chance she got? Did she prefer the depths of the Brazos to your loathsome embrace?"

The angry words spilled out, without thought. Then she saw his face. Oh, God, she thought desperately, what have I done? Never had she seen him so angry. He grabbed her, shook her until she thought her head would snap off. Then he drew his fist back, ready to strike.

She threw her hands to her face, stiffened for the blow. But none came. Cautiously, she peered through her fingers, watching the play of tormented emotion on his face.

"God damn you, woman!" he finally hissed.

He stormed to the door, kicking it open with a black boot, breaking the lock.

"Good morning, Daniel."

The wizened old servant looked shocked as Emilie swept past him through the downstairs hall. She walked sedately into the deserted dining room.

She sat down, unfolded her napkin. At last, she thought, she had scored a victory against that despicable man! It had been well worth the stark terror she had suffered minutes earlier. Of one thing she was certain—she had hurt him. If he suffered only a whit of the pain he had heaped upon her, then she was considerably satisfied.

As Emilie poured herself coffee, Avis Gerouard strolled in. The Creole woman's usually stoic features displayed shock at seeing Emilie. "*Mon dieu*, Madame!" she sputtered. "You're out of your room!"

Emilie regarded the older woman haughtily. "Indeed, Mrs. Gerouard! Do you assume it is normal for me to be kept like a caged animal?"

The woman's eyes grew wide, then she hastily recovered. "I—I'll get your breakfast, Madame."

Emilie smiled grimly as the woman left the room.

When Avis returned moments later with a steaming plate, Emilie studied her curiously. The woman could actually be pretty were it not for her forbidding countenance and mourning attire.

"Do you wish anything else, Madame?" the housekeeper inquired, handing Emilie a basket of muffins.

"You may go, Mrs. Gerouard," Emilie replied airily.

The Creole woman's eyes flickered strangely for a moment, then she quietly left the room.

Emilie smiled. She was learning to get under the skin of that black-haired cat of a woman! And the old witch deserved it!

As Emilie ate her breakfast, she thought again of Edgar's bizarre behavior the previous day. First, he had almost drowned her; then he had made love to her, begging her forgiveness. Who was he—man or demon? Or both?

The answer was quite simple. He was mad. And she, hating him beyond all reason, taunted him mercilessly, drove him to violence. Oh, what a horrendous mess!

If she stayed, she knew sooner or later she would push him too far and he would kill her. That he had made abundantly clear yesterday. She knew the power of the man, yet this morning she had again vexed him, and he had almost, almost—

Emilie threw down her napkin, her appetite suddenly gone. Her options, she realized, were really quite simple. She must find the right moment to make her move.

She left the dining room and entered the front hall, almost colliding with her unsmiling husband as he stepped from the staircase. Cocking an eyebrow, he strode off down the hall.

Oh, dear, she thought. Have I made him more angry by leaving the bedroom?

Cautiously, Emilie followed him. She found him in the office, his back to her as he sat at the desk, shuffling papers. She stood watching him, listening to the creaking of his leather swivel chair.

Then, as if her eyes had bored into his back, he swung around, stood. "You wish something, madam?"

She cleared her throat nervously. "I—well—since you broke the lock on the door, I assumed you did not care—"

"Did not care, my dear?" he interrupted.

"I assumed you did not mind," she continued hastily, "if I left your room."

A wry smile pulled down one corner of his mouth, but his eyes remained cold. "My dear Mrs. Ashland, may I assume you are here to ask your husband's permission to leave *our* room?"

Miserably, Emilie lowered jet eyelashes and did not reply.

He walked toward her, circling her like a great stalking cat, his bold eyes eating into her flesh. After a moment, he moved off, closing the door.

Emilie looked up cautiously, meeting his steely gaze. What was he up to now, the rogue?

"Let me allay your fears, my dear," he murmured smoothly. "It's just as well that you roam the house at will. Sooner or later, I plan to take you in every room of the house."

Emilie gasped and backed away from him. He approached her steadily, his eyes intense, determined. As the rough planking of the wall pushed against her back, she realized that escape was impossible.

Close to her now, Edgar paused, seeming to savor

her discomfort. "Are my embraces so—what was the word, sweet?—loathesome?"

He was next to her now, his hard frame pinning her against the wall, his masculine scent filling her senses. His eyes scorched her face as he whispered, "You're not like Olivia. Or are you?"

Oh, God, what does he mean? she thought. His hand slowly moved down the front of her dress; his body flattened hers against the wall. A low moan escaped her throat—fear, mixed with inevitable desire.

He laughed, low and bitter. "You're ready—just thinking about it, aren't you, love?"

Abruptly, he released her, returning to his desk. "Run along, woman. Your lusting has kept me from my work."

His words hit Emilie like a blinding slap. "Monster!" she hissed. "Oh, I'll run along! Straight back to Houston. I don't care if I have to walk every step of the way!"

She stumbled for the door, but a strong hand seized her arm. "Sit down!" her husband roared.

"No!" she screamed, lashing out at him.

"Sit down, or I'll not be responsible for the consequences!" he threatened, grabbing her wrists.

She stiffened, glowering at him.

Seeing her indecision, he pulled her to the leather settee, pushed her down. "Did you learn nothing yesterday, Emilie?" he asked menacingly, glaring down at her. "Must I keep you under lock and key?"

"Doesn't it matter to you that I hate you?" she spat back.

A vein jumped in his temple. He clenched his fists, then uttered evenly, "You sing a different song in my bed, love."

Her face burned; miserably, she lowered her gaze. "You would—shame me with that?"

He sat down beside her, raised her chin with his hand, forcing her to meet his angry, passionate gaze. "I don't want your damned shame, Emilie. I want you to let go of your stupid pride, and give yourself to me as you truly desire—without reservation."

"No!" she denied, throwing off his grasp. "I *never* wanted you! You pushed me into this marriage! I only want to leave—as soon as possible!"

"Leave?" he hissed. "Where would you go, Emilie? You should be grateful I've provided you with a home."

She jumped up, only to be yanked back down. "Damn it, girl—haven't you a brain?" he snapped. "All this talk of gallivanting about! Don't you realize there are Indians in the woods? That the field hands have recently spotted them near here?"

His words sent chills up and down her spine. "I—hadn't thought—" she faltered.

He scowled. "Aye, you've done precious little thinking, Emilie! As you must be aware, Lamar's soldiers have been pushing the Cherokees from their lands. The stragglers remaining are not in a mood to be amused." He paused, carefully watching her reaction. "Do you know you could be killed?"

"You wouldn't care!" she accused.

He leaned back against the settee, crossing his legs carefully as he eyed her coldly. "I would not find you particularly—attractive—love, minus your scalp."

"Oh!" she gasped, enraged and revolted.

She sprang up, stumbled towards the door. But Edgar pursued her, holding her squirming body. "Do you know what the Cherokees did to David's parents—to Charles and Amelia?'' he asked in a strangely calm voice.

"Spare me the gruesome details!" she spat, struggling against him.

"Spare you? Would you prefer to experience it firsthand?"

Emilie's lip quivered under his hard gaze.

"My brother Charles was the lucky one," Edgar continued in a harsh whisper. "He was scalped—killed—quickly. But Amelia was killed—in a more leisurely fashion." He paused significantly.

She shuddered. "Please—no more. I believe you!"

"Do you, love?" He pulled her hard against him, his hands forbidding escape. "She was raped, Emilie," he hissed between gritted teeth, "raped repeatedly, brutally. Her fingers and toes were cut off one by one, her legs slashed—"

"No! No! Stop it!" Emilie screamed, clapping her hands over her ears.

Edgar yanked her hands away, held them tight. "She was scalped, of course," he continued ruthlessly, "and somewhere along the line—mercifully—she died. By the look on her face, it took a long time."

Tears spilled from Emilie's eyes, but still he continued. "They also slaughtered several of the slaves who didn't run fast enough. Then they tried to burn the house. Luckily, a rainstorm saved our home. When David and I returned from fishing and found their bodies—" he paused, then added raggedly, "the look on David's face has haunted my dreams for many years."

His hold on her relaxed, as if something had died inside him. He released her, turning away.

She threw open the door, fled into the hall; but he was soon beside her, grabbing her arm as she started up the stairs. "That's not the way to Houston, love."

With a choking cry, Emilie threw off his grasp and stumbled upstairs.

Emilie returned to Edgar's room and stood pressed against the door, tears spilling from closed eyes that could not bear to look at his room, his bed.

The brute! First he had shamed her with her body's response, then he had tortured her with the ghoulish account of Indian atrocities. She hated him, hated him!

A sudden breeze swept through the room, washing a sickeningly sweet odor across her. Stifling a sob, she opened her eyes. Then she saw the mirror, the wetness in the middle of the carpet.

And she screamed with horror and revulsion.

It seemed only seconds later that Edgar bolted into the room, his eyes wild. "What the hell—"

He paused; they both stared dumbfounded at the room. Emilie's red dress lay in shreds about the floor. Her mother's rose crystal perfume bottle lay shattered near the dresser, and a choking essence of rosewater was exuded from the wetness on the rug. But Emilie's eyes were focused with horror upon the mirror above the dressing table. It had been shattered—no doubt with the perfume bottle—and the word "whore" had been emblazoned across it with Emilie's rouge stick.

She whirled upon Edgar. "You did it!" she accused hysterically. "You did it—I saw you coming down the stairs after breakfast! You broke my mother's bottle!"

"Emilie—I—how could you think—"

"Don't lie to me, you coward! How could you torment me downstairs, all the time knowing,

knowing—" she choked on her tears.

Edgar knelt, picked up a fragment of rose crystal, muttering, "I had no idea the bottle meant so much to you."

She glared down at him in bitter triumph. "There! You admitted it! It means—meant a lot to me! Just like your blasted vase!"

He stood up angrily. "You think that because you broke the vase I—"

"Yes! Yes! Now, get out of my sight! Get out!"

Edgar threw the fragment down. "All right, I'll leave! Think what you will, but I plan to get to the bottom of this. And when I find out the truth, you'll not like the price I'll exact from you for my forgiveness!"

Moments later, Hallie came into the room. Liberally proclaiming her shock and outrage, she cleaned up the mess. Then she and Daniel removed the shattered mirror from the room.

Hallie returned to find Emilie leaving the room with an armload of dresses. "What are you doing, Missus?" she exclaimed.

"Quit your chattering and help me, Hallie," Emilie replied crossly. "I'm moving my things back to the other room!"

Hallie's eyes rolled wildly with fear. "No'um!"

Emilie spun about, enraged by the girl's disobedience. "Hallie, didn't you just see what Mr. Ashland did to me?"

"Yes'um."

"Then how in God's name do you expect me to stay in this room! Quit talking back and get busy, girl!"

Hallie backed off, her full lower lip quivering. "No'um. Mister Ashland will whup me dead if I

153

touch those things!"

The frightened girl scurried out of the room. "Hell!" Emilie groaned. She realized cynically that her language was becoming as colorful as her husband's.

Without Hallie's help, Emilie carried all her things back to the Blue Room. Then she started putting things away, waiting. She knew that, inevitably, Edgar would storm into the room and they would have a dreadful scene. But this time she would die before she submitted to him!

As Emilie put her lingerie away in the chest, her anger built. The gall of the man! He had pushed her into marriage, kept her his prisoner, taken her against her will repeatedly, almost drowned her. Then, just as he had destroyed her virginity, he had smashed her only material link with her dead mother! He had completed her humiliation by shredding the dress and writing "whore" across the shattered mirror.

Then the cad had the audacity to deny doing it! How could he? The word "whore"—the very word he had used when he saw her in the red dress—was a dead giveaway!

The crowning blow was his announcing that he would exact a price from her for his forgiveness. The insufferable arrogance of the man! As long as she lived, she would never, never ask his forgiveness for anything!

The day passed in slow anguish. After lunch, Emilie tried reading, but only flipped through the pages fretfully. Finally, her boredom turned to fatigue. She removed her dress and napped in her chemise.

She was awakened by a meekly smiling Hallie who brought up a dinner tray. "You seen Mistah Ashland yet, Missus?''

"No, Hallie," Emilie returned woodenly, tying on her wrapper and sitting down upon the day bed.

Hallie put the tray down next to Emilie. "He ain't downstairs for dinner, Missus, so I brung this up for you." Sighing, she added worriedly, "I is glad I ain't a wall of this here house when he come home t'night, Missus!"

Emilie picked indifferently at the ham and rice. "You're fortunate, Hallie. I wish I had the luxury of sleeping in quarters removed from the house tonight."

Hallie's face puckered in a frown. "Missus, you sure 'nuff sleepin' in this bed, 'stead of his'n?"

"Yes, Hallie."

The slave's eyes widened ominously. "Missus, I is scared t' see if'n this house is standing tomorrow! And if'n you is!"

Despite Hallie's protestations, Emilie held to her resolve. She let Hallie help her bathe and get ready for bed.

At nightfall, she got into bed, only to toss and turn fitfully. Finally, drowsiness overcame her. Through the wall, she heard the sound of boots scraping the floor. So the beast had finally returned. . . .

The door crashed open and Emilie jumped awake. Edgar stood before her in his nightshirt. "Get out of bed!"

He moved closer, set the taper he carried on the night table. The candlelight wavered over his hard features, giving him a sinister look.

Emilie glowered at him tiredly. "Must you break down every door in the house?"

In a strangely calm voice, he uttered, "Would you

prefer, sweet, that I break every bone in your lovely body? Get out of the bed!"

"No!"

He took an angry step towards her, roaring, "Mother of God, woman! I told you I didn't break your precious bottle!"

"I don't believe you!"

They hung, for a moment, in an enraged, glaring impasse. Then Edgar lunged for her. She dodged him, jumping out of bed. "Enough!" she shrieked, panicking at the black look in his eyes. "I give up!"

Turning her back on him, she stormed out the French doors, down the veranda, and into his room. She got into the bed, pulled the covers up high, and turned her face to the wall.

She felt the mattress sag as he got in beside her. He touched her back, and she went stiff as death. "If you touch me," she said simply, "I'll kill myself."

"You'll *what?*"

"I mean it!" her voice rose in hysteria. "I'll kill myself! I'll find a way!"

There was a long silence, then he sighed heavily. "Very well, madam. You win—for the moment. I'll not force you to endure my loathesome caresses tonight. But mark my words, Emilie. Leave my bed again and you'll be denied the pleasure of your own suicide!"

The next morning, Emilie sat at the dressing table, staring into the mirror Daniel had brought in from her old room. Edgar had just left, after helping her into her green and white frock. She had been maddened by Hallie's absence—the girl was usually waiting in the hall when they awakened, but this morning she was nowhere in sight. Emilie had been forced to endure Edgar's ministrations, shivering as

156

his hands tickled her back while he buttoned the dress.

Now Emilie was rapidly getting into a snit. She was exhausted and nervous this morning, and her hair was a mass of tangles, due to a fitful, sleepless night. She had grown accustomed to Hallie fixing her hair, and wanted the girl to arrive so she could go downstairs for breakfast.

"Blast the girl! Where *is* she?" Emilie cursed, throwing down the hairbrush.

As if summoned, Hallie squeaked open the door and meekly entered the room. Her cocoa-colored skin looked a decided shade paler. "I'm sorry, Missus," she said humbly, "but I been heavin' all mornin'."

"Heaving?" Emilie asked incredulously, standing.

"Why of course, Missus," the girl continued. "Jacob planted me with his seed."

Emilie colored at her servant's coarse language.

"Ain't you happy 'bout it, Missus?" the girl asked uncertainly.

Her face paling as she thought of her own future, Emilie replied tonelessly, "Certainly, I am, Hallie, if you are. Congratulations."

Emilie's knees were suddenly weak; she sat back down. Hallie walked up, preening brightly as she took the hairbrush. But her mistress missed the servant's smile as her mind rushed to the months ahead. How long could she expect to remain in Edgar's bed and not have him take her? How long—damn her traitorous body!—before she demanded to be taken? Then what? A babe growing within her, history repeating itself. She shuddered at an image of her mother bleeding to death in the farmhouse in Gonzales. How long before her luck ran out? What if it had already?

Emilie set her jaw firmly, staring at her stony reflection. She could not, would not give in to him again! She would prevail, and, somehow, she would find a way to leave Brazos Bend forever!

Chapter Thirteen

April 3, 1841

Two weeks passed. The days became longer, warmer, and Emilie found no solution to her dilemma. After her humiliating scene with Edgar in the office, she realized that simply walking out would be foolish and dangerous. She decided to await David's return, and hope to enlist his aid in leaving Brazos Bend.

Edgar steadfastly insisted that Emilie sleep in his bed, but otherwise, he made no sexual overtures. It seemed implicitly agreed that he would leave her alone providing she slept with him. The nights were long, tortured—they went to sleep with their backs to one another. Dark lines appeared under Emilie's eyes as sleep eluded her night after night.

Whether or not Edgar believed her suicide threat, she did not know. But she was grateful that he had not taken her by force again. To her chagrin, however, he played the situation for all it was worth, coming to bed naked, then snoring loudly through the night, occasionally throwing an arm across her hip or breast. In the mornings he would shave, naked, while Emilie would struggle to avert her gaze from his body. On more than one occasion their eyes had met in the mirror, and Edgar had chuckled, causing her to turn crimson with shame.

She hated to admit it to herself, but he was getting to her. Her flesh missed his embrace, his warmth. During that time her body informed her that she was not to bear his child, and she was tempted to throw the information up to him. Then she realized dismally that her real motive was to tempt him to rectify the situation! Things had come to a pretty pass, indeed, if she were willing to forego her fear of childbearing in order to satisfy her lusts!

Luckily, her pride held firm. Thus, so did her coldness.

Edgar had not again mentioned the broken perfume bottle, despite his promise to find the guilty party. How could he, she often mused bitterly, when *he* was the guilty party? She often wondered if he were insane, and feared a return of his violent behavior. She avoided him whenever possible.

The days passed in slow loneliness for Emilie. She had free run of the house now—she played the piano, read books from the well-stocked library, sewed. But she lacked human companionship, other than Hallie, whose conversational skills were limited. Maria Ramero still hadn't arrived from Nacogdoches, and Emilie was beginning to wonder if something had gone awry, since David had told her the girl should be arriving by the end of March.

So Emilie waited and kept her own company. When the house became too confining, she took long walks about the grounds to relieve the boredom. Surprisingly, Edgar made no attempt to stop her from taking these jaunts, other than warning her not to stray into the woods.

On one particularly pretty late spring morning, as

Emilie returned to the house from a walk to pick some bluebonnets, she ran into Avis Gerouard in the front hallway. "Madame Ashland, there is a caller in the drawing room, and I cannot locate M'sieur Edgar. Do you wish to speak to the gentleman?"

Emilie's spirits soared. A caller! Someone actually coming to visit them in this God-forsaken place! "Of course I will see the gentleman, Mrs. Gerouard."

"Yes, Madame."

Avis left her. Emilie paused before entering the parlor, considering her appearance. Should she change her frock? She eyed her blue gingham critically. It wasn't her best dress, but it would do. Besides, she couldn't wait a moment longer to greet the visitor! Shifting the bluebonnets from one hand to the other, she smoothed down a couple of stray curls, then entered the room.

The man stood with his back to her, gazing out the window. He was tall, almost as tall as Edgar, but of stockier build. His curly hair was a bright red. But he was far more conspicuous because of his flashy clothing—he wore an emerald-green velvet frock coat, crisp white trousers tucked into gleaming black boots.

He turned, then, as if feeling Emilie's presence. He stared at her in utter astonishment, as if a young woman were the last thing he expected to see.

Emilie's eyes took in the handsome, freckled face, the sparkling green eyes. He seemed about Edgar's age—perhaps a bit younger. She studied his starched linen shirt, the black cravat and vest, the green satin waistcoat.

The caller let out a low whistle, breaking the silence. "Jesus!" he breathed. "Where the devil did you come from?" His eyes swept Emilie from head to toe. Then, grinning, he asked, "Those flowers for me, sweetheart?''

His voice, deep and resonant, was full of mocking derision. Infuriated, Emilie somehow managed not to throw the bluebonnets in his face. She spun about and swept out of the room, intent upon having Daniel expel the braggart.

But the caller followed her into the hall. "Miss! Miss, please—excuse my remarks. Please, I meant no harm!''

Emilie turned and eyed the stranger cautiously. The man continued sincerely, "My apologies, young lady, I had no idea Edgar had a woman here—''

"A wife,'' Emilie interrupted haughtily.

The gentleman grinned, displaying even white teeth. "Well, I'll be damned. Old Edgar is remaining true to character—I'll grant him that.''

Emilie drew herself up with dignity. "Please state your business, sir.''

The caller scratched his red head, raising an eyebrow in puzzlement. "I fear I've botched things badly, Mrs. Ashland. Could we not begin anew?'' He bowed formally, then drew himself up, offering his hand. " Aaron Rice at your service, madam.''

Emilie looked suspiciously from Aaron Rice's hand to his face. He smiled back at her—a friendly, contagious smile. She hesitated for a moment, then shook his hand. "Very well, Mr. Rice. You may join me in the parlor.''

Once they were seated, Emilie again asked Aaron Rice his business. "Actually, I'm hunting that husband of yours,'' Aaron returned. "He has something that belongs to me.''

"Oh?'' Emilie prompted as she arranged the bluebonnets in a crystal bowl before her.

Aaron crossed long legs and leaned back in his chair. "Actually, it belongs to my parents. Olivia's portrait.''

"Olivia's portrait?" Emilie repeated, looking up in shock.

Aaron laughed—a short, dry laugh. "Don't you know? No, of course not. Why should Edgar tell you about me? Mrs. Ashland, I'm Olivia Ashland's brother."

"Olivia Ashland's brother!" Emilie echoed.

Aaron frowned. "You *do* know about Olivia, don't you? Edgar's first wife? You know, the one he chased into the river?"

Aaron's words sent shivers up and down Emilie's spine. "You don't have a very high opinion of my husband, do you, Mr. Rice?"

Aaron smiled thinly. "Lady, you're married to him. Do you?"

Emilie swallowed a giggle. The gentleman had a point. "Tell me about—this portrait," she urged, dodging his question.

"Well, it's pretty much as I've already told you. It belongs to my family."

Emilie frowned pensively. "I'm familiar with the entire house, Mr. Rice, but I can't recall seeing—such a portrait. That is, unless it's here and I've overlooked it."

Aaron laughed. "Oh, you wouldn't have overlooked it. No, I'm sure it's stashed in the attic or some such place. Why should Edgar keep around such a—er—painful reminder?"

Emilie eyed the crimson-haired gentleman speculatively. "Tell me, Mr. Rice, if the portrait belongs to your family, why is it here?"

Aaron's eyes narrowed slightly. "You're no mental mite, my fair girl. As it happens, my parents commissioned the portrait with a Houston artist. It was a first anniversary present for Edgar and Olivia."

"I see," Emilie murmured. "So the portrait is actually the property of my husband?"

Aaron bit his lip, then stood up angrily. "What the hell does Edgar want with it? My parents are *old*, Mrs. Ashland. It will mean much more to them, now—it's naught but paint and canvas to Edgar!"

Despite the gentleman's brusqueness, Emilie felt sympathy for him. "Please, sit, sir. I don't like having someone shout down at me. Let's try to discuss this calmly."

Aaron hastily sat down, a flush spreading across his features. "Forgive my outburst, Mrs. Ashland. It's just that we miss Olivia so. Why should Edgar want the portrait? He has you, now, doesn't he?"

Emilie frowned; there was a troubling undercurrent in the man's tone. "Speaking of *now*, why have you waited five years to ask for the portrait?"

"I've been living in Washington D.C. for several years, Mrs. Ashland, lobbying for Sam Houston."

"But Mr. Houston hasn't been president for three years!" Emilie countered in confusion.

"Sam hasn't forgotten his dream of statehood, even though he is out of office and the statehood petition has been withdrawn. When he is reelected, things will really start popping in Washington. I'm only going to be home for a few months, coordinating his campaign."

"I see."

"By the way," Aaron continued, gesturing to his frock coat, "I have a letter from Sam to Edgar. Do you have any idea where your husband is, when he'll return?"

Emilie shrugged. "He's no doubt touring the fields, and may or may not return at lunch time. You might try returning late in the afternoon. However, I would be happy to give my husband the letter, Mr. Rice."

"Oh, no," Aaron replied hastily. "I intend to give Edgar the letter *personally*, to ensure that he will hear me out."

Emilie shivered. There was obviously much animosity between the two men. "Do you dislike my husband so, Mr. Rice?"

Aaron laughed bitterly. "Let's say we've *both* forgotten the concept of brotherly love."

Emilie stood. "I'll tell my husband of your call, Mr. Rice. If your sister's portrait is here—well, I certainly have no objection to your taking it. But then, the decision is my husband's."

Aaron, now also on his feet, took his beaver hat from the tea table. "I'll be staying with friends in Washington-on-the-Brazos for several weeks, Mrs. Ashland. Tell Edgar I'll be back—possibly later today."

After Emilie saw Aaron Rice out, she found that his visit had left her feeling quite unsettled. She went upstairs, tried sewing some seams on the calico dress she was making, but found she could not concentrate.

Olivia's portrait! A new twist to the drama! She tried to conjure an image of Edgar Ashland's first wife. She thought of Aaron, and fashioned a portrait of a creamy-faced sister with sparkling green eyes and red hair. Had Edgar loved her deeply? Did she have the engaging flirtatious manner of her brother? Did she have his temper?

"What were you like, Olivia Ashland?" Emilie asked the walls of her room.

She would find out! Perhaps the portrait *was* in the attic, as Aaron Rice had suggested. It was a small chance, but why not try?

Leaving her room, Emilie went to the door at the end of the hall, which Avis had told her led to the attic. At first the door would not budge, and Emilie feared it was locked. Then it opened with a labored creak.

Emilie climbed the narrow spiral stairs and pushed open the door at the top, entering an oppressively hot room filled with trunks and moth-eaten furniture. Dusty light filtered through dirty dormer windows, illuminating silvery threads of spider webs.

Emilie sighed. Finding anything in the musty clutter would be difficult. But, nonetheless, she began moving items about, searching for anything the size of a portrait. Sweat dripped between her breasts and she sneezed frequently from the dust, but she stubbornly continued.

As she pulled a box from beneath a tattered wing chair, her thoughts strayed to Aaron Rice. He had said he might return today, and seemed a decent enough man. Perhaps, if she could get to know him better, she might enlist his aid in returning to Houston. Yet she must proceed with caution—she had trusted David, only to be abandoned!

Moments later, Emilie was about to despair of her project, when she found a muslin bundle wedged between two trunks. Moving aside one of the steamers exhausted her, and she sat down on the floor, breathing laboriously and staring at the package.

Once rested, she began struggling with the twine stretched taut about the muslin; her hands were raw by the time she completed this task. Then, much to her chagrin, she found that the cloth had been sewn around the package. She ripped open a seam at the bottom, began pushing back the muslin and cotton batting. She uncovered the bottom of a gilded frame. Good! This might be it!

She pushed the wrappings upward. Her heart

raced as she uncovered a brass plaque reading "Olivia." She struggled against the cloth, revealing a woman's torso clothed in an emerald-green velvet dress, with billowing sleeves tied with bows at the elbows. Now she saw the *décolletage*, trimmed with three lime-green satin roses. Olivia would wear green, Emilie thought, just like her brother! Green complements red hair.

With rising anticipation, Emilie pushed the wrappings off the portrait, uncovering the face. "Oh my God!" she choked.

It was like looking into a mirror.

Emilie paced Edgar's room in a rage. The full impact of her visit to the attic moments earlier had dawned upon her.

How dare Edgar do this to her! No wonder Aaron Rice had viewed her with astonishment! Now she understood the irony of his words, "Why should Edgar want the portrait? He has you, now, doesn't he?"

"He has me! The monster!" she hissed through clenched teeth. "Does he think I have no feelings, that I can be used like a brood mare to reenact his demented story of the past? Will he now expect me to bear twins?"

Frantic for something to throw, Emilie grabbed Edgar's shaving mug and smashed it soundly against the wall. "Lunatic! Beast!" she screamed at the fragments.

As if summoned, Edgar tore into the room. "Emilie, what in God's name—"

"You! You!" she shrieked, lunging for him.

A look of horror spreading across his features, Edgar held Emilie at arm's length while she flailed at him repeatedly. Finally, losing his temper, he yanked her close and pinned both hands behind her back. "Well, madam? Explain this insane behavior!"

"Insane! You're the one who's insane!"

He pushed her away violently, causing her to fall against the bed. "Don't ever say that to me!"

Heedless of his reaction, she stood, screamed, "It's true! How dare you do this to me! You expect me to replace Olivia!"

"What?" he shouted incredulously.

"It's true!" she cried. "I've seen her portrait and I know I look like her!"

He took a step back, as if slapped. A mask closed over his features. "How did you find Olivia's portrait?"

"I—I—" Emilie sputtered, "Aaron Rice was here and—"

"Aaron! What the hell was *he* doing here?"

"He—he has a letter for you and he'll be back. He wants Olivia's portrait!"

"Does he, indeed?" Edgar returned sarcastically. "And were you good enough to fetch it for him, madam? Is that how you got dirt all over your face, rummaging through the attic?"

Distracted for a moment, Emilie put her hand to her face. Then she stamped her foot. "That's not the point! Of course I was curious after Aaron's visit! And your—your precious portrait is still in the attic!" She clenched her fists and continued hysterically, "But how could you play this cruel joke on me? Marrying me when you knew I looked like Olivia!"

Edgar sighed, regarding her fury dispassionately. "The resemblance is merely a coincidence, Emilie."

"I don't believe you—you monster!" she spat back. "Why did you marry me so—so quickly—if not because I look like her?"

A vein throbbed in Edgar's temple; his face darkened. "You delude yourself, Emilie," he said hoarsely. "I married you to get you into my bed."

Strangely, his crude remark hurt her unbearably. Tears stung her eyes; her rage melted into a deep ache.

Watching her, Edgar drew a shaky breath as his face softened. "You're not like Olivia at all. No one could be."

His words sliced into her heart. He had told her he married her merely to vent his lusts. Now, he had completed her humiliation by saying no one could replace his lost love. Damn him!

He moved closer. "Actually, it's just as well that you saw the portrait. Sooner or later, you would have learned of the resemblance. Now, let's forget it."

But Emilie, lost in her own painful thoughts, was not willing to forget. "You don't want me, Edgar," she accused bitterly. "You're still in love with Olivia, aren't you? And you find me—inadequate!"

She glared at him, her chest heaving. For a moment, he studied her curiously, then a slow smile spread across his lips. "Why Emilie, I do believe you're jealous!"

"Th-that's ridiculous!" Emilie sputtered.

Slowly, Edgar approached her, his eyes darkening with desire. "Oh, sweetheart, how I've waited for this moment. You want me to make love to you. Don't you?"

"Ooooh!" Emilie gasped, flushing crimson, turning her back on him. Olivia's portrait was forgotten as a new threat made her spine crawl.

He reached her, encircled her waist with his arms, pulled her back against his chest. She stiffened in his arms, swallowing a moan when his mustache tickled her ear.

"Lovely, sweet wife," he murmured, his lips teasing her earlobe. His hands reached around her, cupping her breasts. "You've missed my arms, haven't you? Just as I've missed your silky body beneath me."

His words caressed her and sent chills up and down her spine, while his hands tantalized her nipples through the cloth of her dress. "I've been remiss, Mrs. Ashland. Your show of jealousy calls for a passionate response."

She trembled as his lips travelled down the curve of her neck. But her stubborn pride prevailed. "I-I'm not jealous," she maintained weakly.

He turned her in his arms, his eyes scorching her quivering mouth. "Indeed, darling?"

He kissed her. A helpless cry of defeat died in her throat as his mouth possessed hers. Her lips surrendered and her arms curled around his neck. Oh, how good he felt! Yes, she wanted him, right this minute, hard and naked on top of her, driving into her flesh! She would banish his memories of Olivia! She would show him what a real, live woman was like!

The kiss ended. He drew away, smiling tenderly. "Such a wanton response, love," he teased gently. "Yes, I believe your little snit deserves its proper reward." He turned from her, walked to the door. "Tonight," he added significantly.

He left her there, in the triumph of her utter defeat.

Chapter Fourteen

April 3, 1841

Emilie stood on the upstairs veranda, surveying Brazos Bend and all it meant. Her reaction to Edgar moments earlier had left her feeling numb with defeat—she had given up on trying to squelch her carnal self. Tonight, he would make love to her, and she would receive him with all the loving passion a wife could summon!

Loving? She groaned audibly as the truth dawned upon her. She was in love with Edgar Ashland! All this time, she thought it was David, and it was Edgar—Edgar!

"Oh, God," she moaned aloud, "when did it happen?" Was it in his arms just now, or the first time he made love to her, or, indeed, the day she came to Brazos Bend and watched him come down the stairs?

More importantly, *why* did she love him? Of course, he was a magnificent figure of a man—but that merely explained her desire for him. No, there must be some quality buried beneath his arrogance that made her love him. But what, in God's name?

Was it his pain? Did something inside her know he

did not mean to be cruel, that he hurt her out of his own anguish? She knew how it felt to see the ravages of war, to watch loved ones die. Did she want to heal him, to teach him to love?

Love! Could Edgar Ashland ever love her? Was he capable of anything but hurt?

Despairingly, Emilie returned to the bedroom and studied herself in the mirror. Her image left no doubt—the glow of a woman in love. She loved Edgar Ashland, and if she stayed here with him, her heart would override her reason. The man was not stupid—he would pick up on her feelings, use her love, tear her heart to ribbons. And she would endure it all—for she had lost the power to fight him! She would lie willingly in his bed, bear his children, perhaps die of childbirth as her mother had—

"Oh!" she cried dismally, turning from her reflection. It must not be! It simply must not!

She could have endured it before. When she thought she hated him, at least she had her pride. Now she was stripped of all defenses, the slave of a madman! A madman who wanted her to resurrect a dead woman! And what would happen, when, inevitably, she failed to meet the demands of the role he had assigned her? He had already told her that she wasn't like Olivia at all. How long before he tired of the game and discarded her like a broken toy?

Tears streamed down her face—tears for what could not be—ever. There was only one answer, despite the risks.

And this time she must not—dared not—fail!

Emilie trudged down River Road. She was still on Brazos Bend land, but she had put a lot of distance between herself and the house in the hours since she walked out.

She cursed as a sharp rock cut into the ball of her foot. She paused, removed her slipper, silently reproving herself for not wearing walking shoes. What was more insane, she scolded herself, was not taking a horse! In a ridiculous burst of pride, she had left her wedding ring and decided she wanted nothing of his—not even one of his horses! As her feet could attest, she had regretted that decision at length. Gingerly, she replaced her shoe and continued walking.

Noting the sun's position in the sky, she decided she had about five hours of daylight left. She was thirsty, but not painfully so, having stayed on the edge of the road in the cover of trees as much as possible. But she dared not stray too close to the thicket beyond. She feared the woods—Edgar had ensured that, with his warnings about Indians.

Today the woods were ominously quiet. She stopped several times to listen, but heard only scattered birdsong. She also glanced behind her frequently. If she spotted Edgar, she might be able to hide in the brush. There, at least, not having a horse was an advantage. Soon, she would be off Brazos Bend land entirely, and she doubted he would pursue her past the boundaries of the plantation. After all, Edgar had not left his estate in five long years! His misanthropic ways would be his undoing!

With luck, she would reach Washington-on-the-Brazos by nightfall. Then, she would go to Pastor Fritz, enlist his aid in returning to Houston. She had brought Granny's brooch; selling it might provide her fare. But what would happen once she got home? What if David were at Granny's house? Well, she would simply insist he give her the house back. Once he learned how Edgar had treated her, how could he refuse?

Emilie paused, feeling a sudden unease. She glanced behind her—nothing. She turned to the woods and listened—silence. She scolded herself for letting her nerves get the better of her.

As she continued, her thoughts strayed to Edgar. She was now sure that he had picked up on her feelings this morning. That was why he had announced he would bed her tonight. He knew now that her suicide threat was sheer bravado.

She felt a moment of intense longing for what could have been. Would her future really be better than it could have been with Edgar? "Of course it will!" she scolded herself aloud. "Whatever uncertainties your future holds, leaving that beast of a man is the best decision you've ever made!"

Again, Emilie paused, as if expecting her harsh words to cause Edgar to materialize before her. She glanced about warily, only to discover no sound, no movement. She frowned. She had been ignoring her body's summons for some time now, and could no longer avoid a trip into the woods. She studied the dense tangle of trees and underbrush just beyond her. When she was positive no dangers lurked in the immediate vicinity, she edged into the woods.

When she returned to the road moments later, she gasped sharply when she saw what awaited her. Mother of God, where did *he* come from?

She backed up cautiously, studying him. He did not move, but stared at her with savage black eyes.

She did not know whether to run, and have him pursue her like some great stalking bear, or stand perfectly still, and try to stare him down. He stood with his back to the river—she could race past him, dive for the Brazos—and she would drown! But would that fate really be worse than this?

A mounting panic determined her course. She backed into the woods, then whirled, tearing through the dense growth with all the strength in her body. As she raced off, she caught a last glimpse of him through the corner of her eye—he stood motionless, evidently in no hurry to pursue her.

Branches and vines clawed at Emilie as she ripped tortuously through the undergrowth. Her sunbonnet hung around her neck and her hair streamed in leaf-strewn disarray about her face. She stumbled on the hem of her skirt, fell, then cried out as a bramble pierced her calf. But she struggled to her feet, tore off again, her breath coming in huge gulps. A branch slapped her hard across the face, momentarily stunning her, but her feet continued, unbidden.

Then it happened. A snap, a cry of agony, and she fell on a pile of rotting foliage. Emilie winced, reaching down to touch her foot. She cried out in despair as she realized that her ankle had been twisted, perhaps sprained in the hole in which she had just stumbled.

Heedless of the sound she was making, she sobbed desperately and waited for the inevitable.

She had not long to wait. Moments later, without looking up, she felt his presence in the small clearing. She closed her eyes. The pain would be enough. She could not watch it happen.

A savage hand grabbed her hair, sending pins flying, yanking her to her knees. She opened her eyes in agony, glaring up at him. "Be done with it!" she screamed. "For God's sake, be done with it!"

There was no reaction on the brown face as he threw her back down. There was a bright flash of metal, making his harrowing intent clear.

Oddly, he seemed to descend toward her in slow motion. With numb precision, Emilie's mind committed to memory every detail of the savage who was to kill her.

His face was broad, bronzed, the high cheekbones and hooked nose streaked with red and yellow paint. His black hair, decorated with bird feathers, streamed to his waist. His hard brown body was naked aside from a breechclout and moccasins.

As his hand descended, grabbing her hair, she ironically saw only the gleaming copper bracelets on his wrist. She looked up, ignoring the hard silver flash as her eyes studied the blue and white beads strung around his neck. "Lovely . . ." she muttered inanely.

The world exploded. There was blood everywhere, all over her face, her neck, her breasts. And the savage was upon her. "Mama!" she cried, desperately trying to remember her mother's face. But she could not. Instead, her husband's image loomed before her. In a rattling whisper, she choked, "I love you, Edgar . . ."

She drifted in a black tide. The cool water comforted her. This must be heaven, she thought. I'm being reborn, baptized in heaven. . . .

"Emilie, open your eyes!" a hoarse voice ordered.

Slowly, she did as bid. Her vision was foggy. It couldn't be—but it was! She was still alive, held in strong arms. Now he was going to drown her!

"No! No!" she screamed, kicking and clawing.

He dropped her legs, but held her firmly about the waist. Her bare feet found a foothold on the rocky river bottom. She flailed at him, screaming hysterically, then cried out when a brown hand slapped her across the face.

He held her at arm's length. "Emilie, it's me! For God's sake, it's your husband!"

176

At last, the words penetrated her cottony brain. With a startled cry, she recognized Edgar, and fell, sobbing, into his arms.

They stood there, embracing, for a long time. "The—the Indian?" she asked, when her shaking subsided.

Edgar picked her up, carried her toward the shoreline. "He's dead, love," he stated dully. "That's why I brought you to the river. The blast covered you with his blood."

She shuddered. "I th-thought I'd been scalped."

He said nothing, but his arms tightened about her.

Leaving the river, he put her down under a huge, leafing pecan. A sharp pain seared her right ankle as she put her weight upon the foot. She glanced about, spotted Apollyon tethered to one of the trees shielding them from the road.

Calming a bit, Emilie studied her husband. But his dark faced offered no hint of what he was feeling.

He came to her, began unbuttoning the front of her dress. "W-what are you doing?" she stammered.

His deft hands pulled the frock up over her shoulders. "I'm allowing your dress to dry, love, while I assess the damage," he replied grimly.

"D-damage?" she choked, shivering. Was she some piece of baggage to be studied for misuse? "Can't we go home?"

"No. Not until we get some things settled."

His words made her tremble. She felt utterly defenseless standing before him in her sheer chemise.

He spread her dress across a bush. Then he examined her bruised flesh. He studied her hobbly ankle, affirming that it was merely badly twisted. "You'll live," he pronounced.

He removed his coat, leaned over and spread it on the ground beneath the budding tree. "Sit down,

Mrs. Ashland," he said quietly, standing to face her. "We have a matter to discuss."

His smooth tone unnerved her. She did as bid. He pulled his Patterson revolver from his belt, laid it on the ground as he sat down next to her.

"Aren't you afraid of more Indians?" she asked querulously.

He shrugged, eyeing his gun. "They have more to fear from me, sweet. Besides, Apollyon has a nervous disposition around strangers—especially Indians."

Nonetheless, Emilie glanced about fretfully, folding her arms across her sheer bosom. "How—how did you find me?"

He gave her a hard look. "When I discovered you'd left, I rode after you. From a distance, I saw the Cherokee follow you into the woods. I pursued him and—you know the rest."

A tense silence followed his words. Then, casually, Edgar reached into his pocket, drawing out her wedding ring. "Forget something, love?"

She gulped, looking at him. His eyes defied challenge. She reached for the ring, but he took her hand, placed the ring on her third finger. His hard fingers held hers for a moment, then he released her hand, turning to stare off at the river. Quietly, he inquired, "Have you recovered from your hysterics, Emilie?"

"Yes," she replied shakily, sensing the rage buried beneath his smooth words.

"Are you sure—quite sure—you're all right?"

"Yes."

"Good."

Then, with a quick motion, he grabbed her, dragging her to her knees. He shook her until tears streamed down her face and she feared her neck would snap. "You scared the living hell out of me, woman! Never—never try that again!"

He threw her to the ground. The hard earth hit her, unyielding. "You—you've hurt me!" she accused hysterically.

"Hurt you!" he cried, glaring down at her in angry disbelief. "Hurt you! Have you any idea of the torment I suffered when I saw that savage follow you into the woods? Mother of God, Emilie, I could have lost you—forever!"

"Would you have cared?" she screamed back.

"Would I—have cared—" he sputtered incredulously, his eyes wild. With a ragged cry, he fell upon her, kissing her violently. His mouth ravaged hers with a possessiveness that startled her and left her breathless. "Do you prefer death to this, Emilie?" he asked hoarsely as his lips travelled down her throat. "Do you?"

His impatient hands ripped open her chemise, his mouth closed over a rosy nipple. She moaned softly.

His arms tightened about her. "Why did you leave me, Emilie? Tell me!"

She turned away, but both his hands grabbed her face. "Why, Emilie? Are you so afraid of me?"

Her lip quivered. "Yes! I'm afraid of you!"

"Afraid of—exactly what, my dear?"

"I'm afraid of—what you make me feel and—"

"And?"

"I'm afraid—" she flushed miserably, "that you'll get me with child."

He stiffened; his eyes went cold. Oh, God, I've hurt him! she thought. I didn't want it to come to this!

He studied her silently for a long time. Emilie's heart begged her to tell him the truth—that she loved him, but feared childbirth. But her pride kept her silent, even as she watched angry pride darkening his features.

He sighed. Then, slowly, he pulled off her chemise. She gasped as he lowered himself upon her. His head moved to her breasts, his arms encircled the small of her back. "Would it be so terrible, love, to have my child?"

His lips moved downward. "No, Edgar, please," she pleaded, her heart beating wildly as she realized his intent.

He ignored her as his lips moved inexorably lower.

She suffered a momentary panic, then rapture—a fluttering ache in her loins, sweet and new as the buds bursting open above them. He drove her mad with desire, tormenting her for interminable moments. Her hands swept through his hair as she forgot all but the heat raging within her.

When he moved upward to kiss her, she began tearing at his shirt, all pride abandoned. "Edgar, I want you," she choked.

He drew back to look at her, his eyes glowing softly in the shimmering green-gold light. "Even if it means having my child?"

"Yes—I'm a little frightened—but yes, I do want your child."

"Darling, don't be afraid," he soothed. His hand reached down, unbuttoning his trousers. "Feel how right it is."

The sweet, hot shaft tantalized her for endless moments, while his lips tickled her breasts. Deep inside, she ached to be filled. She arched against him, pleading, "Please, Edgar—"

"So be it, love."

He drove himself into her; she gasped at the wonder of their joining. Their eyes locked, awe-filled, both of them savoring the ecstasy, the melding.

"My—darling," she breathed. The word seemed, somehow, inadequate.

His eyes grew darker—intense, adoring. "Oh, God, Emmie, don't leave me again," he moaned. "Please don't leave me."

Emilie melted. The endearment "Emmie" touched her ear like the sweetest caress. He wanted her—really wanted her to stay with him!

His arms clenched about her and he took her fiercely, deeply, as if to brand her his forever. She welcomed him wantonly, wrapping her legs about his waist, her entire being opening to his hard, searing possession. Suddenly, she wanted to accept all the violence within him, to heal his tortured soul. "Yes! Yes!" she cried, encouraging him with her hands and mouth, even as tears of exultation spilled from her eyes.

It was right, so right! her heart echoed. Only this sweet frenzy could end a day in which she had almost lost her life—and her love! How good he felt, filling her with his heat until she thought she would burst!

His mouth moved hungrily over her face and neck. "You're mine, Emilie, mine!" he whispered.

His hands clutched her buttocks, holding her hard against his final, devouring movements. She called his name brokenly and jerked upward, desperate to join her mouth with his. Their climax was tumultuous, edged in a pain which only deepened the rapture, shattering every barrier between them—

"Oh God!" Emilie cried, as her entire world became one moment, one man.

Chapter Fifteen

April 3, 1841

They rode home in silence. Emilie sat in front of Edgar on the horse—one of his arms was wrapped tightly about her waist, while his other hand grasped the reins.

Evening was approaching. The cool breeze tugged at their clothing as Apollyon trotted under a canopy of limbs shading River Road. Light beams sifted through the branches, showering the lovers with soft, caressing light.

Words were not necessary; they were basking in the afterglow of their lovemaking beneath the pecan trees. Emilie's mind relived the glorious moments when they had been one—every touch, each whisper. "You're mine, Emilie," Edgar had told her, "mine. . . ."

She had given herself to him completely—no particle, no hidden vestige of pride, of self, held back. Did he know—and how could he help but know, now?—that she loved him? She could not see his face to hazard a guess. He had seemed deeply shaken by almost losing her. Was it because he was coming to care for her in some manner, however small, or because he would have missed her services in bed? Would he now be kind, loving, let her into his life? Or would he retreat behind his mask of arrogance?

Edgar turned Apollyon from River Road and they ascended the hillside toward the house. Emilie looked at the stately pink brick mansion, a tiny fear tugging at her heart. They had met in the woods on common ground, a man and a woman giving of self equally. Was there a meeting place for them when they returned? Or were the walls of Brazos Bend filled with too many memories?

Edgar halted Apollyon in front of the house and dismounted. He pulled Emilie from the horse into his arms, his eyes caressing her. "Wait until I get you upstairs," he whispered. "I'm going to ride you until you can't move from the bed." Grinning, he added, "That should solve the problem of your little escapades, madam."

Emilie's heart raced. She smiled tremulously at his words.

Edgar had spoken almost jestingly, but as they climbed the steps, his arm shook slightly about her waist.

They entered the front hall, running into an excited Daniel. "Praise be, Mister Ashland! We feared the missus was dead!" The wizened black man turned to Emilie. "You ain't got yourself hurt, have you, child?"

"I'm fine, Daniel," Emilie replied, smiling.

"Daniel, have the stable boy see to Apollyon," Edgar directed. "Later, I'll need two lads to accompany me to the woods for—a burial. A Cherokee tried to scalp Mrs. Ashland." Edgar's arm tightened about Emilie's waist. "Come, my dear. I'll take you upstairs."

Daniel's eyes bobbed in his nodding head. "Yessir." He frowned. "Mister Ashland, sir, I forgot to tell you there's a gen'l'man waitin'—"

"Well, Ashland, still chasing them away, are you?" a voice sardonically interjected.

Edgar suddenly released Emilie, and both of them whirled to face Aaron Rice. Dressed in the suit he had worn earlier that day, Aaron leaned indolently against the archway to the parlor. His thin smile did little to disguise the malice in his gaze as he stared at Edgar.

Emilie hastily glanced at her husband. His face had gone white; a vein throbbed in his temple.

"Aaron Rice!" Edgar hissed. "What the hell are you doing in my house? Get out, before I—"

Emilie grabbed Edgar's arm. "Edgar—no—please—"

Edgar shook himself free of Emilie's grasp. Emilie cringed, backing away from him.

Edgar's face fell. His eyes sought Emilie's, silently saying, "I'm sorry." He stepped closer to her, drawing his arm about her. Nodding to the butler, he said, "Snake season, Daniel. Do take our *guest* to the parlor, and fetch him a juicy rodent. I'll attend to the *gentleman* after I take my wife upstairs."

Not even glancing at the grinning Aaron, Edgar led Emilie up the stairs. Once they were inside the bedroom, he pushed her against the door, kissing her so suddenly, so violently, that she was breathless. "Don't *ever* cringe from me," he ordered hoarsely.

"You—you frightened me with your anger," she stammered, avoiding his eyes.

Edgar took her face in his hands, tilting her chin until her eyes met his troubled gaze. "Emilie, I know I've been cruel to you in the past. Some of the things I've done—I don't know if you'll ever be able to

184

forgive me. But mark my words, darling. I'm never going to hurt you again. Do you understand? Never!''

He kissed her again, passionately, then drew back, eyeing her possessively. "What's Aaron to you?"

"Aaron!" she exclaimed. "Whatever do you mean—"

"Why did you defend him?"

"Defend him! Edgar, I just didn't want to see you fight him! I should hate it if you killed him and were hanged yourself—"

"Would you, darling?" Edgar interrupted, grinning.

"Oh!" Emilie gasped.

Without her knowing it, Edgar had unbuttoned the front of her dress. Now he was pulling the fabric down, his hands cupping her breasts. "Prove it," he murmured, his lips against her throat. "Show me he means nothing to you—now."

Emilie felt her face heating. "Edgar, please, I can't, not with him downstairs—"

"Let him wait!" Edgar growled, his mouth moving downward.

Emilie groaned as a tantalizing ache spread through her belly. "Edgar—please—get rid of him first!"

Edgar drew back, studying her quizzically. "Get rid of him," he repeated, smiling. "Now that's a task I would relish. Very well, madam, if it means that much to you." He leaned over, kissing the tautened nipples of both breasts. "Take off your clothes, love, and wait for me in bed," he directed, winking as he left her.

Emilie stood motionless for a long moment, breathing heavily. God, she ached for him. It had taken every ounce of control she could muster not to

185

begin tearing his clothes off!

But she was glad she hadn't given in. She wanted the issue of Olivia's portrait resolved.

Olivia's portrait! Should she have said something to Edgar about it before he went downstairs? She glanced at the bed, remembering her husband's words as he left her.

The silvery, romantic spell he had woven about her shattered. Sighing raggedly, she pulled her dress around her breasts and fastened the buttons.

In the parlor, Edgar greeted Aaron Rice coldly. "I believe you have a letter for me, Rice."

Aaron grinned, glancing about the room. "Aren't you going to offer me a chair, Ashland?"

"No, you aren't staying." Edgar extended his hand commandingly. "The letter, please."

Aaron shrugged, drawing an envelope from his breast pocket. "It's from Sam," he said simply, handing Edgar the letter. Aaron walked off, casually sprawled himself across a wing chair.

Edgar studied Aaron with icy indifference, then strode to the window. He opened the envelope and held the parchment up to the light. After studying the contents in frowning concentration, he folded the letter carefully and put it in his breast pocket.

He turned to Aaron. "Tell Sam I'm honored by his request, but the answer is no." He started towards the door. "A pity you aren't staying, Rice. Good day."

Aaron Rice sprang up. "Just a moment, Edgar!"

Edgar spun about, his features darkening. "Have you some affliction which impedes your understanding of simple English, Rice? Let me be blunt—you're not welcome in this house—ever!"

Undaunted, Aaron Rice casually unbuttoned his

186

frock coat, tucking his thumbs into his vest pockets. "Why are you living this—hermit's existence, Edgar?"

"That's none of your God damn business," Edgar drawled.

Aaron whistled, then grinned, casually striding over to the window. "One would think you'd be quite a statesman by now, dear brother," he mocked, moving the lace curtains and gazing out at the grounds, "considering your activities during the War for Independence, as well as your career in England, *Lord* Ashland."

"I'm neither your brother nor a lord—now," Edgar replied brittlely. "As to .war, politics—you and Sam are welcome to both. I got a bellyful of the Texas brand of courage and compassion at the Battle of San Jacinto." His jaw tightened. "But why am I explaining that to you, *brother?* You've no comprehension of war, since you were hiding out at the time."

Aaron turned, flushing hotly. "I'll have you know I was touring Europe, Edgar. Mother—"

"Your mother didn't want her bright-haired boy sullied by battle," Edgar cut in triumphantly. "Can't say I blame her. Fighting is a man's business."

Aaron clenched his fists and sputtered, "Why you—you—"

"Now get out," Edgar ordered stonily, turning to leave.

"Not so fast!" Aaron countered, regaining his composure and hurrying after Edgar. "Not until you give me Olivia's portrait!"

Edgar stopped in his tracks; his back went rigid. He turned to glare at Aaron, his face an iron mask, a vein throbbing in his temple. "Olivia!" he hissed. "How dare you mention her name!"

"Feeling pangs of guilt, brother?" Aaron taunted.

Like a panther, Edgar sprang upon the shorter man, grabbing him by the collar, twisting the green fabric. "Get out, you slimy bastard, before I stuff the God damn portrait down your throat!"

Edgar released Aaron abruptly, and the younger man tottered, putting his hand to his chafed neck. "Give me the portrait, Edgar," Aaron demanded, his voice rising. "You're being cruel to withhold it. You know you didn't give a damn about Olivia!"

Hissing this barb, Aaron flinched, as if expecting a violent reaction from his brother-in-law. But the taller man simply paced off, saying, "You're digging your own grave, Rice."

Edgar turned, taking the pistol from his belt. Calmly, he cocked it, pointed it towards Aaron's middle.

Watching him, Aaron gulped. "See here, Ashland, you're not going to—going to—"

Green eyes wide with fear, Aaron stared down the barrel of the revolver. Then, uttering a ragged cry, he dodged as Edgar calmly fired the weapon. The explosion was deafening—glass splintered in every direction at the window near where Aaron had stood.

"Jesus Christ!" Aaron gasped, clutching his chest, his eyes threatening to pop out of his head. "You're insane, Ashland—insane!"

Aaron dashed out of the room. But Edgar calmly recocked the revolver. His eyes were black; he seemed in another world.

At the sound of footsteps, he raised the gun, pointed it.

Emilie screamed, staring frozen at the pistol aimed at her. Then she spun about, dashing out of the room.

Edgar's face whitened with fright. He stared, horrified, at the gun in his hand. With trembling fingers, he unloaded the gun, placed it in the rack above the fireplace. Then he hurried out of the parlor and raced up the stairs.

He found Emilie on the bed, sobbing. He grabbed her, rolling her towards him. She cringed.

"No, darling, no!" he choked, pulling her close.

She flailed at him, bolting like a frightened colt. "Let me go! You're going to k-kill me—k-kill me!"

He pinned her hands into the mattress, his body holding her still. "No, Emilie! I didn't want to kill you! I wanted to kill Aaron! I thought you were—oh, my God, I could have—" his voice broke and he turned away, releasing her.

Emilie sat up, her hair cascading in disarray to her shoulders, her tear-streaked face aghast. "Aaron! You were going to kill—mother of God, Edgar, you can't just go around murdering people!"

Edgar's face twisted with anger. "The bastard deserved it!" he muttered hoarsely, pounding his fist into the mattress. "Of all the gall—he demanded Olivia's portrait!"

Emilie's eyes grew wide as saucers. She gazed at her husband in amazement, her tears frozen on her face. "You were going to—kill him—over Olivia's portrait?"

Edgar countered, "Aaron had no right—"

"No right!" Emilie cried, her voice rising convulsively. "What of *my* rights? How do you think *I* feel about having the portrait in this house? Having you fight Aaron over it? My God—I can't believe it! You were actually going to murder him over the thing! Why don't you just give it to him, Edgar?"

Edgar sprang up from the bed. "Because it's mine,

not his!'' he snapped.

Emilie was up in a flash. "It's just as I thought!" she accused indignantly. "You still love your precious Olivia! You won't let her go!"

Edgar clenched his fists, fighting for control. "Emilie, you are speaking of matters you don't understand—"

"I won't share you with her!" Emilie screamed.

"And I won't have you dictate to me!" Edgar yelled back.

For a long moment, they glared at each other. Then Edgar grabbed her arm. "Enough of this bickering, damn it! Come to the bed, woman. I'll soon hear from your lips who makes the decisions in this house!"

Emilie dug her heels into the carpeting, throwing off his grasp. "You touch me and I'll—I'll—"

"You'll kill yourself?" he supplied. "I think not, love. If I learned one thing today, it's that you very much want to live."

His shrewd remark knocked her off balance, and for a moment she stared at him speechless, her face burning. Then she recovered, flailing at him. "Then you'll have to rape me!"

His eyes narrowed; he backed off. "Emilie, you mean after what happened today, you would still deny me—just because of Olivia's—"

"Yes!"

"So you're issuing an ultimatum?" he asked, his voice surging with anger. "It's come to rape—"

"Yes! I'm sleeping in my own room until the portrait is gone!"

She expected him to strike her then, so great was his ire. But instead, abruptly, he turned his back on her. He was silent for a long moment, then spoke quietly. "Emilie, why don't you trust my judgment

190

on the matter? I'll promise to give it—serious consideration.''

But Emilie was not in a humor to compromise. ''No!''

She shivered as he turned. But he merely looked tired, sad. ''Very well, Emilie, do as you wish. You'll soon discover you're only punishing yourself. Enjoy your pure, lonely bed.''

His remark seared her deeply. ''And *you*—you may go enjoy your sick memories of Olivia!'' she retaliated ruthlessly. ''I'll *not* be lonely! I've always hated you and—and I still love David!''

Not waiting for his reaction, she fled the room, slamming the door as she raced into the hallway. But as she opened the door to her own room, she heard an object—lamp? pitcher?—smash explosively against the door she had slammed.

The sound was frightful, stripping her senses.

Chapter Sixteen

April 4, 1841

The next morning, Maria Ramero arrived at Brazos Bend. Edgar was out touring the fields at the time, and Emilie, hearing oxen approaching from the distance, went out upon the breezy front porch to greet the travellers. She waved at the newcomers, her hopes soaring. Yesterday's emotion-wrenching events had left her feeling despondent, and she was sure meeting Maria would be just the lift she needed.

As the heavily-loaded covered wagon stopped before the plantation house, a thin, middle-aged man alighted, assisting his plump, black-clothed wife to the ground. Then, a young Mexican woman emerged from the draped recesses of the conveyance and stepped down to join the couple.

Emilie immediately knew that this young woman must be Maria Ramero. The girl wore a yellow gingham dress, complementing her gleaming ebony hair, which fell in cascading waves about her shoulders. She was of average height and slim proportions, her skin having a tawny quality revealing her Mexican blood. Yet as the girl moved closer with the couple, Emilie noted that Maria's eyes were a rich forest green, showing perhaps a Castilian heritage as well. The girl's face was lovely—high cheekbones, a straight, fine-boned nose, and a full mouth.

As Maria spotted Emilie on the porch, she cautiously lowered rich black eyelashes, slanting the older girl a narrow, suspicious stare.

"Welcome!" Emilie called brightly to the three-some, lifting the hem of her green printed frock as she started down the steps. She turned first to the man, who wore a black suit and hat, and a clerical collar. Extending her hand, she murmured, "You must be Reverend—"

"John Wesley Prescott," the man replied in a booming resonant voice which sounded almost ludicrous coming from his frail body. Accepting Emilie's handshake, he then gestured towards the lady. "My wife, Winifred Ruth. We're here to deliver the Ramero girl."

Emilie was a bit taken aback to hear Rev. Prescott refer to Maria as if the girl were a piece of cargo to be dumped. But her composure remained intact as she pivoted to shake Mrs. Prescott's hand and murmured graciously, "So good to meet you both. I'm Emilie Ashland."

Maria Ramero looked up sharply upon hearing the name "Ashland," and Emilie turned to the Mexican girl. "Welcome home, Maria—I'm Emilie," she said softly, giving the girl a warm smile, even as the younger girl stared back at her coldly and silently. Taking a steadying breath, Emilie continued, "I'm sure this will come as a shock to you, Maria, but while you were gone, I—well, Mr. Ashland and I are now married."

At Emilie's announcement, Maria's young face tightened. "You married David?" she half-hissed, in

193

a heavily-accented voice.

"No, no," Emilie put in quickly, confused and shocked by the venom in the girl's tone. "I married your guardian—Mr. Edgar Ashland."

Staring at Emilie stonily, the girl did not reply.

Emilie mentally groaned. The fact that she had married Edgar didn't seem to please the girl any more than the thought that she might have married David. Eager to avoid further unpleasantry, Emilie turned to her two guests. "Please, Rev. and Mrs. Prescott, won't you join us for tea?" She glanced at the eight dejected-looking oxen harnessed to the wagon. "I'll see that the stable boy feeds and waters your team."

The Prescotts accepted Emilie's invitation, and moments later, the four were seated in the drawing room, sipping tea and eating rice cakes. Emilie and Mrs. Prescott did most of the talking, since Rev. Prescott seemed of a taciturn nature. Maria did ask the whereabouts of David and Edgar, but once the girl was told that David was away and Edgar was in the fields, she retreated unsociably to a chair in the corner, resisting all attempts to draw her into the conversation.

"We so appreciate your bringing Maria home for us," Emilie told Mrs. Prescott, as she handed the older woman a second rice cake, still warm from the oven. "I trust your journey was without impediment. We rather expected you about a week ago."

"Oh, I hope you didn't worry, dear," the sweet-faced woman replied. "But we did stop off for several days to visit our daughter in east Texas. Meg lives alone with her husband, on a small homestead in the woods. We worry about them so, what with the Cherokee Wars out there. But Meg and Thomas are doing just fine—and soon John and I shall have our first grandchild.''

"Congratulations," Emilie said. She smiled at Rev. Prescott, but the sharply-featured man merely stared back at her grimly as he sipped his tea. Poor Mrs. Prescott! Emilie thought. Meeting the humorless Reverend made living with Edgar seem almost agreeable by comparison!

"So, from what I heard outside, you must be a new bride, Mrs. Ashland," Mrs. Prescott continued brightly. "When did you and Mr. Ashland marry?"

"March 17th," Emilie replied.

"A newlywed—how exciting!" Mrs. Prescott exclaimed, clapping her small, plump hands. "Isn't it wonderful, John?"

Rev. Prescott merely grunted as he chewed on his rice cake. Meanwhile, Maria abruptly asked, "May I be excused, Señora?"

Emilie turned with dismay to the Mexican girl. "But Maria, you've hardly touched your tea."

"I'm very tired, Señora," the girl replied rather sharply, her eyes like green ice.

Emilie smiled indulgently. "Of course, then, dear. I'll come up to check on you later."

The girl did not reply as she got to her feet and left the room, her head held high. Emilie sighed. It must be quite a blow to Maria's pride to come home and find a strange woman married to her guardian and in charge of the household. Yet it was rude of the girl not to thank the Prescotts for bringing her home, or even say goodbye to them.

Emilie turned apologetically to her guests. "I'm sorry. Maria must not be feeling well."

"We understand, dear," Mrs. Prescott replied, smiling compassionately.

"Mrs. Prescott, we, too, must be going," Rev. Prescott put in importantly, as he downed the last of his tea.

"Oh, must we John?" Mrs. Prescott questioned wistfully.

The morose parson gave his wife a reproachful look. "We must be about the Lord's business in Houston, Mrs. Prescott."

Emilie stifled a giggle at the little man's remark. "You'll not find a lack of the Lord's business there, Reverend."

Again, not a hint of humor softened the man's sallow face as he got to his feet. Exchanging sympathetic glances, the two women also arose, following Rev. Prescott out of the room. Outside on the porch, Emilie chatted with Mrs. Prescott for a few moments longer, while her husband checked on the load of the wagon and the harnesses of the oxen.

"Again, I must thank you for bringing Maria home," Emilie told Mrs. Prescott, laying a hand on the woman's arm. "It saved my husband's nephew a long trip. And I'm sorry my husband isn't here at the moment, since I'm sure he would wish to offer you some recompense for your trouble."

Shaking her bonneted head, Mrs. Prescott replied, "You musn't worry on that account, Mrs. Ashland, Marga Ferguson insisted we accept the girl's remaining tuition for supplies. Besides, it was our pleasure to have the girl along, since we were already coming this way."

Mrs. Prescott paused, a worried expression flitting across her heart-shaped face. Finally, she asked, "The Ramero girl—you will have a care for her, won't you, dear?"

"What do you mean?" Emilie asked, frowning.

Mrs. Prescott sighed as she distractedly brushed a bit of lint from her black homespun dress. "I fear something ails the girl—she stays to herself too much. The whole trip, she hardly said a word to us.

Oh, she was an obedient child, and helped with the chores. But there was no knowing what the girl thought—ever."

"I've noticed as much already," Emilie concurred unhappily. "Maria is an orphan, and she's had a rather difficult life. So I suppose it's not surprising that she seems withdrawn, or that she couldn't get along at school."

Mrs. Prescott nodded, her expression perturbed. "You know, Marga told me the reason the girl was dismissed from school . . ."

"Yes?" Emilie prompted.

The woman frowned her uncertainty. "I'm not sure I should tell you, Mrs. Ashland. It might be passing a judgment on the girl."

"Or it might help me understand Maria better," Emilie countered persuasively.

Mrs. Prescott bit her generously-proportioned lower lip, then nodded. "Well, Marga did tell me the other girls tormented Maria to no end. But what the girl did—" the woman shook her head and clucked to herself—"it was a crime against nature, Mrs. Ashland."

Emilie felt chilled to the bone. "What happened?"

While Mrs. Prescott hesitated, her husband called out impatiently, "Winifred Ruth, we must be upon our way. The devil waits for no man!"

Mrs. Prescott nodded to her husband, then turned to give Emilie a quick, spontaneous hug. "No rest for the weary, dear. Thanks so for your hospitality." Slanting Emilie a final, concerned glance, the woman added, "But do have a care for the girl, Mrs. Ashland."

And before Emilie could question her further, Winifred Prescott turned and hurried down the steps to her husband's side.

* * *

Edgar came in at lunch time, greeting Maria matter-of-factly, planting a chaste kiss on the girl's forehead. As the three sat down to eat lunch, Emilie thought she detected a glint of yearning in Maria's green eyes as she stared at her handsome guardian. Unfortunately, Edgar took little note of either girl during the meal, and Emilie's attempts to engage Maria in conversation were again without success.

Maria left the table early, and Emilie couldn't help but snap at Edgar, "You might have at least shown some interest in the girl! She has been gone three months."

"Oh?" Edgar countered laconically. "I suppose the attention you paid the girl was received with heart-warming enthusiasm."

"I'm not the one she wants it from!" Emilie shot back.

Edgar leaned back in his chair, his dark eyes boldly appraising Emilie. "Perhaps she's not the one *I* want it from," he whispered meaningfully.

Emilie felt a hot flush suffusing her face at Edgar's words, but she refused to be swayed from her purpose. "Will you for once stop thinking of your own satisfaction and consider the girl's position? Maria has come home to find a stranger in charge of her home. Have you no sympathy for the girl?"

For once, Edgar looked taken aback. "Well, I—actually, Emilie, I hadn't given the subject much thought—"

"Oh, the devil with you!" Emilie said disgustedly, throwing down her napkin and getting to her feet. "I might have known you'd be too fascinated with yourself to take any note of the poor girl. I'll attend to the 'subject' myself!"

Before Edgar could reply, Emilie exited the room.

She went upstairs and knocked on Maria's door. "Maria?"

When the girl didn't answer, Emilie again knocked. "Maria, please, it's Emilie."

Finally, Emilie tried the knob, and, finding the door unlocked, she entered the room.

Maria's room was lovely, done in shades of pale yellow, with dark, glossy rosewood furniture. The young girl looked statuesque as the furnishings as she sat on a gold velvet chair near the window, silky light filtering through the sheer panels behind her, casting a deceptive coppery halo about her head.

"You wish something, Señora?" Maria asked, her words clipped and resentful.

"I was worried about you, Maria."

The girl did not reply.

Emilie moved across the room to sit on the edge of the bed facing Maria. "It must have been quite unsettling for you to arrive home to find your guardian married."

The girl shrugged.

Nervously fingering the yellow quilted counterpane, Emilie continued, "Actually, Maria, I initially came here to be your companion. David brought me here—"

"*David* brought you here?" the girl interrupted in a grating tone.

Looking up at the girl's highly indignant face, Emilie struggled not to shudder. "Why yes, Maria. David has been concerned about you. He thought you and I might be friends."

"Where did David find you?" Maria asked suspiciously.

"In Houston," Emilie replied calmly. She went on to explain about her background, her meeting David in March and her coming to the plantation. Then she told matter-of-factly of her marriage to Edgar, leaving out the sordid details.

As Emilie spoke, she felt an increasing uneasiness, for Maria did not seem to be listening. Instead, the Mexican girl stared off into space, her brow deeply furrowed. Then, suddenly, Maria snapped her fingers and interrupted Emilie. "*You* were the reason David sent me away!" she accused, her green eyes brilliant with realization and hatred.

Emilie was caught off-guard by the girl's bizarre remark. "Maria, what are you saying?"

The girl ignored Emily's question as she got to her feet and began to pace in her agitation. "I have wondered why he went so often to Houston and now I know!" Turning to Emilie, she pointed a finger and charged bitterly, "It was you all the time—you he went to see!"

Emilie was stunned, unable to believe the words coming out of the young girl's mouth. "No, Maria, that's not true. As I explained, I only met David a month ago—"

"Liar! *Hija de diablo!*" the girl hissed. "You wanted him all to yourself, *verdad?* So you convinced him to send me away!"

"Maria, you're making no sense," Emily explained patiently. "David sent you to school for your own welfare, not to get rid of you. Besides, there is nothing between David and me. I'm married to Edgar—"

"Ah, *sí,*" Maria interrupted, her eyes cold as ice as she glared at Emilie. "When you got here, you found Señor Edgar to have more money, so you chose him instead."

Emilie shook her head in bewilderment, pleading, "Maria, please listen to me—"

"No!" Maria cut in contemptuously, drawing her-

200

self up with dignity. "You will leave my room, Señora."

Emilie's face fell. "But Maria—"

"Am I to have no privacy, Señora?" the girl demanded.

Emilie sighed and got to her feet, saying resignedly, "Regardless of what you think, Maria, I don't want to get rid of you, and I do want to be your friend. Remember that I'm here—any time."

The girl's only response was to hurry to the door, opening it wide as she stared at Emilie with disdain.

Emilie left the room, shuddering as the door slammed behind her. She trudged wearily down the stairs, her spirits sagging. She had held such high hopes for a friendship between her and Maria, only to have her first attempt to get to know the girl end in disaster.

Yet despite the girl's hostility, Emilie felt sympathy towards her, for she realized how love-starved and insecure Maria must be to resent Emilie so on sight, to draw such unfair, outrageous conclusions about her without hearing her out.

How could she reach the girl?

Emilie paused on the landing, pondering the question. Perhaps when David returned, he might be able to help her better understand Maria. There were so many things she needed to know about the Mexican girl. Why had Maria been dismissed from school? How disturbed was the girl truly?

Continuing down the stairs, Emilie frowned as she remembered Winifred Prescott's warning: "Have a care for the girl, Mrs. Ashland."

Chapter Seventeen

April 23, 1841

On an unseasonably cool, wet morning, David Ashland returned to Brazos Bend. He entered the front hall, shivering; a fretful Daniel took his coat and urged him to warm himself by the fire in the parlor.

As David entered the room, he spotted Emilie sitting in a wing chair, frowning at a seam of calico in her lap. "Emilie?"

She started, stabbing herself with the needle. "Damn!" she cursed. She threw her sewing down, looked up at David with astonished blue eyes, her smarting thumb in her mouth. "So you've returned," she muttered.

He took a step closer, and she noted that he was as handsome as ever—innocent blue eyes, thin, handsome face. His blonde hair curled in damp waves about his face. Despite his mud-spattered boots, his brown suit was immaculate.

As she watched him, nothing tender stirred within her. No, she realized, she truly did not love him. Perhaps she never had.

"Emilie, dear, how are you?" he asked nervously.

She half wanted to jump up and claw his eyes out, damn him to hell for abandoning her. But weeks of estrangement from Edgar had left her feeling raw inside, and, to her horror, she felt tears filling her eyes as she looked up at his warm, concerned face.

He moved closer; illogically, she stood, fell into his arms. For a moment she clung to him, her cheek damp against his ruffled linen shirt, the comforting scent of his shaving soap wafting over her.

Then he sneezed, breaking the silence. She moved away, wiping a tear. "Do go stand by the fire, David. God knows, I'm not feeling kindly towards you, but I don't want your death from the ague on my conscience."

David walked over to the fireplace and held out his hands, glancing at Emilie over his shoulder. "Did Maria get back, dear?"

"Yes. Over two weeks ago."

"And how is she?"

"Oh, the girl is almost as delightful as your dear uncle," Emilie returned dryly.

David turned to face Emilie. "What do you mean, dear?" He paused, his face creasing with worry. "Emilie, you seem—so distressed. Are things that bad between you and Uncle?"

"Bad!" Emilie scoffed, returning to her chair. "No, David, things have not been *bad* at all! That is, aside from your uncle's throwing me in the river and almost drowning me! Aside from his breaking my mother's perfume bottle and taking me by—by force repeatedly! No, everything has been just *lovely* here!"

David's features twisted with incredulous horror. "Jesus!" he gasped. "My uncle did—all that?"

"Yes!" she spat. "I almost died from his cruelty! In God's name, David, why did you bring me here?

203

You had to have known I look like Olivia!''

David's face whitened. ''How—how did you know—''

''Aaron Rice came, demanding Olivia's portrait, and I—found it.''

''I see,'' David gulped.

''Well?'' Emilie pursued. ''Didn't you know I looked like her?''

David slowly walked to the wing chair opposite Emilie, sat down heavily. ''I suppose there was something compelling about you from the very beginning, Emilie,'' he admitted. ''But I truly did not recognize the resemblance until we got here, and you put your hair up—like—like Olivia used to.''

Emilie's eyebrows flew up. ''So *that's* why you were so put off! You must have thought you were seeing a ghost! Come to think of it, your uncle started to pursue me that very evening. It makes me ill just to think of it!''

''Think of what?'' David inquired confusedly.

''Your uncle married me because I look like Olivia!'' she replied exasperatedly. ''He's obsessed with her—when Aaron came, he refused to give him her portrait.''

David frowned. ''I can't say I'm surprised, Emilie. There has always been a great deal of antagonism between Uncle and Rice.''

''Your uncle's fault, no doubt!'' she snapped. ''The man is a beast—the things he has done to me, David—'' she paused, shuddering.

David leaned forward, his face anguished. ''Emilie, I am deeply sorry for my uncle's treatment of you—''

''Sorry!'' she cried. ''Sorry enough to take me back to Houston?''

David colored miserably. ''You know I can't do

that, Emilie.''

"You can't? Why, pray tell?"

David gestured helplessly. "Emilie, be sensible. "You have no way to support yourself, no protector, aside from Uncle—''

"Oh, and he's done a *magnificent* job of protecting me!''

"Besides," David continued shakily, "you are Uncle's wife, now. I can't just whisk you away, contrary to his wishes. Now were you to get his consent to leave, then I could take you wherever you please.''

Emilie's eyes rolled heavenward. "Shall I stop the rain, also?"

David's face was crestfallen. "In time, things may improve, Emilie," he offered lamely.

She shook her head vigorously, got up and moved to the window, noticing that it was now raining heavily. "Your uncle hates me because I remind him of Olivia—and he hates me because I can never be Olivia. It's—it's hopeless.''

David groaned miserably, then rose, coming to her side. "I'm sorry," he whispered. "It grieves me to see you so unhappy, Emilie. But I'm here, now. And I'll stay—until I'm assured Uncle will behave like a gentleman.''

At these words, Emilie laughed until tears filled her eyes. "In that case, I shall expect you *never* to leave!''

David bit his lip, looking extremely uncomfortable. "I'll do what I can to improve things for you, dear." Clearing his throat, he added, "And perhaps we'll be able to make some progress with Maria, as well. Tell me, how has the girl seemed since she returned?''

Emilie gestured helplessly. "David, she's unreachable. After she got here, Lord knows I tried to befriend her. I explained to her how I came to be married to your uncle, but she immediately jumped to all manner of absurd conclusions.''

''What do you mean?''

''She got it into her head that I was the reason she was sent away, and now she hates me for it.''

David's blond eyebrows shot up. ''Surely you jest!''

''I'm afraid not,'' Emilie replied dismally, as she turned and moved toward the settee. ''When I told Maria you and I met in Houston a month ago, she decided that was a lie—that we had been meeting there for some time, that I had even persuaded you to get rid of her.''

David looked thunderstruck as he watched Emilie cross the room. ''But that makes no sense. You're married to Uncle—''

''Oh, I fear the girl thinks I'm trying to steal both of you away from her.'' Emilie sat down wearily. ''Jealousy knows no reason, David. I've tried several times to explain the truth to Maria, but she shuts me out every time. In a sense I can't blame the girl. She came home to find I had taken over.''

David turned to stare out the window, shaking his head in despair. ''It seems I've royally botched things. I thought the boarding school would bring Maria out of herself a bit, help her to get along with other young women of her station.'' He ran a hand distractedly through his hair. ''Perhaps it was too drastic a first move—a convent school might have been a better choice. Lord, I don't know.''

Emilie felt a rush of sympathy for her confused companion. ''Don't be too hard on yourself, David. You tried your best, but the girl is desperately insecure. It's not your fault that she misinterpreted

206

your good intentions."

David turned, looking somewhat soothed by Emilie's words. "You have a point, Emilie. The damage is done, at any rate, so I suppose we must make the best of the situation." He bit his lip. "But there is one thing . . ."

"Yes?"

A glint of pleading in his blue eyes, David said softly, "I think it's best we not mention Maria's failure at school, Emilie."

"Oh, believe me, I haven't," Emilie hastily assured him. "I'm not about to do anything to further antagonize the girl." She eyed David narrowly. "But what did happen at the boarding school, David? Why was Maria dismissed?"

David paled but did not reply.

"Hello, David."

Emilie and David turned to see Maria standing in the doorway. The girl's eyes were fastened upon David, and she seemed oblivious of Emilie's presence. She was exquisitely dressed in a delicate, ivory-colored, lace-trimmed frock. Her ebony curls were piled high upon her head, emphasizing the lovely, classical lines of her face.

"Why Maria! How good to see you, dear!" David exclaimed.

David hurried across the room and briefly embraced the girl, kissing her on the forehead. As the two pulled apart, Emilie caught a flicker of a smile crossing Maria's features as she stared shyly at David, a warm, revealing glow lighting her fine, deep green eyes. David, too, beamed as he gazed back at the girl.

"Maria, won't you come in and join us?" Emilie offered brightly.

As the young girl turned and spotted Emilie across

the room, a mask of defiance closed upon her young face. "Señora Ashland, I did not see you," she muttered tonelessly.

No, you have eyes only for David, Emilie thought. But aloud, she urged, "Come warm yourself by the fire, Maria."

"I do not wish to intrude, Señora," the girl replied, her words laced with hostility.

"You wouldn't be intruding, Maria," Emilie said patiently. "As a matter of fact, I have duties I must attend to, so perhaps you and David—"

Emilie's voice trailed off, as Maria walked out on the older girl in midsentence.

Emilie and David could only shake their heads as they exchanged expressions of bewilderment.

The days of excruciating loneliness ended; Emilie had David's company again. When not helping his uncle with plantation duties, David spent every spare moment with her, as if trying to make amends for the wrongs done her by Edgar. Gratefully accepting David's friendship, Emilie soon forgot his abandonment. The two took long rides together in the buggy, studying the knee-high green cotton plants, counting the color combinations of the rainbow assortment of longhorns. Emilie often invited Maria to go along on the outings, but the girl coldly refused each time.

Another dark cloud loomed on Emilie's horizon— Edgar Ashland. Although he did not forbid Emilie's spending time with David, the brooding Edgar always seemed to be just around the next corner, or beyond the next bend in the road—scowling, silent, staring at them icily. Emilie ignored her husband's aloof behavior, while her mind plotted ways to convince David to take her back to Houston.

Thus Emilie's days passed. The nights were

another matter. When she lay in her big bed alone, when time hung suspended in the darkness, her heart ached for what might have been. Despite Edgar's bizarre behavior, she still loved him. Yet how could she penetrate the defenses he had erected about him?

At night, her soul longed for the man buried inside him; her body hurt with the need he had fired in her. Despite her threats, she knew if he came to her, touched her, she would be lost. . . .

She often dreamed of him beside her, planting feather-soft kisses all over her, entwining his body with hers. She would awaken covered with sweat, and go out onto the veranda to cool off, staring at the open doors to his room. How she would long to go to him, to throw off her nightgown, her pride, to climb into his bed and surrender to whatever the future held. But she did not, could not. Perhaps when he let go of Olivia, she would think. But she knew it was hopeless—her marriage was over.

Thankfully, she saw him very little, avoided him whenever possible. But mealtimes were a particular trial. The family would gather, and Emilie and Avis would converse with David under the scowling countenance of Edgar and Maria.

Emilie grew to expect Edgar's silence, but Maria's behavior seemed contradictory and illogical. She could understand the girl's reluctance to speak with the moody Edgar, yet why did the girl make no attempt to converse with David, with whom she was obviously enamored? To make matters worse, David seemed rather self-conscious around the girl, perhaps because of the disastrous school episode. Emilie frequently tried to draw Maria into her conversations with David, but the sullen girl continued to resist all overtures.

All of that changed one bright late-April morning.

Emilie was descending the stairs when she heard a lilting, silvery voice singing, *"Y quierme, Jesusita, Y quierme, por favor."* Emilie tiptoed into the library, and saw Maria standing at the window singing the lovely melody.

"You have a beautiful voice, Maria," Emilie said, when the girl had finished.

Maria spun about in a swirl of lime-green skirts, a blush heating her face. *"Gracias,* Señora," she replied rather coldly.

Emilie forced a smile, not about to be put off now that she had this small insight into Maria's personality. "You never told me that you sing," she remarked conversationally. She took the girl's arm. "Do come into the drawing room and I'll accompany you on the piano."

Emilie pulled Maria's resisting body across the hallway. "It's just a song taught to me by *mi padre,"* the girl protested.

"Ah, but that's the beauty of folk music," Emilie replied casually, as they entered the parlor. "It's a treasure handed down from generation to generation. What is the song about?"

The girl scowled for a moment, then replied grudgingly, "It is a song sung during the Mexican Revolution, about going to the dance hall."

Maria watched Emilie seat herself upon the swivel piano stool, her young face still creased with suspicion. Yet a glint of yearning escaped the girl's green eyes as she watched Emilie's slim hands drift to the ivory keys. "I have heard you play the piano," she murmured, almost wistfully. Then, dropping her guard even further, she added, "I—I have wanted to learn myself."

"Then you must," Emilie assured her smoothly. Delighted to have the girl's interest and attention at last, she coaxed, "Now sing that lovely song for me!"

Emilie played an arpeggio and nodded to Maria. The girl hesitated, a struggle gripping her features. But when Emilie repeated her introduction, her hands even firmer upon the keys, Maria cleared her throat and began to sing.

Vamos al baile y veras que bonito
Donde se alumbran con veinte linternas
Donde se bailan las danzas modernas
Donde se baila de mucho vacilón.

As the girls finished, they were astonished by the sound of clapping. They turned to find David in the room, a rapt expression on his face. "Bravo!" he commented, looking from one girl to the other. "I knew of your gift, Emilie, but Maria, dear, you have kept hidden a marvellous talent."

Maria blushed, lowering jet eyelashes. "Thank you, David."

Studying the Mexican girl, Emilie felt much sympathy. She realized that the girl was miserably shy around David, and no doubt desperately afraid of being rejected by him, especially since she had misinterpreted his intentions in sending her off to school. Both Maria and David needed a push in the right direction!

Seizing the advantage, Emilie announced, "David, Maria wishes to learn to play the piano. Since you're far more advanced than I, you simply must teach her, don't you agree?"

David flushed. "Well, I—of course—"

"Aren't you free this time each morning?" Emilie pursued.

David glanced nervously at Maria, who was still

studying the carpeting. "Would you like that, Maria?" he asked shyly.

"Yes, David," Maria whispered, "if it is not—an inconvenience."

David's face lit up. "Inconvenience, my hat!" he said cheerfully. "It would be a pleasure to keep my skills from growing rusty." He strode to a cabinet in the corner, opened its doors. Riffling through the stack of papers, he murmured, "Let's see— somewhere here I have some basic scales and chords—"

Emilie tiptoed out of the room, leaving the two to their newly-discovered common interest.

Thus began the friendship between David and Maria. The two met each morning for music lessons, and Brazos Bend was filled with song. At times, Emilie regretted her generous behavior, for David's spending time with Maria left him less time for her. Also, now that Emilie had developed a fragile rapport with Maria, she dared not antagonize her by spending too much time with David, whom the girl seemed to worship.

Emilie's matchmaking worked too well, for soon, David and Maria became devoted companions. Aside from morning music lessons, the two started horseback-riding in the afternoons. Sometimes Emilie would spot them from the upstairs portico, the couple laughing as they galloped down the blue-bonnet-strewn lawn. David invited Emilie to join them, but she declined to intrude, explaining to David that she had little training as a horsewoman.

Emilie's days grew lonelier. As usual, Edgar spoke to her only when necessary, and seemed oblivious to the activities of the household. She read, she walked, she played the piano, but inside she was going crazy

212

with boredom.

Then, a week before David was to return to Houston, an idea occurred to her—she would redecorate the house! If she had no choice but to remain, she would change the house to suit her! David could fetch her the materials!

Emilie walked about the house taking notes—she would move a chair closer to the fireplace, throw a navy pillow across the yellow settee, add lace trim to canopy covers, have slipcovers made for worn upholstery. . . .

Once Emilie had completed her plans, she sought out Avis Gerouard. She found the woman writing out menus in the small anteroom behind the dining room, which the housekeeper used as an office. As Emile entered the room, Avis stood, unsmiling, her black skirts rustling, her brows arched in curiosity.

"Do sit down, Mrs. Gerouard," Emilie urged, taking seat in the slat-backed chair across from Avis at the small board table. Nodding towards the papers spread out upon the whitewashed table top, Emilie commented, "I see you're planning the menus for the next week. May I see them, please?"

Ignoring Emilie's extended hand, Avis Gerouard stacked the papers and murmured, "You mustn't concern yourself with such trivia, Madame. That is why I am here, *n'est ce pas?*"

Emilie frowned. "It is not trivial to me, as mistress of the house. I intend to plan some of the meals myself."

"Is that why you sought me out, Madame? The menus?"

Emilie drew back her hand. Avis's questions reminded her of her purpose in seeking the woman out. She'd best see to that first. "No, that is not why I came, Mrs. Gerouard. I wish to change the decor of the house. I'll be needing two strong lads to move furniture about, and, once Mr. David has made his trip to Houston, I'll need another girl to help Hallie sew draperies and slipcovers."

Avis Gerouard's eyes flickered strangely. "And what does your husband have to say about your—plans, Madame?"

Emilie's eyes flashed with anger. "What do you mean?"

"I take my orders from M'sieur Ashland, Madame."

Emile rapped her fingertips on the table top. "Indeed? Are you saying you'll not do as I ask?"

"Not without your husband's consent, Madame."

Emile shot to her feet, her hands shaking the table. "Why you impertinent old—you'll follow my directions, Mrs. Gerouard, or I'll see to it that you're dismissed!"

Avis stood, studying Emilie with malevolent black eyes. "Are you sure you have that authority, Madame?" she asked, an uncharacteristic, brittle edge in her voice.

Emilie thrust her chin forward as she bit her lower lip. "Of course I do!" she stormed. "How dare you defy me, Mrs. Gerouard! The consequences will be—appropriately severe! Have you forgotten that I'm married to Mr. Ashland?"

"No, Madame," Avis replied steadily, "I've not forgotten."

Furious, Emilie whirled and exited the room, slamming the door. She stamped down the hallway towards Edgar's office.

Damn the woman! The Gerouard woman had the soul—and the sharp claws—of a cat!

Despite her anger, Emilie paused at the door to Edgar's office, reminding herself that she hadn't had a serious conversation with him in over three weeks. What if he assumed she was coming to—no, damn it! She would see to the matter at hand without delay! She refused to be defied by that scarecrow Gerouard woman!

She rapped on the door, heard Edgar snap, "Come in!"

She entered the room slowly, leaving the door widely ajar, remembering her last visit to her husband's office. He stood, turned to look at her, his expression pleasantly surprised, his brown eyes glowing with a tender light.

Her heart fluttered wildly. How handsome he was—the rugged features, the magnificent, muscular frame, the shirt partially open, revealing curly black hair. . . . How easy it would be to fly across the room, into his arms—

But his tender expression vanished, replaced by the usual mocking grin. "Well, Mrs. Ashland, what may I do for you?" he asked, walking towards the door.

She watched his hand take the doorknob. "Leave it open."

He pushed the door shut. "You overestimate your charms, sweet," he said, his face a cynical mask. He sauntered back to his desk, sat down in his swivel chair and leaned back, crossing shiny black boots on top of his desk. He gestured to the leather settee. "Do sit down, my dear."

Emilie clenched her fists and ground her teeth, furious at his cool taunts. No, she decided, she would not let him anger her out of her purpose! She crossed to the settee and sat. Drawing a ragged breath, she blurted, "I want you to dismiss Avis Gerouard!"

Edgar laughed deeply. "Do you, now? How very amusing. May I ask why?"

"I—I can get no cooperation from the woman!" Emilie sputtered. "Since I'm mistress of the house—"

"Are you, love?" Edgar interrupted, undressing her with his eyes. "The last time I looked, my bed was empty."

Emilie blushed to the roots of her hair. "You—you know what I mean," she muttered, lowering black eyelashes.

Edgar chuckled. "Pray continue, Mrs. Ashland."

"I wish to redecorate the house, and Avis says I must get—your consent." She looked up warily.

Edgar gestured indifferently. "You have it. Do whatever you please—short of reducing the place to a shambles."

"But I need the help of the servants, Edgar, and Avis refuses to cooperate!"

Edgar uncrossed his legs and stood, walking towards her. "If you are, as you say, mistress of the house, then you must learn to handle Avis." He sat down beside her, his dark gaze piercing her. "Such eyes you have, love. Like blue diamonds. Astonishing."

Ignoring his silky words and his fiery gaze, Emilie continued nervously, "Will you at least speak with her—set her straight?"

Edgar raised her chin with a brown finger, forcing her to meet his smoldering stare. "No," he replied, grinning, displaying even white teeth. "But you should feel free, love, to try to change my mind."

"Oh!" Emilie gasped. She jumped up just in time to avoid Edgar's mouth as it descended towards hers. She hurried to the door. "You're despicable!"

She grabbed the doorknob, but he was instantly beside her, pinning her against the door. His masculine scent filled her senses; her knees went weak as his hard frame pressed into her softness.

She trembled as his lips moved to her ear. "God, how sweet you are!" he breathed. "Emilie, darling, come upstairs with me now," he whispered, his voice sincere, pleading.

For a moment, she was swept by a delicious lassitude, a wave of tenderness. His mouth moved close to hers; his breath was warm upon her lips.

Then she remembered, pushing against his chest. "Will you get rid of the portrait? If not, you'll have to rape me!"

He backed off, his face darkened with anger. "The God-damned portrait again!" he stormed. "Emilie, I *don't* want you to replace Olivia—that fabrication is strictly in your mind! I've other reasons for not giving the portrait to Aaron!"

"Yes! You still love her!" Emilie spat.

"Jesus Christ!" he hissed, striding off, fists clenched. "Must you be such a trial to me, woman?"

Seeing his distress, Emilie hastily argued, "Edgar, why don't you let me go? David's returning to Houston in a week, and—"

He spun about. "Let you go!" he muttered. "Let you go—with David! Woman, if it's rape you want, simply mention *that* idea again!"

Uttering a cry of frustrated rage, she stormed from the room.

Chapter Eighteen

Later that day, Emilie sought out Maria. She had decided a length of gold dimity David bought her in Houston was particularly suitable for the Mexican girl, and she was planning to offer to make the girl a dress, hoping the gesture would help bridge the gap between them.

When a knock at Maria's door proved fruitless, Emilie went downstairs, running into David in the central hallway. "Have you seen Maria?"

David nodded as he hung his jacket on a peg in the hallway. "Yes, dear. Maria and I just returned from our afternoon ride, and she's still down at the stable. After we cooled down our horses, she decided to stay and give them both a good brushing."

"She's brushing the horses?" Emilie repeated, raising an eyebrow in curiosity. "That's an odd way for a young woman to spend her afternoon."

A wry smile tugged at David's mouth. "Maria has quite a way with animals, Emilie. But it's strange you should say that. Olivia used to say the very same thing."

"*Olivia?*"

"Yes. Seven years ago, when Maria's father was first hired on to take charge of the stable, Maria was at his side every minute. But Olivia put a stop to that, saying that a stable was no place for a girl of ten, that Maria might see something—" David nervously cleared his throat—"indelicate."

Despite herself, Emilie giggled. "Well she might. It's interesting, though, that Olivia was concerned about the girl's welfare."

"Aye. She took a fancy to Maria for a time. Olivia bought the girl clothes and dolls, taught Maria to speak English—that sort of thing."

"How kind of her. But you say only for a time? Did Olivia's attitude change?"

David stared at Emilie blankly for a moment. Then he snapped his fingers. "Good grief, Emilie, I just remembered that some important papers arrived in today's post. I must show them to Uncle immediately. If you'll excuse me?"

"Certainly, David." Emilie frowned as she watched David hurrying down the sun-spotted hallway. Somehow, she suspected he went off not in search of the urgent correspondence, but to dodge her questions about Olivia.

A look of puzzlement on her face, Emilie left the house and crossed the breezy, spring-scented lawn to the stable. She creaked open the weather-beaten door, slanting a square beam of sunshine upon the hay-strewn floor. Dust hung heavily in the air, and Emilie wrinkled her nose at the pervasive manure smell as she started down the long row of stalls. She glanced in each cubicle, seeing only horses munching on hay and grain. "Maria?"

As she approached the end of the building, she heard low humming of the Spanish tune Maria had sung for her weeks before. "Maria? It's Emilie."

219

Abruptly, the humming stopped, and the plank gate to a stall swung open. Maria, wearing a frayed black velvet riding habit, stood staring at Emilie, her brow deeply puckered. "Yes, Señora?"

Emilie took a deep breath and smiled. "I wanted to have a word with you, if I might."

Maria's eyes narrowed. "I'm brushing David's horse, Señora."

"I see. May I join you for a moment?" Emilie glanced skeptically at the large brown sorrel. "That is, if the horse doesn't mind."

Surprisingly, Maria laughed. "Copper is *un cordero*—a lamb, Señora. Do not fear—he won't harm you."

Emilie eyed Maria with new respect. "You know horses make me nervous, don't you?"

The Mexican girl shrugged and stepped back into the stall, taking the brush to the side of the large animal, murmuring low, indistinguishable words in Spanish, which seemed to soothe Copper.

"What have you to tell me, Señora?" Maria asked, without looking in Emilie's direction.

Emilie hesitantly stepped into the stall, closing the gate. "Well, I've a lovely length of gold dimity, Maria. I thought it would make up into a nice frock for you."

"How kind," Maria replied in a flat tone. "But do not trouble yourself, Señora. Señor Edgar provides quite generously for my needs."

Emilie had a sinking feeling that she would get nowhere with the girl. But she squared her shoulders and plunged on. "I realize that, Maria. It's just that—well, David bought me the length, but it's perfect for your coloring—"

Suddenly, Maria turned to stare at Emilie, her green eyes hard, her full-lipped mouth tight. "I do not need the charity of your castoffs, Señora!"

Emilie mentally groaned as the girl again turned to brush the horse. She could kick herself for not thinking before she spoke. Mentioning that the cloth was a gift from David was precisely the wrong thing to do!

But as Emilie watched the Mexican girl groom Copper, she witnessed an immediate transformation—the eyes which had been so cold seconds earlier now softened as the girl again whispered to the horse.

Emilie decided upon a new tack. "You have a gift with horses, Maria. David told me your father trained you."

"*Sí*, Señora."

"He also told me Olivia Ashland was very kind to you at one time. Is that true?"

Maria's expression grew guarded, yet she went on casually enough, "Oh, yes, Señora Olivia was good to me. Once, soon after we came, she asked me to come live in the big house. She called my father a nogood, who only drank and played his guitar all through the night. But the señora—she didn't understand."

"Understand what?" Emilie asked, astonished that the Mexican girl should grant her this small insight into her past.

Maria turned to stare at Emilie, but her eyes seemed to connect with a scene much further away. "That the music soothed me, Señora. For years after *mi padre* left, I did not sleep well."

Maria turned and began vigorously brushing Copper, her young face again tight, as if she regretted her admissions to Emilie. Emilie's heart wrenched for the lonely girl—why had Maria's father deserted this beautiful child? Emilie half-wanted to embrace Maria, to tell her that it was all right, that she had a friend, but she knew the girl would heartily resent any show of affection. Years of rejection had forced Maria to build staunch defenses against the outside world.

"I'm sorry, Maria," Emilie finally said. "I'm sure you miss your father terribly. But he has a fine daughter I'm sure he would be proud of. And he passed on to you his wonderful talent with animals."

Maria glanced at Emilie sideways, and Emilie thought she noted some mellowing of the girl's features. Seizing the advantage, she added, "I've also noticed you're an expert horsewoman, Maria."

"*Gracias,*" came the cautious reply.

"In fact, I'm a bit envious. You see, I grew up on a farm, and rode only an old plow horse. I'd love to—I mean, I'd be most pleased if you would be so generous as to teach me to ride."

The Mexican girl laughed shortly as she hung Copper's brush and leaned over to check his supply of water and grain. "That is an honor I shall save for your husband, Señora Ashland. He might be jealous that his new wife should spend so much time away from him, *verdad?*"

That remark nettled, and Emilie struggled to keep her patience. "I disagree, Maria. I think my husband would be pleased if we became better acquainted."

Maria laughed mirthlessly, straightened and stared at Emilie with indifference. "You do not know Señor Edgar very well."

Emilie scowled. "What do you mean?"

"Señor Edgar is the type of man who wants his woman waiting for him. He was that way with Señora Olivia, also."

Emilie hastily digested this revelation. "You mean Edgar resented Olivia's being with you?"

Maria's deep green eyes flashed with bitterness. "With anyone, Señora. You have never seen a more jealous man. Señor Edgar forced Señora Olivia to quit entertaining, because he could not stand to see anyone else with his wife."

Emilie listened in perverse fascination. "Surely Olivia resented that. Surely she tried—"

"Oh, she tried, Señora. She tried—and you would not believe the fights between her and your husband. I would hear them sometimes at night, their screams travelling all the way to our cabin. I think Señor Edgar used to beat her."

"You don't mean—but Maria, you have no proof—"

"Señora Olivia is dead, isn't she?" Maria cut in, her eyes gleaming with triumph. "And Señor Edgar was there at the time, wasn't he?"

Emilie gulped, totally arrested by Maria's words, unable to think of a reply.

"Think on that for a time, Señora," Maria concluded, driving home her point. "I would advise you not to let Señor Edgar see you spending much time with David, or me. Your husband's patience is not limitless."

Emilie was silent, her face deeply lined. Her worst fears about Edgar seemed to be well-grounded. Maria was obviously frightened of the man—and for good reason, too.

"You must excuse me now, Señora, I must check on Peligra," Maria said.

Lost in troubled thought, Emilie automatically followed Maria out of the stall and down the long corridor leading towards the door.

"You wish to see Peligra also?" the girl called over her shoulder.

Emilie frowned. "I beg your pardon? Oh, you

223

mean the Arabian I see you riding every day. Yes, I'd like to see her. She's quite a beauty."

"She is." Maria swung open another stall door and smiled. *"Buenos tardes, corazon."*

Emilie watched Maria step into the stall and carefully examine the hind leg of the beautiful, chocolate-brown mare. "She has a cut—from a bramble," Maria told Emilie, pointing at a reddish gash on the mare's beautifully shaped leg. "It's healing well, but I must prepare more of the salve *mi padre* taught me to make."

Emilie smiled as she watched the girl move forward and whisper to the horse. Maria's face was rapt, her eyes adoring as she embraced the mare's sinewy neck.

"Come on in, Señora—say hello to Peligra," Maria coaxed.

Emilie stepped into the stall. But the horse snorted nervously, and began tapping the dirt floor with its sharp hooves. "I don't know, Maria," Emilie said dubiously.

But Maria continued to whisper low, soothing words in Spanish to Peligra, as she stroked the mare's mane. Soon, the horse calmed down. "You are safe, Señora," Maria reassured Emilie. "Arabians are high-strung creatures, but she will get used to you."

Emilie edged closer to Peligra, and, as Maria promised, the tall, majestic animal remained placid. Emilie arrived at Maria's side near the front of the stall, and carefully studied Peligra's noble head—the dark, widely spaced eyes, the broad forehead tapering to a narrow muzzle. Hesitantly, she reached out and touched the animal's coarse, warm flank. Peligra did not flinch, and Emilie began to feel more confident.

"I suppose I must be getting back," Emilie told Maria. "But do remember that any time, I would be happy to help you make some clothes, Maria. By the way, do you know how to sew?"

Maria glanced at Emilie, and Emilie detected a glint of yearning in the girl's eyes. *"Un poco*—not well, Señora." The girl turned, again murmuring to the horse, foreign guttural words Emilie did not understand.

"Well, if you don't need a dress, perhaps a new riding habit, then—"

Suddenly, Emilie gasped and moved backward, for Peligra abruptly became very nervous, snorting and tapping the stall floor once more. Even Maria drew away from the fiery-eyed mare.

Emilie gulped. "Maria, I think you'd better—Oh, God!"

Emilie jerked backwards against the wall, for now Peligra was stomping the ground, growing enraged. "Good Lord, Maria, please—"

But Maria remained motionless, staring at the other girl implacably, even as the rampaging animal reared above Emilie.

Emilie screamed, closing her eyes, throwing her arms about her face as she waited for Peligra's sharp hooves to come crashing down upon her!

Emilie heard a hysterical whinny, then a voice exclaimed, "Oh, my God—Emilie—Maria!"

A dull, thudding sound followed, then, abruptly, all grew silent. Emilie cautiously opened her eyes and saw David standing at the door of the stall, looking thunderstruck. Opposite him, Maria stood with a hand on Peligra's mane. Both girl and horse looked incredibly unruffled, as if nothing had happened.

David slowly entered the stall, eyeing the horse warily. "Emilie—Maria—are you both all right?"

The aftershock hit Emilie. Her heart pounded so frantically she thought it would burst in her chest. "Maria's—horse—tried to trample me," she told David, her voice crackling. She managed to catch her breath, and her fear surged into anger. She whirled upon the Mexican girl. "Maria—why did you just stand there and let it happen?" she hissed.

Maria shrugged, her face emotionless. "Peligra surprised me, Señora. I suppose I panicked—I could not think what to do."

"Until David appeared!" Emilie retorted in a hoarse whisper. "You acted quickly enough then!"

The girl did not reply—not even a flicker of feeling crossed her smooth Spanish features.

David inched forward, nervously clearing his throat. "Emilie, dear, let's get you back to the house."

Emilie hesitated for a moment, glowering at Maria. Then she sighed angrily. "Very well, David. I want to get as far away from here as possible!"

A malevolent smile curled Maria's lips as David led Emilie out of the stall. At the gate, David turned and nodded to the Mexican girl. "Maria, we'll talk later."

Once they were outside, Emilie exploded to David. "Oh, David, it was horrible! She just stood there and let the horse rear above me! I don't know what would have happened if you hadn't appeared."

David's face twisted with conflicting emotions as they walked towards the house. "Emilie, what are you saying? Maria explained that she panicked—"

"The devil she did! She was savoring every second of my terror—until you came! Why did you come, anyway, David? Didn't you trust Maria alone with me?"

David glanced sharply at Emilie. "Of course I did.

I came to get Copper—Uncle asked me to check on the hands in the north field.''

Emilie studied David carefully as they neared the house, noting the tension etched in his thin, handsome face. "David, there's much you're not telling me," she accused.

David sighed heavily. "Well, I suppose Maria did surprise me a bit."

"How so?" Emilie prodded.

"It just seems odd that she would allow anyone around Peligra—under the circumstances."

Emilie stopped in her tracks, grabbing David's arm. "What circumstances?"

Halting beside her, David looked miserable. "Well, Peligra always has been unpredictable, and now—well, she's with a foal. Uncle bred her with Apollyon." He added without conviction, "But I'm sure Maria thought she knew what she was doing—"

"Of course she did!" Emilie cut in sarcastically. "Tell me, David, what does the name 'Peligra' mean?"

David stared at his feet. "It's—it's the Spanish word for 'danger,' " he mumbled.

Emilie groaned, gesturing her frustration. "David, please, don't be a fool! You're covering for the girl, and it's only doing her—and me—harm." Moving closer, she touched his arm and continued vehemently, "I want you to tell me why Maria was dismissed from school."

He looked up furtively. "Emilie, I don't think you want to know—"

"Tell me!"

David's face fell, and he nodded sadly. "Very well, Emilie. In her letter, Mrs. Ferguson explained that one of the girls nettled Maria ruthlessly. And Maria . . ."

"Yes?"

David sighed, then blurted, "Maria went into the girl's room one night and cut off her hair."

"Merciful heavens!" Emilie gasped.

Chapter Nineteen

May 9, 1841

The grandfather clock in the hallway of Brazos Bend chimed two strokes. All was quiet, all dark, save for the single light flickering in the library.

Edgar Ashland sat upon the silk brocade settee, his boots crossed on the rosewood table before him. His frock coat was unbuttoned, his cravat askew. He was very drunk.

"Damn the girl!" he muttered for the dozenth time. He took a deep draw of fiery brandy from a crystal snifter. "Bar me from her bed, will she? Dictate to *me,* a gentleman and a lord, will she? Damn her eyes, the little hellcat!"

He stood then, swayed as he walked towards the sideboard. He put his brandy glass down next to the crystal decanter, then caught the mahogany edge to keep his balance. He eyed the near-empty decanter in puzzlement, then waved it off unsteadily. "You've had enough for one night, dear Ashland," he told himself, staggering back to the settee.

He collapsed and closed his eyes, surrendering to euphoria. But images of Emilie shimmered and swayed in his mind—Emilie, in a pretty yellow dress, her bright blue eyes laughing at him, Emilie, naked in his bed, her arms held out to him, inviting. . . .

He jerked upright. Jesus! How had the girl bewitched him so? He hadn't felt this way when he married her—she was merely a pretty minx to share his bed. Or had the reasons gone deeper? What of her resemblance to Olivia? Had memories of his first wife influenced his decision to marry Emilie, his behavior since?

Funny—when he saw Emilie now, he didn't think of Olivia at all. He wanted Emilie for herself—charming, guileless, serenely beautiful. But could she come to care for him? Hell—it was too late. She insisted she loved David, and, besides, he had ruined his chances with his cruel behavior.

Or had he? He remembered the day he shot the Cherokee. As the savage collapsed upon Emilie, he thought he heard her whisper, "I love you, Edgar." Was it possible—had he heard correctly? "Nay," he told himself, with a bitter laugh. "The girl was crazed at the time. If she, indeed, said the words, they meant naught."

Edgar groaned, holding his face between his hands. No, she could never love him. The things he had done to her—raping her, locking her up, throwing her in the river! How could she forgive him? How could he hope to make her understand the reasons—his confusion, his torment, his guilt?

He thought of the day he almost drowned her. His mind had recoiled since that day, forbidding thought of his harrowing deed. But tonight, his inhibitions were washed away, and the truth splintered his brain—

Emilie, thrown screaming into the black depths of the river. Emilie, gasping for breath, crying for help—

He had dashed to save her. Off came the boots, the coat. The water rushed up to meet him—he dove down, thought for a terrifying, interminable moment that he had lost her—

"You bastard!" he choked. He got to his feet, his head swimming as he moved to the sideboard. He stared at himself in the mirror on the wall, clenching his fist at his bleary-eyed countenance. "You God-damned bastard! Throwing the girl—your own wife—into the Brazos! This time there was no war to excuse your despicable behavior!"

The war! Just thinking of it, he was swept by dizziness. He turned from the sideboard and collapsed into a wing chair near the fireplace. He had been cruel to Emilie then, too. Needlessly cruel, despite the dangers. He remembered her kneeling in the mud, clinging to a cross next to a mound of dirt. A freshly-filled grave—her mother. What of her father? he now wondered. Where had *he* been—off soldiering? No, David had told him Emilie's father died at the Alamo! Mere days before she lost her mother!

"The poor babe!" he groaned aloud, his fingers digging into the upholstered chair arm. "What if she remembers? Ashland, you should be drawn and quartered for your heinous behavior!"

Edgar began to piece together the story of Emilie's life as he knew it. She had lost both parents, and was then dragged off by a brutal soldier—Edgar Ashland. She had lost her grandmother, then was coerced into marriage with—Edgar Ashland. Then she had been flagrantly abused, physically and emotionally, by—Edgar Ashland!

How she must hate him! How she must fear him! No wonder she had twice attempted escape. If he had one ounce of decency left, he would let her go! Let her go!

But he could not! Damn his soul to hell, he could not! He could put a pistol to his own head with much greater ease!

She had asked him to let her return to Houston—with David! If he did—he knew how that little drama would eventually end. David was quite fond of the girl, and disapproved of his uncle's behavior.

Damn the boy! He and Emilie were too close for comfort already! But what could he do—throw his own nephew out of the house? That would only alienate Emilie further. Besides, the boy owned half the estate and would defend his rights; he was reserved, but no coward. And, dash it all, he loved the boy! He had promised himself to do his best by the lad after Charles and Amelia were killed.

No, he could never force David to leave. But, oh—it was torture to watch David and Emilie together! How long before Emilie convinced David to take her away? How long, indeed, before his own behavior convinced David to take her away?

And what of Aaron Rice? How long before *he* began skulking about again? How that green-eyed idiot would love to get his slimy hands on Edgar Ashland's wife! If he knew Rice at all, the man had not given up on getting Olivia's portrait, and would use any means to get it—including Emilie!

"The portrait!" he moaned. "I should burn the bloody portrait!"

Yet burning it would solve nothing, alienate everyone—

He was defeated at every turn. He could not give in to Aaron, to Emilie, without sacrificing his pride. And he was a proud man.

Was there no hope? Would he never get Emilie

back again? Would he never feel her beneath him, soft and warm, know again the sweetness of her surrender?

If only he could bed her, perhaps then he could make her his wife again! He knew her body—every curve and valley, every vulnerable spot. With his manhood buried deep inside her, she would agree—to anything! God, how he longed to devour her!

Yet she had vowed he would not have her, except by force. And he could not—would not—hurt her like that again. But he wanted her so—ached for her. If he could get her to submit physically, she might be his again in every way.

He remembered being with her beneath the giant tree near the river. Their lovemaking had been intense, culminating in an ecstacy he had never known before. They had hung there, all defenses shattered, two people becoming a single being, a united soul—

Yes! He must get her to surrender to him once more! Then he would never let her out of his bed again! When she became angry, he would melt her with his kisses! He would never let her withdraw from him again!

He thought of her now, upstairs sleeping. Was she embracing the pillow, her lower lip petulant, as it often was when she slept? Which nightgown was she wearing? Did she have the sheet drawn about her, or were all her curves visible through the sheer fabric of her gown?

"Oh, God!" he groaned, standing. He would have her! By God, he was her husband, and he would have her! Now!

He staggered into the black hallway and groped his way up the stairs. He would smother her protests, kiss her into submission. He would ride her until she promised to be his—forever!

He stumbled through the upstairs hall. But when he got to the door of her room, he stopped, his limbs shaking. "Best proceed with caution, old man," he warned himself.

He creaked open the door, then closed it and stood dead still inside the room. When the mad beating of his heart subsided, he heard the sound of her steady breathing. Good. She hadn't awakened.

Quietly, he removed his boots, then tiptoed toward the bed. When his eyes adjusted to the dimness, he made out her sleeping form, his breath catching in his throat as he viewed her. She lay on her stomach on the counterpane, her nightgown twisted about her middle, revealing her long, silky legs, teasing him with the lower curves of her hips. A wealth of moonlight-streaked curls framed her face and cascaded down her back.

Trembling, he sat down beside her. Gently, he turned her towards him; she moaned slightly. He perched himself on his elbows, leaned over and kissed her. He tasted the sweetness of her lips and began to drown—

She jumped awake; her entire body went stiff. She tried to cry out, but he smothered her mouth with his own, grabbing her hands when she tried to flail out at him.

She resisted and he kissed her harder, ruthlessly, forcing her mouth open with his teeth. But she did not yield; she did not soften. Her body was corpse-rigid beneath him—

He released her hands, drew back and stared at her. She gasped for air, sobbing, huge tears streaming down her face.

"Emmie, let me," he whispered. "Darling, please

let me—''

But she continued to cry fearfully, her hands now limp against the pillow—

Mother of God—she was terrified of him! She felt nothing for him—but fear! Wordlessly, he got up, staggered out of the room, the sound of her piteous sobs ringing in his ears, the taste of her tears in his mouth.

He entered his own room, staggered to the bed, collapsed. She feared him—hated him! There was nothing left, nothing to save! He would go downstairs now, load the pistol and blow his brains out!

Why? Why? Because he loved her! He loved her! What an idiot he had been! He loved her, yet he had murdered every chance he could have with her!

He would die, now—oh, God, he wanted to die! But he couldn't move—his legs were dead weight beneath him. He was even a failure at killing himself!

Weakly, he pounded his fist against the mattress. "Oh, God, Emmie, I love you," he choked. "What have I done? What have I done?"

Chapter Twenty

May 9, 1841

Emilie smiled indulgently, smoothing her pink dimity skirts about her. "No, David, you can't simply give the list to the man at the general store," she scolded. "As I've tried to explain, the color and fabric selections are of the utmost importance."

David scratched his head and gazed in consternation at the long list in front of him. He and Emilie had spent the last hour in the parlor going over the long inventory of fabrics and other sewing supplies Emilie wanted bought or ordered in Houston. "Let's see, *navy* blue," he muttered.

Emilie giggled. "Yes, that's for this room," she replied excitedly, stroking the smooth silk brocade of the settee where they sat. "Can't you imagine some splashes of dark blue against this yellow settee, complemented by a bowl of bluebonnets on the tea table?"

David groaned. "But *navy* blue," he repeated. "I'm familiar with velvet, Emilie, but what color is navy?"

Emilie smiled at her confused companion. David had been good to agree to get the supplies she wanted in Houston, and she was quite excited about being able to occupy her time redecorating the house. It kept her mind away from her painful thoughts about Edgar—and Maria.

In particular, she was frightened about being alone with Edgar while David was gone, especially after last night. But Edgar's daring behavior the previous night had also convinced her that her husband was capable of taking her any time if he truly wanted to—whether David was there or not.

"Emilie?"

Emilie left her thoughts and turned to the befuddled David. "Let's see—navy. It's darker than your eyes. Your eyes are more the color of the sapphire blue silk I want to fashion some roses to display after bluebonnet season. You'd best make a note of that."

As David began scratching away on the parchment, Emilie continued, "Navy is—well—the color seamen wear. I know—it's the color of Captain Porter's coat!"

"I beg your pardon?" David asked, looking up in bewilderment.

Emilie's eyes sparkled mischievously. "You do remember Captain Porter from the steamboat? Won't you be seeing him on the trip to Houston?"

"Ah, yes, the good captain," David replied, his brow furrowed.

"You must have a good look at his coat," Emilie instructed. "Or borrow it!" she added teasingly.

"Very well—Porter's coat. Now what of this sea green you mention—"

"Sea green is the color of the ocean, of course. You have seen the ocean, haven't you? And note that it is to be a watered silk. What else would one have in a sea color? Be sure to look for the shimmer

237

in the fabric.''

David frowned, his fingers crackling the parchment nervously. ''Heavens, Emilie, it will be all I can accomplish not to botch up all these colors. You mustn't expect much when it comes to shimmers and what-not—''

Smiling warmly, Emilie covered David's hand with her own. ''I have every confidence you'll bring me exactly what I want!''

Looking down at Emilie's hand on his, David flushed. Then he glanced up, returning her smile.

''Good morning, Señora Ashland. David.''

Seeing Maria in the doorway, Emilie hastily released David's hand. ''Good morning, Maria.''

Studying the girl, Emilie reflected that Maria looked coldly, distantly beautiful. The girl's gleaming ebony tresses were piled on top of her head; her full-skirted white muslin dress was trimmed with delicate green embroidery. One tawny, beautifully shaped hand clutched a music book.

For a moment, Maria's eyes locked with Emilie's, raw defiance meeting grim determination. Though deep inside, Emilie felt a stab of fear at seeing the Mexican girl following the frightening incident at the stable yesterday, she outwardly displayed no emotion. She'd be damned if she'd let the girl intimidate her! It was time Maria accepted the fact that Emilie was now a member of the family, not an unwelcome guest who could be bullied into leaving!

To Emilie's relief, Maria was the first to turn away. Nodding to David, the Mexican girl said stiffly, ''I have studied the musical terms, as you wished, David. Is it not time for our lesson?''

David stood, looking flustered as he took his beaver hat from the settee. ''Ah, yes, our lesson, Maria. I'm afraid I must apologize, my dear. I must

238

shortly leave for the landing or risk missing the *Belle.*"

"I see," Maria replied with a trace of bitterness. Glancing at Emilie, she continued disdainfully, "Since you and Señora Ashland have been involved with matters *muy importante* all morning, your time is no longer available, *verdad?*"

"Maria," Emilie offered smoothly, "I would be happy to help you with your piano while David is gone."

Maria turned to glare at Emilie, her green eyes shooting darts. She was now tapping one satin-slippered foot impatiently, her jaw thrust forward in indignation.

Realizing she had nettled the girl further, Emilie added, "You could surprise David with your progress when he returns, couldn't you?"

The Mexican girl's eyes narrowed perceptibly. *"Tal vez,"* she conceded noncommittally.

"Well, nephew, can I get a moment of your time, or are you too busy flirting with every female in sight?"

The three turned to see Edgar standing in the doorway. Emilie's heart jumped into her throat as she gazed at him. Showing no evidence of wear from his drinking the night before, he was more handsome than ever. His broad face was smoothly shaven, his mustache neatly trimmed. His black, collar-length hair reflected the sunlight streaming through the front windows. He wore a white, open shirt, revealing his muscular chest, the matting of black curls. Below, dark trousers clung snugly to his sinewy legs.

Emilie studied him with her usual astonishment—he was so handsome that every time she looked at him it seemed a startling new experience. If

239

only he were as beautiful inside as he was outside! she mused sadly.

For a moment, his dark, deepset eyes held hers, as if he were trying to bore into her head, read her feelings. She gulped, wondering if he would make some mention of the previous night in front of the others.

Then David spoke. "Good morning, Uncle. What is it you wish?"

Slowly, Edgar's eyes released Emilie's. He turned to David. "I've a long list of supplies we'll be needing in the coming months. You'll join me in the office, Nephew?"

"Of course, Uncle. As it happens, I have a matter to discuss with you before I leave." He glanced significantly at Emilie. "Excuse us, ladies?"

As the two men started to leave, Edgar paused, turning to Maria. "Have you asked David to bring you back some pretty cloth, kitten?" he asked. He grinned, winking at her. "You're blossoming into quite a woman, my dear. I'd enjoy seeing you in some lovely new frocks."

Maria blushed, lowering black eyelashes. "*Gracias,* Señor Ashland."

Edgar started out of the room, instructing David, "Don't forget, Nephew, some lengths of cloth for Maria. And don't mind the cost."

David threw Emilie an apologetic look and shrugged, leaving the room.

Emilie bolted to her feet, hands on hips. Was this her punishment for refusing Edgar the night before—to be humiliated while his eyes literally unclothed Maria? He had never before called the girl "kitten"; the pet name had rolled off his tongue caressingly. The nerve of the man—asking David to spare no expense buying for Maria, yet not asking him to bring back anything for his wife!

"Señora, I believe I shall accept your kind offer of music lessons," Maria remarked.

Emilie only half-heard the girl's words. Frowning, she turned to Maria. "I beg your pardon?"

The girl beamed at Emilie. "Music lessons, Señora. I shall accept your offer. Yes, I do believe David will be quite pleased with my progress." Looking straight at Emilie, she added pointedly, "As will Señor Edgar. Did you hear, Señora? He finds me quite a woman now."

Issuing this parting barb, Maria gracefully swept out of the room. Emilie clenched her fists, resisting with great effort an urge to chase the girl down and strangle her.

Emilie began to pace. "I must remember that Maria is an orphan," she hissed to herself. "I must remember that she was forced to live with Edgar Ashland!"

She stopped near the tea table, stamping her foot, kicking the cabriole leg. "But so was I!" she raged. "So was I!"

A loud crash interrupted her thoughts. She looked down in dismay to find she had shaken a crystal bowl to the floor—tiny glass fragments covered her slippers and large, jagged pieces lay nearby.

"Hell," she groaned. "Now what shall I put the bluebonnets in?"

Chapter Twenty-One

May 9, 1841

Emilie sat upon the front porch of Brazos Bend, rocking as the day faded. The evening breeze wafted across her, bringing the delicious scent of cedar mixed with honeysuckle.

She had had all of the house she could take. The day had been ominously quiet after David departed. She spent the time worrying about how Edgar would treat her now that her "protector" was gone. Would he lock her up again? What new, bizarre twist might his behavior take?

Her worries had been somewhat assuaged at dinner—Edgar had been in a jovial mood, laughing and flirting with Maria as if the two of them shared a well-kept secret. Emilie had been shocked and angered by his unusual garrulousness—especially since he ignored her completely.

Unlike last night. For the dozenth time, she relived the horrible, frightening moment when he was in bed with her. She had awakened to find his teeth cutting into her mouth, his body crushing hers. Then he had begged her, "Let me. . . ." She trembled at the memory. She had wept, terrified of him. He was so strong—she feared him when he held her so hard, especially after hearing Maria's warnings about Edgar yesterday.

"Emilie!"

Emilie almost jumped out of her chair at the sound of her husband's deep, commanding voice. Her head shot up; she saw Edgar standing next to her, staring down at her in frowning disapproval.

He sat down in the rocker next to her. "I've been looking all over the house for you, woman. I had almost decided you were out tempting another redskin to divest you of your golden tresses!"

Emilie looked wearily at the indignant stranger beside her. "I've only been out here rocking, Edgar. It's hardly an act of treason."

"Very well, don't get in a snit," he replied, lowering his voice. "But in the future, Emilie, kindly keep me better informed of your activities."

Emilie sprang up from her chair, her eyes shooting diamond-blue sparks. "Oh—you're unbearable! Must I get your permission every time I go for a walk, or take a bath?"

He grinned. "Yes, of course. I might wish to join you—for your bath."

Her husband's bold words made Emilie blush profusely. Hearing him chuckle, she whirled and started for the door.

"Sit down," he ordered quietly.

She grabbed the doorknob, but he was beside her, his large brown hand covering hers. "Would you prefer sitting in my lap?"

Gritting her teeth, Emilie returned to her chair. For a long moment, they each rocked silently, listening to the creaking of the chairs and the chirping of birds. Then Edgar took a cheroot from the pocket of his frock coat. Emilie watched as the match illuminated his face, the wavering light making his features harsh, almost sinister.

After a while, Edgar chuckled. "We're like an old married couple," he commented. "What will we be like, my dear, say twenty-five years from now? Will we be rocking—here—on this same porch? Let's see, my hair will be quite gray by then, I 'spect. Yours—will be as golden and silky as ever. Of course, there will be quite a collection of grandchildren cavorting on the lawn."

Emilie turned, eyeing her husband icily. "You're assuming a lot."

"I expect—a lot," he replied silkily, blowing smoke across her. "There, don't bite your lip. I've no plan for your immediate ravishment, my dear. As I assured my nephew before he left this morning—you're quite safe."

Emilie couldn't resist retorting, "Perhaps David should have been more concerned about Maria's safety!"

"Maria?" Edgar asked innocently. "What has *she* to do with any of this?"

"Edgar, if you have any honor at all," Emilie gritted, "you'll not trifle with the girl's affections. She's been through enough!"

"My dear, I have no idea what you're talking about," Edgar replied with consternation.

"No idea, indeed!" Emilie fumed. "You've been flirting with the girl all day, leading her on—"

Edgar laughed. "You're jealous!"

"I—I'm not jealous!" Emilie stammered. "If you've played this little game to arouse my jealousies you've failed—dismally! I'm simply Maria's friend and will not have her used by the likes of you!"

A vein throbbed in Edgar's temple. Emilie realized with satisfaction that her verbal shot had scored.

"Used!" he growled. "Just what sort of man do you take me for?"

"A man thoroughly capable of seducing a seventeen-year-old girl—if you haven't already!"

Edgar grabbed her arm. "Well, madam, if your opinion of me is so—low—perhaps I should fulfill your expectations!"

"Let go of my arm!" she whispered hoarsely, her hard eyes gripping his.

Strangely, he released her immediately and turned, staring moodily at the landscape, biting down hard on his cheroot. But moments later, when she quietly tried to leave, he said firmly, "Don't."

Sighing angrily, she sat back down.

His eyes fixing upon a tree in the distance, he said calmly, "The truth is, Emilie, I've been thinking about what you said the day Maria returned from school. You're right—I've ignored the girl. I'm simply trying to perk her up."

Emilie studied her husband intently, astonished by his sudden honesty. "That may be your goal, Edgar," she told him carefully, "but remember that the girl is love-starved. You must be careful how you approach her, for she could easily misinterpret your attentions. The girl needs friends her own age."

Edgar scowled. "David placed Maria in school, and, as you know, the results were disastrous. Pray tell, what would you suggest, madam?"

"We should start taking her to social functions—and inviting people over—"

"How cozy," Edgar interrupted testily.

She studied his face, but his expression was unreadable in the gathering darkness. He stood, throwing the cheroot down on the porch. She watched the sparks die as he ground the cigar beneath his boot.

"Coming in, Emilie?"

"I shall, shortly," she replied, defiance creeping into her tone.

For a moment, he stood motionless. Then, slowly, he came towards her in the darkness. Oh, no, she thought, what will he try now?

She sat tensely still. She felt his mustache tickling her ear, then he was gone.

Was she hearing things? As his mouth touched her ear, she thought she heard him whisper, "Forgive me for last night."

Later, Emilie slept without peace, caught in the grip of the nightmare again. She found herself back at Gonzales, desperately searching for her mother amid the fire and ruin. Edgar came, riding a black horse, which reared dangerously above her. Dismounting, he grabbed her, dragged her to the river. Then he threw her in and she was drowning . . . drowning in the dark, surging coldness. . . .

Yet this time, curiously, she was not alone—a small babe lay in her arms! Her heart breaking, she clutched her tiny, dead brother, as the blackness sucked them deeper. . . .

"Emilie."

Emilie sat up, screaming for air. She sobbed uncontrollably for a moment, then paused, gasping for her breath as she realized she was safe in bed.

"Emilie, what is it?"

She saw Edgar—standing in the archway to her room, outlined by the moonlight streaming in from the veranda behind him. He was naked to the waist, his dark trousers rippling in the breeze. His face was in shadow, his hair streaked with shimmering silver.

He was real, not a monster. She held out her arms.

"Hold me," she sobbed.

He took a step towards her. "Love, if I come to you—you know what will happen," he said thickly.

"Yes," she whispered. "Please—hold me."

He rushed to her side, pulled her into his arms. She curled her arms around his neck and clung to him, drinking in his comforting manly smell, feeling the hard strength of his powerful body.

He looked down at her, his dark eyes disturbed. "Your nightgown is soaked, love. What is it? Why are you trembling so?"

She shivered and clutched him tighter, laying her head against his shoulder.

His hand stroked her hair as his lips brushed her ear. "A nightmare, darling?" he coaxed. "My God, you were screaming like someone had thrown boiling water on you. Won't you tell me about it, love?"

She drew back, stiffening. "No," she choked, tears streaming down her face, "I can't. I want to forget. Please—make me forget."

He sighed raggedly. "Sweet Jesus—we can't have these tears, love. You were meant for kisses, not tears. Yes, darling—forget."

And his mouth descended upon hers.

It was meant to be, inevitable . . . these were the thoughts that filled Emilie's head, even as her lover's hard, warm body set her senses swimming. Deft hands removed her nightgown, strong arms pulled her tightly against him. He rolled on top of her, and darts of pleasure shot through her as his muscular chest flattened her breasts. His hands swept through her hair as his tongue explored her mouth.

His kiss ended and he buried his face against her throat. "God, Emmie," he breathed, "I'd forgotten how sweet you are—how soft—"

But she did not allow him to finish; her hands

took his face, bringing his mouth back to hers. Her tongue pushed past his smooth teeth, into his mouth; she heard him moan softly.

Emilie's heart was overflowing. How beautiful it felt to be in his arms again, after the weeks of alienation and bitterness, after the terror of the nightmare. She opened to him, her hand reaching for the buttons on his trousers, her body coaxing him to take her quickly—

The instant he filled her, she felt an explosion of rapture so intense, it banished all pride, all fear. And she wanted more—to lose herself in him entirely, to forget, utterly. She became a wild thing, gone mad with passion.

He rose to match her ardor, taking her with sweet violence, making her cry out in mingled joy and torment. All reality became the glorious sensations of their coupling—of his manhood surging deep inside her, of their lips melding in hungry, searching kisses. They moved together in a perfect primitive rhythm, until together they found the blissful satiation that only complete abandon, total surrender can bring.

They fell asleep still joined.

Emilie awakened in the darkness. During his sleep, Edgar had rolled off her. Studying his form outlined in the moonlight, she found he looked peaceful, vulnerable, his mouth thrust forward in an almost boyish manner. She was not used to seeing him thus—unguarded. She leaned forward and kissed his mouth lightly. He stirred slightly, possessively throwing an arm across her breasts.

Gently, she moved his arm. Then she got up, donned her wrapper, and tiptoed out onto the veranda.

For long moments she gazed at the trees swaying in the night breeze, ghostly images playing upon the cascading Spanish moss. She listened to the symphony of crickets and birds.

Why had she ever fought him? she asked herself. Didn't it always end this way, resolved by his strong body claiming hers?

She jumped as warm arms closed about her waist. "Don't be frightened, love," Edgar whispered from behind her, his hands cupping her breasts. "Trouble sleeping again?"

"No—well, I guess I'm just restless."

The breeze swelled and blew across them, sending shivers through the trees and down Emilie's spine.

Edgar's arms tightened about her. "Did I hurt you tonight?" he asked gently.

"I'm fine."

"Sometimes I forget my own strength," he whispered, his hands moving down her body possessively. "I want to make you so completely mine, I forget that I can hurt you."

His unusual honesty warmed her, even as his boldness made her tremble.

Edgar turned her in his arms. Her hands moved from the coarse fabric at his waist to rest lightly on his chest as she gazed up at him.

"Can you tell me about the nightmare now, darling?" he asked.

Her mouth quivered. "N-no."

He drew her securely against him, running his hands through her hair. "Perhaps in time you'll come to trust me," he said. But his voice was sad.

"I just—can't right now, Edgar. It's too painful," she offered weakly.

He tucked her head beneath his chin. "Poor babe. You've been through a lot, haven't you? It must

249

have been hell for you, losing both your parents, then your grandmother.''

She pulled back. "How—how did you know?"

"David told me,'' he replied, gazing down at her seriously.

She gulped. Did he know about Gonzales, did he remember her?

"I want to know all about you, Emilie,'' he continued gravely. "Your family—your childhood.''

"Why?''

His eyes flickered strangely, then narrowed. "Would it be so incredible that I might be coming to care for you?'' he asked, with a trace of bitterness.

She did not answer.

"Please, Emilie, won't you tell me of your past, the memories that make you scream in your sleep? It might draw us closer, darling.''

"But will you tell me of *your* past?'' she countered.

He stiffened. "That's different.''

"It's not different! You want me to be close to you, yet you won't tell me of the things that torment you. You try to kill me every time I mention her name—''

He drew back from her, his hands shaking as he held her shoulders. "Emilie, when will you believe me? I'm never going to hurt you again—*never!*''

She looked up at him, biting her trembling lower lip.

Sighing heavily, he released her. "Is there no common ground for us, love?''

Seeing his torment, something seemed to break inside her. I don't care, I love him! her heart screamed. "Yes,'' she whispered, "there is.''

She curled her arms around his neck and drew his mouth down to hers. At first he seemed startled, then he returned her kiss, his hands untying her wrapper and drawing her breasts against his naked chest.

The kiss ended, leaving them both breathless. "Oh, lady," he whispered against her ear, "there may not be words for it yet, but I feel so close to you."

His words brought tears to her eyes. He swept her up into his arms. "Come back to my bed, Mrs. Ashland. Where you belong."

It happened the moment she lifted her head from the pillow—a wave of nausea so intense, she stumbled out of bed in the half-light, dashing for the basin.

Moments later as the spasm subsided, she felt Edgar's hand on her shoulder. Her face burned that he should see her thus. "Get Hallie!" she ordered hoarsely.

"Darling, let me help you—"

"Please!" she pleaded desperately.

He released her. She heard the rustle of his dressing gown, the door opening, his soft command, "Attend your mistress," as he left.

Hallie ministered to Emilie, then led her back to bed. "Missus, are you with babe?" she asked, grinning broadly.

Emilie's heart thudded as she sat down upon the bed. Of course, that was the answer—Edgar had gotten her with child! She had been so preoccupied these past weeks, she had failed to take note of the fact that her monthly time was late. Calculating the weeks, she was swept by a horrible sinking sensation. Yes, she was pregnant—that would explain the nausea. And the nightmare?

Emilie shivered as Hallie drew the covers around

251

her. "You go back to sleep, now, Missus," the servant directed. "You need bushels of sleep these next weeks."

A tear slid down Emilie's cheek. She shook, recalling the dream—the images of fire and death.

"Ain't you happy, Missus?" Hallie asked confusedly.

"I'm going to die," Emilie said dully.

"Die?" the slave gasped. "What kind of talk is that? You're going to please Mister Ashland with a fine son. You ain't going t'die any more'n I am with this babe. You rest now, Missus. No more talk of dying."

"A son," Emilie repeated mournfully. She remembered dreaming of the wee baby boy in her arms. Her brother? No—her child! "My poor baby," she sobbed, clutching her pillow.

Emilie sat at the dressing table as Hallie attended her coiffure. She felt utterly numb after a morning in bed.

Edgar walked into the room, closing the door. Emilie felt his gaze, but did not look up. After a moment, he asked Hallie, "You are finished?"

"Yessir," the black girl replied, hurrying out of the room.

Emilie heard Edgar walk across the room, felt his hands upon her shoulders. He leaned over, his eyes meeting hers in the mirror.

"You should be in bed," he scolded gently. "You're ill."

She stood, turning to face him. "I'm pregnant," she said flatly.

He smiled. "So I've surmised."

She turned and walked to the window, staring moodily at the midday brightness.

"Is that fate so horrible, love?"

She did not reply. Her fingernails dug into the red velvet draping the window.

He came up behind her, wrapped his arms around her waist. His lips brushed her neck. "Now you'll give me my son," he whispered.

She spun about and pushed him away, glaring at him incredulously. "Your son!"

He chuckled. "Well, it's apt to be one or the other, don't you agree, love? Besides," he cajoled, "the damage is already done. At least you have nothing more to fear on that score for a while. Who knows, you might enjoy our lovemaking more—"

"More! You mean you plan to continue to take me now that you've had your way with me?" Her voice rose in hysteria. "But I'm forgetting, aren't I? You'll want to continue to—to practice upon me, as sooner or later I'll be required to replace *both* of them!"

Edgar's face twisted in bewilderment. "Emilie, what on earth are you talking about?"

She began to pace in her agitation, ignoring him. "Now I'll give you your son!" she seethed. "I should have known better when you said you were marrying me to share your bed and bear your sons! I'm to replace both your sons, just as I'm to replace Olivia!"

Edgar grabbed her arm. "Stop it, Emilie, you don't know what you're saying!"

"Yes, I do!" she raged. "I won't be Olivia! I won't give you your sons back. I—I—I'll have a girl!"

Edgar clutched her tightly by the shoulders, his face desperate. "Listen to me, Emilie, I don't expect you to be Olivia!"

She stamped her foot. "Yes, you do! You won't

get rid of her portrait! You still love her!'' Her eyes were bright with tears, and a spasm gripped her stomach, but she continued convulsively, ''I'm going to run away and have a girl and you won't even care!''

He listened to her words, horror spreading across his features. ''You're hysterical. You should be in bed.''

''No!'' she sobbed, struggling to push him away. ''I'm leaving you! I won't give you a son! I won't!''

He turned her firmly; she tried to yank away. ''Be still!'' he growled.

She wept, but obeyed him as he unbuttoned her dress and pulled it over her head. She clutched her chemise as he pulled her to the bed.

''Believe what you will, madam,'' he told her firmly as he pushed her down, ''but I'll not have you getting hysterical and becoming ill.'' He pulled the covers up to her neck. ''Your face is white as this sheet. Next, you'll have a raging fever!''

Emilie clutched the sheet and looked up at her grim husband. ''Would you care?''

''I care!''

''You care—about the son you want!''

''I care about you!''

He sat down beside her, his eyes boring into hers. ''You're to stay in bed all day, do you hear me, Emilie? I'm fetching that servant of yours, and I'll skin her alive if she as much as lets you sit up. Do you understand?''

''Yes,'' she said weakly, suddenly exhausted by the emotional scene. She turned away from him, hoping he would leave.

But he leaned over; she felt his mustache tickling her ear. ''When you feel better,'' he whispered, ''get rid of the damn portrait.''

Startled, she turned, only to see the door closing. Had she heard him right?

A frown of puzzlement on her face, she laid her head back upon the pillow, obeying her husband.

Chapter Twenty-Two

May 12, 1841

Emilie sat upon the settee in the parlor, her brow puckered as she gazed at the note in her lap. Three days previous, she had sent a lad to Washington-on-the-Brazos to seek out Aaron Rice. Not wanting to give Edgar a chance to change his mind, she had written Aaron requesting that he come get Olivia's portrait.

As if she hadn't read the note a dozen times this morning, Emilie leaned back and studied the reply Aaron sent back.

My dear Mrs. Ashland,
   I am greatly pleased to hear that your husband has condescended to relinquish my sister's portrait to its rightful owners. You are most kind to invite me to your home to fetch it. I shall happily anticipate attending you on the day and hour appointed.

                   Your obedient servant,
                   Aaron Evans Rice

Emilie laid the note on the table next to her, impatiently tapping her fingernails on the smooth mahogany. She had not told Edgar of Aaron's impending visit, greatly fearing his reaction. After all, he had almost killed the man the last time he came. Consequently, she had suggested that Aaron come late in the morning, knowing Edgar would most likely miss his visit entirely. She would conclude the appointment quickly, then the portrait would be gone. But what of Olivia's memory?

Emilie bit her lip. If only she could know what Edgar truly felt! Other than telling her she could get rid of the portrait, he made no mention of Olivia. He claimed he cared for *her,* Emilie, but what did he mean? Was he really coming to love her, or did he care for the child she bore, the replacement for the sons he had lost?

Instinctively, her hand went to her stomach. Her feelings about being pregnant were mixed. There was the primal wonder of knowing she bore a human life, a small miracle within her. Yet lurking in the background was the vivid memory of her mother's death, the fear of history repeating itself. And there was resentment against Edgar—did he want her for herself, or was he using her to relive the past?

But the greatest fear of all centered upon the child itself. Would he (or she?) be like Edgar? Would their child be as unpredictable, as violent as her husband? At times, she truly doubted his sanity. Were such tendencies hereditary?

Her softer nature often overrode her fears. After all, she loved her husband, despite his faults. At one time, she would have done anything to escape him, but now, especially since he had given in on the portrait, she had no desire to leave him.

Yet how she wished she could be honest with him!

She remembered the night on the veranda, when he said, "I feel so close to you." If only they could have that kind of closeness outside their bedroom! She knew she had hurt him with her anger about being pregnant, yet how could she trust him with her true feelings? How could she tell him of her nightmares, in which *he* was the demon?

Perhaps in time, they could be honest with each other, she consoled herself. For the present, she would have to be content with what they had. Actually, Edgar had been most considerate towards her since they had discovered her pregnancy. He had been tactful about her daily bouts with nausea, and had surprised her by coming to check on her while she rested during the day.

She was beginning to catch glimpses of a tender, protective side to his nature. In fact, the night after they realized she was pregnant, he had shocked her by offering to cease making love to her until after the child was born. She remembered the moment well, the tightly reined need etching his face. She had surprised herself by going to him and wrapping her arms around his neck, saying, "I have no desire to contend with you in a black mood for the next several months."

She smiled at the memory. She had felt so happy then, at his caring enough to be gentle with her. Yet later, doubt had seeped in—had he *really* not wanted to hurt her, or was his concern directed toward the precious life inside her? Although she felt no jealousy toward the babe she bore, she wanted Edgar to care for both of them as individuals, not as characters in a play he was orchestrating.

The clock in the hallway began to chime, drawing Emilie out of her thoughts. She realized the hour she expected Aaron would soon be upon her. There was no more postponing the unpleasant task—she must go to the attic and bring down Olivia Ashland's portrait.

She left the parlor, slowly climbing two flights of stairs to the attic. Inside, the room was as hot and musty as she remembered. The portrait lay just where she had left it, the wrappings scattered about.

She got down on her knees, gathered up the muslin and cotton batting, deliberately avoiding Olivia Ashland's face. Finally, with a ragged sigh, she turned and stared at the canvas. This time, the previous eerie feeling did not come. She realized with some relief that her resemblance to Olivia Ashland was not as striking as she first thought.

It was the same face—yet it was very different. It was an implacable face, a cautious face, the smile playing upon the thin lips coyly, as though laboriously wooed. The face was narrower than her own, the features more sharply delineated, the nose longer, the eyebrows thinner, arching more provocatively.

Olivia appeared older than Emilie by at least five years, demonstrated by the tiny lines around her mouth and eyes. Had she lived, she would be in her early thirties now, Emilie mused.

The greatest resemblance between Emilie and Olivia was in the color of the hair—bright gold—and the astonishing dark brown eyebrows and eyelashes. But Olivia's eyes were different—a deep, midnight blue—almost the unfathomable ebony of the Brazos, Emilie thought with a shiver. She sighed. Her own face was almost childlike compared to the worldly maturity of the woman smiling at her from the canvas, the lips promising to guard all her secrets well.

"Will I ever know what happened between you

259

and Edgar?'' Emilie asked the portrait. "Why did you run away from him, Olivia?"

But the portrait smiled back malevolently, as if promising eternal silence.

"To hell with you!" Emilie snapped, turning to the wrappings piled on the floor. Sneezing as the dust flew, she laid the cotton batting across the portrait, then slipped on the muslin cover.

"Goodbye, Olivia," she said.

Emilie collapsed upon the settee, gasping for breath. With distaste, she eyed the bundle leaning against the parlor wall. The portrait had been heavy—she had been foolish to try to drag it down two flights of stairs herself. Edgar would surely lock her up again if he knew she had carried out such an arduous task.

Edgar! She had spent much longer than she should have in the attic. Aaron was now late, and Edgar might soon appear for lunch!

She jumped as she heard a knock at the front door. If that were Aaron, she must get rid of him quickly!

Emilie stood just as Daniel showed Aaron Rice into the parlor. "My dear Mrs. Ashland, how lovely you look today!" the redheaded Rice greeted her.

Emilie extended a slim hand, accepting Aaron's fleshy grasp. "Good morning, Mr. Rice," she replied, giving him a cool smile.

Gesturing to one of the wing chairs, Emilie sat down upon the settee. Aaron sat down across from her, crossing one black-and-white-striped leg over the other.

Emilie studied him, her lower lip twitching. As usual, Aaron's manner of dress was outlandish. His coat was of white wool—the ruffles on his linen shirt edged with bright green embroidery. A crimson taffeta bow tie topped off the outfit, clashing garishly with his red, curly hair.

Aaron grinned as his twinkling eyes swept Emilie. "My, what a picture you make this morning, my dear. Blue is undoubtedly your color. It makes those incredible eyes of yours—all the more enchanting."

Avoiding Aaron's frank gaze, Emilie felt a blush heating her face as she smoothed her blue silk skirts about her. She was painfully conscious of the fact that she had chosen a dress that revealed a generous portion of her breasts. "Thank you, Mr. Rice. Now may we—"

"Call me Aaron," he interrupted smoothly.

Emilie twisted her fingers nervously. "I appreciate the friendly overture, Mr. Rice, but our acquaintance must necessarily be—brief." She pointed to the wall and rushed on, "The portrait is over there, wrapped and ready to go."

Following the direction of Emilie's outstretched hand, Aaron looked critically at the bundle.

Emilie stood. "I'll call Daniel to help you load it."

Aaron got to his feet, eyeing Emilie curiously. "Why so hasty, Mrs. Ashland? I've only just arrived."

"I don't wish to be rude, but—"

"But you don't want Edgar to know I'm here," he supplied, grinning devilishly.

Emilie lowered dark eyelashes, studying her white satin slippers. "Yes," she conceded.

Slowly, Aaron approached her. His forefinger raised her chin. "So you've fallen for the old boy, have you?" he asked, a strange light flickering in the emerald depths of his eyes.

His breath wafted across her, smelling sourly of whiskey. She wrinkled her nose in distaste, astonished that any man should smell of spirits so early in the day. Squaring her jaw, she backed away from his touch. "I hardly think my relationship with Mr. Ashland is your concern, sir."

Aaron dropped his hand, the troubling light in his eyes now replaced by a cynical gleam. "Edgar's a lost cause, you know." He turned, nodding towards the bundle against the wall. "You're sending home Olivia's portrait. But can you send home her memory?"

Emilie fought to control a rising anger as she glanced from the bundle to the sardonically smiling Aaron. "Sir, you abuse my hospitality."

Aaron sobered somewhat at her ire. "Forgive me, lady," he said sincerely, "you're far too pretty a young woman to abuse—in any manner. Please accept my heartfelt apologies."

Emilie flung her hands wide in exasperation. "Very well. But please—take your package and go!"

He ignored her, moving closer. "Far too pretty," he repeated, the peculiar light again in his eyes. "Jesus, how you look like her!"

Emilie gasped sharply.

"You've seen the portrait and you know you look like her, don't you?" Aaron asked, his whole face growing animated.

"Yes, but what does that—"

"Then surely you know Edgar is only using you," Aaron continued crudely. "What you need is a man who can appreciate your charms." He snapped his fingers, and his eyes grew wildly excited. "A man like me! Let me take you away from here, Emilie!"

Emilie stared at Aaron Rice in shock. His face lit up and determined, he seemed very serious about his outrageous offer. Outrageous? Only a few weeks past, she might have jumped at the chance to leave

262

with him!

Emilie clenched her fists and told him sternly, "Sir, you are being—unpardonably forward! Kindly take your portrait and leave!"

Suddenly, Aaron laughed; the spell broke. The enthusiasm faded from his features, and he grinned sheepishly. "Can't blame a man for trying," he chuckled. "Christ, what a beauty you are! My dear, you have smitten me, utterly!"

Despite the man's boldness, Emilie found a smile tugging at her lips. At least Aaron was forthright about what he wanted, not temperamental and devious, as Edgar often was. It was refreshing to be able to talk to a man without constantly fearing he would fly into a rage. Although she had known Aaron only briefly, she realized she would miss him simply because he was another human being—someone she could talk to.

Aaron sighed. "Well, I suppose I've no further excuse for detaining you, Mrs. Ashland." He turned toward the bundle. "On to the task at hand."

But as he reached for the portrait, he paused, then again snapped his fingers. He turned, smiling broadly, his eyes sparkling mischievously. "By jove, I've forgotten to thank you, my dear."

In two strides he was next to her, pulling her hard against his stocky frame. Emilie was too shocked to react as his mouth landed squarely on her parted lips; the vile taste of his kiss made her nauseously weak.

"Well, Aaron, have you a secret desire to bed your late sister?" a sarcastic voice demanded.

Aaron and Emilie sprang apart, both of them whirling to face Edgar, who stood unsmiling as he leaned against the doorway.

Emilie gulped in horror, trying to open her mouth

to speak. But no words would come.

Aaron's face turned as bright red as his hair, and he clenched his fists in rage. "By God, Ashland, I'll kill you for that!"

Edgar smiled cruelly. "Interesting words, coming from a dead man!"

Aaron dived for Edgar; Emilie screamed, drawing her hands to her face. Edgar calmly dodged the bulkier man, and Aaron was sent flying into the hall. Hearing furniture overturning and a bowl crashing in the entry hall, Emilie swallowed a hysterical giggle.

Aaron bolted back into the room, his face livid. He swung at Edgar like an angry bear. But Edgar dodged his blows deftly, his face grim as he punched the shorter man squarely across the jaw.

Emilie sought shelter in the farthest corner of the room as the fists flew. As the punching and groaning increased, she shut her eyes and covered her ears. Edgar would kill Aaron, of that she was sure. And then he would kill her.

Suddenly, there was silence. Cautiously, Emilie peered out at the room. Furniture was askew—broken glass scattered about. Aaron lay on his stomach on the floor.

Emilie gasped, then looked up the tall frame of her husband. Blood dripped from one corner of his mouth as he gazed at her steadily, a cruel promise in his black eyes.

She gulped, her heart beating wildy. "D-did you kill him?"

Edgar, glaring at her, did not reply. "Daniel!" he thundered.

The old black man scurried into the room, his eyes white with fright. "Yes sir?"

Edgar jerked his head toward the portrait. "Take the gentleman's—property—to his buggy!"

The servant nodded vigorously. "Yes, Mister Ashland!" he said, attending to the task.

Emile gritted her teeth as she watched Edgar boot Aaron in the belly. When Aaron began to groan, Edgar leaned over and roughly dragged him to his feet.

Aaron shakily grasped his middle as Edgar propelled him out of the parlor. Emilie heard Edgar growl, "Next time, Rice, don't count on such gentle treatment!" Then the front door slammed.

Emilie heard Edgar's boots hitting the wooden floor of the hall. She dashed out in time to see him open the door to his office.

"Edgar, wait!"

He scowled at her as she hurried towards him. She put her hand on his arm.

Shaking off her grasp as if she were an offending insect, he inquired hoarsely, "My dear, do you have suicidal tendencies?"

He turned his back upon her and entered the office, slamming the door.

Chapter Twenty-Three

May 12, 1841

Emilie sat under a cedar tree, plucking petals from a buttercup. Though the sun was sinking low in the sky, heat hung oppressively to the landscape, a sign of rapidly approaching summer. Emilie stared moodily at fading flowers and parched grass—rain was badly needed. As if Edgar were not already in a black mood—now he would have the cotton crop to worry about.

She had not seen him since the dreadful scene that morning. Now that night was approaching, she feared what would happen when he came to their room. And she was angry—too angry to trust herself alone with him. He had treated her with cold hatred, as if she had deliberately tried to seduce Aaron Rice! He had even hinted that he was ready to kill her!

She threw down the stalk of the flower and plucked another plum-colored blossom. All the dearly gained progress between her and Edgar had died, like the tender blossom she now pulverized between her thumb and forefinger.

Emilie stood. Brushing grass off her skirts, she walked back to the house. The hot air blew across her face. Her lips felt dry, cracked, and she tasted sand as she moistened them with her tongue. Yes, summer was coming—a long, hot siege.

Entering the front hall, Emilie heard a dissonant scale being pounded out in the drawing room. She tiptoed to the doorway, and surreptitiously watched Maria practicing her scales in frowning concentration. With a beginner's enthusiasm, the girl punched out each wrong note in loud discordance.

"May I help you, Maria?" Emilie offered.

The girl jumped, throwing a slim, honey-colored hand across her bosom. *"Madre de dios!* You gave me a start, Señora!"

Despite herself, Emilie giggled at the younger girl's unguarded reaction. "Forgive me, Maria. You attack your practice with such—gusto. May I ask why you have such an interest in music?"

The girl studied Emilie narrowly. *"Mi padre,"* she murmured, after a moment. "My father was a gifted musician, Señora. He played the guitar."

"I see," Emilie replied. "We must get you a guitar also."

For a brief, revealing moment, Maria's green eyes lit with longing. Then she hastily lowered black eyelashes.

"Did your father ever perform with his guitar?" Emilie pursued.

Maria idly played a soft scale with one hand. *"Sí,* Señora. Sometimes he would play at the *cantinas,* when he couldn't get work with the horses. In San Antonio, I danced while he played, and gathered up the coins the men threw at us."

Maria's young features grew taut as she spoke, and Emilie felt a rush of sympathy for the girl. She conjured an image of a proud young Mexican girl in ragged clothing, being forced to pick up the coins drunken men threw at her feet. Emilie suspected Maria was deeply scarred by some of the experiences of her childhood years.

Although Emilie hungered to learn more about Maria's past, her instincts told her that this was not the right moment. But she did feel compelled to reach out to the young girl again in friendship. "Maria, as I said the other day, I'd love to help you with your piano while David is gone. And you've a lovely voice—you must let me play for you so that you may practice your singing."

A mask closed over Maria's features. "Perhaps."

Hearing the front door fly open, both girls stiffened. Unsmiling, Edgar Ashland strode into the room. Ignoring the girls, he walked purposefully to the sideboard, clanging glassware as he grabbed the brandy decanter and a snifter. He left the room as abruptly as he had come.

Emilie stood and started to follow him. Then, hearing the door slam down the hallway, she sank weakly upon the settee, her heart racing. Suddenly, an explosion of silver fireworks spouted in front of her eyes, and for a dizzying moment, she was sure she was going to faint. She held her head in her hands, trying to steady herself.

A warm hand closed over her own. "Emilie, *que pasa?*"

Emilie looked up to see Maria seated beside her, a look of curiosity in her eyes. The girl had never before called her "Emilie," and it warmed her heart.

Emilie smiled wanly. "It's nothing, Maria. I was simply dizzy for a moment. You see, I'm pregnant."

"Encinta!" Maria repeated, her eyes narrowing. "Ah, I see. You are *encinta* and not steady on your feet." She stood. "I will call Señor Edgar to carry you upstairs."

Emilie struggled to her feet, her eyes widening. "No, Maria," she pleaded, gripping the younger girl's arm to keep her balance. "You mustn't disturb him. He's angry at me!"

Maria arched a black brow. She seemed shocked that Emilie should say Edgar was angry, as if she were not at all perturbed by his storming about clattering bottles and glasses. "Why is he angry?" Then, as Emilie tottered, Maria grasped the pregnant girl's wrist. "First sit down, Señora, before you faint indeed."

After they were both seated, Emilie explained, "My husband's angry at me because Aaron Rice visited today. Edgar walked in just as Aaron was trying to kiss me."

"*Ojos de diablo!*" Maria exclaimed. "You are lucky to be alive, Señora!"

"Edgar told me as much," Emilie muttered grimly. She leaned forward imploringly. "But it wasn't my fault, Maria. Aaron was forcing his attentions upon me—"

"Ah, *sí,*" Maria interrupted with a knowing smile. "You have much power over men, Señora."

"Then the next time Aaron Rice calls, *you* handle him!" Emilie countered briskly.

Surprisingly, Maria giggled. Emilie swallowed a gasp. She had always known the girl was beautiful, but when Maria smiled, she was spellbinding. Her face glowed and her dark eyes sparkled.

"Why, Maria, you're lovely when you smile! You have perfectly charming dimples. Yes, I do believe I'll turn *you* over to Aaron Rice next time, and see how well you fare!"

Maria laughed, a deep, melodic laugh. Emilie felt close to her then; the scene poignantly reminded her of happier times with her girlfriends at school in Houston.

But after a moment, Maria frowned. *"Por supuesto,* Señora, I have no interest in Señor Rice."

"I know—I was teasing," Emilie replied. She almost blurted out, "You're in love with David, aren't you?" but thought better of the idea. Perhaps, instead, she should level with the girl, possibly assuaging some of Maria's fears.

Emilie took a deep breath and abruptly confided, "Maria, I'm in love with Edgar."

The girl gazed at Emilie hard and steadily. She started to speak, then bit her lip. Finally, she said, "If you still wish to help me with the music practice, Señora, perhaps—perhaps *mañana.*"

Emilie tossed and turned fitfully. She realized the night had aged considerably, and that she and the tiny life growing within her desperately needed rest. But Edgar had not come to bed, and she simply could not sleep.

If only he would talk to her! Even a good row would clear the air, perhaps righting things between them. This silent treatment baffled her—she did not know how to reach him, what to expect next.

Emilie turned and for the hundredth time punched down her pillow. Putting her head back down, she caught his essence emanating from the pillow next to her. Inexplicably, she began to cry. Why was she so emotional lately?

Suddenly, lightning illuminated the room, followed closely by booming thunder. As if on cue, the door swung open and Edgar entered, his face illuminated by the taper he held. He kicked the door shut and blew out the candle. She heard his boots scrape the floor, then a bang and a curse as he stumbled. She heard him sit down, heard his boots drop with a thud. Lightning flashed, wavering across his face, making his features harsh, frightening. Emilie shook at the sound of rolling thunder; but the noise seemed no louder than that of her heart roaring in her ears.

He walked across the room, stopped. She saw him outlined in a pool of moonlight streaming in from the French doors. The silvery light, gauzy from the imprint of the curtains, shone softly on his magnificent nakedness, but did little to mellow the determined set of his features.

Lightning ignited the room. The wind swelled, blowing open the French doors, billowing the curtains crazily, sending ghostly images across his body. He did not move.

She knew he could not see her—the bed was shadowed by the canopy. But how could he fail to hear the frantic pounding of her heart?

Thunder crashed, and he came to her. The mattress sagged as he got in beside her. He grabbed her roughly, pulled her hard against him and kissed her demandingly, his mouth tasting heavily of brandy. She accepted his ravagement of her mouth, forcing herself not to push him away, knowing that would only enrage him.

His hands twisted her hair, springing tears to her eyes. His mouth moved to her ear. "Did you enjoy your little flirtation with Aaron today, madam?" he whispered harshly.

She choked, "I wasn't flirt—"

"Hush!" he commanded, sealing her open mouth with his lips.

Rain began to fall, sounding hard as hail on the roof above them. He pulled back and glared at her, lightning blazing across his face. She blinked back tears, her lips burning from his kiss.

"Surely I've been remiss, madam, if my lovemaking leaves you seeking your satisfaction elsewhere," he said ruthlessly. "A matter I intend to remedy—at once!"

She jumped as he ripped open her nightgown. His mouth closed upon a breast. His arms clenched about her middle, and she feared he would squeeze her in two.

"Edgar, please don't hurt me!" she begged breathlessly.

Abruptly, he went limp, as if all the rage inside him died. He released her, turning to sit up at the edge of the bed, his head in his hands. "Christ, Emmie, the last thing I want to do is to hurt you!" His fist pounded the mattress. "But I do it, don't I? I hurt you, when I really want—I want—"

He stood, went to the French doors, closed them against the pounding rain. He moved to the chair, sat down, picked up his trousers.

Her heart hung in her throat as she watched him. She must let him go, she realized. He was not human, but a demon, come to sear her flesh with his, to devour her. She must let him go.

She got to her feet, dropping the shredded gown. She went to him, stood between his legs.

He looked up at her, his eyes intense, quizzical.

She reached out and touched him where she knew him to be most vulnerable. "Darling, tell me what you want," she whispered.

His trousers hit the floor. He drew her forcefully downward, the coarse hair of his thighs rubbing against her buttocks. His mouth fastened upon hers, and she tasted the rain on his lips. His fingertips caressed the satin of her back, her legs, then his arm moved to tightly grasp her hips, pulling her inexorably closer—

She felt a momentary chill of fear. He was so

strong, so full of violence, he could easily snap her spine. Yet she was putting her trust in him, letting him have his way entirely. . . . She sighed deep in her throat, swallowing the brandied heaven of his kiss, as her hands swept through his hair, stroking the silky moistness—

Yes, she would die for him, let his love consume her! She would give herself without reservation—there was no other choice!

He drew her hand to his erect manhood. She stroked it gently with her fingertips, feeling the hard smoothness, the ridged tip. Then her hand tightened about it, felt it pulse, grow harder, larger. He moaned and his kiss grew deeper.

His hand parted her legs; his fingers teased the bud of her passion. The arm clasping her hips tightened, pushing her forward against the penetration of his fingers. He pressed her breasts together between his chest and face, tickling and sucking the nipples with his tongue and lips.

The combined stimulation was electrifying. Desire cut between her thighs, a torment demanding the sweet pain of consummation. Her bottom moved against his fingers, his thigh, as her hand stroked the base of his hard shaft, and moved gently lower. . . .

He pulled her to her feet. His hands clutched and lifted her buttocks. Her feet left the floor, and his hips locked beneath her. She gasped as he lowered her upon his manhood, slowly, by glorious inches, until he probed her so deeply that she thought he must be touching her very soul.

He laughed, a laugh of joy, wonder. The rain beat out its cadence, and they hung there, her toes barely touching the floor, their eyes embracing.

"This—is what I want," he whispered.

He lowered her to the floor, all the while deep

inside her. She slid downward, curling her legs around his waist, her back feeling the rough rub of the rug. Lightning flashed and thunder boomed as her lover pounded out the hard rhythm of the rain. Rapture exploded inside her and she fell back, spent. But he laughed, for he was not finished. Again and again, he demanded her total, passionate surrender. He rode her hard to the moment of ultimate release. She climaxed with him and they hung together, suspended in a moment of time, a flash of light.

Afterwards, she lay with her head on his chest, too awed to speak. Finally, she murmured, "The storm is abated."

He chuckled, stroking her moonlight-streaked hair. "Aye, love, it has, indeed."

The sweetest memories drifted through Emilie's half-conscious mind. "Say you are mine," he whispered, his body possessing hers deeply. "I'm yours—believe me," she promised. "I believe you," he murmured to the rhythm of his thrusting, "I believe you. . . ."

Emilie awoke, smiling. The room was warm, filled with sunshine. She felt totally relaxed, her stomach not gripped by the usual early morning spasm. Sitting up, she stretched languidly. Then she gasped as she spotted her husband nearby, stretched out in the bathtub.

Grinning, Edgar drew the sponge down a muscular arm. "What a sleepyhead you are, my darling," he teased. "How you slept through all that interminable clatter is beyond me—what with the maids coming and going with buckets and all that sloshing." He winked at her. "But then, you sleep the sleep of a well-satisfied woman, eh, my love?"

She got out of bed, eyed him petulantly as she tied

her wrapper. "You've stolen my bath," she accused. "Why aren't you out riding in the fields?"

"I'm being lazy this morning. Besides, why waste all this heavenly warm water?" He smiled at her. "How prettily you pout, sweetheart. Come kiss me."

"But you're all wet!" she protested.

He blew her a kiss, grinning wickedly. "Wet and soapy, and very slippery. An interesting state, wouldn't you agree, love?"

"Oh, you're evil!" she objected. But she took a step closer, her lips twitching. She studied his rugged face with its shadow of whiskers, his muscular chest with its matting of curly black hair. Her eyes travelled downward, but the soapy water forbade further exploration.

He chuckled. "Curious, love? Then come join me!"

She felt her face burning. "Oh—I couldn't!" she sputtered. "That would be—I mean, how decadent!"

"Decadent!" he repeated, his eyes laughing. "Is this the same wench who demanded my services last night?" He leaned forward, extending his hand. "Come. I'll settle for a kiss, then."

"Well—" she eyed him and decided he was irresistible—"all right."

She stepped forward tentatively, leaned over and brushed her lips against his. But he grabbed her and pulled her downward. With a startled cry, she splashed into the water beside him.

"Edgar, how dare you! What if the servants—"

"They wouldn't dare!"

"Look what you've done to my wrapper—"

"Aye, love, it's all wet and transparent around your breasts—Jesus Christ, what a woman you are!"

275

"Don't throw it on the rug! Now there will be a stain, I must—"

"No!"

"But you're all whiskery, you're scratching—"

"All the better to put my mark on your flesh, my love."

"Edgar, stop it! This is sinful, this is—Oooh!"

"Sorry, love. I warned you that I was slippery."

Spring died, and summer crept in, hot and oppressive. Rainfall was heavy for the rest of May, and the cotton crop thrived. June brought heat and less frequent, but thorough, cloudbursts.

Emilie thrived like the plants. The days of nausea passed—her cheeks bloomed, her belly began to curve gently outward. She seemed possessed of boundless energy.

In many ways, she and Edgar were no closer; nothing had been affirmed, no words of love spoken. But he treated her gently now. They were not confidants, or friends, but, oh, they were lovers!

Edgar introduced her to joys of lovemaking she had never known existed. All pride, all pretense vanished as he drew her into his arms each night. They devoured each others' bodies with the thirst of exiles returning from a desert. Words seemed unnecessary—their lovemaking said it all. Emilie relaxed and enjoyed the smooth, intimate period between them. For now, she realized, their closeness in bed had to be enough. Perhaps when the babe came—

What would happen, Emilie often wondered, when her child was born? Would she then find out whether Edgar wanted her and the child for themselves? What if the babe were a girl? Would Edgar's fantasy be shattered? Would he be driven over the edge, to madness?

Despite Edgar's kind treatment of her, fear still lurked in the corners of her mind, and sometimes, like cobwebs, it crept outward, in memories of Edgar's previous abuse. He seldom even raised his voice now, but sometimes she could see the violence thinly veiled in his face, ready to boil to the surface with the least provocation.

But when the threads of fear clouded her mind, she swept them away, keeping herself busy with happier pursuits. She saw Maria frequently now; the two of them were developing a tentative rapport. They met each day in the drawing room, where Emilie would help Maria with her chords and scales. Afterwards, Emilie played the piano while Maria sang beautiful songs in Spanish.

One morning, as they relaxed after the music lesson, Emilie decided to risk asking the Mexican girl more about her background. "A few weeks ago, Maria, you mentioned San Antonio," she began. "Did you and your father live there long?"

Maria straightened a ruffle on her peach-colored frock and eyed Emilie guardedly. "Papá and I lived there—perhaps a year. We lived in many towns in South Texas—wherever we could find work."

"I see. My parents took me to visit San Antonio once, while we were living in Gonzales. I loved the city, with its Spanish flavor—the beautiful missions. Tell me, what part of town did you and your father live in?"

"The oldest part—La Villita, Señora. *Mi padre*

and I worked at Señora Bustamante's fandango hall, playing the music, singing and dancing." Maria smiled wistfully. "Sometimes during the day while Papa slept, I walked to San Fernando Cathedral near the plaza. The sisters there were kind to me—they taught me to read, and how to pray to the Virgin Maria."

"I'm glad they were there for you, Maria." Emilie bit her lip, then plunged on. "But tell me—your father—was *he* kind to you also?"

The young girl's eyes darkened. "He did his best, but he was a man. He could not be a mother to me, Señora."

Emilie frowned, sensing there was much Maria was not telling her. "You know, Maria, you and I have a great deal in common," she said carefully. "I think perhaps we could help each other. You see, I am an orphan, too. My father was killed at the Alamo, then when my mother found out, she went into shock and died of a miscarriage. Your background is similar, Maria. Your mother—I mean, David told me—"

"That my mother died bearing me?" Maria asked, her voice rising as she strained forward in her chair. Her green eyes gleaming strangely, she added, "Tell me, Señora, does it frighten you to be pregnant?"

A chill gripped Emilie's heart at the Mexican girl's words. There was a frightening quality in Maria's eyes, making Emilie vividly recall the day she was alone with Maria in the stable, and the horse almost trampled her.

"Maria!" Emilie gasped, at last finding her voice. "How can you—that remark was cruel!"

Surprisingly, the Mexican girl's eyes flickered with remorse. "You are right, Señora. I apologize."-The girl got to her feet and went to the window, gazing soberly out at the sunswept lawn of Brazos Bend. "It was wrong of me to alarm you. But sometimes life can be very cruel."

Emilie was about to reply, when a masculine voice interjected, "What better greeting for the weary traveller than two lovely ladies!"

Both girls turned to see David standing in the archway. Maria's troubling question for the moment forgotten, Emilie smiled as she studied him, deciding he had never looked more handsome. He was dressed in a black frock coat and buff trousers, his blonde hair glowing in the light filtering in through the parlor windows, his blue eyes sparkling with excitement.

Amid cries of greeting, he strode into the room, kissing both girls on the cheek. Once the three were seated, he asked conversationally, "What has been happening here during my absence?"

Emilie waited for Maria to speak, but the younger girl was staring at David dazedly, frank admiration in her dark green eyes.

"Maria and I have been practicing our music," Emilie answered. "Wait until you hear her—you'll be so pleased with her progress."

"Good," David replied, smiling shyly at Maria. "I found you a music book in Houston, Maria—all the most recent songs in Spanish."

"Oh, *gracias,* David!" Maria exclaimed, clapping her hands. She smiled at him, displaying dazzling dimples. "I can't wait to see it. *A veces,* I hunger for something to read."

Emilie frowned confusedly. "But Maria, the library is full of books!"

Maria's face fell as she lowered her gaze. "I do not read *en ingles,* Señora. The sisters taught me *en español.* As for the other school . . . there, I fear I learned *nada.*"

There was an awkward silence, then Emilie announced perkily, "Then we must remedy that situation at once. David, now that you're back, you can take over the music lessons, and I'll teach Maria to read and write in English."

David grinned at Maria. "I'm at your service, *Señorita.*"

The day passed in great excitement. The supplies from Houston were unloaded, and Emilie joyfully sorted through the bolts of cloth David had brought her to redecorate the house. She scolded David for bringing her new dress lengths as well, for her wardrobe was now teeming with frocks she and Hallie had sewn. David also brought Maria at least a dozen lengths of cloth, and, to Emilie's delight, Maria accepted the older girl's offer of help with a new wardrobe. Emilie was again pleasantly surprised when the Mexican girl said she would like to learn to applique pillows and cushions for the redecorating project. At last Emilie felt she was making real progress in getting to know Maria.

But David's bringing Emilie the supplies she wanted brought up a sticky problem—she could no longer avoid a confrontation with Avis Gerouard. After her disastrous talk with Avis, she had made no further attempt to gain control of the household, but now she had to ensure the woman's cooperation.

Late in the afternoon, Emilie found the housekeeper in her office behind the dining room. Emilie took a seat at the small table where Avis was working, and immediately approached the business at hand. "Mrs. Gerouard, I'm planning to redecorate the house. I'll immediately be needing a girl to help Hallie with some sewing. And, for the next few days, I will need the services of two strong lads to move furniture, take down drapes and so forth." Emilie gazed at Avis steadily. "I also wish to inform you that Mr. Ashland and I are expecting a child. A nursery must be prepared, and baby clothes made."

At the mention of the child, Avis's eyes glittered with an emotion approaching defiance. But she said civilly enough, "Congratulations, Madame."

"Thank you, Mrs. Gerouard." Driving home her point, Emilie added, "My husband has said I may do whatever I please with the house. Should you have any doubts, do speak with him yourself."

The housekeeper's angular features tightened. "That will not be necessary, Madame. M'sieur Edgar has already spoken with me."

Though shocked by this revelation, Emilie was not about to lose her advantage, and continued briskly, "Additionally, Mrs. Gerouard, I shall be approving the menus from now on. You will please meet with me in this room each Monday morning."

The older woman tapped her fingernails on the white board tabletop, her out-thrust lower lip betraying her chagrin. "You are not pleased with the cooking, Madame?"

Emilie shrugged. "The food is fine. However, my preferences differ from your own. You will meet with me Monday, then?"

"Certainement, Madame."

Emilie stood. "I shall be in the drawing room for the rest of the afternoon. You may send the servants I requested in to see me there."

"Oui, Madame."

The only smudge on Emilie's otherwise flawless day was Edgar. When her husband came in from the fields, he greeted David pleasantly enough, but his attitude toward Emilie became suddenly, decisively chilly—especially as he stared dispassionately at the luxurious gifts David had brought her. Throughout dinner, he was glumly silent, frowning, as Emilie, David and Maria chatted cheerfully. Several times, Emilie caught Edgar eyeing her covertly, his dark eyes piercing her. Once, she smiled back brightly, but he only scowled as he gulped his brandy. He left dinner early, abruptly, the brandy decanter in hand.

David leaned across the table towards Emilie, his brow creased. "Is everything all right? Uncle hardly touched his food."

Emilie reached for David's outstretched hand. Then she noticed Maria watching them petulantly. "It's all right," she assured David, withdrawing her hand. "I'll see to him."

Emilie got up and left the room, but David stopped her in the hallway, laying a gentle hand on her shoulder. "Emilie, has my uncle been abusing you?" he asked in an urgent whisper.

Emilie turned, a smile tugging at her lips at David's melodramatic remark. "No, David."

He released her, sighing. But his brow was still puckered, thoughtful. "Dear, could we step into the library for a moment? I've been wanting to have a word with you all day."

Once they were inside the cozy room and seated upon the settee, David continued worriedly, "I've been thinking, Emilie, about what I did to you—leaving you with Uncle. It was flagrantly thoughtless. Perhaps I should set things right, take you back to Houston."

Emilie smiled. How ironic—the words she had prayed for for months. Now they were meaningless. "But I've no wish to go back to Houston, David. I'm in love with your uncle."

David's brows flew up. "You are?"

"Yes, David."

David scowled at Emilie's revelation, and she studied his tense face with concern. Did David share some of her doubts about Edgar? Maybe his question about Edgar "abusing" her wasn't as silly as she first thought.

"David, Maria once told me Edgar had a violent temper—with Olivia," Emilie remarked. "Maria even said she thought Edgar beat his first wife. Is that true?"

David nervously shifted his weight on the settee, then said woodenly, "Maria has a healthy imagination, dear. You mustn't concern yourself with such folly."

"Folly? How can you call it folly when you just asked me if Edgar has tried to harm me? I must be concerned because—" Emilie took a deep breath—"because I'm carrying your uncle's child."

David half-smiled at the announcement, but his deep blue eyes were still troubled. "Congratulations, dear," he murmured. "I hope—I trust the child's coming will be a good omen for us all."

As David leaned over to plant a brotherly kiss on Emilie's cheek, a deep voice boomed out from the doorway, "Take your damned hands off my wife, Nephew!"

Both Emilie and David jumped, jerking about to face a grim Edgar at the doorway. Maria stood a foot or so behind him, a smile of triumph on her face.

As Edgar strode into the room, David sprang to his feet. "Sir, I was simply congratulating Emilie about the child—"

"Splendid. Now get the hell away from her!" Edgar barked, stopping a foot away from David, his fists clenched at his sides. Turning to Emilie, he said threateningly, "Madam, I'll have a word alone with you in our bedroom."

Surprisingly, David stepped between Edgar and Emilie and said vehemently to his uncle, "Sir, you've been drinking. I'll not risk your harming Emilie, or the child—"

"Emilie—and our child—are none of your damn business, Nephew!" Edgar roared. "Now stand aside before I knock you through the wall!"

Emilie's jaw dropped. She was astonished by her husband's bloodcurdling display of temper, as well as by David's staunch protectiveness. Realizing physical blows were imminent, she hastily got to her feet, placing her hand on David's arm. "David—it's all right. Edgar and I will settle this between ourselves." Turning to stare boldly at her husband, she added, "Your uncle won't hurt me."

Studying Edgar's brooding face, Emilie thought she actually detected some softening in his features at her words.

"Very well, Emilie, if you're sure—" Emilie heard David murmur.

"I'm sure." Emilie turned and left the room with Edgar. As they entered the hallway, Emilie spotted Maria still standing there. "Thanks, Maria," she whispered sarcastically.

But the girl merely stared at Emilie innocently as the couple passed.

Once they were inside their bedroom, Edgar went straight to the brandy decanter, pouring himself more brandy and hastily gulping it down.

Looking at the near-empty decanter on the bedside table, Emilie said, "I must compliment you on your nourishing repast, m'lord."

Though she had hoped to humor him, Edgar was

not impressed. Putting down the empty snifter, he turned to her and ordered, "Take off your clothes."

His verbal shot scored. Emilie stamped her foot at his arrogance. "You have no right—"

"I have *every* right!" he cut in, his eyes wild as he started towards her. "You're the one who has been flaunting what's rightfully mine, first to Rice and now to David! Well, Mrs. Ashland, tonight your husband will get his fair share of the favors you bestow so freely on others!"

He stopped within inches of her, hands resting at his waist as he stared at her with a fierce resolve. Emilie shook a fist at him and cried, "That's not true! Next you'll be accusing me of trying to seduce Pastor Fritz!"

He laughed humorlessly. "You were certainly dressed for the role the day you tried to run away with him." Turning with deliberate indolence, he started for the bed. "Speaking of which, I repeat—take off your clothes."

"Damn you!" she hissed back, shaking with rage, her eyes flashing blue fire. "First you don't speak to me all day, then you nearly kill David over a perfectly innocent display of affection, and now you have the unmitigated gall to order me into your bed!"

"Precisely." He turned and smiled thinly, but his eyes defied challenge. "You came up here with me, didn't you? My dear, you should know by now that you're a fool to walk through our bedroom door if you plan to hold back—anything."

With those audacious words, he unbuttoned his shirt and shrugged it off. Despite herself, Emilie felt a chill of titillation as she studied the ripple of muscles on his powerful chest.

She watched him sit down on the bed and remove

his boots. As he swung his sinewy legs up upon the bed, he asked nastily, "Do you need assistance undressing?"

Emile bit her lip, struggling with conflicting emotions. Oh, he was insufferable to treat her so! Yet she found her eyes irresistibly moving to his magnificent form on the bed, and her fingers treacherously aching to unbutton those well-fitting trousers. Her softer nature urged her to go to him, reminding her that he *was* her husband, and had every right to expect her services in bed. But why did he have to be such a cad about it?

A petulant mouth her only outward expression of defiance, Emilie unbuttoned the front of her dress. She removed her dress, chemise and undergarments, then shivered, feeling the heat of Edgar's bold gaze as she took a filmy white nightgown from her dresser and pulled it over her head.

"You won't be needing that," he said.

Emilie pulled the nightgown downward and smoothed it about her with trembling fingers. She went to sit on the edge of the bed, a good two feet away from Edgar.

"Come closer," he urged from beside her.

She did not move, but looked up at him cautiously. His expression appeared a bit kinder, though still cynical. "Edgar, why did you ignore me today?" she ventured. "Are you jealous of David?"

"Should I be?" he countered.

Emilie half-smiled as she studied her husband's moody, tight face. "Why Mr. Ashland, I *do* believe you're jealous!"

Edgar, however, was not amused; his hard fingers grabbed her wrist, pulling her across him onto the mattress. Perched on his elbow, he stared down at her. "I repeat—*should* I be jealous, my dear?"

She looked up at him, mesmerized by the lamp-light gleaming in his unfathomable brown eyes, her senses filling with the smell of him—half-brandy, half-man. "You have no reason to be jealous, m'lord," she murmured.

But his brows knitted; he did not smile. "Do you still love him?" he demanded.

Emilie did not reply, now perversely luxuriating in his distress. She reached upward, stroking the square line of his jaw with her fingertips.

Edgar grabbed her hand. "Damn it, Emilie, don't be coy with me! I want to know if you're in love with David!"

His eyes were half-crazed with passion now, and Emilie suddenly ached for an end to the game. She smiled up at him, her blue eyes bright and sincere. "I thought I was—once. But nay, I do not love him," she whispered.

She longed to tell him that it was he, Edgar, that she loved, but the words somehow froze in her throat. She still half-feared he would use her love, that a part of him still wanted to destroy her.

Edgar sighed heavily, then abruptly pulled Emilie astride him, tugging her nightgown over her head and flinging it on the floor. He smoothed her rich blonde curls about her shoulders, then his hands took her breasts, his fingertips tantalizing the nipples to an unbearable tautness. Meanwhile, his eyes moved ever so slowly down her body, lingering for long, searing moments at strategic points, until she was sure she would succumb to madness. . . .

Emilie's heart raced frantically. She half-wanted to withdraw from him, to fold herself away from this very vulnerable position, to retreat from the relentless penetration of his eyes. Yet she knew that the very unconditional intimacy she feared was also what she most desired. There were *ways*—ways of showing him her feelings—ways that went beyond words—

He unbuttoned his trousers; she trembled as his hard maleness teased her naked softness. She felt a blush suffuse her entire body as his large, brown hands took her hips, pulling her snugly against his heat.

She looked down at him, her eyes silently telling him she hurt for him. He looked up at her, his eyes glowing with desire and possessiveness.

"You say I have no reason to be jealous," he whispered. "Now prove it."

She did not hesitate, her eyes locked with his as deeply as their bodies were joined.

Chapter Twenty-Five

June 29, 1841

The buggy with its three occupants inched down River Road toward Washington-on-the Brazos. The day would be a scorcher—the sun's rays burned through the canopy of tree limbs shading the road. The warm air bore the heavy odor of summer vegetation.

Emilie glanced at her two silent companions. Maria sat next to her, her tawny hands demurely clasped in her lap. The girl wore the purple and plum calico dress she and Emilie had just finished sewing. The color suited Maria's dark beauty perfectly, the gathered neck and sleeves, the fitted waist setting off her figure to perfection. She wore a pale pink satin poke bonnet lined with lime-green lace and tied with black satin ribbon.

Next to Maria sat David, dressed in a honey-brown suit, a buff-colored broad-brimmed hat on his head. He looked over to smile at Emilie briefly, shyly, his blue eyes darkening perceptibly. Then he turned, clucking to the team.

David's friendly overture was not lost on Maria, who bit her pink lower lip as she surreptitiously eyed him. Watching the two of them, Emilie swallowed a sigh and fanned herself with the lace fan Pastor Fritz had given her. Although she had assumed the fan was lost the day Edgar threw her in the river, she had recently discovered it tucked away in her lingerie drawer. She had realized Edgar must have sent someone back that day to retrieve it. Would she never understand the man?

He had also baffled her yesterday by agreeing to let her attend church in Washington-on-the-Brazos. Emilie had decided it was time they had an outing and met some of the townspeople, and had nervously approached Edgar with her idea. Surprisingly, he had voiced no objection, but had refused to accompany them, obvious disapproval in his eyes.

If he disapproved, that was his misfortune, Emilie now told herself. Let the man be a recluse if he wished, but it was unfair to expect the rest of them—especially Maria—to follow his misanthropic ways!

Emilie put her thoughts of Edgar aside and scrutinized her own appearance. Like Maria, she had chosen calico for the outing—the blue and yellow print she selected was a fitting complement for her hair and eyes. She wore a dark blue silk bonnet and white crocheted gloves. She had given Maria a pair of beige gloves, but she now noted that the girl had tied them to the drawstring of her reticule rather than wearing them. A small gesture of defiance, perhaps? True, Maria had been behaving more coldly towards her since David returned. That very night, in fact, the Mexican girl had gotten Emilie in trouble with Edgar.

Emilie half-smiled to herself—perhaps, considering the incredible night of passion which resulted from Maria's treachery, her "thanking" the Mexican girl had not been at all inappropriate at the time! Yet Maria had doubtless planned a more violent ending to her little intrigue, Emilie realized. Emilie would never forget the day in the parlor, when Maria asked, "Does it frighten you to be pregnant, Señora?" Maria's eyes had seemed to glow with an evil light at the time, as if the girl took distinct pleasure in Emilie's suffering.

There was so much about Maria that Emilie didn't know—and couldn't trust. But one thing Emilie was sure of—she must be careful around the girl. As she once again recalled the terrifying experience in the stable, and remembered the reason the girl was dismissed from school, Emilie realized she could not put anything past this troubled, enigmatic young woman—even harming an innocent, unborn child in order to hurt Emilie.

Emilie sighed, wrenching her mind from her troubling thoughts, and thinking instead of their imminent arrival in Washington-on-the-Brazos. She hoped the three of them would make a favorable impression on the townspeople. She and Maria owned fancier gowns, but the village of Washington-on-the-Brazos was quite poor, if memories of her view from the steamboat served her correctly. Although David had told her there were some wealthy planter families living in the vicinity, she doubted many of the women were able to acquire Sunday frocks as fashionable as the ones Granny Rose had sewn for her.

David turned the team from River Road onto a crude trail carved through the trees. Emilie and Maria gripped the seat of the buggy as it bounced over roots and rocks in the roadway.

Soon, they reached a large opening in the woods—the village of Washington-on-the-Brazos.

Emilie's memory proved accurate—the town consisted of several shanties and a few frame buildings. The stump-dotted street ended abruptly on the western bank of the Brazos.

"This is Ferry Street," David told the girls. "Yonder, where the road ends, is La Bahia crossing, where Andrew Robinson operated his ferry in the thirties." Pointing towards a ramshackle building with a high, pitched roof, he added, "That's the hall where the delegates met to sign the Declaration of Independence."

Gazing at the dilapidated structure, Maria giggled. "A most unusual place to begin a new nation."

"Whoa!" David ordered the team, as they reached the end of the street. They stopped in front of a small frame church. David alighted and tied the team to the hitching post. Then he assisted Emilie and Maria out of the carriage.

Lifting their skirts, the girls walked with David through the dusty swept churchyard towards the board steps. Emilie smiled as she viewed the blooming marigolds around the whitewashed building. A young family nodded a friendly greeting as they entered the church just ahead of them—the wife and two small daughters wore homespun, the father buckskins and a coonskin hat.

As they entered the church, all eyes turned to regard the threesome curiously. Emilie noted that most of the people were dressed like the young family they saw on the steps, although a few families were more elegantly attired.

They sat down near the front, just as the black-robed parson climbed the pulpit. Nodding smilingly at Emilie, the round-faced Pastor Fritz began addressing those assembled in a heavily accented voice. Seeing the man, Emilie pushed back memories of her last encounter with the parson—the day that ended in nightmare.

Emilie resolutely tried to enjoy the hymn-singing, but the crowded building was distractingly uncomfortable. The pews were hard, with backs so straight they seemed to tilt forward; the clarified rawhide covering the windows did little to keep out the heat and the fat, buzzing flies. Emilie fanned herself vigorously, longing to be outside under a tree.

As she listened to the parson, Emilie remembered marrying Edgar in the parlor of Brazos Bend. The wedding had been so rushed—she had drifted through the ceremony like a sleepwalker. Emilie looked around the church sadly—crude as it was, what a difference it would have made had she and Edgar said their vows here, in God's house!

After the service, several of the townspeople came forward to greet them, urging them to come back again. Much to Emilie's displeasure, however, the people addressed her or David, ignoring Maria conspicuously.

Later, on the front steps, the three greeted the parson. Pastor Fritz expressed his joy regarding Emilie's improved health, and Emilie, biting back a rueful smile, promised they would soon return to church.

The three were approaching the carriage when they were stopped by a thin, graying woman in a black silk dress. "Good day, Mr. Ashland," the woman addressed David. She turned to study Emilie with inquisitive gray eyes. "Pastor Fritz has informed us there has been a wedding at Brazos Bend."

Tipping his hat to the black-bonneted lady, David replied, "Mrs. Alder, may I introduce my uncle's bride, Mrs. Emilie Ashland—and Miss Maria Ramero."

Mrs. Alder extended a bony hand to Emilie. "How do you do, Mrs. Ashland? I'm Grace Alder."

Emilie shook the older woman's hand. There was something she instantly disliked about the woman—perhaps the grating quality of her voice. "I'm pleased to meet you, Mrs. Alder," she murmured.

Grace Alder tilted her head toward Maria. "She your maid, honey?" she asked Emilie.

Emilie's jaw tightened. "Miss Ramero is my husband's ward," she said archly.

Grace Alder shrugged. "And where is your husband this morning, Mrs. Ashland?"

Biting her lip, Emilie sternly reminded herself that she would be living in this community for some time. Yet she was strongly tempted to tell off this nosy old hen! "My husband is at home, Mrs. Alder," she said stiffly. She couldn't resist adding, "And where is Mr. Alder?"

Emilie detected a flicker of irritation in the older woman's eyes. "My Henry was still abed when I left this morning," the woman replied nervously. "He and our houseguest—Aaron Rice—were up late last evening—er—studying the scriptures."

Emilie swallowed a giggle at this astounding revelation. So Aaron was staying with the Alder family. Wherever he was, she was sure he did not study the Bible last night!

"You know Aaron, don't you dear?" Grace Alder continued. "He told us of his visit to Brazos Bend, and of your startling resemblance to Olivia Ashland." The woman laid a hand across Emilie's arm, clucking in sympathy. "My dear, it must be a trial for you, living with that man! I simply could not believe the way he mistreated poor Aaron. Now things were vastly different when Olivia was alive.

After—the tragedy, we tried to keep in touch with Edgar, but our efforts were in vain." She sighed resignedly. "I don't suppose Edgar will ever get over losing Olivia and the wee ones. The guilt must be killing him. Don't you agree, my dear?"

"Ladies, we must be getting home," David interjected nervously, watching Emilie firmly disengage Grace Alder's hand from her arm.

Grace Alder turned to David, ignoring Emilie's scathing look. "But won't you and Mrs. Ashland—and the girl, of course—come home and join us for Sunday dinner?" she asked him sweetly.

"Another time, perhaps, Mrs. Alder," David replied, smiling as he led both girls away.

Once they were in the buggy going home, Emilie exploded. "What an old witch! How dare she be so nosy!"

David nodded, his face grim. "You were wise not to call her on it, Emilie. Folks live an isolated, boring life in these parts. Many a dowager would kill for a small bit of gossip. Grace Alder could turn a lot of people against you, Emilie. Be careful of her."

Emilie gritted her teeth. "Aye, there's venom in her tongue. But I'll not let the old biddy walk all over my face—or insult Maria!"

Maria, who had not uttered a word most of the morning, now turned to regard Emilie coldly. "If I wish your help, Emilie, I'll ask for it!" she said waspishly.

Already pushed to the limit, Emilie found her sympathy for Maria evaporating. Throwing her hands wide in exasperation, she returned the girl's glare. "Maria, sometimes you're no better than a spoiled child!"

Maria could only gape at the older girl in stunned silence.

* * *

Emilie expected Edgar to be cross when they got home, and braced herself for another assault upon her already frayed nerves. But when they arrived, he astonished her by smiling and hugging her. "You look so pretty," he whispered, gently kissing her cheek.

Late in the afternoon, he again shocked her by asking her to go for a walk. She agreed cheerfully, and they held hands as they walked toward the river. Although they strolled along in silence, Emilie was delighted that he should want to spend time with her outside their bedroom.

Emilie sadly noted that the wildflowers were gone, the air thick with the smell of summer greenery. They walked through the trees camouflaging the river and stopped near the banks of the Brazos. As they sat beneath the limbs of a lofty sycamore, Emilie looked down at the water—the river flowed calmly today, a silvery gray in the late afternoon light.

Emilie felt Edgar's eyes studying her. "Did you enjoy your outing?" he asked.

Emilie returned his gaze cautiously. He was leaning against the tree, his arms crossed on his knees, his white shirt rippling in the gentle breeze. Her heart fluttered at the frank appraisal in his dark gaze.

"Our excursion was quite pleasant," Emilie replied. "Won't you join us next time?"

Edgar shrugged, frowning. "Did you see Aaron Rice today?" he abruptly asked.

"Of course not! What makes you ask such a question?" Emilie countered, scowling at him. Had Maria been up to her shenanigans again? she wondered.

"It's not easy to forget the sight of that slimy cur with his hands on you. I frequently regret that I did not draw and quarter the bastard."

Edgar uttered the words casually, but his eyes were filled with a murderous resolve, and a chill shot through Emilie. She gulped, but did not reply.

Edgar studied her hard for a moment, then extended a brown hand. "You're too far away, my dear. Come closer."

Emilie cautiously scooted closer to Edgar, smoothing her yellow skirts about her.

Edgar slid an arm about her waist. "Won't you stay here with me—next time?" he whispered in her ear.

His possessiveness warmed her, but she pulled back a bit, asserting her independence. "I want to get to know the people of Washington-on-the-Brazos."

Edgar frowned thoughtfully as he toyed with one of the gold curls cascading down her back. "And were they so unusual—or entertaining?"

"No," she admitted. "But I'm returning, nonetheless. It's important, for Maria's sake. And we should start entertaining at the house, Edgar—invite people her age."

Edgar picked up a twig, snapped it in his hand. "We'll see."

For a moment they sat silently, listening to the flowing river, the sounds of nature surrounding them. Then Edgar said slowly, "I feared you might go—and never return."

Emilie leaned forward, startled by her husband's frank revelation. "Then why did you let me go?"

His hand moved beneath her mane of gold hair to stroke her neck. "I can't keep you in chains."

"At one time you tried to," Emilie reminded him.

298

His hand grew still. "Are you still afraid of me?"

"I—I don't know."

His arm moved to her waist. "You have night-mares—you won't tell me about them."

"I—I haven't had them since—" she bit her lip, feeling a blush heat her face.

"Since we've been making love again?" he supplied.

She lowered her head and nodded.

He lifted her chin, and her bright blue eyes met his deep-set, troubled brown gaze. "Does that mean you are happy with me? Or have you truly thought of leaving me?"

"Where would I go?" she asked. "Besides, we now share something I can't leave behind."

Emilie turned away, grimacing. She did not like to think of giving birth to the babe growing inside her—the thought filled her with fear, and brought a vivid recollection of her past nightmare of Gonzales.

Edgar's hand slid down her belly. "Do you want this babe growing within you?"

"I—I—what difference does it make now?"

Edgar scowled. "Emilie, you're dodging me! Why won't you tell me what you're thinking?"

"Why won't you?" she countered.

Sighing angrily, he stood, extending his hand to her. "Let's go home."

As they walked back to the house, he again asked her, "I must know, Emilie—are you content staying here with me?"

She smiled as she gazed at his intense face. "I'll stay with you, Edgar."

His brow creased, he seemed dissatisfied with her answer. They continued walking in silence.

After a while, she remarked, "Edgar, I was thinking today at church, about how I wished we had married there, instead of here, in the parlor."

His brows shot up. "You were?"

"The wedding was so rushed—and my thinking was rather befuddled, at the time. It's almost as if I never married you."

Frowning, he pulled her close, his hand touching the small mound of her belly. "Even with this, you feel we're not married?"

She nodded. "Even with this. It's not as if we said our vows in the church, before God."

They walked silently for a moment, as a flock of blackbirds flew over their heads. Finally, Edgar remarked, "I had no idea you were so religious, my dear."

"I can't deny my upbringing, Edgar." She sighed. "I miss my church in Houston. You know, our new building was finished mere days before I left town. But I never got to see the new edifice—neither did my grandmother."

"And that is why you attended church today?"

"Yes. Yet it's not the same, in Washington-on-the-Brazos. The people are different—Pastor Fritz is so very different." Smiling wistfully, she continued, "In Houston, our minister was a giant Swede with wooly silver hair and a booming voice. His sweet little wife would play the piano in a loud, discordant fashion—" she paused, giggling. "I often thought of offering her piano lessons. Yes, I suppose I miss them, as well as our friends in the congregation—the socials, the quilting bees."

His brow puckered, Edgar stared at the sun sinking in the west. "I can see, my dear, that you have needs I cannot supply," he said resignedly.

She stopped. He paused, turning to look down at her sadly, the fading light casting a coppery halo about his head.

She stood on tiptoe, kissing him on the chin. "You must remember, Edgar, that you supply the most important of my needs," she whispered.

He gazed at her curiously. Removing his arm from her middle, he took her hand and stared at the gold band on her finger. Her breathing stopped as she waited for him to say something.

But he simply frowned, lacing his fingers with hers as he turned to lead her up the hillside towards the house.

He held her hand tightly.

But nothing was asked.

And nothing answered.

"No, don't kill him! Don't kill him!" she screamed.

Emilie jerked awake in the darkness; she was wild with fright, and someone was shaking her.

With a choking cry of relief, she recognized Edgar clutching her in the moonlight-bathed bed. "Oh, darling—darling!" she cried, throwing her arms around his neck, clinging to him.

He drew himself upright, pulled her into his lap, smoothing her nightgown about her legs. "There, there," he soothed, stroking her back. "You had the nightmare again, didn't you, love?"

She stiffened, as memories of the harrowing dream splintered her brain. "You brought it on," she accused hysterically, "with all your questions today!"

She could instantly feel the constriction in his chest at her unfeeling remark. "I'm sorry," she whispered in a quavering voice. "I'm not being fair. It's just that I was—so terrified," she choked. "I thought the dream would not come again."

"You must talk about it, darling—tell me," he

urged gently. "Then perhaps it will never come again."

She gulped, drew back. "You think so?"

He nodded in the silvery darkness.

She felt too fearful, too vulnerable to reject his suggestion, and blurted shakily, "It was horrid, Edgar, the worst one yet! Pastor Fritz was there, and that nosy biddy from church—"

"*Who?*"

"Grace—Grace something or other! And the people from Washington-on-the-Brazos—and Gonzales. They were m-murdering me—and my baby!" she finished, sobbing convulsively.

His arms grew rigid about her. "Oh, no, love!" he gasped. "You poor darling! Are you truly so frightened—about the child?"

"Yes! Yes!" she cried.

She sobbed her heart out to him then, telling him of watching her mother die in Gonzales, of her fears since discovering she was pregnant, of the dream in which she and her babe were dead. But she omitted his role in everything. He listened, his eyes sympathetic, serious.

When she finished, he sighed breathlessly. "God, Emmie, I thought all this time you were terrified of *me!*" His fingers brushed the tears from her face as he continued firmly, "Emilie, listen to me. You're a healthy girl and you're *not* going to die. Neither is our child. I'll not permit it. Do you understand?"

"Yes," she replied tremulously. Looking at his determined face outlined in the moonlight, she could almost believe that if Edgar Ashland would not allow her to die, so it would be.

He pressed his lips against her hair. "Push the demons from your mind, love. And remember—I shall be here, all night, to keep them at bay. Now, you must sleep—and dream dreams as lovely as you are.'' His hand caressed her cheek. ''Close your eyes.''

She looked up at him quizzically, saw his warm eyes glowing in the darkness. Sighing, she lowered black-lashed eyelids.

He tucked her head under his chin. ''Let me take you on a journey, my love,'' he whispered. ''Just let your mind drift.''

Relaxing in his strong arms, she lay pliant, receptive. In a soothing voice, he began talking to her of England—of rolling hills, chestnut trees and laurel, of mists in the morning, the configuration of stars in the heavens at night.

Listening, nestled in his warmth, she soon fell asleep, dreaming beautiful dreams.

But he sat wakeful, holding her, his expression deeply troubled as he gazed down at her in the darkness, his fingers stroking her moonlight-washed hair.

Chapter Twenty-Six

July 2, 1841

The sun hung brightly in the middle of a cloudless sky, pouring down upon a rider racing up the hillside on a brown sorrel.

David Ashland pulled his horse up near the house and hurried inside. "Daniel!" he called as he entered the hallway.

As the wizened old man appeared, David directed, "Fetch the stable boy to care for my horse. Mind you have him give Copper a good rubdown—he's had quite a run this morning."

David hurried toward the dining room, his boots pounding the wooden floor. As he tore into the room, those present eating lunch turned to view him with curiosity.

Emilie studied David as he swept past her, emanating the strong odor of leather and horseflesh. His hair was wind-tossed and dull, his face dusty, creased with worry.

"Uncle," he began in an agitated voice, "there are squatters on our range!"

Edgar Ashland raised an eyebrow at his nephew. "Indeed?"

"There's two dozen or more of them—erecting lean-tos and shanties on my hillside."

Edgar smiled. "Well, we can't have that now, can we? What manner of folk are these—squatters?"

"They are *mexicanos*, five or six families, best as I can judge. They must have moved in during my last trip to Houston."

"And did you inform these folk as to where they are trespassing?" Edgar questioned.

David bit his lip. "You can't expect me to take on all of them single-handedly, Uncle. I've returned home for help."

"Help!" Maria interjected angrily. "*Madre de dios!* Why do you assume these people are cutthroats and thieves, David? They will not give you trouble—I'm sure they've been pushed off their land before!"

All present turned to stare at Maria, stunned by her sudden ire. "But Maria," David protested, "it's *our* land, not theirs. I'll not have been camping on my hillside!"

Maria stared sullenly at her napkin.

Edgar remarked, "You are planning to ranch that land in the future, aren't you, Nephew?"

Maria's head shot up, her eyes flashing coldly at David and Edgar. "Land, land! You and your uncle own six *leguas* of land, David! Why are you quibbling about one hillside?"

"Maria, David has a point," Edgar explained patiently. "Today a hillside—tomorrow the entire estate could be crawling with squatters. We can't afford to ignore this sort of thing."

"Uncle's right, Maria," David asserted. "And besides, why are you defending these people? They are the ones in the wrong, not us."

Maria squared her shoulders as she looked up at

David, her eyes bright and proud. "They are my people. Who else is to defend them?"

Suddenly, Emilie clapped her hands, her eyes sparkling. "David—I've an idea. Since you want to start ranching the longhorns, why don't you hire these people to help you?"

Maria smiled as she caught Emilie's enthusiasm. *"Sí*, David, that is exactly what you must do! My people have been *vaqueros* for centuries! I beg of you, do not turn them away!"

"But I've no idea what manner of folk they are," David protested uneasily.

"Then let's find out," Edgar suggested, "*after* lunch. In case none of you have noticed, Avis is glowering at all of us, as we are letting her gumbo go cold. So, nephew, if you will—clean up and join us for lunch. We'll ride out to the prairie this afternoon."

David flushed. "Sorry, Avis," he told the Creole woman, smiling sheepishly. He nodded to his uncle. "This afternoon, then."

A buggy followed by three horsemen travelled down the road weaving through the cotton fields. David drove the harnessed grays, a bonnetted girl on either side of him. Edgar and two slaves rode behind them, rifles sheathed to their saddles.

In the cotton fields, slaves attended the waist-high cotton plants; fuzzy white growth was beginning to appear on the healthy green stalks. Overhead, the skies were bright, cloudless, the sun beating down hotly on the backs of the travellers.

Soon, the group turned from the road and started out across the prairie. Moments later, Emilie was shocked to view a settlement which appeared thrown upon the hillside. Several lean-tos of sticks and cloth had been pitched. Chickens and pigs and small children in homespun scurried about.

As they drew nearer, Emilie scrutinized the scene carefully. Four lean-tos had been erected, and a cabin was being started by two men pounding stakes into the ground. Nearby, two women were thatching reeds for a roof. Another woman was attending meat on an open spit, and an older child was grinding corn.

The group from Brazos Bend halted and dismounted close to the small settlement. The *mexicanos*, spotting them, ceased work. Dark, inquisitive eyes stared at the approaching visitors.

A man came forward from one of the lean-tos. He looked tired and old, but his straight shoulders and proud gait showed him to be a man of great dignity. Dressed in a dirty white shirt and frayed black velvet jacket, he wore silver-studded brown chaps and dusty hand-tooled boots; his silver spurs jingled as he approached them.

The man removed his *sombrero*, revealing silver-streaked black hair. His face, though dirty and creased, had the high cheekbones and classically-etched proportions of the aristocrat. *"Buenos tardes, señors y señoritas,"* he began in a deep, lyrical Spanish voice. He looked around expansively. "To whom do I have the honor of speaking?"

Edgar Ashland stepped forward and offered his hand to the older man. The Mexican looked shocked for a moment, then he hastily accepted the handshake.

"I'm Edgar Ashland, owner of this estate. And who are you, sir?"

The older man drew himself up with dignity. "I am Don Lorenzo de la Peña." He gestured about him. "My companions are my family and some of the *vaqueros* we employed on our estate near the Rio Grande."

"I see," Edgar replied thoughtfully, stroking his mustache. "You say you have land in South Texas?"

"I had land, sir," Don Lorenzo replied sadly. "After the war, our land was stolen from us by a group of cutthroat *especulados*. They killed my oldest son and several of our *vaqueros*. We have been travelling north ever since, trying to find land and resettle ourselves. We were hoping to homestead this land where we are camping."

While Emilie and David exchanged worried glances, Edgar said firmly, "This land is not available, Señor de la Peña. It belongs to me and my nephew. You would have been wise to investigate before trying to settle here."

De la Peña smiled grimly. "The authorities have not been very—shall we say—cooperative, Señor. We have had little luck gaining information on available lands. In most towns, we have been urged—if not forced—to leave."

Edgar frowned, but made no comment.

Don Lorenzo sighed. "Do not concern yourself, Señor Ashland. I am a man of honor. Unlike others I know, I do not steal another man's land. My wife and several of the others are ill with *la fiebre* at present, but as soon as they can travel, we shall be gone."

Edgar glanced meaningfully at David. "Well, Nephew? I leave it in your hands."

David stepped forward tentatively. "Señor de la Peña, perhaps we could work something out."

De la Peña studied David Ashland appraisingly. "*Sí*, Señor?"

David hesitated, then sighed as he saw the silent pleading in Maria's eyes. "Señor, I intend to begin

308

ranching these lands. Perhaps some employment could be arranged for you and your companions."

The older man's eyes narrowed. "I have lived all my life as a landowner, Señor. It is as such that I wish to die."

"I sympathize," David replied. "But you've been hunting land for what—five years? Perhaps it's time you settled for a while, saved your money."

The older man nodded slowly. "Your point is well-taken, Señor."

"With your help, de la Peña, I could possibly have my first drive to New Orleans this fall."

"*Sí, es possible*, Señor," the older man replied noncommittally.

"Well, what say you?" David pursued.

"May I have some time to think, Señor Ashland? I am not a man to make hasty judgments."

"Of course. May I expect your reply tomorrow, then?"

Don Lorenzo nodded gravely. "*Sí, mañana.*"

Don Lorenzo watched as the group prepared to leave. Gesturing to the east, Edgar asked, "By the way, de la Peña, what are those two mounds yonder?"

"Cherokees," the Mexican replied. "They were trying to steal our—" he smiled—"your meat, Señor."

"Rather lazy of them, wasn't it?" Edgar quipped. "The few Indians left in these parts generally leave us alone if we stay out of their way. But it may be a different story out on the prairie. We've never fully explored our lands."

"That is not right, Señor," de la Peña replied sternly. "Land, like a good woman, should be cultivated."

Edgar winked at Emilie, then told David, "Heed

the words of a man of experience, Nephew."

The next day, David, Emilie and Maria returned to the encampment of the *mexicanos*. This time, their buggy was followed by an ox cart filled with supplies. Emilie had asked Edgar if they might take some food and cloth to the settlers, and he had surprised her by kissing her forehead and saying, "Surely, love, whatever you wish. How thoughtful you are. But mind you stay well away from anyone with the fever."

As the two conveyances stopped at the encampment, several small children came forward to eye curiously the treasures in the ox cart. Emilie looked at them sadly—the little ragamuffins needed new clothes and nourishing food.

The visitors dismounted. Jacob and another black lad began stacking the supplies next to a lean-to.

Don Lorenzo came forward, frowning. *"Que es esto?* We do not want your charity, Señor," he told David.

"Regardless of whether you choose to stay or not," David replied, "you can't work—or travel—without food."

Several women had crept over to examine the supplies. They prattled happily in rapid Spanish as they fingered the bolts of cloth, the sacks of cornmeal, the jars of canned foods.

Don Lorenzo snapped his fingers in irritation. *"Silencio!"* he ordered the chattering women.

The women immediately ceased their pattering and moved away, faces downcast.

Don Lorenzo strode off to study the supplies, his shoulders held high, his hands clasped behind his back. Then he turned to David, his mouth tight. "We are tired of the nomad life, Señor Ashland. We will work for you—for a time. *Pero* the cost of the supplies must be deducted from our wages. *Comprendes*, Señor?"

"Whatever you wish," David returned. He glanced about at the sea of dark eyes watching them intently. "I take it you make the decisions for the others?"

De la Peña drew himself up with dignity. "*Por supuesto*, Señor. I am *el patrón.*"

"I understand. You will be my foreman, then."

"On my *rancho*, I had three *mayordomos*, Señor."

David sighed. "Times have changed, de la Peña."

"*Sí*, Señor Ashland, they have."

"You will come to the house this afternoon, then, so that we may discuss the matter further?"

"*A su servicio*, Señor."

David glanced around expansively. "You may erect housing anywhere you wish hereabouts, except—" he pointed at the clearing on the rise above them—"yonder."

"Ah, *sí*, Señor," de la Peña replied sagely. "When we arrived here, I told my wife Doña Elena that—*allí*—there will be someday *un gran hacienda. Verdad*, Señor?"

David grinned. "Aye. I think we'll get on just fine, Señor de la Peña."

"I'm so delighted about David," Emilie told Edgar that night in their bedroom. "Don Lorenzo de la Peña can be an intimidating fellow, but David handled him beautifully! And you should have seen Maria's eyes glowing as she watched him!"

Edgar grinned. "Ah, our little Maria seems to have big eyes for my nephew." He playfully slapped Emilie on the derriere. "Turn around."

She turned, felt his deft fingers unbuttoning her dress. "It was so kind of you to let us take the supplies to them, Edgar. Maria and I talked to the women before we left—well, Maria did most of the talking—and you simply can't believe the deprivations and cruel treatment these people have suffered. They were ecstatic about the simple items we brought them."

Edgar turned her, pulled the dress over her head and threw it aside. His hand slid down the smooth cloth of her chemise, patted her belly. He winked at her. "You're growing fat with my seed, woman."

She blushed.

He chuckled, his dark eyes dancing with merriment. "Will you *never* lose your shyness with me, love? No, don't—ever. You should see your face—all alive and eager. It warms my heart to see you so happy!"

She threw her arms around his neck. "Oh, Edgar, I *am* happy, I truly am!" she breathed. "If only—" she drew back and looked up at him. She wanted to say, "If only you loved me, as I love you," but the words hung in her throat.

"Yes? What is it, Emilie?"

She started to reply, then, suddenly, she jumped away from him.

He frowned. "Love, what is it? Do you feel ill?"

Emilie stood stock still, her mouth and eyes like three saucers as her hand held her stomach. "It moved, Edgar! My baby moved inside me! Here! Feel it!"

Edgar placed his hand on the small mound of her belly. His eyes smiled down at her. "Aye—I can feel the fluttering—like a tiny bird beneath my hand."

A tear slid down Emilie's face. "My baby's alive—healthy."

"Of course, love. How else would it be?" he asked confusedly.

She choked, "But I was so afraid he was dead—"

Edgar pulled her close. "Emilie—don't talk that way!"

She looked up at him, her face intense, pleading. "Edgar, if I die, take care of my baby for me."

He scowled and grasped her face. "Damn it, Emilie, you're not going to die! You're going to live, and care for *our* baby. Do you understand?"

"Yes, Edgar," she replied, trying to sound convincing. Deep inside her, the tremulous motion began again. "My baby's alive," she cried joyfully, her eyes bright with wonder. "How good it feels to have him move inside me!"

Edgar laughed in amazement. Touching the tip of her nose with his index finger, he said wickedly, "Get undressed, woman. It's time for *me* to move inside you. And how good *that* will feel, eh, love?"

"Oh, Edgar!" Laughing, Emilie moved off to the dresser to get her night clothes.

Edgar studied her with devotion as she removed her chemise. "Have you started making preparations for the babe's arrival?"

Emilie turned as she pulled a pale blue batiste nightgown over her head. "Oh, yes, Hallie and I have been sewing for several weeks now, and old Eben has already begun work on a crib." She tied her blue wrapper, then extended her hand to Edgar. "Come see the room Hallie and I have been fixing up as the nursery. I wanted it to be a surprise, but what the heck!"

"I'd love to see the room, sweetheart."

Together, they crossed the hallway to a former guest room. Edgar lit the lantern and stared about at the cheerful room. The corner bedroom sported six tall, narrow windows, all now curtained in a bright blue and yellow calico trimmed with eyelet lace. The same fabric covered a far wall, obviously reserved for the crib. A day bed, rocking chair, wardrobe and dresser completed the furnishings, and a blue and gold rag rug on the floor added warmth.

"My, you and Hallie *have* been busy," Edgar commented with admiration, as he moved off towards the dresser. He opened the top drawer, pulling out a tiny linen gown which was seamed with perfect blue cross-stitching. "To think the creature will fit into something this tiny," he said shaking his head.

Edgar was refolding the gown, when Emilie came forward and took it from his hands. "No, you're wrinkling it," she giggled.

Replacing the gown next to the others, Emilie frowned at a ragged edge of fabric protruding from the back of the drawer. Tugging on the cloth, she pulled out an alien object, then dropped it, gasping. "Oh, my God! Where on earth did that come from?"

Both she and Edgar stared horror-stricken at the small lump on the floor—it was a ceramic-headed doll, its face smashed into a grotesque countenance, its body ripped and slashed, stuffing protruding from an arm that had been torn off. There was no doubt that the toy had been deliberately and sadistically disfigured.

Emilie blinked at the horrible knife marks all over the mangled mass. It seemed a desecration that someone would do such a thing to a doll—and putting it in the baby's dresser made the symbolism even more frightful! Backing away from the appalling sight, she turned to Edgar in outrage. "It's-it's sickening!" she cried. "Who could have done something so malicious?''

Staring at the doll, Edgar did not reply, but a vein throbbing in his temple revealed the intensity of his emotion.

"Edgar, you know something about this, don't you?'' Emilie accused, hysteria tinging her voice as she pointed towards the doll. "I can tell by your face that you know who did this! Tell me!''

Edgar turned to her, his features dark with brooding. "Emilie, don't work yourself into a panic over a raggedy old doll. Perhaps one of the black children accidentally left it there—''

"No!'' Emilie cut in, infuriated by his dodge. "Someone intentionally mutilated that doll and left it in the baby's dresser to frighten me! And you know damn well who did it! Who are you protecting, Edgar? Your mistress? Or is there more than one of them?''

"Emilie!''

He reached for her, but she backed away, her eyes full of distrust as she studied him. Someone in this house really hated her—and her coming child! The very thought of her precious babe succumbing to the same fate as the doll was enough to make her physically ill. Who detested her so? Maria? Avis?

"You're covering for someone, Edgar!'' she reiterated. "Unless you did it yourself!''

His features twisted with disbelief, and he gestured in supplication. "Emilie, what on earth are you saying? How could you think—''

"Then *why* don't you tell me who did it—or who broke my mother's perfume bottle? You know I'm frightened about the baby, but sometimes I think that you—I think—that you hate me—because I can't be her—'' Her voice broke, and she finally succumbed to tears.

Two strong arms closed about her. "Hush!" Edgar ordered gently. "You don't know what you're saying, Emilie."

She clung to him. "Oh, God, Edgar, you're right! I don't know what I'm saying! Sometimes I think I'm losing my mind!"

"Come, love. Let's get you out of here."

He blew out the lamp and led her back to their bedroom. Moments later, she lay beside him beneath the covers, still shivering and weeping. He held her and stroked her back with his fingertips. His voice was deeply troubled as he asked, "Do you really believe I would do such a thing, Emilie?"

"No! No, of course not!" she choked.

"You know how much the babe means to me. . . ."

"I know." *I only wish I meant as much*, she added to herself.

"I shouldn't have railed at you so," she continued in a shaky whisper, "but when I saw that horrid doll, and thought of the babe like—like that—I was scared, so confused."

"I know, Emilie. And I'll see a stop put to it," he replied vehemently.

"Then you *do* know who—"

"I said I'll put a stop to it, Emilie. For now, you must simply believe that—and trust me."

She started to reply, then hesitated, sitting up in the darkness and putting her hand on her stomach.

Edgar sat up beside her. "Did the babe move again, love?"

"Yes."

He placed his hand over hers on her belly. "Our baby's alive, Emilie. And we're alive, too. You must think of only that." He pulled her closer, his hand raising the hem of her gown. "I'm going to make love to you now," he whispered intensely. "Mad, passionate love—until you forget all else!"

She stiffened. "No, I don't want to—not after—"

"You want to." He cradled her against him protectively, his mouth hot on hers, his hands bold and possessive beneath her gown.

She groaned, kissing him back fiercely, smothering her own terror. "Yes, I want to! God help me, I always will!"

Book Two

Chapter One

September 12, 1841

David Ashland walked through the rotunda of the
St. Louis Hotel. He paused to gaze up at the copper-
plated dome, decorated with Canova murals. In
startling contrast to the opulent surroundings,
several slaves stood on the dais beneath the dome,
their eyes downcast as an auctioneer sold them to the
assortment of gentlemen bidding.

David left the hotel. A brisk fall breeze greeted
him as he started down Chartres Street. Peddlers,
businessmen, and finely dressed ladies with servants
in attendance strolled down the *banquette*. David
gazed in wonder at the European-style buildings with
their iron-lace balconies, doors open to patios
brilliant with lush greenery and flowers.

David had never seen a city like New Orleans, not
even in his travels to the east. The romantic
metropolis, with its combined French and Spanish
personality, seemed distinctly foreign and intriguing
to him.

He continued through the Place D'Armes, gazing
up at the dominating St. Louis Cathedral with its
three lofty towers. Then he turned south and
followed Decateur Street into the French Market.

A gigantic hubbub of activity greeted David under the huge shed. Shawl-draped Indians peddled their crafts; old Negro women sold berries; farmers displayed fruits and vegetables. Everywhere was noise, the mixture of Spanish, French, and American voices, and the strong odor of fish.

David stopped at a sidewalk cafe and ordered coffee and *beignets*. As he sipped the strong, delicious *cafe au lait* and ate the delectable sugar-dipped doughnuts, he reflected on the last few weeks.

The cattle drive from Washington-on-the-Brazos had been a success. They arrived in New Orleans yesterday with more than a thousand head. David had already negotiated the sale of the cattle to a merchant who planned to slaughter the beef for meat and ship the hides north. Patting his breast pocket, David smiled, thinking of the ten-thousand-dollar bank draft he now carried.

The money had been well-earned. He and Señor de la Peña had spent the balance of the summer rounding up the herd. It was back-breaking work in the intense heat, and they were slowed down by a Yellow Fever epidemic.

David frowned as he remembered the frightening weeks when so many were ill. Tragically, three of the *mexicanos* died—one of the *vaqueros*, a mother and child. Maria came out to the small settlement to help during the worst of it. She was a remarkable girl, David now realized, thinking of the day she wept in his arms after Señor de la Peña's small nephew succumbed to the disease.

Emilie had wanted to help also, but Edgar had strictly forbidden this, or to let her nurse some of the slaves who were also ailing. Luckily, no one in the family had fallen prey to Yellow Jack or malaria. With cold weather approaching, both diseases were now on the wane.

David's thoughts drifted to Don Lorenzo de la Peña; he and the *mexicano* had become good friends over the summer months. The astute foreman had taught David all about the ranching business— cutting, branding, grazing. De la Peña's tireless direction got the herd across the treacherous Louisiana swamps. He anticipated trouble by keeping the longhorns tightly bunched, and scouts on constant lookout for Indians. David realized he never could have made the drive without his capable *mayordomo*.

To show his gratitude, he had arranged for rooms for de la Peña and his son Enrique at the St. Louis. Last night, he had taken Don Lorenzo and Enrique to dinner at the newly established Antoine's, where the threesome had dined on snails *bourguignon*, chicken Rochambeau, and other delectables. David enjoyed seeing de la Peña and his son brightly dressed, enjoying the luxuries of happier days.

Smiling as he remembered the delightful evening, David took the last bite of his sugar-coated doughnut, then left the small restaurant. He strode out of the large shed, brushing past old women shopping with baskets, their heads covered with brightly colored *tignons*.

As David walked back toward the hotel, he paused by a small shop whose sign read, "Madame Antoinette Darcy, *Couturiere*." David frowned for a moment, then removed his hat. Studying his reflection in the shop window, he straightened his black string cravat and buttoned a button on his brown frock coat. Then, grinning, he entered the shop.

A dark-haired young lady in a flowing green gown came forward. "*Bonjour*, M'sieur. May I help you?"

David smiled shyly at the pretty girl. Her large eyes and beautifully proportioned face reminded him of Maria. "Yes, miss. Are you Madame Darcy?"

The young girl giggled, clapping beautifully shaped hands. "Oh, no M'sieur. Mamá is at the bank this morning. I am Mam'zelle Liliane. And to whom do I have the honor of speaking?"

David bowed. "I am David Ashland, Mam'zelle." Straightening, he glanced about at the tables and shelves stacked with bolts of cloth. "I am here to purchase a gown—two gowns. Do you have any frocks already made up?"

"*Oui*, M'sieur, a few," the girl replied, her brow puckered. "But it would be far better, if you would bring your wife in to be measured and fitted."

"It's not my wife, and she—they can't come," David stammered.

Again, the French girl giggled. "Your *amor*, then, M'sieur? Two of them you say? But of course, a handsome gentleman like you must have to fight off the ladies!"

David flushed. Normally, he would be put off by such blatant curiosity, but the young girl's guileless, engaging manner was utterly charming. "The gowns are for my uncle's wife, and for another young lady, who is my uncle's ward. They're both in Texas, at Washington-on-the-Brazos."

"Ah, you are from Texas, M'sieur. *Que fascinant!* What type of gown interests you?"

"Well, the frocks are to be presents—a bit of a celebration of my first cattle drive."

Mam'zelle Liliane's eyes danced merrily. "You are a rancher, M'sieur? *Que romantique!*"

David smiled. "I have in mind something rather fancy—cost is not important. But I can't wait—we shall be leaving for Texas tomorrow."

The girl knitted her black brows. "*Oui*, M'sieur, you cannot wait. Oh, I know! Mamá carries a small line of gowns from designers in Europe. *Très coûteux*, but as you say—"

"Expensive is fine," David returned smoothly.

The French girl smiled her appreciation. "*Bien*, M'sieur. About what size are these two very fortunate young ladies?"

David appraisingly studied the pretty young girl across from him. "My uncle's wife is much your size, but perhaps two inches taller. Only there is a small problem. . . ." David gestured awkwardly to his stomach.

Mam'zelle Liliane laughed. "She is *enceinte*, M'sieur?" Noting David's nod, she continued, "As you say—a small problem. Let me think." She snapped her fingers. "Ah, I have just the thing. *Excusez moi, s'il vous plait?*"

"Of course."

David watched the excited girl flounce to the back of the shop in a rustle of green skirts, disappearing through a curtained doorway. He smiled. Intense, proud, yet charmingly girlish, Mam'zelle Liliane reminded him of Maria. Seeing the French girl made him realize he missed Maria—he had become much better acquainted with the girl over the summer months through music lessons and their shared interest in the *mexicanos*.

Mam'zelle Liliane swirled back into the room, carrying a light blue frock. "Feast your eyes on this, M'sieur Ashland." She held the gown up, the stiff petticoats swishing. "Just the thing for the little *maman*. The Empire style."

David gazed in awe at the shimmering frock Mam'zelle Liliane held up. It was of ice-blue taffeta, the exact color of Emilie's eyes. The daringly cut *décolletage* was highlighted by a white satin rose between the breasts, its petals edged with pink embroidery. The dress was tied beneath the bodice with a deep blue velvet ribbon, then billowed to the floor in full lines, a white lace overskirt veiling the delicate blue. The sleeves were fitted to the elbow, where they were tied with matching blue velvet ribbons adorned with miniature pink and white roses. Below the flowers, the sleeves flounced to the wrist, veiled with white lace to match the skirt.

"C'est magnifique?" the girl questioned, her dark eyes dancing with delight.

"Yes, *magnifique*," David agreed. "But what of the length?"

Smiling coyly, Mam'zelle Liliane held the dress up to her shoulders. The skirt trailed the floor by a good two inches.

David nodded. "Perfect. I'll take it."

"Que excellent! Mamá will be pleased!" The French girl carefully hung the dress on a rack. "Now, M'sieur, for the other young lady. Your *amour?"*

David grinned. Somehow, he couldn't bring himself to correct the delightful young lady's misconception. Or was it a misconception? "Maria reminds me very much of you. Something you would choose for yourself would look lovely on her, I would think."

"Maria? Your *amour* is Spanish?"

"Mexican."

"Ah, I see. I seem to remember we have something—*pardon*, I do remember!"

Again, the young girl swept out of the room, her face bright with excitement. Moments later, she returned with a red and black gown thrown across her arms.

323

"For the señorita!" she exclaimed. "It is from the finest *couturiere* in Spain, M'sieur." Her face animated, she held the blazing garment up to herself.

David smiled dazedly as he looked at the vision before him. The dress was of red satin, low-necked, full-skirted, with a tightly-fitted waist and a black lace overskirt. Looking up at Mam'zelle Liliane's face, he had the eerie sensation of seeing Maria's features instead. How beautiful the girl would look in the gown!

Then, studying the full skirt, David frowned. "It's a bit long, isn't it?"

The French girl shrugged off David's remark and smiled. "Ah, M'sieur, a minor adjustment, the hem. Both gowns shall be ready tomorrow—and properly packed. For you I shall burn the midnight oil."

David chuckled. "You're quite efficient, Mam'zelle Liliane."

"*Merci*, M'sieur."

Laying aside the dress, the girl walked over to a shelf and pulled down a box. Approaching David, she said, "These articles were also sent from Spain with the gown. Behold!"

The French girl placed the box on a table and removed the lid. David watched her pull out a beautiful black lace *mantilla* sewn to an ebony comb.

"Yes!" David said excitedly. "I'll take it!"

Mam'zelle Liliane giggled. "But there is more, M'sieur. The *piece de resistance*!"

Thus saying, she pulled a fan from the box, spread it out and held it coyly just beneath her chin. David noted the shimmering ebony sticks, the red lace fabric. Moving closer, he studied the satin medallion picturing a beautiful young señorita with dark hair and laughing eyes. "Maria!" he breathed.

Looking down at the medallion, Mam'zelle Liliane

arched a delicate black brow. "Ah, the satin cameo reminds you of your señorita. Your *amour est perfection, n'est ce pas, M'sieur*?"

"My love," David repeated reverently, smiling to himself. "Ah, yes. She is perfection."

Chapter Two

Emilie sat at the writing table in the library. She frowned as she sealed the last of the invitations she was sending to Washington-on-the-Brazos the next day. She stood and stretched, rubbing her aching back.

Sitting back down heavily, she began organizing the invitations in a box in front of her, reminding herself that she must ask Jacob to wait for a reply at each house tomorrow. Although the *fiesta* was two weeks away, she had much to do, and must let Doña Elena and the other *mexicano* women know how many people to expect.

Thankfully, she knew at least one couple was coming—her guests of honor. Emilie had written the Houstons weeks earlier, and only today, Margaret Houston's reply had arrived in the mail. Emilie reached across the desk and pulled the parchment envelope from its position of safety tucked between two books against the wall. As she opened the envelope, she wondered what Edgar would say if he found out the Houstons were coming. She sighed—he would no doubt be furious. Difficult though it was, she would adhere to her decision and not tell Edgar his old friend Sam was attending the *fiesta*. Then, when the Houstons arrived, she would simply have to hope her husband was enough of a gentleman not to toss them out.

For the tenth time that day, Emilie read Margaret Houston's note: "Sam and I shall be most honored to accept your kind invitation for the first. . . ." Emilie smiled as she replaced the note in the envelope and laid it on the desk before her. She couldn't wait to meet Margaret Houston—she had heard that the general's wife was a great lady, and had dramatically changed her hell-raising husband.

Yes, she was delighted the Houstons were coming—their presence would ensure the success of her *fiesta*. Hers? Actually, the *fiesta* had been Maria's idea. The girl remembered such celebrations from her days in San Antonio, and when she suggested to Emilie a night of feasting and dancing when the *vaqueros* returned, Emilie cheerfully agreed. A night of gaiety was certainly in order after the hot months of fever and tragedy. But more importantly, the affair would bring Edgar Ashland into contact with the outside world again.

Emilie's project over the summer months had been to get Edgar to go out socially again, to meet the townspeople. Unfortunately, she had failed dismally. Although he let her and Maria go to church, to candy pulls and other such activities, he steadfastly refused to leave the plantation himself.

"Well, if you won't leave, my love, I'll bring the world to you," Emilie now said firmly.

In a sense, she and Edgar had been drawn closer over the summer months. Yet there was still much unresolved between them, so many things Edgar wouldn't share. She still didn't know if he wanted her and her child for themselves, or to resurrect the past. And the mysteries of the shattered mirror and the mutilated doll still clouded their relationship.

Emilie shuddered as she remembered her frightening experience with Edgar in the nursery. When she returned to the room the next day, the doll was gone, and no further incidents had occurred. Had Edgar remained true to his word and confronted the culprit? Who had he approached? Maria? Avis Gerouard?

For several days afterward, Emilie was sure Maria must have been responsible for the episode. But then she remembered that the girl was away from home months earlier when the mirror was smashed. The incidents were equally malicious and secretive, making Emilie suspect a single perpetrator. Was Maria then innocent in both cases? Or did more than one person at Brazos Bend hate Emilie?

The night Emilie discovered the doll, she had felt so terrified and revolted, she had even accused Edgar of the misdeed. But her fears had faded over the summer months. Now, the incident seemed so far removed, she sometimes wondered if Edgar wasn't right all along—that one of the black children had left the doll there—

"Where's that woman of mine?"

Emilie started guiltily as she heard Edgar's voice in the hallway, hastily stuffing Margaret Houston's note into the box of invitations before her.

"Oh, there you are. Are you planning to stay up until the cock crows, madam?"

Emilie turned to look at her husband, who stood grinning at her from the doorway. Despite his gaiety, she could see the fatigue etched across his features— supervising the cotton harvesting was demanding much of him mentally and physically.

"I've just finished the invitations, Edgar," she told him as she stood. "Are you tired?"

Edgar grinned indolently as he crossed the room. He pulled her up into his arms and patted her derriere. "If you're asking for the night off, love, the answer is no," he said wickedly.

Emilie smiled, her fingers toying with a button on his shirt. "It is good of you to let me and Maria plan the *fiesta* for David's return," she told him.

"Anything to put a smile on your face," he replied lightly. "Ouch!" he continued in mock outrage, placing his hand on her swelling stomach. "The little beggar is starting to come between us, eh, love?"

Emilie looked up at her husband's smiling face, at the laugh lines around his eyes. He had been good to her this summer. Impulsively, she reached upward, hugged his neck tightly.

"What's this, love? Feeling afraid again?"

"No," she said. "I was just thinking."

"Yes?"

She pulled back a bit to look up at him. "It's been a good summer, Edgar. You've been—most kind to me."

"Do my ears deceive me, madam? Words of praise coming from your lips?" His words were casual, but his voice shook slightly.

"It's true," Emilie continued. "I can't complain — except when you wouldn't allow me to nurse Hallie's mother when she took the fever."

Edgar lifted her chin and looked down at her sternly. "Emilie, you carry my—our child. You have no right to take such risks."

She sighed. "You're probably right."

"How is Hallie taking her mother's death?"

Emilie looked up in surprise. Never before had Edgar shown a solicitous attitude toward the servants. "She'll be all right. She's quite great with child right now. The baby will distract her."

Edgar patted her belly. "Aye, and soon she'll have two to attend to."

"Two?" Emilie asked in surprise.

Edgar chuckled. "Don't go thinking I'll let the babe demand all your time, woman. I, too, shall be needing your services, especially during the cold winter months when the fields are barren." He leaned over and kissed her ear. "Your field will not be barren for long, love."

"Edgar!" Blushing crimson, she pushed him away.

He chuckled. But Emilie's heart thudded when he didn't follow her, instead turning to the desk and idly flipping through the invitations in the box. "Henry and Grace Alder," he read, "Pastor Heinz Fritz. Are you inviting the entire village, love?"

Emilie moved to his side. "Let's go to bed, Edgar. It's late."

But, to Emilie's horror, Edgar had already pulled out the letter from Margaret Houston, and was now staring at the return address in scowling concentration.

He held the envelope out to Emilie. "Care to explain this, love?"

Emilie sighed miserably. "It's a letter from Margaret Houston, accepting my invitation to her and her husband for the *fiesta*."

"I suspected as much." Edgar tossed the letter upon the writing desk. "And tell me, love, why did you invite the Houstons? Are you a friend of theirs?"

Emilie gestured in exasperation. "Don't bait me, Edgar—you know I'm not. But Sam Houston is a good friend of yours—or he would be, if you quit shutting him out."

Edgar's face tightened in anger. "Who I choose as my friends is my own business, Emilie. I'll not have my wife meddling in my affairs!"

"Oh, you're impossible!" she sputtered. "I hardly consider it meddling that I invite the President-Elect of the Republic and his wife to a social event at Brazos Bend. I would think that as mistress of the plantation, it would be my duty to do precisely that. Besides, how can you talk of choosing your own friends—you haven't any!"

His face was now deeply creased with scowl lines. "I have you Emilie," he said, almost sadly. "And you're all I want—or need. I just wish you felt the same way."

Emilie felt tears brimming in her eyes, for she was deeply moved by Edgar's words. Never before had he said so openly that he wanted and needed her.

Before she could reply, he asked her, "Why aren't I enough for you, Emilie?"

Her heart twisted at his words, and she drew closer, placing her hands on his strong shoulders. Their eyes met, the silent questions exchanged in their glances emphasizing the differences between them.

At last Emilie spoke, choosing her words carefully. "You *are* enough for me, Edgar—in many ways. But I can't live the rest of my life cut off from the outside world. It's not healthy for any of us, particularly now that the child is coming."

Edgar sighed in resignation and moved off to blow out the lantern. Emilie followed him, gently placing her hand on his arm. "Edgar, please, let's not go to bed angry."

Edgar extinguished the lamp and abruptly turned, pulling Emilie into his arms. "You mean I can have you to myself all the night through?'' he demanded. ''Or will your guest list—and dreams of future social conquests—be swirling in your head?''

Emilie laughed. "Oh, Edgar, don't be such a bear! Of course I shall think only of you tonight. But—but may the Houstons come to the *fiesta?*"

He was silent for a long moment in the darkness. At last he mused, "Perhaps I'll not bar them from my house—but I'm in need of some convincing.''

"Oh, thank you, Edgar!" she breathed, clutching him tightly. "As for the convincing—I shall certainly try, though I am very tired.''

Edgar chuckled, leaning over and sweeping Emilie up into his arms. "Good. You won't be able to fight me.''

"Edgar—I'm too heavy!" she protested as he carried her out of the room.

"Bosh! You're a feather!"

She languidly curled her arms around his neck as he started up the stairs. "I wouldn't, you know," she whispered in his ear.

"Wouldn't what?"

"Wouldn't fight you.''

His arms tightened about her.

Chapter Three

September 20, 1841

"Yes, Hallie, it's perfect—now!" Emilie exclaimed, clapping her hands.

"Can I get down now, Missus?" a deep voice tremulously asked.

Emilie giggled as she looked up at Jacob, who stood unsteadily perched on the ladder leaning against the wall. "Of course, Jacob! I quite forgot you in my excitement at seeing your handiwork. Do get down at once—Hallie, steady the ladder."

Hallie stepped forward and grasped the ladder, her large belly pressing against the wooden slats. As her husband stepped down, she fingered the fresh folds of yellow and white chintz now draping the window. "I like this here yeller stuff, Missus. It lets the light pass, like the Lord intended."

From where she stood across the room, Emilie smoothed down the matching counterpane on the bed. "Aye, Hallie, the entire house was so gloomy when I came," she commented, nodding toward the folds of dusty red velvet heaped on the floor, "with all the heavy fabric shrouding the windows, blocking out the light. How different the place seems now!

It's a happy house, isn't it, Hallie?"

Hallie and Jacob smiled and nodded at one another. "Yes, Missus, with you and Mister Ashland t'gether, and babes a'comin'!" Hallie agreed.

A frown pulled at the corners of Emilie's mouth. She wished she could feel as happy, as confident about her pregnancy as Hallie did about her own. Pushing her thoughts aside, she asked Jacob, "Are you happy about the coming event?"

Jacob beamed. "Yes'um." His ebony eyes turned toward the thick mounds of red velvet on the floor. "What should I do with that, Missus?"

Emilie shrugged. "I don't care."

Hallie let out a whoop of delight, and she and Jacob began gathering up their treasure.

Emilie giggled. "You could make something nice for your cabin."

"Cabin, hell, Missus!" the black girl returned gleefully. "I outfit the whole family for Christmas—'cludin' this babe when he present hisself!"

Emilie smiled as the two happy servants hurried out of the room with the velvet. She went to the mirror and took a critical look at her appearance— the gold curls piled on her head, the pink and plum calico dress with ruffled bodice. Smoothing the full skirt over the mound of her belly, she turned and took one last, appraising glance at the room. How cheerful, cozy it looked now! But would Edgar like it?

Sighing, Emilie left the room. Walking down the hall, she peeked in at other bedrooms. Everywhere was brightness—crisp new fabrics of rose and beige and mint green, new curtains, new slipcovers, new coverlets. Indeed, Brazos Bend seemed a new house—her house now.

Emilie stopped off at the nursery, admiring the oak crib Eben had just finished. The room was now ready for the babe's coming—the dresser filled with handmade garments, cheerful, lace-trimmed pillows and stuffed toys adorning the daybed and rocking chair. The fact that she and Edgar had discovered the mutilated doll there months before seemed unreal now amid all the airiness.

Leaving the nursery, Emilie strolled down the stairs, humming a happy tune she had heard Maria singing. She walked into the parlor, admiring the blue cushions thrown against the settee. Peeking into the dining room, she feasted her eyes on the new green linen seat covers on the mahogany chairs; Maria had spent many hours this summer embroidering flowers on the cloth. Emilie was very grateful for the girl's help.

Hearing hoofbeats, Emilie went back into the parlor to peer out the window. Fingering the crisp white lace curtains, she spotted Maria galloping up on a mustang pony.

Emilie swept out onto the porch just as Maria dismounted from the brown pony. The girl's face was bright and animated, her raven curls falling in radiant dishevelment about her face.

"Well, Maria, you're getting much use of the pony Don Lorenzo gave you!"

"*Sí*, Emilie," Maria replied. She handed the animal's reins to Daniel, who had just creaked out the front door. As the girls watched the bent old man lumber off towards the stable, Maria continued, "Peligra will drop her foal any day now, so I am grateful for Don Lorenzo's generosity."

Emilie stiffened slightly at Maria's words, wondering if the girl had deliberately referred to the horse Emilie so feared. Maria remained an enigma to

Emilie—at times, the girl could be surprisingly friendly, yet on other occasions, Maria was cold or even hostile.

Deciding to give the girl the benefit of the doubt, Emilie nodded approvingly at the rawhide divided skirt and matching fringed shirt Maria wore. "I see you're also enjoying the *gaucho* Doña Elena sewed for you."

"Yes, Emilie," the girl replied. "In fact, your *gaucho* is almost ready also."

"My gaucho?"

Maria frowned. "Oh, dear—I was not supposed to tell you. After seeing my outfit, Señor Edgar asked Doña Elena to make you a *gaucho* also—for after the *bebé* comes. Now I've spoiled the surprise, haven't I?"

Emilie scrutinized Maria suspiciously. Though her heart was warmed by her husband's thoughtfulness, something in Maria's tone of voice was distressing. She strongly suspected the girl took secret pleasure in revealing Edgar's planned gift. If only she could know what the girl was really thinking! "I'll look forward to receiving my *gaucho*—and to riding with my husband," she murmured. Forcing a smile, she added, "You know, Maria, you've really changed this summer."

Maria smiled, lifting her head high. "I'm among my people now."

"And aren't we your people?" Emilie asked a bit sadly.

The girl didn't answer, instead drawing a scrap of parchment from the pocket of her skirt. "Oh, I almost forgot. The list of supplies you wanted. The señoras will be making *tamales*, *menudo*, *chili*—oh, it will be *un fiesta grande* for David and the *vaqueros!*"

Emilie sighed and took the list from Maria. At least she should be grateful that being around the Mexican women had changed Maria for the better, giving the girl new confidence and enthusiasm. Emilie's brow puckered as she studied the list. "But Maria, it's all in Spanish—I can't read this! Your lesson for the morning will be translating this!"

Maria shook a finger at Emilie. "No, Emilie, Mexican food *should* be described in Spanish. Your lesson for the morning will be learning what all the words mean."

Emilie smiled, pleased by Maria's good humor. *"Touché."*

The girls turned to enter the house, but both whirled when they heard the sound of many approaching hoofbeats. Maria clapped her hands in joy as they gazed down the hillside at the band of returning *vaqueros.*

"David! David!" Maria called, waving her arm gaily.

Laughing her own excitement, Emilie studied the Mexican girl. Yes, there was no doubt about it. The glow about the face, the adoring eyes—the girl was head over heels in love with David!

The band pulled up in front of the house—an assortment of tired, dusty riders, frothy horses and grumbling oxen leading the supply cart and the tattered chuckwagon.

David dismounted and hurried towards the girls. There was a new assurance in his gait, Emilie decided, as new as his *vaquero* dress—black boots, leather *chapparreras*, matching fringed jacket.

He went straight to Maria and pulled off his *sombrero.* "Hello, *chica!*" he greeted her, leaning over to kiss her cheek.

Emilie bit her lip to keep from giggling as she

337

stared at the two of them. David's brown hands held Maria's as their eyes locked—his dark, possessive, hers dancing delightedly.

As if to reward David for the endearment in Spanish, Maria whispered, "*Bienvenido*, David."

Leaving the two to moon over one another, Emilie turned to Señor de la Peña, who was still on his horse. "Don Lorenzo, how went the trip?"

Don Lorenzo smiled at Emilie as he tipped his *sombrero*. "Quite successfully, Señora."

"Good. Won't you come in and join us for coffee?"

"*Muchísimas gracias*, Señora, but I am anxious for *mi familia*. You understand, *verdad?*"

Emilie nodded. "Of course. But you and Doña Elena must join us for dinner some evening soon."

"We would be enchanted, Señora," de la Peña replied gallantly. "Until then—*adiós.*"

"*Adiós,*" Emilie returned.

As Don Lorenzo and his company trod off, David seemed to come out of his trance. "Ah, Emilie, dear, hello!" he said sheepishly, sauntering over to plant a kiss on her forehead. "You've grown more beautiful during my absence—if that's possible!"

A black lad came forward to lead away the two horses David had tied to the post. "Just a minute, Ben. I've some packages to take off the gray, here."

The boy helped David remove two large round boxes from the horse, then led the animals off.

David grinned, his blue eyes sparkling as he approached the two girls with the presents. "Come inside, ladies. I've a surprise for the two of you."

The girls giggled and teased David as the threesome went inside. Once in the parlor, David leaned against the piano and watched the delight of the two girls as they opened the boxes.

"Oh, David!" Maria breathed. "I've never in my life owned a dress such as this." She lovingly caressed the folds of red satin and black lace. *"Está magnifica!"*

"My pleasure, dear."

"David, you must read minds," Emilie squealed incredulously as she held up the blue dress. "Maria and I were wondering what we would wear for the *fiesta*, and now we know!"

"Fiesta?" David questioned.

Emilie winked at him. "You shall see, sir," she said enigmatically. Looking down at the dress once more, she cooed, "David, it's truly the most exquisite gown I've ever seen!"

"Is it now, love?"

Emilie spun about to see Edgar standing near her. In her excitement, she hadn't heard him enter the room. He stood dressed in his black riding suit, his handsome features impassive.

Ignoring her husband's moody remark, Emilie swirled about, swishing the shimmering blue taffeta. "Edgar! Look what David brought me for the *fiesta!*"

Edgar caught her about the waist, pulled her against him. "Did he now, love?" His brow creased, he touched the satin rose on the daringly cut *décolletage.*

He released Emilie abruptly, strode to David. "Greetings, Nephew. How went the journey?"

David shook hands with Edgar. "Quite well, thanks, Uncle. I've a large draft for our accounts in Houston."

Edgar shrugged. "The money is yours, of course."

"Well, I did rather fancy using it to build my own house," David admitted shyly.

Edgar cocked a black brow. "Moving out, are you, nephew? Starting your own *rancho?* You'll need a woman to sweep that new house of yours, won't you? Emilie's taken—" he stared pointedly at his wife—"which leaves—well, Maria, what have you there?"

Smiling radiantly, Maria looked up at Edgar. One hand held the lace *mantilla*, the other the fan. "Oh, Señor Edgar, David has brought me the most beautiful gown!"

"So I see, Maria. How generous of him." Edgar turned to Emilie. "May I have a word with you in private, Mrs. Ashland? David and Maria can occupy themselves playing—the piano, or whatever."

Emilie started to protest, but Edgar firmly took her elbow, guiding her out of the room. She hurriedly gathered the blue dress against her, so she would not trip going up the stairs.

They entered the bedroom and Edgar closed the door, turning to stare at Emilie grimly. "Put it on."

"I—what?" Emilie stammered.

"The dress. I want to see you in it."

"But Edgar, it's for the *fiesta*—why are you—"

"God dammit woman, don't argue with me! Put it on!"

Emilie gulped and stared back at him in astonishment. For months he had not so much as raised his voice to her. Obviously, her luck had run out—something had spurred the violence inside him.

"Do you like the way I've done the room?" she asked, hoping to distract him.

He scowled. "Must I undress you, sweet?"

Sighing angrily, she unbuttoned the front of her dress and pulled it over her head. He watched unsmiling as she struggled with the voluminous blue frock. She finally got it down around her, then

340

began struggling with the buttons in the back. He crossed to her, turned her, buttoning the dress ungently.

As he backed off, she turned and gazed at him warily. His hard eyes swept her from head to toe, coming to rest upon her bosom. "Just as I thought. You're not wearing it to the *fiesta*."

"*What?*"

"You're beautiful in it, of course." He began to pace, his face determined. "The babe is hardly noticeable with all those layers of petticoats." He turned to her angrily. "How your breasts keep from falling out of the damn thing is beyond me! You're not going anywhere dressed like a high-priced strumpet!"

"A—a—how dare you!" Emilie cried back. "My breasts may be pushed high by the stays, but I assure you, sir, they are in no danger of—of falling out, as you so delicately put it!"

"Hah!" Edgar snorted. "It's a dead issue, my dear, since you're not wearing the frock—ever—unless in the confines of our bedroom, when you are wanting—er—prompt satisfaction!"

She stamped her foot. "What do you expect me to do? Wear a flour sack?"

He shrugged.

"I can't insult David this way!"

"Insult David!" He threw his arms wide in exasperation. "Has it occurred to you that David has insulted *me* with his—intimate gesture? Let him find his own woman!"

"You're just jealous and angry at David for bringing it!"

"Damn right, I'm jealous! And if you wish to save the dress from certain burning, keep the damn thing out of my sight!"

"But you're not being fair!"

"Fair? Is it fair to have the whole countryside gaping at my wife's bare bosom?"

"They won't gape!"

Edgar laughed bitterly. "They'll gape."

"You're one to talk after the way you gawked at me the day I came here!"

"That's different. You're my woman!"

"I wasn't then!"

"You are now!"

They stood, both with clenched fists, glowering at each other. Then Edgar strode forward and grabbed Emilie. "You are *my* wife, Emilie! I'll not have you whoring after half the countryside!"

"Whoring!" she raged, kicking him forcefully. "You monster! I'll not have you dictating to me! I'm wearing whatever I damn well please!"

Wincing, he jumped away, his face white with disbelief as he grasped his shin. "You would strike me, woman?" he hissed incredulously. "You would defy me and wear the dress?"

"Yes!"

Abruptly, he straightened. His jaw quivered, then tightened; a vein jumped in his temple. "I should beat your delicate derriere, Mrs. Ashland! But, regrettably, I must bow to your condition!"

He angrily strode toward the door.

"You're hateful!" she shot at him.

He turned, his hand gripping the doorknob. "And you're a willful, disobedient wife! Very well, madam, play the hussy! Enjoy your little *fiesta*. But if your brazenness makes it necessary for me to murder half the gentlemen guests—let it be on your conscience!"

Chapter Four

October 1, 1841

"More coffee, Señora Ashland?"

Emilie smiled up at Doña Elena, who stood at the hearth stirring an enormous bubbling kettle of spicy *menudo*. The amply proportioned Mexican woman had an elegant simplicity about her as she stood in a gathered-off-the-shoulders white dress and colorful apron, a beaded rosary hanging from her neck.

Emilie placed her white enamel cup on the board table top. "Thanks, no, Doña Elena. You have filled me up with your excellent coffee and—" she paused, staring at the tin plate in front of her, the yellow flecks from the meal she had just eaten—"what is it you call this delectable custard?"

Doña Elena wiped her large brown hands on her apron. "*Huevos reales*, Señora."

"*Huevos reales*—that I must remember." Smiling, Emilie scolded, "But it was not necessary for you to feed me, Doña Elena. Now I've breakfasted twice this morning!"

"*Un almuerzo para usted*—and one for the *bebé, verdad?*" Doña Elena asked, winking at Emilie.

The Mexican woman turned and stirred the boiling

stew with a wooden spoon. Watching her, Emilie felt bathed in serenity; someone else was in charge, responsible—a kind, loving presence. Emilie glanced about the homey room—the rows of neatly shelved canned goods, the bright printed curtains adorning the rawhide-covered windows. Once, she had lived in a farmhouse such as this, had known love, the warmth of belonging.

"You make a good home here for Don Lorenzo," Emilie remarked.

"*Gracias*, Señora," Doña Elena replied, beaming. "For five long years I pray to the *Virgen* Maria for *mi casa otra vez*. Now, Señor Davíd has made our dream come true."

Emilie stood stiffly, rubbing her back. "You and your people have worked hard for that dream, Doña Elena. That you must remember. Now, my friend, I must get home."

Emilie walked with Doña Elena out onto the breezeway. A mild fall breeze swept across the dog run; Emilie pulled her white wool shawl about the shoulders of her dark blue long-sleeved dress. She glanced at the open doors across from her—the cozy parlor, the inviting bedroom. A wave of nostalgia swept her—oh, to go climb into that bed, curl up, sleep, go back all those years—

"Behold, Señora—the cuttings, the seeds you brought me!"

Leaving her thoughts, Emilie went down the board steps to join Doña Elena in the swept yard. She breathed in the smell of the spice garden and the blooming marigolds adorning the house's exterior. Leaning over, she touched a huge sunshine-yellow blossom. "You are gifted, Doña Elena. You must tell me your secret. Our marigolds never get this large at Brazos Bend."

Doña Elena blushed and nodded toward the ground. *"Abono de pollo,"* she murmured with a coy smile.

Emilie laughed and shook her head. "You think of everything, my friend."

"Well, Señora, I sweep the yard each morning, *así—*" she smiled, shrugging.

As the two women started up the hillside, Emilie glanced approvingly at the small settlement. The lean-tos were gone, replaced by several small cabins and the larger de la Peña residence. Children, chickens and pigs were everywhere. In the distance, several *mexicanos* were busy plowing a winter garden.

Emilie turned and looked up at the clearing, where David, Maria and a half dozen *mexicanos* were preparing the grounds for the evening's feast. The sounds of hammering and happy voices filled the air.

Touching Doña Elena's arm, Emilie asked, "Do you have everything you need for tonight?"

"Sí, Señora, " the older woman replied. "The women have been working for days grinding the *masa* and rolling the *tortillas.* All will be in readiness tonight."

"Good," Emilie replied. "It will be quite a feast. Several of the ladies from town are also bringing dishes." Emilie grimaced, rubbing her lower back. "Doña Elena, thanks again for your hospitality. I'm going to get David to take me back, now."

Doña Elena laid a brown hand on Emilie's arm. *"Sí,* Señora, *lo comprendo.* The *bebé* lies heavily on your belly, *verdad?"*

Just then, Maria came rushing down the hillside, her ebony curls flying in the breeze, the fringe of her rawhide *gaucho* flapping behind her. "Hello, Doña Elena—Emilie!"

Emilie smiled as the girl stopped next to them. She had never seen Maria happier—her cheeks were pink, her green eyes sparkling.

"Doña Elena, I cannot be still this morning!" the Mexican girl gasped. "*Esta noche* will be *un fiesta grande, verdad?*"

Doña Elena wrapped a brown arm around Maria's waist. "Calm yourself, *chica*, or you will be *en su cama* before nightfall. *Vamos*, I will get you some coffee."

Emilie bid Doña Elena and Maria farewell. Watching the two walk off arm in arm, Emilie thought they looked much like mother and daughter. Continuing up the hillside, she breathed deeply of the fall-scented air. The day was mild, pleasant, and the night would undoubtedly be cool, a beautiful evening for merriment.

How much more beautiful it would be were she and Edgar getting along, she mused sadly. He had been cold to her ever since David brought her the dress.

Emilie frowned pensively as she approached the clearing. Her husband was now an aloof, frightening stranger. During the summer months, when they were so close physically, the memories of his previous violence had evaporated. But now that they were no longer making love, the old fears crept back.

"Emilie, doesn't it look grand?" David called down to her.

Emilie looked up at David, who stood perched on top of a ladder leaning against a tall oak. "There," he said, placing a brightly colored lantern on a nail. He deposited his hammer in his apron and carefully climbed down.

As he descended, Emilie glanced about the clearing. There were long board tables under the trees, and in the center the grass had been pulled, the ground swept for dancing.

"You look tired, dear—ready to go home?" David asked.

"Yes, thanks. Everything seems in readiness here."

"Agreed," David grinned. "It will be quite some celebration. Most everyone from town is coming, but the real *coup de grace* was your getting the Houstons to come. It was worth taking Uncle's grumbling about it for weeks, wasn't it, dear?"

Emilie laughed dryly. "Aye. I think your uncle fears Sam Houston may persuade him to get involved in politics again."

David laid his tool-filled apron on a board table. "All to the good if he does, dear." He turned, cupped his hands about his mouth as he shouted, "Enrique, Jorge, *hasta luego!*"

In the distance, the two *mexicanos* turning beef on a spit waved their farewells as David led Emilie down the hillside.

Riding home in the buggy, Emilie studied David through the corner of her eye. How he had grown up over the summer months! He had the assurance of a man, his shoulders squared, his head held high. Now, as he turned to smile at her in recognition of her perusal, there was none of the old tenuousness or flushing hesitation. The deep blue eyes gazing at her from beneath the brim of the *sombrero* were the probing eyes of a man. Surprisingly, Emilie felt her face heating. She turned away. Quite a role reversal—David making *her* blush!

Presently, as they stopped in front of the house, Emilie was shocked to see an elegant black carriage in the driveway. "Seems we have guests," David remarked casually as he helped her down.

Emilie smoothed her dress and hair nervously as they entered the house. They walked into the drawing room, where Edgar and a couple were seated.

Edgar stood. "Ah, Emilie, David. Come meet our *guests*," he instructed, smiling wryly.

Emilie turned, swallowing a gasp as she stared at the big man who now stood next to her husband. He was very tall, exceeding her husband's height by an inch or two. She was immediately captured by the piercing, eagle-like eyes, deeply recessed beneath bushy brows. The nose and face were broad, the mouth firm and wide beneath the graying mustache.

The man's clothing was as fascinating as his face. He wore a black silk velvet, gold-trimmed suit. His cravat was of silver and black taffeta, tucked into a crimson waistcoat. He held in his hand a broad-rimmed Panama hat decorated with a flowing plume.

"Sam, Margaret, meet my wife Emilie and my nephew David," Edgar said. "Emilie, David, Sam and Margaret Houston."

Why, of course! Emilie told herself. Who else could this towering man be but the famous General Houston?

Emilie stepped forward, extending her hand, which Sam Houston shook firmly. "Ah, my dear Mrs. Ashland, a vision you are! I would be instantly smitten had my dear Esperanza not already stolen my heart!"

Emilie followed Houston's adoring gaze to the settee, where Margaret Houston sat smiling back at him. Emilie hadn't even noticed Houston's wife—the room seemed filled with the dominating presence of the General.

Emilie rushed to sit by Houston's wife. "Mrs. Houston—welcome," she said graciously, extending her hand.

Shaking Emilie's hand, Margaret Houston smiled, a peaceful smile which lit her thoughtful violet eyes. "Do call me Margaret, dear."

"And you must call me Emilie," Emilie replied, studying Margaret.

Mrs. Houston was a beautiful woman, Emilie decided. She was about Emilie's age, and possessed the dignity and grace of a great lady. She was dressed in a lavender silk dress that perfectly complemented her soulful violet eyes. Emilie knew at once that she would like this lady.

"Esperanza," the General called from across the room.

"Yes, Mr. Houston?" Margaret replied.

"I'll be having a word with Edgar in private, if you ladies will excuse us?" Houston winked at Emilie.

"Of course, General," Emilie returned.

As the general followed Edgar out of the room, Emilie decided he must be in his early fifties, at least twenty-five years older than his bride. Yet they seemed a well-matched pair, his commanding energy balanced by her radiant tranquility.

David excused himself to continue preparations for the *fiesta*, and Emilie returned her attention to Margaret Houston. "Your husband is a very dynamic man, Margaret. It's no wonder he has been reelected to the Presidency. By the way—congratulations."

"Thank you, Emilie. It's been an exciting two months. After Sam won the election, we were entertained royally by the citizens of Washington County. And we've been gadding about quite a bit, what with Sam selecting his cabinet. I'm really longing to return to Cedar Point."

"Cedar Point?"

"Sam has built me a home there. We'll be summering there from now on." Margaret looked shyly at her lap. "Sam's hoping my health will be improved. I was constantly ill in Houston."

"Houston? I lived there until last spring. Funny we never met."

"Oh, my dear, I was ailing all last winter and spring. The fever, you know."

"Yes, I know," Emilie replied sadly. "My grandmother died of the fever right before we—I left the city."

Margaret Houston laid a delicately boned hand on Emilie's arm and smiled sympathetically. "I'm so sorry. You're fortunate to be married to Mr. Ashland and living further inland. There are epidemic deaths along the coastline and bayous each year. Mr. Houston's hoping that—with my improved health—we'll soon be expecting a family of our own, as you and Mr. Ashland are." Margaret beamed as she went on happily, "My dear, you must be ecstatic! When is the little angel expected?"

"Well, I spoke with the doctor the last time I was in Washington-on-the-Brazos. He said the first of the year." Emilie met the kind gaze of her new friend, knowing instinctively that she could trust this fine lady. "It frightens me a little," she admitted.

"My dear, I'm sure that's perfectly normal with the first wee one. But you'll see. You're going to have a perfectly normal, healthy baby and a delighted husband!"

Emilie considered Margaret Houston's words. Would Edgar indeed be happy, would they be drawn closer after the babe's birth?

Avis Gerouard walked in, carrying a silver tea service. "Although you didn't call for me, Madame,

I thought refreshments in order," she said pointedly. "Do you wish me to serve?"

Emilie bit back a frown of irritation. Efficient Mrs. Gerouard—she had compensated for Emilie's excited negligence! "Thanks, no, Mrs. Gerouard. You may leave the tray on the tea table. *I* will serve."

After Avis swept out of the room, Margaret astonished Emilie by giggling. "My dear, you rather dislike that woman, don't you?"

Emilie wrinkled her nose and smiled back. "Oh, she's a witch—always skulking about, dressed in black. The woman's a walking funeral!"

Margaret laughed. "You've got spunk, Emilie. I do believe we shall be the best of friends."

Emilie smiled warmly as she poured Margaret a cup of tea. "Aye, the very best," she agreed solemnly. "By the way, Margaret, that name the General calls you—'Esperanza.' What does it mean?"

Her violet eyes serene, Margaret replied, "It's Spanish for 'the one I have waited for.' "

"How romantic," Emilie breathed, sighing wistfully. " 'The one I have waited for.' "

"Were you expecting us, Edgar?" Sam Houston asked.

The two men stood facing each other in the library.

"As you know, my wife invited you," Edgar replied tensely. "I was rather irritated when I found your reply in the post."

"Irritated?" Houston questioned confusedly.

"Irritated at my wife, not you," Edgar put in quickly. "She invited you without consulting me."

Sam Houston waved Edgar off. "Fiddlesticks,

man. How can you be angered with that vision of loveliness I just had the pleasure of meeting?"

Edgar laughed ruefully. "That vision of loveliness, as you call her, is a little hellcat." Edgar gestured to a chair. "Take a seat, Sam. Brandy?"

Sam Houston folded himself into a large Jacobean wing chair. "Thanks, no, Edgar."

Edgar raised a black brow. "Not drinking, Sam?"

Houston pulled a hartshorn vial from his breast pocket. "I've only my bitters to comfort me now." Taking a swig, he grimaced. "I asked that housekeeper of yours to fetch me some orange peel. Makes it a bit easier on the palate."

Edgar sat down in the chair across from Houston and sipped his brandy, a smile of curiosity tugging at his lips. "Why are you drinking that poison, man?"

Sam returned Edgar's gaze, his eyes bright with sincerity. "Oh, but I promised my Esperanza that I would give up hard spirits."

Edgar laughed deeply, slapping his knee with a large brown hand. "Good Lord, Sam, you really are smitten! I never thought I'd live to see the day that a hard-drinking man like you would give it up for a pretty girl. Why, I well remember the day you almost fell off the Yellowstone into the Brazos—"

"Enough!" Houston ordered hoarsely, holding up a large, bony hand. "What's past is past."

After knocking perfunctorily, Avis Gerouard entered the room and handed the General a china saucer containing several pieces of orange peel.

"Bless you, good woman," Houston said gratefully.

Avid nodded and left.

Houston chewed on the peel and took another swig of bitters. Edgar laughed until tears sprang to his dark eyes. "Assuaging your conscience, old friend? What is that brew you swig—half alcohol?''

Houston scowled. "Back to the matter at hand, Ashland. I take it you're not delighted to see me?''

Edgar shrugged. "If you mean would I have invited you—the answer is no.''

"But why, man? What has happened to you?''

"Nothing has happened to me,'' Edgar replied indifferently. "I simply prefer the company of my own family.''

Sighing, Sam Houston recapped the vial and replaced it in his breast pocket. "Ah, Edgar, man, pray reconsider. End this—retreat—of yours. I need you—Texas needs you.''

Edgar frowned. "Like she needed me at San Jacinto? When I helplessly watched our *noble* soldiers butcher six hundred Mexicans?'' His hand tightened on the chair arm. "Jesus, Sam, I'll never forget those piteous cries—'Me no Alamo—no Goliad!' The battle was won, Sam, won hands down, yet my own men threatened to kill me if I denied them their revenge!''

Houston nodded sympathetically. "Aye, Edgar, I, too, tried to stop the slaughter. But you must bear in mind that the Mexicans were also cruel—especially at Goliad.''

"My point exactly,'' Edgar said stiffly. "It's a cruel age—I want no part of it.''

Houston stood up in agitation. "But it's men like you who can change things!''

Edgar gulped his brandy, glowering at Houston. "Bosh!''

Throwing his arms wide in exasperation, Houston strode off to the window, composing himself as he gazed out at the plantation lawn. "Edgar, I need your help.''

"I surmised as much from the letter brought to me

by Rice.''

Houston turned. "Oh, yes, Aaron. I can't say I was surprised by your reply. That boy botches up everything. Which brings me to the position I have in mind for you. I want you to replace Aaron in Washington.''

Edgar smiled wryly. "Indeed?''

"That rascal has not advanced our cause one whit,'' Houston went on heatedly, "what with his drinking and womanizing. We need a *man,* a true *statesman,* in Washington, and who better than a former member of the House of Lords?''

"That—was then.''

"Don't refuse me entirely, man,'' Houston urged. "Think it over. Why next spring, you and that lovely wife of yours—and your wee one—could be in Washington. The capital is a lovely place in the springtime.''

"How romantic,'' Edgar replied sarcastically.

Sam Houston forcefully strode toward Edgar, looking down at him sternly. "Man, we need you. Must I get down on my knees and beg? Lamar is leaving the Republic in a desperate state. The treasury is bankrupt, with millions in worthless Redbacks flying about. That fool has the Indians on the warpath, not to mention rubbing salt into Santa Anna's wounds with that ridiculous expedition into Mexico—God only knows what has happened to those poor misguided bastards! To top it all off, the seat of government is now in Austin, right on the edge of civilization, subject to constant Indian attack. And wouldn't it be a feather in Santa Anna's cap to raid the place, capture the heads of state? I tell you, Ashland, the Republic is tottering on the brink of ruin! We must have protection, and statehood is the only answer. We need a man like you to get some action in Washington.''

Edgar shrugged, draining his brandy snifter. "A pretty speech, Houston. You always were an orator. I remain, however, unimpressed.''

Houston returned to his chair, sitting down heavily, his shoulders drooping. "Edgar, man, do you remember that time on the Yellowstone during the war? When we discussed our dream for Texas—our star of destiny?''

Edgar frowned thoughtfully. "Aye, Sam. Whiskey puts foolish ideas in a man's head.''

"Not foolish, Edgar. That dream can still be realized—with the help of men like you.''

Edgar stood and walked to the sideboard, pouring himself more brandy. "Thanks—but no thanks.''

Sam Houston sprang to his feet. "Edgar, what has happened to you? Was it the death of your wife and sons?''

Edgar gritted his teeth. "That—I prefer not to discuss.''

But Houston continued, undaunted. "Has your bride changed nothing? By the way, how did you come to be married to the girl?''

Edgar scowled. "That's none of your Goddamn business.''

Houston laughed heartily. "I see you've not lost that temper of yours, man. Always did appreciate your forthright manner.'' He started toward the door. "Well, I'd best collect Margaret and get started back to the village. We're expected for lunch.''

Edgar cocked an eyebrow. "You're not staying?''

"Oh, we'll be returning for the festivities. But we're staying with Rice's friends in Washington-on-the-Brazos, the Alders. By the way, do you mind if Aaron tags along this evening?''

Edgar glowered. "Rice and I are not on speaking terms. Aside from which, I do not like his salacious interest in my wife."

Houston laughed, clapping a broad hand on Edgar's shoulder. "From the way you were looking at that girl, I'd say you don't want anything in pants around her. But have a heart, man. Aaron is a bit down in the mouth now that I've informed him he's been demoted to chief errand boy in my coming administration. He needs cheering up."

Edgar shrugged. "Whatever you wish."

Sam paused, eyeing Edgar speculatively. "Hey, Ashland, 'tis a shame you can't inform Aaron that you're taking his place," he commented shrewdly.

Edgar smiled bitterly. "Aye, that *is* a pity."

Late that afternoon, the bedroom was silent as Edgar and Emilie dressed. Wearing only her chemise, Emilie walked to the wardrobe and opened its doors. She took out the ice blue taffeta frock and turned, smothering a gasp as she saw her husband staring at her.

Never had he looked so handsome—and never so coldly angry. He was dressed in a chocolate brown velvet suit that exactly matched his dark brown eyes. He wore a beige satin waistcoat, pleated white linen shirt and black string cravat. He stood leaning indolently against the tallboy, one shiny black boot crossed over the other.

His eyes seemed to eat holes in her flesh. "I'm asking you one last time—don't wear the dress."

Emilie did not reply. Instead, she swept the dress over her head, then looked up at him rebelliously. "Will you fasten it?"

His eyes flickered, but he said nothing.

Emilie shrugged, starting for the door. "I'll call Hallie."

He grabbed her arm. "Hell, turn around!"

Emilie spun about, but, to her surprise, instead of fastening the gown, Edgar pulled it up over her head, then tossed the rustling garment upon a chair. She whirled to face him. "What on earth—"

Edgar swept her up into his arms, his face grim. "If your aim is to market your wares to the countryside, you'll not find my response lacking!"

He carried her to the bed, a terrible resolve in his eyes. "No! No!" she cried, realizing his intent. She couldn't risk a physical struggle with him at this point! As he laid her down, she pleaded, "Edgar, please—the baby—"

"I'm not going to hurt you," he replied hoarsely, casting aside his coat and vest and unbuttoning his shirt. "But it will be my pleasure to remind you whose bed you belong in."

Emilie angrily sat up. "You're being cruel, Edgar. You know I can't risk running away or fighting you!"

"It seems I have you where I want you at last." He discarded his shirt and sat down beside her on the bed, his determined hands taking her shoulders and pulling her closer. When she stiffened, he cursed, "Damn it, Emilie, I told you I won't hurt you!"

She stared up into his dark, ruthless eyes, her own gaze bright with hurt and defiance. "The scars you leave don't show."

Curiously, his expression softened at her words, and she saw a reflection of regret in his deep brown eyes as his hand reached upward to rest upon the back of her neck. "Perhaps you're right, Emilie," he said poignantly, his eyes glazed. "Perhaps we'll destroy each other, love."

"No!" she cried. But she was too late, for he firmly pulled her forward, capturing her lips with his. He kissed her demandingly, even as his hands quickly untied her chemise.

As soon as his warm, hard chest contacted her breasts, and his hand moved boldly to her pelvis, she knew it was hopeless. They had not made love since David returned with the gowns, and her body hungered for him. It galled her deeply that he was taking her to prove a point, but it was not within her power to resist him. For in the back of her mind lurked the horrible fear that this might be the last time they ever made love. She knew she would not give in about the dress—there was too much at stake there. He had crushed her pride one time too many!

Edgar, too, seemed to sense how close they were to complete estrangement, for he made love to her with surprising gentleness, kneeling above her so as not to hurt her or the babe, riding her slowly as he clutched her breasts and kneaded the nipples.

Lying beneath him so open and vulnerable in the silky late afternoon light, Emilie was close to the emotional breaking point. Edgar did not make things easier for her—he turned her face when she would not look into his eyes, and he watched her ever reaction to his thrusting with unnerving fascination. His provocative, languorous pace finally drove her to a frenzy of passion, and she begged him to put an end to it. When he hesitated, she arched upward brazenly to feel him to the hilt, and he groaned and brought them to a quick, shattering climax, all the while intently watching her as she cried out in ecstasy, tossing her head from side to side.

Afterwards, they hung together for a long moment, gazing into each other's eyes with sorrow and resignation, knowing they must now return to the reality of their failing marriage, and that they might never again know such a bittersweet, intimate moment. . . .

At last, Edgar rolled off her. "Nothing has changed, has it?" he asked bitterly.

"Oh, God!" Emilie groaned. She felt raw inside with conflicting feelings—her love for him, her resentment of his arrogant behavior. Her wounded pride won out. "Do you think everything can be solved simply by bedding me?" she demanded fiercely. "Don't you know there's more to a marriage than that?"

In a quick, angry motion, Edgar sat up on the side of the bed, reaching for his clothes. "Yes—there's much more to a marriage—like a wife honoring her vow to obey her husband!"

"A husband is supposed to honor his wife, too, not call her a whore just because she wants to step out in public!"

He now stood by the bed, shrugging on his shirt. "To hell with you—do whatever you damn well please." He grabbed his coat and vest and headed for the door. But as he opened it, he turned to issue a final warning. "I want you to remember what happened between us just now, Emilie. Remember well—and may your memories keep you warm!"

He was gone, the door banging behind him.

Later, after Hallie helped Emilie get into her gown, she stood alone at the dressing table, thinking of what had transpired between her and Edgar. Sometimes Edgar was no better than an overgrown child! she thought bitterly. They were entertaining for the first time, yet he had to shatter her nerves with the emotional, heart-wrenching scene moments earlier!

Emilie looked in the mirror, scrutinizing her party frock carefully. True, the blue gown exposed a generous portion of her ripening breasts, the stays pushing the firm globes up tauntingly. But many of her dresses boasted a low-cut *décolletage*. Why had Edgar thrown a fit over this particular one? Simple— David had given it to her!

Of course, Edgar's jealousy did prove that he had some feeling for her. But how—as a possession, a bedmate to bear his sons? Was his opinion of her so low that he became enraged every time another man was present? Well, by God, she would not stand for it! She had done nothing to merit such a lack of faith.

She quickly ran the hairbrush through her gold tresses, then calmed a bit as she went about the delicate task of piling the curls on top of her head. She would not have Hallie's help with her coiffeur this time, since the heavily pregnant slave had looked exhausted moments earlier, and Emilie had sent the girl off for a nap. Emilie scowled as she worked, finally managing to pin the springy locks down, and securing them with a blue ribbon. Taking Grand-mother's gold and sapphire brooch from the dressing table, she looped a blue velvet ribbon through the clasp. She hung the brooch around her neck—it rested a few inches above the white satin rose in the valley between her breasts.

Emilie donned silk stockings and white satin slippers, then stood back and admired her handi-work. True, her pregnancy was concealed by the Empire lines of the gown. But it was not a strumpet staring back at her from the bevelled glass. She saw instead a grand lady—her head held high, her shoulders squared, her gown elegant, luxurious.

The mistress of Brazos Bend.

Chapter Five

October 1, 1841

Emilie took David's arm and stepped out of the
buggy. The sun was sinking in the west, casting an
amber glow in the clearing. Board tables, covered
with brightly patterned oilcloth, were lined up in a
large square beneath the trees. In the center, the bare
earth was swept and firm, readied for dancing. The
spicy, succulent smell of Mexican food drifted up the
hillside from the cabins below. To the side of the
clearing, two *mexicanos* turned the side of beef, as
they had all day.

Emilie glanced back at David, who was reaching
up to help Maria out of the buggy. He wore the
black, silver-studded jacket, *calzoneras* and *sombrero* of a Mexican *cabellero*. As he took Maria's
arm, he smiled up at her, his eyes darkening to a
midnight blue.

Seeing the object of David's attention, Emilie was
not surprised by his amorous reaction. Never had
Maria looked more stunning! Her ebony tresses
were piled high on her head, secured with the black
comb and veiled by the lace *mantilla*. Her smooth
olive skin had a pink flush of excitement, her green

eyes danced merrily. Her ripe young breasts, thrust high by the stays of the red and black gown, jiggled as she flounced out of the buggy, and Emilie heard David gasp under his breath.

Maria spread her black and red fan and waved it over her face vigorously. "Oh, David, I am burning! Surely it will be cool later, *verdad?*"

David grinned and Emilie giggled. "Surely you must be *burning* with excitement, Maria, for it's getting cool already," Emilie told the girl.

Emilie pulled her lacy shawl about her as she stepped into the clearing. "All is in readiness," she commented. She turned to David. "Any idea where your uncle is?"

David frowned. "He and Apollyon were nowhere in sight when we left." He stepped closer and patted her arm. "Don't fret yourself, dear. He'll come."

Emilie was about to respond when she heard excited voices talking in rapid Spanish. The three spun about to see a procession of Mexican ladies entering the clearing, carrying huge crocks of food covered with bright cloths.

"Doña Elena!" Maria shouted, running to throw an arm about the waist of the older woman.

"Chica!" Doña Elena returned brightly. *"Su bata es mas hermosa!"*

While Emilie watched, David and Maria helped the Mexican ladies place the dishes on the tables. The half-dozen women were similarly dressed in gathered-off-the-shoulders gowns; the bodices were white, the full skirts and sleeves of vividly patterned fabric. Several children now frolicked about the table, their dark heads bobbing in and out of the draped oilcloth.

Emilie guessed the townfolk would soon be arriving. Settlers, *Mexicanos,* assorted children—

there should be a good threescore present for the festivities. Threescore, yet she had eyes for only one, and he might not even come!

"Emilie!" Maria called out. "The men are coming! *La musica!*"

Seeing Maria's exuberant face, Emilie forgot her own worries. Don Lorenzo and a half-dozen *vaqueros* entered the clearing. Don Lorenzo wore a crimson velvet jacket and black *calzoneras*. The others were dressed in similar finery—leather *chapperreras* adorned with tassels, *sombreros* trimmed with bright, multicolored bands. "La Musica!" consisted of a young man with a violin and an older *vaquero* sporting a guitar.

As the men laughed and visited with the women, the first family from the village pulled up in an oxen-drawn wagon. Two homespun-clad children ran for the clearing, squealing gleefully. They were followed by their calico-gowned mother and their buckskin-clad father. The parents greeted Emilie and added a dish of fried chicken and a jug of corn whiskey to the delectables collecting on the tables.

The dusk deepened; more families arrived. David and two of the *vaqueros* lit the lanterns hanging from the trees. The two Mexican musicians began to play, and to the delight of everyone, Don Lorenzo led Doña Elena into the clearing, and the two performed the slow, decorous *fandango*. Soon, they were joined by other Mexican couples. The villagers showed a lively interest in the dancing, tapping their feet to the rhythm, but they did not actually mix with the *mexicanos*.

Emilie visited gaily with the guests, but inside she was filled with a deepening dread. What if Edgar did not show up at all? What greater insult could he fling upon his wife than to desert her side for such an important event? Surely he would come, she kept telling herself—surely. But the voice of rising panic inside her kept reminding her that it would be more in character for him to simply go off in a huff and not appear at all. After all, he had not stepped out in society for five long years!

Emilie was thinking of this, twisting her fingers nervously, when she saw the Houston carriage pull up. Sam alighted, wearing the same suit he had worn that morning, his palmetto hat in hand, his tufty, silver-gray hair catching the fading light. He assisted Margaret out of the carriage. She wore a pink mull gown with gathered bodice and full skirt and sleeves. Her hair was drawn back to the nape of her neck; rich auburn curls cascaded down her back.

A buggy, escorted by two riders, pulled up alongside the Houston conveyance. A bent old man, toting a fiddle, climbed down and assisted a thin, black-gowned lady. Emilie recognized Grace Alder, and decided the burly man climbing off his horse nearby was her husband.

But her attention was soon seized by the other rider, who now almost fell from his mount. The gentleman, clothed in an emerald-green frock coat and black and white striped trousers, tottered as his feet hit the ground. When he regained his balance, he pulled off a wide-brimmed hat. Emilie gasped as she recognized Aaron Rice.

Suddenly, someone grasped her from behind, pulling up the lacy shawl, which had slipped down around her shoulders. One brown hand tucked an edge of fabric between her breasts, while the other hand tightly encircled her neck and shoulders with the crocheted wool.

Shivering, Emilie turned to look up at an unsmiling Edgar.

"Well, Mrs. Ashland, shall we greet our guests?" Her husband had arrived.

"Oh, my dear, you are a vision!" Margaret Houston told Emilie.

"My thoughts about you exactly!" Emilie returned brightly. Through the corner of her eye, she watched Sam Houston clapping a broad hand on Edgar's back while the two shook hands.

"Good evening, Mrs. Ashland," a shrill voice interjected.

Emilie turned to nod at Grace Alder. "How good to see you, Mrs. Alder." She smiled curiously at the two men standing next to Grace.

"Meet Father and my husband, Henry," Grace said offhandedly.

Emilie shook hands with the grizzled "Father" and the robust Henry Alder. Seeing the whiskey jug Henry Alder held in his other hand, Emilie swallowed a giggle, remembering the day when Grace Alder told her Henry and Aaron had been up late reading the scriptures.

Aaron Rice now staggered up; Emilie suppressed a shudder as his whiskey breath engulfed her. She backed off, but he astonished her by planting a heavy hand on her shoulder. "Hello, m'dear," he said unsteadily, grinning crookedly.

Emilie spotted her husband nearby, glaring at them blackly. Trying to unobtrusively push Aaron away, she smiled nervously at her guests. Her heart thudded as she watched Edgar take a quick step forward. But Sam Houston intervened, striding quickly to Aaron. He grabbed the younger man by the coat and said gruffly, "There, boy, take your hands off Ashland's wife before he makes *menudo* of you." Propelling Aaron toward the clearing, he ordered, "Go find one of the *señoras* to fetch you some strong coffee, and mind your manners or I'll send you home!"

For a moment, Aaron glowered at the towering Houston. Then he grumbled sheepishly, "Yes, sir," and started toward the clearing.

"A harmless enough lad when kept in his place," Houston commented. He winked at Margaret. "Come, *Esperanza*. Shall we dance?"

"I see you have Mexican music," Grace Alder sniffed disdainfully, staring at Emilie. "Didn't no one tell you Father fiddles and Henry calls all the dances here'bouts?"

Emilie was about to reply, but Houston again intervened. "Ah, Gracie, don't go getting in a snit. Let poor Henry wet his whistle a while first, else you'll have him calling till he's hoarse. Besides, I've a hankering to try that fancy Mexican *fandango*—" he smiled at Margaret—"haven't you, my dear?"

"Certainly, Mr. Houston," Margaret replied. She turned to Emilie. "We've food in the carriage. Shall we set it out, dear?"

Emilie nodded, smiling. "Aye. How thoughtful of you. We'll eat once everyone has arrived."

The group collected the covered dishes and entered the clearing. After the food was deposited, Sam and Margaret Houston joined the dancers, imitating their deliberate, graceful movements. Following the Houstons' lead, other couples from the village entered the clearing. As the whiskey began to flow, the whites and *mexicanos* intermingled, swirling about and laughing.

Emilie stood at the edge of the clearing as night set in. So far, she had declined all dancing partners. She was waiting—perhaps foolishly—for Edgar to come forward and ask her to dance. Her husband stood

366

apart from the others, leaning against a tree in the shadows, smoking a cheroot. Although she couldn't see his eyes, she felt his stare, especially moments earlier, when Aaron Rice asked her to dance. Thankfully, Aaron had taken Houston's advice and sobered up, and had politely accepted her refusal.

Emilie sighed and turned her attention to the couples dancing. She smiled as she watched David and Maria swirl about. Their cheeks flushed with excitement, their eyes bright and alive, they seemed the perfect couple—and totally in love. Oh, if only she and Edgar could now be so happily joined! she mused wistfully.

Suddenly, the twosome she watched became a threesome; Edgar tapped David on the shoulder. As David stepped aside, Edgar bowed deeply to Maria, smiling devilishly. Emilie heard Maria's name drift across on the night breeze in her husband's deep, caressing voice. Watching Edgar and Maria join hands and clasp arms to the elbow, Emilie fumed inside. How dare he! She had turned down every man present, yet he had the gall to ask another to dance!

David walked up, grinning sheepishly. "Well, it's nice to see Uncle—participating."

Emilie gritted her teeth and turned to David, grasping his arm. "Dance with me, David!"

A look of surprise crossed David's features. Then he recovered, grinning, leading her into the clearing. As they moved, the shawl slipped down about her shoulders; David's face reddened, then he hastily removed his gaze from her upthrust breasts. Emilie swept about to the scintillating music, flirting with David gaily. But, unfortunately, Edgar seemed to take no notice of them as he led Maria about the clearing.

When the dance ended, Doña Elena came forward and spoke to Edgar. Edgar clapped his hands to gain everyone's attention, then announced, "Ladies and gentlemen, the feast awaits."

A roar of appreciation swelled from the crowd, and all present fell into line to be served. The guests were served plates heaped with *tamales, menudo,* chicken, barbecued beef, beans, and other delectables. They then took seat upon the numerous rawhide-bottomed chairs which had been rounded up and lined up about the tables. The Mexican musicians strolled about, playing a soothing ballad as everyone ate.

Sam and Margaret Houston insisted that Emilie sit between them. Edgar shocked Emilie by sitting down next to Margaret and carrying on a lively conversation with the pretty general's wife. Emilie seethed inside. While she was not angry with Margaret, she was furious at Edgar for ignoring her so shabbily.

Watching Emilie pick at her food, Sam Houston leaned over and whispered, "Things are not well between you and Ashland, eh, young lady?"

"Aye, things are not well," Emilie repeated sadly.

Houston affectionately patted Emilie on the back. "Things will improve with the babe's coming—you'll see," he said with fatherly concern. "When he's bouncing the proof of your devotion on his knee, he'll soften a bit. Right now, he's just crazy jealous to kill anything in pants that has eyes for you. It's obvious the man's totally smitten with love for you."

Emilie's jaw dropped. "Oh, I think not, General!"

Sam Houston laughed heartily. "But of course you can't see it, Emilie," he whispered confidentially. "You're blind in love with him also!"

Emilie's face fell. "Is it so obvious?"

Sam Houston leaned forward, chuckling. "Tell him you love him, girl—then watch the transformation."

Emilie opened her mouth to reply, but stopped when she heard Edgar's deep laughter and Margaret Houston's gay retort. Oh, how her heart hungered for him—and how her hands longed to wring his neck!

Once everyone had dined, the guests moved back to the edge of the clearing, patting full bellies. Visiting with Margaret, Emilie studied Maria through the corner of her eye. The girl was talking animatedly with the Mexican musicians. Suddenly, Maria dashed into the clearing in a whirl of bright skirts, and the grinning musicians began playing a soulful Spanish melody.

A hush fell over the crowd as the guests turned to watch Maria dance rhythmically. She swayed to the beat, swirling about the clearing, the red lace fan veiling her bright, excited face. The musicians increased their tempo and the music swelled. Maria stamped her feet and began moving her arms, brandishing the fan provocatively, her bright eyes flashing.

All present watched the beautiful young woman in stunned silence, as her red and black skirts flew about. Then a cheer went up as she pulled the *mantilla* from her head, and her ebony tresses fell about her face and shoulders in radiant dishevelment.

The music quickened and her movements grew frantic. She had the entire audience enthralled, but her eyes told everyone that she was dancing for one man alone—David Ashland.

Emilie studied David and smiled. His face was filled with wonder—he was watching Maria as if he had never seen her before. He moved forward through the crowd like a man in a trance, his eyes captivated by the beautiful young *señorita*.

The music stopped; applause and cheers swelled from the crowd. Maria stood with her arms upraised, her face flushed; she panted for air, her chest heaving. The night breeze rippled her skirts and played with the black tresses falling about her face and shoulders.

The gathering hushed as David Ashland stepped into the clearing, his eyes the dazed eyes of a sleep-walker. Seeing him, Maria smiled and held out her hand. David hurried to her side; the two stood staring at each other, transfixed.

It was then that the crowd began to roar. They whooped, they hollered, they stamped, they clapped. "Hey, boy, shall we be fetching the parson this fine eve?" Sam Houston yelled.

The two turned, staring at the crowd like a couple of frightened deer. Then David leaned over and whispered something in Maria's ear. Laughing, their hands clasped, the two dashed out of the clearing.

The guests went crazy, cheering as the two darted into the woods. Then someone shouted, "Attention, friends! Attention!"

All present turned to look at General Houston, who stood in the clearing, one arm around the Mexican violinist, the other around the guitarist. "Folks, let's show these extraordinary musicians our appreciation!"

Cheers and applause roared from the crowd. Finally, Houston held up his hand for silence. "Ladies and gentlemen, let's let these boys rest and get some well-deserved vittles. Now that our generous Mexican *compadres* have taught us their courtly *fandango,* let's show them how Texans dance. Henry Alder, put down that jug and get out here!''

Amid cheers and laughter, a flushed Henry Alder entered the clearing, followed by ''Father'' toting the fiddle. Once the crowd calmed, Henry called, ''Ladies and gentlemen, choose your partners and we'll do-se-do!''

All present dashed excitedly for partners. While Henry called, ''I'm Going Away to Texas,'' the guests frolicked Texan-style, dancing and singing the chorus, ''Oh dear me, Oh dear me!''

But a few feet away, the *fiesta* might not have existed; two young people had eyes only for each other.

''How did you learn that fancy Spanish dancing, Maria?'' David asked wonderingly.

A smile played on Maria's lips. The two stood a few feet from the merriment, concealed from the others by trees, a pool of light pouring upon them from the lantern in the branches above.

''When I was young, my father sometimes played his guitar at the *cantinas,''* Maria explained. ''Sometimes, I would dance and collect the money thrown by the *cabelleros.''* She frowned.

David took her hand. ''But that is all over, now, dear,'' he said soothingly. ''You never have to do that—dance like that—again.''

She looked up quickly, wistfully. ''You did not like my dancing, David?''

His fingers trembled as he held hers; his eyes darkened as he stared down at her eager, expressive face. ''Oh, God, Maria, I loved it!'' he whispered in a quavering voice. ''But I'd prefer you dance for me alone, my darling. Christ, you're beautiful!''

With those words he pulled her into his arms. His limbs shook as he pressed her warm softness against him. Their hungry lips met, melded, and deep sighs rose simultaneously from their throats. She wrapped her arms around his neck and stood on tiptoe to press herself against him.

Suddenly, he stiffened, gently pushing her away. "Maria—I've forgotten myself," he said hoarsely, stumbling off toward the clearing.

Maria stamped her foot, feeling rejected, bewildered. *"Madre de dios!* Damn! Did my lips burn holes in his?"

She smoothed down her coiffeur, then stomped toward the dancers.

From her position across the clearing, Emilie watched David and Maria return separately. He looked stunned, she furious. But Maria had no sooner gotten into the clearing when she was grabbed by Edgar, who whirled her into the strains of "Liza Jane."

Watching the two of them, Emilie fumed. At first Maria followed Edgar methodically, petulantly, but soon she responded to his gaiety, smiling, flirting with him with her green eyes.

"Wish to dance, dear?" David asked from beside her.

Emilie jumped; she had been so preoccupied watching her husband, she hadn't even noticed David's approach.

"Why, of course, sir!" she responded perkily, taking his arm.

Emilie laughed bravely as they whirled through the steps. The Mexicans and the Texans now mingled freely, and sang together to Henry Alder's direction as they square-danced.

All I want in this creation,
Pretty little wife on a big plantation.

But as the strains of "Black-Eyed Susie" died and the dancers began to "Shoot the Buffalo," Emilie found herself quite breathless, and begged David to stroll with her for some air. She grabbed her shawl from a chair and they left the clearing.

"Are you all right, dear—I mean, the babe and all?" David asked solicitously, walking with her in the semi-darkness close to the merriment.

"Oh, I'm fine, and the babe's kicking up a healthy ruckus," Emilie replied. She shivered, wrapped her shawl tightly about her shoulders and neck. "But I don't know how much more of your uncle's coldness I can take," she finished sadly.

David sighed, but did not reply. They strolled, listening to night sounds—locusts, owls, crickets, heard to the accompaniment of the loud revelry nearby.

"He didn't want me to wear the dress," Emilie admitted, after a while. She stopped, gazed up at David earnestly. "Was I so wrong?" she asked, pulling the shawl back against her shoulders. "It is a lovely dress, is it not? Tell me—do I look the strumpet?"

"Of course not," David assured her quickly. "Your dress is no more *risqué* than that of any other lady here."

"If I had known he would react this horribly, I wouldn't have worn the blasted thing," she went on irritably. "But sometimes Edgar tries to control me too much!"

David grinned sheepishly, his face outlined in moonlight. "Well, in a way, I see his point. As a matter of fact, I was just telling Maria that I prefer she dance for me alone."

Emilie eyed David with fresh interest. "Ah, Maria dances beautifully, does she not? Do you think that you and she might—well someday—"

"Perhaps," David said hoarsely, staring at his boots.

Emilie gestured toward the clearing. "And what do you think of your uncle flirting with her the entire evening?"

David shrugged. "Uncle means nothing by it. Maria is like a daughter to him."

"Are you sure?" Emilie asked with disbelief.

"I'm certain. He's in love with you."

Emilie gulped, her heart fluttering. "Did he tell you that?"

"He didn't have to."

"Oh, David, I wish I could believe that! I wish—oh, David, I love him so!"

Suddenly, inexplicably, she found herself in his arms, tears streaming down her face.

"There, there," David soothed awkwardly, patting her hair.

"I don't know what to do, David. Please, tell me what to do," she pleaded, between sobs.

"*Sí*, David! By all means, tell her what to do!"

At the sound of Maria's sarcastic voice, the two sprang apart, like lovers caught in the act. They whirled to discover the Mexican girl standing a few feet away from them, her eyes shooting daggers.

"Señor Edgar sent me to find you," Maria continued in a grating tone. "Señora Houston is going to sing for us. If you two are—finished—join us, *por favor*."

Tilting her head defiantly, Maria swept away from them in a swirl of red skirts and ebony curls. Exchanging sympathetic glances, David and Emilie followed.

As Emilie entered the clearing, a brown hand grabbed her arm, and she was pulled back against a tree in the shadows. "Staying warm, love?" Edgar asked nastily, his dark eyes fastened upon her bosom.

"Let go of me!" Emilie demanded, trying to slip away.

"I take it my services this afternoon left you still lusting, Emilie?" he continued in a dangerous, hoarse voice.

"Stop it! Stop it!" she hissed back. "People will hear—"

"Let them hear!" he roared. "Let them know that you're *my* property, mine alone!"

"No! You don't own—"

Pulling her close, he kissed her, silencing her protests. His kiss was fierce, stealing the breath from her lungs, his mouth tasting heavily of liquor and passion. Moments later, when he pulled back slightly to stare down at her in the darkness, she could only pant to catch her breath.

"Emilie, come home with me," he whispered.

"Damn you, Edgar!" she cried back, clenching her fists. "Have you lost your mind? You know I can't simply leave our guests! You're drunk and making no sense! Let me go!"

Surprisingly, he moved off, his eyes unreadable in the near-darkness. "So be it, Emilie. But remember—I'll have no man's desserts!" He turned on his heel and left her.

His words so enraged Emilie, she yanked off her shawl and tossed it upon the ground. She reentered the clearing, her head held high. Thankfully, no one seemed to have taken note of her altercation with Edgar so close to the festivities. To the contrary, all eyes were now fastened upon Margaret Houston.

The pretty general's wife was seated on a rawhide-bottomed chair in the center of the clearing, and surrounded by a horde of admirers, including her towering husband. Moving closer, Emilie caught the lilting strains of "Green Grows the Laurel." Listening, Emilie tried to calm herself. Margaret had eyes only for the general as she strummed her guitar and sang in her sweet, lyrical voice.

> Green grows the laurel, all sparkling with dew,
> I'm lonely, my darling, since parting from you,
> But by the next meeting I hope to prove true,
> And change the green laurel for the red, white and blue.

The General winked at his wife, utter devotion lighting his fine, eagle-like eyes.

Margaret then launched into a livelier tune, "I'm Bound to Follow the Longhorn Cows." The crowd laughed and clapped in rhythm, joining in on the chorus. When Margaret started to rise, concluding the performance, the crowd roared their appreciation, demanding an encore.

Margaret smiled serenely and agreed. "For our Mexican friends," she announced. *"El Amor Que te Tenía."*

Margaret strummed the chord, then began the haunting Spanish ballad. Nearby, David leaned forward and asked Maria, "What do the words mean?"

For a moment, Maria stared moodily into space, ignoring David. Then she turned, looked contemptuously at Emilie as she translated Margaret Houston's words.

> The love I had for you, my dear,

Hanging from a branch remained.
A strong whirlwind came along, my dear,
And branch and love took away.

Margaret paused between verses, strumming a chord as she called out, "Maria! Your guardian tells me you've a beautiful voice. Pray, join me!"

Emilie heaved a sigh of relief as Maria, after a moment's hesitation, walked off to join Margaret.

As the lovely duet concluded, Sam Houston expostulated, "Beautiful, Esperanza—Señorita Maria!"

Amid the cheers of the crowd, Sam Houston helped his wife to her feet. "Now that Father and Henry have been refreshed, let's cut a caper, folks!" Houston shouted.

The settlers hurried to fetch partners as Henry and Father again took the stage. David pulled Maria into the clearing, and Aaron Rice sauntered up to bow in front of Emilie.

"May I have the honor, Mrs. Ashland?" he asked silkily.

Emilie eyed him warily. He looked sober enough as he smiled at her, flashing even white teeth. Glancing about for her husband, she spotted him joking with one of the villagers as he hefted a whiskey jug.

She looked back at Aaron. Why not! She had already refused the man thrice this evening. Besides, Edgar had demonstrated that his opinion of her could fall no lower.

She smiled and took Aaron Rice's arm. "Certainly, sir."

They whirled to "Buffalo Gals" and "Skip to my Lou." But during the final strains of "The Gal I Left Behind Me," Aaron astonished Emilie by pulling her through a gap between the tables out into the woods.

"What are you doing?" she hissed, trying to shake off his grasp.

But his fingers held her wrist in an iron grip.

"There, lady, don't be frightened," he said in a low, soothing voice. "I merely want to talk with you."

"Why can't we talk in the clearing?" she demanded, trying to shake off his fingers.

Abruptly, he released her. "In case you hadn't noticed, lady, that husband of yours was looking murder at us while we danced."

"I noticed," she returned dryly. "He'll no doubt be storming after us at any moment."

Aaron grinned. "Not to worry, lady. I waited until his back was turned to whisk you off to safety."

Despite herself, Emilie giggled. "He can act like a great, enraged boar at times," she admitted.

Emilie watched a flash of silver as Aaron drew a flask from his breast pocket and put it to his lips, taking a deep draught before he returned the container to his frock coat.

Emily cleared her throat nervously. "Did you get your sister's portrait to your parents?"

Aaron looked at her blankly.

"Your sister's portrait—did you get it home?" she repeated, twisting her fingers.

Again, the strange, vacant look. "Livvie—Livvie's portrait," he said, after a moment. He took a step closer to her. "You know, you look God-awful like Livvie, my dear."

He slurred his "L" each time he said "Livvie," and Emilie began to wonder uneasily if he had imbibed more than she thought during the evening. "Were your parents pleased?" she asked, her voice rising.

He did not reply, but stood gazing down at her, an eerie, almost fanatic gleam in his gaze. For a frightening moment, Emilie thought he must be mad—he seemed to stare at her with the green eyes of a demon.

Cautiously, she backed away from him.

Suddenly, he laughed, his features clearing. "There, now, don't scurry off like a scared rabbit. You've simply reminded me of some—painful memories. Do stay, Mrs. Ashland. As I said, I've a matter to discuss with you."

Emilie frowned, hesitating. "Very well," she said, at last. "But please be brief."

Nodding, he took a step closer, gazed at her longingly.

"Well, sir?" she snapped irritably.

"Jesus, you're a pretty thing," he breathed.

"Sir, you forget yourself," Emilie retorted acidly. "What have my looks to do with any of this?"

"Everything, my dear," he returned smoothly. "Ashland treats you rather shabbily, doesn't he?"

"That's hardly your concern, sir!" Emilie retorted, whirling about to leave him.

But again he caught her wrist. "He treats you shabbily, doesn't he?" he reiterated, a tense edge in his voice.

"Let go of my arm!" she shot back indignantly, struggling to free herself, panic welling up in her chest.

He held her in tow, ignoring her flailing arms. "I'll wager he beats you—or worse!" he continued in an excited whisper. "Come closer, I will see if you have scars, my dear."

He pulled her toward him and she pushed against his chest, horror spreading across her features. "You're drunk—mad!" she gasped.

He laughed, a wicked laugh. "Mad with love for you, lady," he whispered hoarsely. "Tell that bastard Ashland to go to hell and come away with me—now! I'll treat you right, I promise."

She struggled wildly, but he merely laughed again. "Come closer, lady, and spread your legs for a real man!"

She cried out as he yanked her forcefully against him. Suddenly, he stiffened, his hand roughly grabbing her belly. "What's this—a brat?" he growled. Then he laughed the awful, evil laugh again. "No matter. We'll ship the little bastard back to Ashland."

Emilie started to scream, but Aaron smothered her mouth with his own. His mouth had the foul taste of whiskey, and a wave of nausea swept her. For a horrible moment she was sure she was going to faint; her arms fell limply at her sides. She heard a low chuckle in Aaron's throat as he mistook her lassitude for a response. One of his hands gripped her buttocks, squeezing painfully, while the other fumbled with her breasts.

Suddenly, Aaron was yanked violently from her, went flying into the underbrush. "Enough, by God!" Edgar roared.

Emilie would have screamed had she not felt so weak as she tottered and stared at her enraged husband. Even in the dim light, she could see the whiteness of fury spreading across his features.

Then his eyes darted to her breasts, turning black as coals. "Cover yourself, woman!"

Emilie gasped in horror as she looked down to see her breasts freed from the cover of her gown. She covered herself hurriedly, while the corner of her eye caught Aaron struggling up from the bushes where Edgar had thrown him.

She heard her husband yell, "Rice, prepare to die!"

Emilie looked up wildly, then screamed as she saw Aaron Rice draw a wicked-looking Bowie knife from a sheath concealed beneath his frock coat. Ignoring Emilie's cry, Edgar eyed the knife soberly. "Are you such a coward, Rice, that you don't trust your own fists?" he inquired coldly.

Aaron Rice laughed bitterly, his eyes gleaming with bloodlust. "For years I've waited for this opportunity, Ashland," he hissed excitedly. "Now I'm going to cram this knife up your ass for killing Livvie!"

Edgar's features blackened. "You Goddamn bastard!" he thundered, lunging for Aaron.

"No, Edgar! He'll kill you!" Emilie shrieked.

But it was too late. Edgar grabbed for the knife and Emilie screamed, sobbing hysterically as she saw blood spurting from Edgar's wrist. But if Edgar felt any pain, he did not show it as his blood-covered hand closed over Aaron's on the knife handle. Suddenly, he lunged powerfully against Aaron, and the next thing Emilie knew, Aaron was down, screaming in agony, the knife pinning him to the ground through his shoulder.

"What the hell is going on?" Sam Houston shouted incredulously.

Houston and several of the men hurried up to stare at the scene aghast. The general strode purposefully to Edgar. "Well, Ashland?"

Looking at Houston, Edgar swayed. "Rice—my wife," he said woodenly, clutching his wrist.

Houston looked from Edgar to Emilie's tear-streaked face. He then strode over to Aaron, kneeled beside the flailing, moaning man. "Hang on, boy. This is going to hurt like hell."

Houston pulled the knife from Aaron's shoulder. Blood spurting from his wound, Aaron let out a harrowing scream, then passed out.

Houston stood, pointed the blood-stained knife toward Edgar. "Yours?"

"His," Edgar returned hoarsely.

Houston tossed the knife into the bushes. "Makes it rather open and shut," he commented dryly. He turned to Henry Alder. "Henry, you'd best send someone to ride for the doctor, then fetch Aaron on home. There, David, catch your uncle before he faints."

Emilie gasped as she watched David grab Edgar's good arm. Her husband's face was white, drawn, his blood flowing to the ground in a steady stream.

Margaret Houston and Maria rushed up. Taking in the scene quickly, Margaret hurriedly ripped strips of linen from her petticoat. She handed a strip to Maria, nodding toward Edgar; then she kneeled by Aaron, binding his shoulder.

Emilie watched as Maria bandaged Edgar's wrist, praying that her husband would not die. She ached to go to him, but her body was swept by waves of shock and nausea, and her feet seemed rooted to the spot.

She watched dazedly as Sam Houston and Henry Alder gently placed the limp Aaron into the Houston carriage. "Margaret, be a dear and go dispatch the crowd," Houston called over his shoulder.

Margaret hurried off toward the clearing, where several couples were still dancing to the accompaniment of the lone fiddler.

Emilie shivered as a firm arm clasped her about the shoulders. She looked up into the compassionate eyes of General Sam Houston. "Don't worry, my dear," he soothed. "Ashland will live."

But she could only stare at him stupidly, tears streaming down her face.

Then she saw Edgar stagger by, his face ghostly white as David supported him on one side, Maria on the other. Her heart seemed to break inside her; she stepped forward.

"Let me help," she choked.

"No!" he hissed, glaring at her with hatred.

Emilie looked desperately at David; he gazed back sympathetically, but shook his head. She stepped away and let them pass.

Sam Houston's arms closed about her. "There, sweetheart," he comforted, stroking her hair. "He'll come around in time. Go home now, and tell him you've eyes only for him."

"Oh, God, he's going to die!" she wept.

"Nay, sweetheart, nay," Houston consoled. "Ashland's too mean to die."

Hearing footsteps, Emilie turned to see David approaching with Don Lorenzo. She rushed to his side.

"Maria and I are taking Uncle home now," David told her.

"But I want to come, too!" she pleaded.

David sighed, taking Emilie's hand. "Let it go for now, dear," he urged gently. He nodded toward his *mayordomo*. "Don Lorenzo and his wife will fetch you home."

Emilie nodded desolately and watched David hurry off.

The Houstons hastily bid Emilie farewell and left with the Alders and Aaron; the crowd dispersed quickly.

As the de la Peña wagon headed toward Brazos Bend, Emilie sobbed her heart out in Doña Elena's comforting arms. "Oh, I'm a wicked girl, Doña

Elena! Stupid and willful! He told me not to wear the dress, now thanks to my stubbornness, he's badly wounded.''

"There, *chica,* do not put the blame on yourself," Doña Elena comforted, patting Emilie's back. "The one with the red hair, he is wicked. I saw it in his eyes—*ojos de diablo.* He would have pressed his flesh on yours if you wore the sack from the corn."

Emilie looked up at the motherly Doña Elena. "But it *is* my fault! I never should have danced with Aaron. Oh, God, now Edgar may die!"

"No, *chica,* no," Doña Elena assured her, tucking Emilie's head under her chin. "Señor Ashland is a strong man. He will live to enjoy the *bebé* you bear him in good health." She went on firmly, "And so must you."

"Aye," Emilie whispered, sobering at Doña Elena's words. As if voicing its assent, the babe within her kicked. "I must bear his babe," she continued thoughtfully. Then her eyes brightened. "And I must tell him I love him. Yes, that's it! I must tell him I love him before it's too late. Don't you see, Doña Elena? He was mad with jealousy because he doesn't know—that I have eyes for him alone! Oh, Don Lorenzo, hurry, hurry, before it's too late!"

Emilie heard Don Lorenzo chuckle in the darkness. "Hush, *chica,* and rest," Doña Elena scolded gently, clucking to her. "No more talk about being too late. Go home and tell that man of yours you love him, *por supuesto.* Then enjoy the rest of your lives together!"

Emilie hurried up the stairs as fast as she safely could. But when she dashed into the bedroom, she froze in her tracks, shocked to see Avis sitting by the bed, open book in her lap.

"Leave us!" she ordered hoarsely, moving closer to study her husband's wan, sleeping face.

"But Madame, I've been instructed to remain here all night!" Avis retorted brittlely.

Emilie whirled on the woman. "Get out of here, you blackhaired scarecrow!"

Avis Gerouard drew herself to her feet with dignity. "Madame, I have my orders," she bristled.

Emilie was about to demand *whose orders* when she heard Edgar moaning. She turned to him, her heart in her eyes as she watched his eyelids slowly open. He stared at her blankly.

"How are you feeling, darling?" she whispered.

A scowl spread across his features, puckering his brow and tightening his pale lips. "Get out of my sight!" he hissed weakly.

"Don't say that, darling, please!" she begged.

He raised himself on his elbows, grimacing with pain. "Get her out!" he ordered Avis.

Avis grabbed Edgar's arm and tried to push his shoulder back down. "M'sieur, no—you'll injure yourself!"

"Get her out of here before I kill her!" he roared, pounding his wounded fist on the mattress, then gasping, falling back with the pain.

Avis Gerouard turned to Emilie, her eyes for once filled with emotion, pleading. "If you value his life, Madame, please go."

Emilie stared at Avis's desperate eyes. "You're in love with him, aren't you, you old hag?" she whispered.

Avis Gerouard's eyes smiled in cruel, dark triumph.

Emilie turned, leaving the room without looking back.

But as she entered the hallway, she suddenly jerked to a stop, as a frightening odor filled her senses. She glanced about in near-panic, then rushed across the dark hall, following the direction of the smell.

She threw open the door to the nursery. "Oh, my God—no!" she cried.

She tore back into the hallway, almost colliding with David, who was now rushing towards the nursery, his eyes wide.

She clutched his arm frantically. "For the love of heaven, help me, David! The nursery's on fire!"

Chapter Six

December 5, 1841

"Come, Emilie, relent and join us today. You do need an outing, dear."

Emilie smiled bravely at David, who sat across from her at breakfast. Next to him sat Maria, her green eyes downcast, her face petulant as she picked at her sausage and eggs. Edgar had already departed to the plantation gin, to supervise the baling of the season's last cotton for shipment on the *Belle* tomorrow.

"Perhaps you're right, David," Emilie conceded. "I'm sure the change of scenery would help. But I feel so—awkward these days," she concluded, eyeing her large belly. "Best I stay home."

"Bosh!" David said briskly. "Don't let the babe's coming give you shy ways, now. No other woman hereabouts would stay home on that account."

Emilie frowned. "It's not just that, but—"

"We insist you come," David interrupted firmly, "don't we, Maria?"

Involuntarily, Emilie shivered as she watched Maria turn and give David a resentful look. But David stared her down, his blue eyes immutable.

"*Sí*, David," she murmured at last, turning hard eyes upon Emilie.

Emilie stared unsmiling at the Mexican girl. Maria had been hatefully cold to her ever since the *fiesta*, when she found Emilie and David embracing. Emilie often wondered if the girl were even responsible for the fire in the nursery afterwards.

David reached across the table to pat Emilie's hand. "Settled, then." He pulled a watch on a chain from the pocket of his brown frock coat. "I'll see to the readying of the team. If you ladies can be ready in, say, an hour's time?"

The girls nodded and the three adjourned to get ready. Emilie walked wearily up the stairs, pausing on the landing to rub her aching back, her heart pounding from the exertion. She carried the babe quite low in her belly now, and it moved and kicked mightily, especially at night.

Emilie braced herself with a deep breath, then trudged on up the stairs. In the upstairs hallway, she paused at the door to the nursery, then sighed heavily and went into the room.

It hadn't been a bad fire—David and Daniel had managed to extinguish it before other rooms of the house became involved. But the nursery itself was ruined.

Emilie walked about, studying the charred walls where the bright curtains had once been. She and Hallie had spent weeks preparing the cheerful lengths of calico, only to have to discard the damage panels. Thankfully, most of the handmade clothes in the dresser were saved, but the furnishings and rug were seared and had to be discarded.

What had caused the fire, they still didn't know. But David had pointed out a smashed oil lantern on the floor, surmising that one of the servants had carelessly left it lit and that the wind from an open window had knocked the hurricane lantern over, starting the fire.

Emilie seriously doubted the fire was an accident, however. So much remained unexplained. For instance, all the servants swore they hadn't even been near the room that day. And why hadn't Avis Gerouard, across the hall with Edgar at the time, heard the lantern breaking? When questioned by Emilie, the Creole woman had claimed she heard nothing. "My hearing has not been the same since a bout with scarlet fever a few years past, Madame," the housekeeper explained offhandedly.

Was this true? Or did Avis lie to cover her own treachery?

At least Emilie was sure Edgar had no knowledge of the fire's origin, since he had lain gravely wounded at the time. Although she assumed Edgar was informed about the fire, she had not mentioned it to him—nor he to her—since they had not been on speaking terms since the *fiesta*.

Emilie stared for a last time at the emptiness and ruin. The room had been swept after the fire, the furnishings removed, yet Emilie had given no orders to repair the damage. She had no intention of letting her baby sleep in this room—ever! The very thought of another fire made her blood run cold. No, her child would sleep with its mother.

Emilie left the nursery and entered her own bedroom. Closing the door, she smiled as she eyed Hallie sitting upon her chair near the blazing fire, nursing a tiny black babe. The infant, in white shirt and diaper, sucked greedily, tiny fists flailing against its mother's bosom.

"How is he this morning, Hallie?" Emilie asked.

Hallie smiled broadly. "Oh, he's hungry as a bear

after winter, Missus." Studying Emilie's face she frowned. "Missus, your eyes look like you been punched flat out. I'll get up and help you to bed."

"Don't you dare, Hallie!" Emilie scolded, shaking a slim finger at the slave. "You're to see to little Jacob first, you understand?"

"Yes'um, Missus," Hallie grinned. "Lil' Jacob's mighty lucky to stay with his mammy all day. The other chillun' stay with Aunt Sarah whilst their mammies are workin'."

"A babe belongs with its mother," Emilie said firmly, her hand reaching for her own belly as she felt the baby kicking.

"Oh, Missus, that rascal of yourn is fightin' to bust loose, ain't he?"

Emilie sat down at the dressing table, drawing the hairbrush through her golden tresses. "Aye, Hallie."

"You wait and I'll do your hair, Missus," Hallie called.

"No, Hallie. I'm going to a house-raising today, and we're leaving shortly. I'll tend my hair and you can help me dress presently."

Looking in the mirror, Emilie caught Hallie's reflection, the puckered black brow. "You up to cavortin', Missus?" the slave asked worriedly.

"Of course, Hallie. After all, you were dancing circles around us all up to the day you delivered."

"I know that, Missus. I'm healthy as an ox, but you—"

"So am I!" Emilie snapped back, her lower lip thrust forward as she threw the brush down on the dressing table.

Hallie lowered her chocolate brown eyes and fell silent.

Emilie picked up the hairbrush, mentally rebuking herself for being short with the servant. Her emotions were so mixed up these days! Her life had been miserable ever since that cursed *fiesta!* It was an unusual night now when she did not cry herself to sleep.

Piling golden ringlets on top of her head, Emilie thought of the events since the unfortunate evening in October. Edgar had quickly recovered from his injury, and was up and about in less than a week. The Houstons had come to visit before leaving for Cedar Point, and had informed Emilie that Aaron Rice was also recovering from his shoulder wound.

If only emotions could heal as easily as flesh! Emilie mused sadly. Since the *fiesta,* she and Edgar had been totally estranged. After his outburst that night, she had avoided him for several days, sleeping in her old room. As his health improved, she was considering returning to his bedroom. But the very day she planned her move, she was shocked to find all of her things deposited once again in the Blue Room. She remembered storming downstairs, finding him in the office.

"Why have you moved me out?" she had snapped at him as he sat at his desk.

A bitter smile had twisted his lips. "Madam, you have already selected separate sleeping quarters."

"*I* selected separate sleeping quarters! *You* ordered me out of our bedroom!"

He had shrugged.

"Edgar, are you just going to push me aside like this?" she had asked hoarsely.

He shuffled some papers, then opened the ledger. "Precisely."

"You can do this—after all we've meant to each other? Why won't you listen to my side of the story?"

He slammed the ledger shut, rising to glare down at her. "Madam, I suggest you leave before I say—or do—something unforgiveable!"

She had fled him in tears.

Emilie now shivered at the memory. The weeks following the angry scene brought no improvement in Edgar's behavior. She began to feel invisible; she longed to leave him.

And she would have left long ago—despite her love for him—were it not for the babe. Like it or not, she and Edgar shared the tiny life they had created; they were bound together by blood. She doubted Edgar would let her leave with the babe, and she certainly would not just leave it behind. Someone in this house hated not only her, but the babe, also!

A tear trickled down Emilie's cheek. Perhaps she would die in childbirth, she thought bitterly. That would solve everything. Edgar would get the babe he wanted, be rid of the wife he hated.

Oh, I'm a wicked girl to think of death! she scolded herself. It would be a sin to leave her precious babe to be brought up by her alienated husband. Besides, if her labor were troublesome, the babe might die, too. . . .

Later, as Emilie was leaving the house, Edgar astonished her by opening the front door just as she reached for the knob. Studying her in her gray wool dress and matching cape, he cocked an eyebrow and asked humorlessly, "Going somewhere, love?"

Seeing him there, standing in a pool of sunshine, his black hair gleaming, his rugged features more handsome than ever, she fought back a rising weakness. Biting her lips, she asked defensively, "Do you care?"

For a moment, an angry spark flashed in the depths of his brown eyes. Then he he held the door wide that she might pass.

Chapter Seven

December 5, 1841

On a rise near River Road just south of the village, a small clearing had been carved out of the woods. Three dozen settlers had gathered in the cool, breezy weather to help the recently arrived Leggett family build a home. The men were busy felling trees, splitting wood, sawing and nailing. The women tended the children as they prepared the feast to be consumed at noontime.

Emilie sat in a rocking chair on the edge of the clearing, a tiny boy fast asleep in her arms. Little Ned Leggett had nearly collapsed from the excitement of knowing his family would move out of their crude lean-to and into a brand new cabin by evening. Now he was deep in slumber, although how he could sleep through the din was beyond Emilie.

Emilie rocked and hummed softly to herself, studying the wee lad in her arms. How angelic the tot looked, his tiny mouth puckered, his cheeks as rosy as a cherub's, his long jet eyelashes still against his face. She stroked the small head, ran her fingers through the ebony curls. Would Edgar's child look like this?

She sighed as she rocked, her mind drifting to another rocking chair, another place. She had been longing to return to Houston lately. David had visited there several times, and had informed her that everything at the house was just fine. Yet she hungered to see the house for herself, to rock her babe in Granny Rose's chair. But would Edgar let her go?

Edgar! He spoiled everything! Of course he would never let her leave with the babe. After all, hadn't he told her he wanted to marry her "to share my bed and bear my sons?" Obviously, he cared not one whit for her, else how could he treat her so callously? It broke her heart to love him so, yet have him act as if she did not exist!

She fought back tears as she recalled the beautiful summer they had shared. At times they had seemed so close, she had almost expected him to tell her he loved her. Indeed, it had been on the tip of her tongue to tell him herself many times. Oh, why hadn't she? Yet would it have changed things? His actions had proved that he thought her no better than a common strumpet. No, had she told him, he might have laughed in her face!

A cheer swelled from the crowd, and Emilie glanced up to see that the *puncheon* floor had been completed. Patting each other on the back, the men began sanding the split logs they had laid flat-side up. While they knelt on the cedar, several others began erecting the sides of the cabin.

"Well, Mrs. Ashland, fancy running into you again."

Emilie gasped as she looked up to see Aaron Rice staring down at her, his bright green eyes shaded by a palmetto hat.

"Mr. Rice—what are you doing here?" she asked

with surprise.

Aaron chuckled and lifted the tails of his white wool frock coat, seating himself on the log next to her. Removing his hat, he gazed up at her curiously, his crimson curls blowing in the cool breeze. "What kind of greeting is that for the man your husband almost killed?"

"He had cause," Emilie returned shortly.

"Perhaps," Aaron conceded. "But you could at least inquire about my health."

Emilie shrugged. "Why aren't you helping the other men?"

He rubbed his shoulder and feigned a woeful look. "Some cad tried to separate my arm from my shoulder. This cold pains me right to the bone."

Ignoring his complaint, Emilie questioned, "Why are you here, anyway? I thought you went with the Houstons to Cedar Point."

"I did. But Grace and Henry invited me up for Christmas. Besides, Houston has little use for me these days. As you may know, he offered your illustrious husband my position in Washington." Aaron smiled grimly. "Of course, I bear Edgar no ill feeling for it."

A smile of triumph tugging at her lips, Emilie was silent.

"Anyway, the Alders and I are going to Houston's inauguration on the 13th." Aaron looked up, sweeping Emilie's form with insolent eyes. "You and Edgar attending?"

Ignoring his barb, Emilie asked, "Why aren't you going to be with your parents for Christmas? You seemed so—concerned for their welfare—before."

Aaron shrugged. "You're full of questions today, aren't you?" He leaned over and picked up a stick, began making etchings in the dirt. "The folks are old

396

and infirm, not to mention being strict Baptists, to boot." He grinned. "I must prefer Henry's company."

"So you can *imbibe* freely?" Emilie asked sarcastically.

"There's no harm in a man having a drop now and then," Aaron put in defensively.

"Certainly there's no harm—in a drop."

He frowned, then glanced at the small form in Emilie's arms. "Practicing for the blessed event?"

Emilie bit her lip. "You'd best go. You'll wake him."

Aaron stood, brushed off his black trousers. "Very well, Mrs. Ashland. But before I join the others, I'd like to—well—I wish to express my apologies for being forward with you that night in October. I'll not apologize for the harm I did your husband—he well-deserved it. But you—you are a lady and deserve better treatment at my hands. I do not usually act in such an ungentlemanly fashion, but I was drunk and, well, one thing led to another. . . ." His voice trailed off lamely.

Emilie raised a brown brow and looked up at Aaron Rice coldly. "Your apology is heard, Mr. Rice—but not accepted."

He sighed heavily. "Can't say I blame you for being angry with me, my dear." He leaned over, his green eyes glittering with determination. "But if that scoundrel Ashland gets to be too much for you, just send for me. I've come to be quite interested in your welfare, Emilie, and I assure you, you'd be well-treated at my side." He covered her hand with his large, fleshy one.

She threw off his hand. "Are you out of your mind?"

His eyes flickered strangely. "Out of my mind

with love for you, my dear. In case you hadn't noticed, I was smitten the first time I saw you."

Emilie's jaw dropped. She was about to issue a sharp rejoinder when the tiny lad in her arms began to whimper in his sleep. She cooed to him, rubbing his back and nestling his face against her shoulder. When he quieted a bit, she glowered up at Aaron. "Leave!" she hissed.

He grinned, bowed extravagantly, then clapped his palmetto hat on his head. "I'll expect to be hearing from you, my dear."

Emilie glared at his back as he walked off assuredly. A gust of wind swept through the clearing; she shivered, clutching Ned tightly with one arm as she leaned over to grab his blanket from the basket at her feet. But as she bent over, she froze, her eyes captured by a shape etched on the bare earth.

She shuddered. Aaron had carved an "L" in the dirt.

When the three of them arrived home late that afternoon, Emilie was exhausted. It had been a busy, noisy, nerve-fraying day. Emilie had enjoyed visiting with the villagers, but Maria had shot her angry glances every time she spoke with David.

Now Emilie lay limply on her bed, thinking she was too tired to move—ever again. She pulled the covers about her and shivered; winter would soon be upon them full force. How she missed Edgar's warmth, his arms! Would she have her babe here, in this cold bed, without him to comfort her? What if she died, never saw him again, never again knew the feel of him making love to her, never held the precious life within her?

Tears trickling down her face, she fell asleep, dreamed. . . .

Later, she shook awake in the darkness, her heart pounding with fear. The horrid dream had come again—the nightmare of Gonzales! Lately it haunted her all too frequently. The houses would explode—fire was everywhere—she and her babe were dying. And Edgar was above them—watching them drown!

Trembling, Emilie got out of bed; she stumbled about, lit the lantern. Her teeth chattering, she donned her slippers and a wool sweater. She settled down with a book—she wasn't hungry tonight, and had no desire to see Edgar.

Presently, there was a knock at her door. She called, "Come in," and was shocked to see her husband enter the room.

He frowned, hugging himself with his arms. "What are you doing up here alone? This room is freezing!"

"I'm just reading," she returned defensively.

He strode toward her purposefully, his features grim. Leaning over, he swept her up into his arms, carried her to the bed.

"What are you—"

"You're staying in bed until this room is warm," he said firmly, pulling the covers up to her chin.

Her eyes grew wide as she watched him walk to the fireplace, kneel to start the fire. His sudden solicitousness startled her.

"Why didn't you eat dinner?" he demanded, his back to her.

"I wasn't hungry."

"No doubt," he returned testily. "I've already reprimanded David for his faulty judgment. You shouldn't be gadding about this close to your confinement."

So his concern was for the babe! "Yes, indeed, sir, I must remember that I'm required to deliver you a normal, healthy heir. Never mind if I die in the process!''

Edgar stood, turned. ''Quit talking nonsense, Emilie,'' he said, his voice crackling like the flames in the grate. He drew closer. ''Don't you *want* to have a normal, healthy babe, my dear?''

She gulped. ''Of course,'' she conceded. She looked up at his handsome face, the dark eyes, the puckered brow, the firmly set mouth. Her heart seemed to jump into her throat as she asked, ''But what then, Edgar?''

He scowled. Surprisingly, he leaned over and kissed her forehead. ''I'll have Avis bring you a tray. Get some rest.''

And he left her.

But Emilie was no longer tired. Again and again, she relived the moment when Edgar came to her room. He had kissed her—touched her for the first time in months! Was it possible that he cared for her in some small way?

Surprisingly, she found she was hungry when Avis brought her dinner. Later, she decided to take her tray downstairs, hoping the exercise would tire her out. But she paused as she stepped from the staircase, hearing voices in the library. Recognizing Edgar's voice, she stood still and listened to the muffled sounds.

''Why must you remind me?'' Edgar asked in a low voice.

She heard a woman reply, ''Ah, but you wish to be reminded. No, M'sieur?''

M'sieur! Avis Gerouard was whispering with Edgar!

''It's over, Avis. Can't you remember that?'' Edgar hissed.

''Can you remember *this,* M'sieur?'' a husky

feminine voice replied.

There was a silence, then she heard Edgar groan, "Goddamn it, Avis, don't tempt me this way! Now look what you've done!"

She heard Avis laugh in a silky manner she would have thought the woman incapable of. "But of course, M'sieur. I haven't lost my touch, *n'est ce pas?*"

But Emilie didn't hear his reply; a loud crash interrupted her eavesdropping. With horror, she looked at the shattered dishes at her feet. Clapping a hand over her mouth, she dashed up the stairs as quickly as her cumbersome shape would allow.

As she rounded the landing, she heard Avis curse, *"Nom de dieu!* That clumsy oaf Hannah has again broken the dishes and scurried off! This time I take a switch to her!"

Emilie entered her room, collapsed upon the bed, pounding her fist into the mattress. Edgar—and Avis! Oh, the man was detestable! He had been making a fool of her with the housekeeper! Oh, she hated him, hated him, hated him! She sobbed convulsively, wiped her cheek with her sleeve. "Damn it, he's not worth your tears!" she scolded herself. "Not worth it!"

Once she calmed a bit, she got up and prepared for bed. Wearing her wool gown and wrapper, she frowned at her reflection as she brushed her hair. Her marriage was over, she realized. How could she stay, knowing what she now knew? She would confront Edgar tomorrow—and hopefully, he still possessed some small shred of honor and would let her go.

The fire in the grate had died down; she trembled as she blew out the lantern and hurried to bed. Huddled under the covers, she started as she heard the door opening and closing in the next room, the sound of Edgar's boots hitting the floor.

She watched the embers burn out in the grate. Oh, how she wished the love within her could die as easily as the fire!

She was drifting off to sleep when she heard voices in the other room. Frowning, she sat up, shaking off drowsiness. She strained her ears, but could hear only muffled sounds.

She got up, tiptoed to the wall, laying her ear against it. "What the hell do you think you're doing now?" she heard Edgar hiss.

She heard Avis laugh seductively.

"So you'd like a hard ride, would you?" she heard him demand.

Emilie dashed for the bed, tears stinging her eyes. She could listen no more.

Chapter Eight

December 6, 1841

The next morning, as Emilie left the dining room after an early, solitary breakfast, she was shocked to see Avis Gerouard going out the front door in a black travelling cloak and bonnet. "Where are you going, Mrs. Gerouard?" she asked confusedly.

The woman turned, eyeing Emilie as coldly as the breeze that now swept thorugh the open door. "I'm leaving, Madame."

"Leaving?" Emilie repeated, following Avis outside. Emilie shivered, clutching her shawl tightly about her blue wool dress as she noticed Avis's trunk on the edge of the porch. "But why—where are you going?"

Avis shrugged. "The *Belle* is due at the landing this morning, Madame. I'll travel to the Gulf, then book passage for New Orleans." She slanted a grim look toward Emilie. "I'm going home, Madame."

Emilie frowned, digesting this information. Last night, she had heard Avis Gerouard seducing her husband. Now, the housekeeper was leaving. Interesting.

"Why are you leaving, Mrs. Gerouard?"

403

Avis glanced off nervously, avoiding Emilie's eyes. "Where is that lazy *négre* with the buggy? Any moment now, I'll be hearing the steamboat's bell, and that worthless lad is *absént!*"

Emilie studied the Creole woman carefully. In startling contrast to her usual self-possession, Avis was nervously tapping a foot, shifting her black parasol from hand to hand. Her jaw quivered slightly, defying the usual stern set of her features. But her eyes were shaded beneath the brim of her bonnet, unreadable.

"Why are you leaving, Mrs. Gerouard?" Emilie repeated.

Suddenly, Avis whirled, yanking loose the black satin bow at her neck, pulling off her bonnet and facing Emilie with black eyes blazing. The winter breeze pulled wisps of curls loose from her restrained *chignon,* giving her countenance a certain aloof allure. Emilie swallowed a gasp, realizing the housekeeper possessed a cold, haunting beauty.

"Do you really wish to know why I'm leaving, Madame?" Avis asked nastily.

"Yes!" Emilie retorted, her voice unwavering. "Did my husband dismiss you?"

Avis laughed, a cold, cruel laugh. "No, Madame, he did not dismiss me. *Au contraire,* he begged me to stay—in his bed last night!"

Avis paused, gazing at Emilie arrogantly, her black eyes gleaming. Emilie bit her lip, but otherwise showed no emotion. So Avis Gerouard was showing her true colors at last! she thought with a certain perverse fascination.

Avis took a step toward Emilie. "I'm leaving, Madame, because I will not share him with you." She added pointedly, "He wants the child, not you."

Emilie squared her shoulders. "If that is true, Mrs. Gerouard, why didn't he marry *you?*"

Avis sniffed disdainfully, glancing rudely at Emilie's large belly. "I am barren, Madame. It is of great importance to M'sieur Edgar to have sons—an heir. He knew that my marriage to Henri was fruitless. Therefore, he chose you—as a sort of brood mare."

Emilie ground her teeth, noticing Jacob with the buggy. "I think you'd better go, Mrs. Gerouard!"

Avis shrugged. *"Certainement,* Madame." She smiled cruelly. "But he'll send for me, you know. If you're wise, Madame, you'll give him his child and leave before he fills your belly again. But then, perhaps you are without pride, Madame. Do you prefer being used?"

"Go to hell!" Emilie hissed.

Smiling smugly, Avis started down the steps. "By the way, Madame, I wish to apologize for breaking your perfume bottle," she called back casually.

Emilie rushed down the steps, grabbing Avis's arm. *"You* were the one?"

Firmly disengaging Emilie's fingers, Avis began putting on her bonnet. *"Oui,* Madame."

"But why?" Emilie asked incredulously.

"I wanted you to leave, of course," Avis replied with silky sarcasm, tying the bow.

Emilie's blue eyes grew coldly brilliant with realization. "You mutilated the doll—and set the nursery on fire!" she accused. "You—you were jealous because I could give Mr. Ashland the child you couldn't!"

But Avis merely shook her head and laughed as she paused at the bottom of the stairs, turning to stare at Emilie with icy indifference. "No, Madame, I did neither of those things. I'm sure you'd like to believe that all your troubles are departing this morning, but such is not the case. You have no friends in this house, Madame.''

''That's not true! I—''

''But as I said, Madame, I do apologize for breaking the bottle,'' Avis interrupted rather impatiently. ''I am a good Catholic and I do not wish it on my conscience.''

''You're a good—and you you don't want it on your conscience!'' Emilie sputtered in amazement. ''You apologize for smashing my mother's perfume bottle, yet you feel no guilt for seducing my husband?''

Avis accepted the wide-eyed Jacob's arm and climbed into the buggy. ''That's different, Madame. I had him first.''

Emilie's jaw dropped. ''I can see, Mrs. Gerouard, that I do not know you at all.''

Avis Gerouard leaned back in the buggy and chuckled down at Emilie. ''Ah, Madame Ashland, I pity you. It is your *husband* that you do not know at all.''

Emilie stood aghast, watching the conveyance clatter off down the driveway. Once the buggy disappeared into the trees shrouding the river, Emilie walked numbly up the stairs and into the house. Avis Gerouard's cruel remarks splintered her brain— ''You have no friends in this house, Madame . . . It is your *husband* that you do not know at all . . . He begged me to stay—in his bed last night!''

Was it true? Had Edgar and Avis been having an affair all this time? Did he love Avis? Could she bear to ask him?

She moved through the downstairs rooms like a sleepwalker. He was nowhere in sight. She started up the stairs, her mind exploring, her heart breaking.

She must leave this place. That was all she knew. She must leave.

She knocked on his door, heard his deep voice call, "Come in."

She entered. He stood drying his face with a towel. He was naked to the waist—her eyes moved familiarly over the muscles of his torso. For an insane moment, she had a desire to rush into his arms, to beg him to say it wasn't true.

She steadied herself, watching the familiar sardonic grin mask his emotions.

"Good morning, my dear. To what do I owe the pleasure?"

She stared at him numbly.

"Well—speak up, Mrs. Ashland. I must get to the *Belle* to make sure Ben has gotten all the bales loaded."

"And to tell Avis goodbye?" she choked.

He cocked a black brow. "Are you mourning Avis's departure, my dear? I could have sworn there was no love lost between the two of you."

"Why did she go, Edgar?" she asked, her voice breaking.

He stroked his mustache thoughtfully, his eyes narrowing. "Don't you know, love?"

"No! Quit playing games with me, Edgar! Tell me!"

He stared at her strangely, his dark eyes glittering with an emotion she couldn't name. Then he sighed, turned and walked to the wardrobe. He opened the doors, and his reply was muffled as he leaned forward to hunt for a shirt. "No," she heard him say.

A chill swept through her body as she watched him put on his shirt. He walked over to her, stood staring down at her with eyes that were gentle, thoughtful now. Reaching out, he touched her hair, smoothed down a stray curl. "You're so beautiful, love, when the light catches your hair just so," he murmured. "What's this? You're shaking like a freezing kitten!" And he pulled her into his arms.

She wanted to push him away, damn him to hell for taking another woman to his bed. But she was swept by a lassitude, a tide of tender feeling.

She felt his lips brush her forehead, then move gently to her ear. His hands caressed her back, warming her. "There, love, let me take you to the bed and hold you until you cease your trembling."

His words touched her; tears sprang to her eyes. She relaxed, let him lead her toward the bed. Then she remembered, and froze.

The bed! The very bed he had shared with Avis! She shoved him away. "What of Avis?" she demanded.

He frowned. "Forget Avis."

"No!" she shot back. "I can't! I won't! How dare you suggest holding me when you don't care for me at all!"

There was a long silence. He did not deny it, but stood staring down at her perplexedly. "Is that what you think, love?" he finally asked.

"Yes!" Her body shook with emotion and her eyes burned. "I want to go back to Houston! Edgar—let me go."

An unfathomable emotion flickered in the depths of his eyes—fear? anger? She could not read it, for the look vanished as quickly as it had come.

He crossed to the door, opened it, his features grim. "Of course, madam—by all means, run home! But leave the child."

Chapter Nine

It was a mild Christmas day. Emilie strolled near the house. She had been consumed by a growing restlessness the past several days; Hallie had warned her that her time would soon be upon her.

Emilie agreed; the babe had sunk low in her belly. It moved infrequently these days, as if resting up for the birth. All was in readiness for the babe's arrival; Eben had built a cradle for the corner of Emilie's room, and Hallie had helped Emilie finish making baby clothes.

Emilie pulled her shawl tightly about her lavender wool dress as a cool wind swept about her. She plucked a leaf from her hair, watched it drift off in the breeze. As she walked, the crisp turf snapped beneath her feet; the season's first freeze days earlier had turned the landscape hay-yellow.

There would be little celebrating this Christmas day, she thought sadly. With Avis gone, Emilie had not the strength for extensive preparation; it was all she could do to keep the servants at their tasks lately. And she had little help today, as most of the slaves were resting up from the traditional harvest ball held for them in the barn Christmas Eve. David had chopped and decorated a small cedar tree for the parlor, but it seemed a pathetic attempt at festivity.

Besides, what was there to celebrate? Emilie's relationship with Edgar had been cold as a Texas norther since Avis departed. She had taken his refusal to comment on his relationship with the housekeeper as an admission of guilt. And surely any courtesy he condescended to show her now was merely for the babe's sake.

The babe kicked sluggishly; she again thought of its imminent arrival. She still had the nightmares of Gonzales—she often awakened sobbing in the middle of the night. Each time, she shook with terror; each time, she managed to restrain herself from rushing next door into Edgar's bed, his arms.

She did not want the nightmare to come true. She did not want to die and leave the babe, if it lived, to be raised by Edgar. She felt a great bond toward this life within her. She wanted to hold it, nurture it. Edgar hated her; Maria had turned on her. But the child was part of her—the child would love her.

"Good morning, Emilie," a feminine voice called.

Emilie turned to see Maria coming down the hillside. The girl was gaily dressed this morning, her green silk dress terraced with ruffles, her black satin cape gleaming like the ebony curls piled on her head.

Emilie waited for the girl, shocked that Maria should speak to her so civilly. "Merry Christmas, Maria," she said when the girl got to her side.

"David wishes you to return to the house," Maria said rather sullenly. "He has made some eggnog, and he wishes us to sing the carols I have learned on the piano."

Emilie smiled. Dear David. He did his best to keep things cheerful. "I'm glad to see you and David such good friends, Maria.''

The Mexican girl thrust out her lower lip. "No thanks to you, Emilie!''

Emilie sighed tiredly. "Maria, believe me—I have no designs on David. All I wish is to leave this place—with my child. But that seems to be impossible.''

Suddenly, Maria glanced off. "Perhaps not, Emilie. Your *admirador* approaches.''

Emilie turned. She frowned as she spotted Aaron Rice driving a buggy up the hillside. "Him again! What the hell does he want?''

Aaron Rice pulled his team up near the two girls. Removing his beaver hat, he smiled broadly down at them. "Good morning, ladies.''

"What are you doing here?'' Emilie snapped, hands on hips.

Aaron chuckled. "Why, I was just on my way to give Edgar my greetings,'' he drawled sardonically.

"Fiddlesticks!'' Emilie shot back.

Undaunted, Aaron grinned engagingly, leaned forward. "May I offer you ladies a ride back to the house?''

Emilie bit her lip as her cold blue eyes swept him. Despite her chagrin at Aaron's unwelcome presence, it was all she could do not to laugh out loud at his outrageous attire. He wore a crimson velvet frock coat edged with gold satin piping, black and white striped trousers, a fluffy ruffled white shirt, and a garish gold and green taffeta bow tie.

Maria stepped forward. "Your buggy is small, Señor. There is not room for all of us.'' She smiled venemously at Emilie. "But I'm sure Señora Ashland would be delighted to join you.''

Emilie whirled, glaring at Maria. Sometimes the girl could be no better than a little prima donna!

411

Maria went on tauntingly, *"Que pasa,* Emilie? Feeling pangs of guilt?"

Emilie gritted her teeth, glowering at the smiling girl. Then, rising to Maria's bait, she reached out and grabbed Aaron Rice's outstretched hand, climbed into his buggy.

Aaron laughed triumphantly. "Tell Edgar I've a Christmas present for him!" he shouted down at Maria.

Before Emilie could wonder what Aaron's cold words meant, he jerked the reins mightily, and the buggy lurched forward. But the team headed toward River Road, not Brazos Bend!

"Where are you taking me?" Emilie demanded, hanging onto her seat as they jolted down the hillside.

Aaron Rice shifted the reins to one hand, his face grim. He reached for his belt; Emilie gasped as he pulled out a revolver. "Take the reins!" he growled, brandishing the weapon.

She stared at him, her jaw dropping. "Aaron, what on earth—"

"Take them, damn you!" he snarled, forcing the leads into her hands.

The whiskey on his breath engulfed her; she fought for control. "Aaron, you're drunk. Put that gun away before you hurt someone, and let me out of this buggy!"

The horses slowed as the reins lay limply in Emilie's hands. Aaron laughed wickedly, pushing the gun against her belly. "Oh, but I intend to hurt—someone. Now get this team moving before I blow the little bastard out of your belly!"

Emilie gasped in horror. She looked back desperately, saw Maria watching them impassively. She realized with a sinking despair that the girl could not see the gun from where she stood.

The metal barrel probed Emilie's belly, hurting her. She heard Aaron cocking the revolver. "Drive the team to River Road—now!" he demanded harshly.

With a cry of anguish, Emilie snapped the reins, sending the team flying. She kept her eyes on the road, trying to keep the racing horses out of the trees. A million hysterical thoughts whirled through her brain. Would Maria tell Edgar about Aaron, or simply remain silent? Even if she told him, would he care? Would Aaron shoot her any second now? Oh, her baby—her poor, poor baby!

Struggling with the reins, she eyed Aaron through the corner of her eye. He was clean-shaven, neat, as usual, but there was something very different about him today. Yes, it was the eyes! They glowed with a strange, maniacal light! The light she had caught a glimpse of the night of the *fiesta!* Yes, he looked insane!

"Aaron, why are you doing this?" she asked, forcing herself to sound calm. "You know I don't want to go away with you—"

"Oh, I'm not taking you far!" he interrupted, laughing an odd, rather high laugh.

Emilie gulped. Mother of God—what did he mean?

"Faster!" Aaron growled, shoving the gun into her until she cried out.

Emilie worked the reins; the team flew down River Road, jostling both of them.

"You know Houston dismissed me!" Aaron said in a strange, high voice. "On his inaugural day, no less!"

While one hand still held the gun, Aaron reached into his breast pocket and pulled out a flask. He popped the cork with his thumb and took a large draught.

Without thinking, Emilie sarcastically asked, "Did your liquor consumption have anything to do with your dismissal?"

Aaron's jaw tightened; Emilie knew she had made a mistake. Setting the flask between his bouncing legs, he slowly, deliberately slapped her hard across the face. She winced, her head spinning from the blow.

Drawing her dizzy head upright, she heard him snarl, "You've a sharp tongue for a wench with a gun at her belly." She saw him draw back his frock coat and touch a sheath at his belt. "Perhaps I should blunt it a bit with my knife."

Emilie's heart jumped into her mouth. She turned, driving the team hard; she heard Aaron chuckle.

As they flew past bare trees and crisp undergrowth, Emilie's mind boiled. What on earth was Aaron planning to do? Had he lost his mind utterly? Oh, God, help me, Edgar! her mind screamed silently. If there's anything felt between us, feel it now! Save me, darling, save me!

She cried out as Aaron again prodded her belly. "Houston wants Ashland, not me," she heard him grumble. "Everyone wants Ashland. Even my darling Livvie."

Emilie turned, her eyes growing huge. "Your—darling—Olivia?"

Aaron's green eyes gleamed as he gazed back at her. "She only married him to make me jealous, you know. What a temptress she was! My Livvie, my sweet, darling love. None other could compare to her beneath me!"

"Oh my God!" Emilie choked. "You—and Olivia?"

Aaron laughed at her revulsion. "None other could compare," he repeated. "But I may give you a try, dear girl, before this day is over!"

Waves of shock and nausea engulfed Emilie. The man had done—intended—wicked, unspeakable things!

"Stop the horses!" Aaron suddenly snarled.

Emilie pulled the team to a halt near a curve in the road. Aaron jumped down, pointed the pistol at Emilie's face. "Get down!"

She hesitated, then struggled not to trip as he reached up and yanked her out of the buggy. He pulled her toward the river. As they passed a large tree, she saw the gray marble marker in the distance. He had brought her to the spot where Olivia and the babes drowned! But why?

"W-what do you intend?" she stammered in rising hysteria.

He laughed, but did not reply. Dragging her to the marker, he pressed her against the cold rock, then shoved the pistol in his belt, pulling a length of cord from his trousers pocket. He yanked her arms around behind the marble; she cried out as the cord cut into her wrists.

"You really played into my hand, dear girl," he bragged as he worked. "I wasn't quite sure how to whisk you out of the house!"

Emilie winced. "Please—you're cutting off the circulation!"

"Good," he said. He strutted about in front of her, took another long draught of liquor. Grinning down at her, he asked, "Comfortable, my dear?"

"You're despicable!" she spat back.

"Oh, not as despicable as I intend to be!" he returned excitedly. He paced about the small clearing, talked as if to himself, "What I'm trying to

415

figure is who to kill first—you or Ashland.''

"Oh, sweet Jesus!" Emilie choked.

He turned and grinned down at her, his green eyes gleaming insanely as he rubbed his hands together.

"Why, Aaron? Why?" she gasped hoarsely.

He pulled out the revolver, watched the light play on the barrel. "Six shots in this new Colt," he said casually. "I rather fashion three each. T'would be jolly to shoot Edgar right in the—" he paused, grinning evilly and bowing extravagantly—"oh, but I'd best remember there is a lady present. You catch my delicate drift, don't you, my dear? I don't have to be explicit, do I?"

Emilie quivered with revulsion and shook her head, but Aaron smiled and drew closer, pressing the revolver to her lips. "Do I?" he repeated.

"No!" she choked, the sound of her voice ringing down the metal barrel, her eyes riveted on the pistol.

He chuckled and sauntered off. "Aye, the first bullet shall be for Ashland. Then, I think I shall let him watch the fun while I open up your belly for his perusal."

Tears streamed down Emilie's face as she realized Aaron's harrowing intent. "How can you do this?" she screamed hysterically. "I know you hate Edgar, but to hurt an innocent child—"

"Ah, but there's the rub, my dear!" he interrupted haughtily, drawing closer and waving the gun in her face. "What did Edgar do to Olivia's babes— indeed, to Olivia herself?"

Aaron threw his head back, finished off the flask of whiskey, angrily throwing the container down the river bank. Then he moved closer, hovering over her. A wave of nausea swept her as his vile breath filled her nostrils.

"Edgar chased my darling Livvie into the river!"

he hissed in rage. "He murdered her—and her babes! Now it is my mission that justice be done! An eye for an eye, my dear. I'm paying Edgar back in kind for what he did to Livvie! Then the river shall sweep away the evidence, just as it saved dear Edgar from the hangman!" He pointed the gun at her belly. "Too bad you're not having twins, my dear. But then we shall shortly find out, shall we not?"

"Oh my God!" Emilie screamed. "You can't truly mean—oh my God! Aaron, please, Olivia's death was an accident! Edgar didn't—"

She froze; both fell deathly silent as they heard hoofbeats approaching. Then Aaron laughed, leering at Emilie. "Your husband approaches, my dear. Prepare to accompany him to hell!"

Emilie cried out as Aaron sauntered off. Oh, it was hopeless! she realized desperately. Even if the rider were Edgar, he had no way of knowing Aaron was armed! He would walk straight into an ambush!

Her heart wrenched as she heard Apollyon neighing. Seconds later, Edgar dashed into the clearing. His eyes were wild; never had she seen him more angry.

He spotted Emilie and raced toward her. "Edgar, he's going to kill you!" she shrieked.

He paused, spotted Aaron off to the side. "Rice, let my wife go!" he shouted angrily. "This is between you and me!"

Aaron laughed; Edgar continued toward Emilie. But he stopped as a bullet bit the dirt in front of his foot.

"You'd best stop, Ashland, before I blow your lovely wife's head off!" Aaron shouted, moving forward.

Edgar's features contorted in horror; a vein jumped in his temple. "Let her go, Aaron!"

Aaron continued forward, his hand shaking as he held the gun, one corner of his mouth jerking as he smiled cruelly. "Let her go—like you let my Livvie go?" he asked shrilly. "Aye, I'll let her go, Ashland. When you're both floating face down in the river!" He took a step closer. "I was just explaining to your wife that I intend to blow your balls off, dear Ashland. Then I have—er, plans—for your wife. I'll give her my best shot—in more ways than one. But don't worry, man. I don't intend to kill her. That would deprive you of the pleasure of watching her drown."

"By God, enough, you bastard!" Edgar roared. And he dived for Aaron.

Aaron laughed and levelled the pistol at Edgar's middle just as Emilie screamed, "No, Edgar!" The scream seemed to distract Aaron for a split second, but the gun exploded as Edgar grabbed his arm.

Emilie gasped with momentary relief as she watched the bullet harmlessly hit a tree. But then she sobbed convulsively as she saw the two men on the ground struggling with the gun. Her entire life flashed through her mind as she watched Aaron point the gun at Edgar's chest.

She could watch no more. She began to sink to the ground. "Edgar—my darling babe—goodbye," she murmured.

The gun blast was the last thing she heard. Yet it seemed distant, from another world.

Chapter Ten

December 25, 1841

The pain jerked her towards consciousness, ripping across her lower belly. "God help me!" she moaned, tossing her head from side to side. "He's killed my baby! Killed—my baby!"

"No, Emilie no!" someone whispered.

Emilie opened her eyes to find herself back in her own room, in bed. She looked confusedly from Maria to Hallie.

Maria, sitting in a chair next to the bed, reached out and took Emilie's hand. Drawing the hand to Emilie's belly, she said, "Feel, Emilie. Your baby lives inside you. He is trying to enter this world. Now you must help us."

Emilie struggled to sit, then fell back as another contraction gripped her. Suddenly, she went rigid. "Edgar?" she questioned, her eyes darting wildly from one woman to the other.

Maria reached out and smoothed down Emilie's gold curls. "Calm yourself, *pobrecita*. He is fine. He—killed Señor Rice."

Emilie sighed heavily. "Thank God Edgar's alive."

Maria leaned closer, and Emilie saw the tears in the girl's green eyes. *"Lo siento,* Emilie,'' she whispered. "To think that for a moment I thought of not telling Señor Edgar—'' She shuddered, tears spilling down her cheeks. "I did not know the man was such a monster. Forgive me for not trusting you, Emilie.''

Deeply touched by the girl's emotion, Emilie held out her arms. The two embraced, but then Emilie stiffened as another, harder pain clenched her belly.

Maria pulled back and glanced worriedly at Hallie.

"Sit up, Missus,'' Hallie said, stepping forward. "We've got to get you undressed before that babe of yours delivers hisself in your skirts.''

Emilie looked down at her fully clothed body. "How long have I been back?''

"Just a few minutes, Missus. I heard of fast birthings, but that babe of yours is out to beat 'um all.'' She reached for the buttons at Emilie's back. "I think the shock set him on his way.''

"Is he all right,'' Emilie gasped.

"Raise up your arms, Missus. 'Course he's all right.''

"But I don't feel him moving!'' Emilie wailed.

"He ain't got much room at the moment, Missus.''

The two women undressed Emilie and put her in her nightgown, then laid towels beneath her thighs. Hallie placed several pillows behind Emilie's head and shoulders. "There, you sit up a bit and spread your knees. You more com'terble that way.''

But Emilie stiffened, crying out weakly as a hard pain grabbed her belly. She felt as if a huge, cruel hand were trying to jerk her insides out.

Hallie wiped the beads of perspiration that had popped out on Emilie's forehead. "Missus, you got to flow with it. It ain't going t'git better."

"Merciful heavens, I'm dying!" Emilie cried, reaching out to clutch Maria's hand.

Hallie spread Emilie's legs and looked down. "Hush this talk of dying, Missus. You got a babe to raise. Don't go talkin' nonsense."

Long moments of strong, closely spaced contractions followed. Emilie gasped as she felt the babe moving forcibly downward. She tensed against the pain, making it worse. Somewhere in the back of her mind, a voice scolded that she must be cutting holes in Maria's hand with her fingernails. But the girl did not move from her side.

"Oh, God!" Emilie panted. "Edgar—get Edgar!"

"Hush, Missus, it wouldn't be fitting," Hallie said matter-of-factly. "Now you push—hard!"

Emilie let out a scream as the pain split her in two. After a moment of wrenching hurt, she fell back weakly.

She was exhausted. She heard pounding somewhere—was it her heart breaking apart? Then she heard a tiny voice crying out. But she was too tired to lift her head! "My baby—bring me my baby!" she begged weakly.

Moments later, Hallie stood above her, holding a small, bundled form, her dark eyes gleaming as she smiled from ear to ear. "You got a girl, Missus," she announced.

Hallie placed the blanketed infant in Emilie's arms. Emilie moved the cloth aside and studied the perfect little body, stroked the fuzzy blonde hair on the tiny head. Tears rolled down her cheeks.

"A girl," she murmured.

She fell in love as quickly as she fell asleep.

While Emilie labored, Edgar paced the parlor,

gulping his brandy. "That Goddamned bastard Rice!" he raged to David for the tenth time, his boots eating the carpeting.

Despite the coldness of the room, Edgar had cast his coat upon a chair; his white linen shirt was partially unbuttoned, his cravat askew. "If he's hurt Emilie in any way—or the babe—by God, I'll cut his wretched corpse into mincemeat!"

David crossed to Edgar, grabbed his arm. "Steady, Uncle. It's over now. I'm sure both the babe and Emilie are fine. You'd best quit your pacing and gulping before you work yourself into a drunken frenzy. Of what use would you be to Emilie then?"

Edgar looked wildly at David. Then he sighed, handed the younger man his brandy snifter. He walked unsteadily to the settee, sank upon it, running his hands through his hair.

"And to think of how I've treated her—all these months—because of that bastard!" He pounded his fist upon the settee. "God, how stupid could I be? I should have known that slimy scoundrel was plotting his revenge all these years. But I went crazy at the *fiesta*—when I saw his hands on Emilie! I thought she—I thought—" he finished weakly, burying his face in his hands.

"There, Uncle, all is not lost," David consoled him from across the room. He put the brandy snifter on the tea table. "You've plenty of time for making amends."

Edgar looked up desolately. "Do I, David? Emilie's frightened—her mother died in childbirth. I've heard her sobbing at night—I've ached to go to her, but this damnable pride of mine held me back. Besides, I'm sure she hates me after all I've done." His eyes grew desperate. "God, David, why do I treat her so? I—I love her!"

Smiling, David sat down in the wing chair next to the crackling fire. "Yes, Uncle, I know. Why don't you tell her, after the babe is born? You might be surprised by her reaction."

"Aye, I'll tell her," Edgar agreed. He went on sadly, "But whatever she wishes—so be it. I'll not hurt her—ever again!"

Suddenly, both men jumped as they heard a scream coming from upstairs. Edgar was up in a flash, his eyes crazed. "Oh, Jesus, she's dying! I must go to her!"

David jumped up and grabbed Edgar's arm. "No, Uncle, you mustn't. You'll only get in the way! Hallie said they'd call you if they need you!"

Edgar jerked at David's grip. "Let me go, Nephew! I'd hate to deck you, but, by God, I'm going to my woman!"

David sighed, releasing Edgar.

Edgar dashed upstairs, cursing when he found the door to Emilie's room locked. "Let me in!" he growled, beating on the door.

Moments later, Hallie cracked the door, staring at Edgar in consternation. "What you want, Mister Ashland? We ain't finished."

Edgar pushed against the door. "I heard her scream—stand aside, girl!"

"Nossir!" Hallie retorted, bracing her weight against the door. "You got a daughter now, but it ain't fitting for you to come in till we've done!"

Edgar went limp. "A—daughter?" he whispered. Through the crack in the door, he glimpsed the bed, saw Emilie asleep, a small bundle in her arms.

"Yessir. Now you wait."

And Hallie shut the door.

Edgar leaned against the door, a smile spreading

across his face. A daughter! Emilie had lived! The babe had lived! A daughter—his very own little girl!

Presently, Hallie opened the door. "You can come in now, Mister Ashland," she directed solemnly.

Edgar walked into the room. Maria got up from her chair near Emilie's bed. She rushed to Edgar, her eyes glowing; he took her in his arms.

"Oh, it is a happy day, Señor! Congratulations!"

"Thanks, Maria," he whispered, a catch in his voice.

Edgar sat down in the chair next to the bed. Hallie came forward and took the bundle from the sleeping Emilie; she put the infant in Edgar's arms.

"We'll go now, Mister Ashland," she said. "You call if you need us."

Edgar heard the women gather up linens and leave. He sat stiffly as the tiny form moved in his arms; he looked down cautiously. With a trembling hand, he pulled the blanket away from his daughter's face. Oh, how perfect, how beautifully formed she was! He reached out and touched the fingers of a small fist; the tiny hand closed possessively over his finger.

"Quite a grip you have, little one," he told his daughter, his voice quavering. "You look much like your mother, you know, with your golden hair and dark eyelashes. I can't wait until you open those little eyes of yours. Will they be the same blue as your mother's? I think you will be quite beautiful, my darling."

He held the babe for long moments, watching with fascination the movements of her tiny limbs. Presently, the infant fell into a deep slumber. He rose and tiptoed to the cradle, carefully placing his daughter inside it.

He went back to his chair, turned his attention to

his wife. She slept peacefully now, dark eyelashes resting against her cheeks. But she was so white—so pale! He reached out and caressed the wealth of gold curls spread out against the whiteness of the pillows. His hand stroked her warm cheek, then moved to the vein at her throat, feeling the pulse, as if to assure himself that she had survived the birth. He leaned over and kissed her forehead, his eyes misting over. "Thank you for our daughter, my love," he whispered.

He sat back, then, watched her sleep. As the long moments passed, he considered his entire relationship with Emilie.

He had married the girl to satisfy his lusts. He had dealt with her frivolously, used her shabbily. But he hadn't counted upon falling in love with her. Was there any hope left? Could she ever love him in return? Or was it too late?

He must do what was right. There were two of them now. He mustn't risk destroying both of them. If Emilie truly didn't want him—he could no longer hold her against her will.

"Give me another chance, Emilie," he whispered fervently. "Please."

Her eyelids fluttered; she stirred, pulling the sheet to her neck. Then she became still again.

He rose, went to the cradle to check on his daughter. Watching her sleep, he thought of the years ahead. Her first pony. Her first beau. Would he be there to watch? For if his love could not hold his daughter—and her mother—he must let them both go.

He reached down and stroked the fuzzy hair on his daughter's head. How would he feel, he wondered, if someone treated her as callously as he had treated Emilie? Simple—he would lay open any scoundrel who abused his daughter the way he had mistreated her mother! He drew his hand back, shaking, and started toward the door. Christ—he didn't deserve either of them!

"Edgar?" Emilie called weakly.

He turned, saw she was awake, and rushed to her side.

Emilie watched her husband approach the bed. Why had he been leaving? she wondered. She studied his face as he neared her. His forehead was creased, his face looked tired. And very sad.

Then she remembered. He had counted on a son.

She glanced about the room nervously, spotted her daughter in the cradle. "Why is she over there?" she asked her husband as he sat down in the chair near her.

"She's sleeping," he replied.

"I want her," she told him, her voice cracking.

He rose and went to the cradle, brought the small bundle back to Emilie. "Your daughter looks much like you, love," he whispered as he placed the infant in her arms.

Emilie drew back the blanket and studied the baby, as if to assure herself that her child was indeed alive and healthy. She watched Edgar sit down, again saw the sadness in his eyes. She looked down at the babe to hide the tears that burned her eyes, threatening to spill over.

He was disappointed. Of that she was certain. She had failed to replace the sons he had lost. He had no more use for a daughter than he had for her! He had put the babe away in the corner, as if the sight of her offended him!

Edgar cleared his throat. "Aaron's dead."

"Yes, I know," she replied, her eyes still downcast. "Thank you for saving my life—and hers."

"I only wish I could have killed him a hundred times over, love."

Emilie stroked the soft foot of her tiny daughter. "The man was vile," she agreed. She looked up at him slowly. "He—told me about himself—and Olivia. How you must have hated him for that!"

Edgar frowned. "Do you think that is why I killed him?"

Emilie lowered black eyelashes. "I'm sure you didn't want him to harm me—or your son."

"Daughter," he corrected.

She looked up, her lip quivering. "At the time—you thought it was your son."

Edgar's brows knitted. "Emilie, what nonsense are you talking? Are you saying I wouldn't come after you if I knew you were carrying a girl?"

"Yes!" she cried. And to her horror, tears began streaming down her cheeks.

Edgar stood, reached for her. "Emilie, how can you think—"

She pulled away, clutching the infant to her breast. She was exhausted, she hurt, something seemed to snap inside her. "Don't touch me!" she sobbed. "I can't take any more of this! I just want to go home!"

Edgar sat down heavily, his face crestfallen. "Home? Isn't this home to you, Emilie?"

"No!" she wailed. "Whenever was it home? You forced me to marry you, you kept me against my will. I thought for a while that we—but then you turned on me! How can you call this my home when I never chose you—or any of this? I'm not your wife—I'm—I'm your prisoner!"

Edgar ran a hand through his hair, helplessly watching her sob. Once she quieted a bit, he said resignedly, "You're right, Emilie. I have no right to expect you to stay with me—not after all I've done."

"Then let me go, Edgar."

"Go?" he repeated woodenly, his brow furrowed. "But where would you live, my dear?" He looked at the babe sleeping in her arms. "And what of her?"

"I'd go back to Houston—to Granny's house. And I'd take her with me."

Edgar frowned; his eyes darkened. "Houston— you and the child alone? I don't know, Emilie."

She caught her breath convulsively. "Edgar— please—let me go."

He reached out and took her hand. "Is it truly what you want?"

"Yes!" she whispered.

He released her hand, stood and went to the window, staring at the bright day outside. "You may go then, of course, my dear," he said huskily. "But you are wrong. You are not the prisoner. I am."

He turned and left the room.

Chapter Eleven

December 25, 1841

Emilie slept most of the day, while Hallie sat vigilantly by her side. She awoke late in the evening, picking at her dinner.

Maria came in as Hallie was removing Emilie's dinner tray. The girl looked unusually solemn as she stood inside the door, clutching a small green bundle tied with red yarn. "Emilie, may I speak with you alone?"

Emilie nodded towards her servant. "Hallie, why don't you go feed Lil' Jacob, and get something to eat yourself?"

"Yessum."

After Hallie left, Maria still stood awkwardly by the door. Emilie smiled weakly and extended her hand. "Come sit by me, Maria."

The Mexican girl nodded, but stopped off to gaze at the baby for a moment before coming to Emilie's side. She hesitantly sat down beside Emilie on the bed, putting the bundle down next to them. "Your baby is very beautiful, Emilie—she looks much like you," the Mexican girl said, avoiding Emilie's eyes.

"Thank you, Maria," Emilie said, warmed by the girl's remark. "Now—what did you want to tell me?"

The girl looked up, and Emilie was shocked to see tears in Maria's green eyes. "I'm leaving, Señora," she announced. "My bags are packed."

"What?" Emilie asked incredulously.

Abruptly, Maria burst into tears. "I am a wicked girl Señora. I—I used not to think of such things, but now that Doña Elena has taught me my prayers—I am sure I am damned to hell for what I have done!"

Emilie's heart went out to the young girl, and she sat up in bed, laying a comforting hand on Maria's shoulder. The movement hurt badly, and she realized she was physically and emotionally unprepared to deal with the young girl's problems. But she took a deep breath and soothed, "There, Maria, don't cry. What could you have done that was so horrible?"

"So many things, Señora—evil, terrible things." Maria caught her breath, then spilled out her pain. "Several times I told Señor Edgar that you were flirting with David or Señor Rice, when I knew it wasn't true. And last spring, the day you were with me at the stable, I lied to you about Señor Edgar mistreating Señora Olivia, and then I—I deliberately spooked Peligra. I did not want to hurt you, Emilie, only to scare you away."

"I see," Emilie murmured. "You know, Maria, I've suspected all these things for some time, and I've long since forgiven you."

"I do not deserve your forgiveness," Maria choked miserably, wiping her tears on her sleeve. "There's—there's much more." She looked up at Emilie, her eyes anguished. "I—I am responsible for the fire in the nursery, Emilie."

Emilie fell back weakly against the pillows. "Tell me what happened, Maria."

The Mexican girl took a handkerchief from the pocket of her green gown and nervously twisted the linen with her fingers. *"Dios* forgive me, I went back to get the doll."

"The doll? You mean you put the mutilated doll in the baby's dresser?"

The girl nodded forlornly. *"Sí,* Emilie. But that was not the doll I went back for." The girl gulped, then went on unsteadily, "It's a long story, Señora, so perhaps I'd best go back to where it started. Last summer, when I found out you were *encinta,* it—it angered me. I slashed the doll and put it in the nursery to scare you. It was cruel of me, Emilie—cruel because I knew you were frightened about the *bebé*. Afterwards, I thought much of my wickedness. And you were good to me then, teaching me to read, to sew, to play the piano. I became all torn up inside. Part of me still hated you for coming here. Yet part of me wanted to believe you were truly my friend. I couldn't sleep nights thinking of my sin, and it was then that I knew I had to make amends for what I had done with the doll. So I made a new cloth doll for the *bebé,* from scraps of material we used to make the dresses. The day before the *fiesta,* I put this new doll in the baby's dresser. That is the doll I went back for after the *fiesta.*"

"But why did you go back?"

"Why?" the girl choked. "Because I saw you in David's arms that night, Emilie. I thought you had played me for a fool all along. Anyway, I went back to the nursery as soon as we arrived home, while the others were tending Señor Edgar's wound and getting him to bed. I lit the lantern and put it on the dresser. But the drawer stuck when I tried to open it. I yanked on it, and it opened, but the lantern—'' the girl paused, shuddering.

"The lantern tipped over and crashed onto the floor?" Emilie supplied.

"Sí" came the whispered reply. Maria looked up at Emilie, her eyes bright with tears, half-crazed with pain.

"So the fire started. Why didn't you tell anyone, Maria?" Emilie asked softly.

"I was just getting to that. I ran to the door and started to open it, but when I saw you coming up the stairs—I can't explain it, Emilie, something snapped inside me. I hated you at that moment for what you did with David—and I hated you because I thought you were responsible for Señor Edgar being wounded. And I was afraid if anyone found out I started the fire, I would be cast from the house. So I waited until you were inside Señor Edgar's room—then I left the nursery and closed the door." Finishing her tale, Maria began to cry heartbrokenly.

Emilie patted the girl's hand. "There, Maria. You mustn't be too hard on yourself. But I do wish you had told someone. You wouldn't have been punished, you know."

Maria glanced up quickly, "Oh, I would have told, Emilie. I went to my room, but within a minute I knew I had to do something, or someone might be hurt. So I went back into the hallway—but by then, you and David had already discovered the fire."

Emilie sighed. "You must forget it, Maria. You didn't intend to set the fire, and you tried to do the right thing in the end. And remember, please, that I have no romantic interest in David—he was only comforting me about Edgar the night of the *fiesta.*"

"I know that now, Emilie. And to think I blamed you for what Señor Rice did to Señor Edgar that night, when that man—was a monster—*loco*—"

Even the mention of Aaron Rice made Emilie's insides clench in pain. "Let's not think of him, either," she put in hastily. She forced a brave smile onto her face. "Tell me, were you able to save the doll you made for the baby?"

At last Maria, too, smiled, nodding as she wiped her tears with her handkerchief. *"Sí,* Emilie, I took it with me the night of the fire." She picked up the green bundle from the bed and handed it to Emilie. "I hope it will be to her liking."

"I'm sure it will be." Emilie unwrapped the bundle. "Oh, Maria, it's beautiful!"

The doll had been laboriously fashioned of cloth and yarn. The detailing was exquisite—meticulously cross-stitched features, a red-checked dress and white muslin pinafore covered with myriad miniature embroidered roses. The tiny feet even sported red felt slippers, and small red ribbons adorned the yellow yarn hair.

"Oh, Maria!" Emilie repeated, touched to the heart, her vision of the doll blurring with tears.

The two women embraced, both weeping. In that very moment, each could feel a deep, unshakable bond growing between them.

"Maria, you must have spent hours and hours on this!" Emilie exclaimed, when at last they drew apart. She gave the girl a curious smile. "But how did you know my child would be a girl?"

Maria sighed. "Oh, I had a feeling, Emilie."

As Emilie stared back into the girl's green eyes, she felt as if she were seeing Maria for the first time. She saw naked vulnerability, desperate insecurity, as well as deep emotional scars. Of course, Maria would fear the child would be a girl! Emilie suddenly realized. A girl child would be most threatening to

433

Maria's place in the family. Emilie realized Maria must think of Edgar as a father—a father who had never shown her the love and attention she so desperately needed. And because of this neglect, Maria had never really grown up—inside, she was still a little girl. When she found out Emilie was pregnant, she was jealous of the baby, much as any child would resent the intrusion of a new family member!

It was all pathetically tragic. Yet the fact that Maria had sewn the doll proved that there was hope—it demonstrated how loving and sensitive the girl was capable of becoming.

Emilie realized that beneath the girl's bravado, she hungered for reassurance. Taking Maria's hand, she said, "You must never again be afraid you will be asked to leave Brazos Bend. No one—not Edgar, not anyone—will ever ask you to go."

Again, Maria began to cry. "I know now that Señor Edgar will not. I found out after the *fiesta*."

Emilie looked at Maria with sharp interest. "What happened?"

"After Señor Edgar recovered, he took me aside and questioned me about the fire. I broke down and admitted what happened. I knew he would send me away, but instead, he did a strange thing. He hugged me and told me how relieved he was that it was an accident, after all. Then he said what you said—to forget it."

Emilie shook her head in amazement. Edgar had actually investigated the fire! Could it be he cared more than she thought? Yes, she realized bitterly, he cared. He was willing to go to any lengths to protect his heir. Doubtless, he wouldn't have bothered had he known the child would be a girl!

Emilie shook off her dismal thoughts and again turned to Maria. "You see, my friend, you are secure here. Edgar wants you to stay—and David does, too.''

Maria nodded solemnly. "I know, Señora. I was a foolish girl to doubt David, but when he sent me to school, I thought he did not want me here. . . ."

"When precisely the opposite was true, Maria," Emilie put in gently. "David knows someday you'll be a great lady, and he merely wanted you to have an education in keeping with that station." She paused, studying the Mexican girl thoughtfully. "Maria— I've often wondered—what truly happened to you at the school?"

Maria looked up, her proud young mouth quivering. "The girls were cruel to me, Señora. One in particular egged the others on. She told them horrible things—that I had *piojos*—lice—that *mi padre* fought with Santa Anna, that I—I slept with the gardener." Maria's voice trembled with emotion as she continued, "All were lies, Señora! But it was wrong of me to do what I did to her, cutting off her hair. . . ."

Feeling intense compassion for the young girl, Emilie squeezed Maria's hand, saying sincerely, "If you realize that, Maria, that's all that truly matters. Besides, the girl learned a valuable lesson about gossip, and I'm sure her hair has grown back by now." Smiling, she added, "Now, my friend, you must forget what's past and be happy. And no more talk of leaving, you hear? Brazos Bend is your home."

Maria stared at Emilie in wonder. "I can't believe after all I've done you still want me to stay?"

"I never wanted you to leave," Emilie explained. For a moment, she was tempted to tell Maria that she, Emilie, was leaving. Yet she did not think she

435

could bear any more emotional upheaval this day. She realized Maria truly needed her, and it wrenched her heart to think of leaving the girl. Yet she must think of her small, helpless babe first of all.

Evidently, Maria sensed how exhausted Emilie was, for she patted the older girl's hand and got to her feet. "You rest now, Señora."

But at the door, the girl turned, staring at the carpet. "There is one more thing, Emilie. About—about David."

"Yes? You're not still afraid that David and I—"

"No, no, that is not what I mean. I mean—if David knew what I have done to you. . . ." Maria's voice faded miserably, then she looked up in torment. "He loves you so, Emilie—"

"He loves you, too, Maria." Watching a glimmer of hope light Maria's fine eyes, Emilie continued, "What happened between you and me, Maria, is just that—between you and me. I've no reason to tell David—ever. Whether or not you feel you must tell him is something you'll have to decide on your own. But I would caution you about one thing. Don't punish yourself, Maria. You've suffered enough already."

A look of complete understanding flashed between the two women, then Maria whispered, "God bless you, Emilie."

The words were barely audible, and Maria left the room in tears. But this time, both she and Emilie knew that the tears were not of sorrow, but of exultation, as something was healed in Maria's anguished young soul.

When Emilie was ready to retire, Hallie brought the babe to her. "She's gettin' a mite fussy—she wants her mammy," Hallie said, grinning. "Put her to your breast, Missus. Tho' she ain't gettin' much from you t'night. I feed her later if she's a fussin'."

Emilie opened her gown, put the small, whimpering babe to her breast. She watched with wonder as the small mouth rooted to her nipple. "Gracious! She sucks strongly!" Emilie exclaimed.

Hallie grinned. "Didn't think a mite like that could suck so pow'ful, did you Missus? You don't let her take too much a' you these first days, or you be mighty sore!"

The door opened; Emilie stiffened as Edgar entered the room. Neatly dressed in a black suit, he carried two wrapped packages. He nodded to Hallie. "I wish to speak with my wife—alone."

Hallie left, closing the door. Emilie's heart thudded as Edgar approached the bed.

"Can't you come back later?" she asked. "I'm nursing the baby."

"So I see," he replied. He placed the packages on the bed next to her, sat down in the chair near her. His eyes studied the suckling babe. "I'm staying," he said matter-of-factly. "I won't get to see you—thus—when you're gone."

Emilie lowered her gaze, feeling her face burn. Was he hinting that he would miss her? Perhaps. But then her pride stubbornly reminded her that he would never have let a son go. She had failed him by having a daughter. Now he was letting her go, because he never wanted her anyway.

"Have you thought of a name for her?" he asked.

She looked up. "I'd thought of calling her Camille Barrett, for my mother."

"Camille Barrett," he repeated thoughtfully. "Yes, I like it."

They fell silent then, listening to the sound of the baby feeding. Presently, the infant fell asleep; Edgar stood and took the baby from Emilie, gently placed her in the cradle.

Sitting back down, he asked, "Aren't you going to open your presents?"

She looked at the two packages on the bed. "Oh, I'd quite forgotten them," she murmured. "Who are they from?"

"Me," he said, smiling kindly.

She gulped—how handsome he looked when he smiled—she could almost—almost—

She picked up the large box, hastily untied the ribbons. She smiled as she pulled out a fringed leather riding *gaucho*.

"I had Doña Elena make it for you," he explained.

"Yes, I knew," she replied, stroking the soft buckskin.

He cocked an eyebrow. "You knew?"

"Yes, I'm afraid Maria spilled the beans to me right before the—*fiesta*."

He sighed. "No matter. I thought you might need it. That when you were better we might ride together." He paused, gesturing resignedly. "Open the other one."

Grateful to have the awkward exchange over, Emilie put the large box aside and turned to the smaller one. She gasped as she unwrapped a crystal bottle. She held it up, watching the lamplight sparkle upon the planes and angles.

"I know it's not exactly like your mother's bottle," Edgar was saying, "but it's a close match, isn't it love? I had David look far and wide for the rose-colored crystal. And, of course, it's filled with the finest Paris perfume."

Emilie stared at the beautiful pink bottle, and began to melt. She wanted to throw her arms around him, tell him she would stay, even if he never loved her.

But then she remembered the reason the first bottle was broken—his mistress, Avis. Before her—Olivia. How could she share him with the ones who had come first? How could she, when he would never confide in her, would never forget the past? No, she could stay in this house of secrets no more.

"Thank you, Edgar. Both presents are lovely."

He stood. For a moment they gazed at one another—his eyes were dark with sadness, hers bright with tears. He leaned over, his lips brushed her forehead.

Her heart screamed, Edgar, ask me to stay! Please, ask me to stay!

"Merry Christmas, love," he whispered.

Chapter Twelve

February 14, 1842

Emilie smiled. "Of course you may rock her, Margaret."

Emilie buttoned the bodice of her blue wool dress and snugly wrapped tiny Camille in a pink and white crocheted blanket. She stood with the babe, crossed to meet Margaret in the middle of the room, transferring the small bundle into her friend's arms.

Emilie turned, took a cotton cloth from the tea table, followed her friend to the rocking chair. "There, let's put this across your shoulder, Margaret. We can't have the baby spitting up on that lovely lavender frock."

"No matter, dear, but thanks," Margaret said as she settled herself in the chair, her silk skirts rustling. She put Camille against her shoulder, patted her back.

Both women giggled as the baby burped loudly. Tiny Camille looked around, then cooed in assent with the women, causing them both to laugh deeply.

"How alert she is!" Margaret exclaimed. "And look how she holds up her head! Why, the mite is not yet two months old!''

"Aye, she's a healthy, happy babe," Emilie agreed warmly.

Emilie seated herself upon the settee. She glanced about at the parlor—Granny's parlor. Every peg on the wall was familiar, as were the crisp gingham curtains, the rough cedar floors. Familiar, beloved—home.

"It's hard to believe we've been home almost a month," Emilie murmured, stroking the rough red wool of the settee.

Margaret shook a slim finger at Emilie. "You were a foolish girl to travel so soon after Cammie's birth. Although I must admit that your friendship has been a godsend these past weeks, with Mr. Houston gone in Austin."

"Aye, we're both without men at the moment, aren't we?" Emilie agreed. She went on wistfully, "Just wish I could look forward to seeing Edgar again, as you must look forward to seeing your Sam." She smiled at her friend. "And you mustn't scold me, Margaret. Cammie and I had to travel when we did, or wait several more weeks for the *Belle's* return. That—I could not bear. Besides, David was with us, as well as Hallie and Jacob."

Margaret's violet eyes met Emilie's sympathetically. "You poor dear. Did Mr. Ashland never even hint he wanted you to stay?"

"No. We were strangers those last weeks. As I've told you, Margaret, he no longer cared what I did after Camille was born. When I saw his face after she came, I knew I had to leave him. He looked so disappointed, and I—I just couldn't take any more. My leaving simply confirmed what we'd both known for ages. Our marriage was a mistake."

Margaret shook her head, clucking softly. "Oh,

my dear, you aren't thinking of living apart permanently, are you?"

Emilie shrugged. "In truth, Margaret, I haven't thought much of the future. Before I left Brazos Bend, I avoided Edgar as much as possible—I wasn't about to say anything which might make him change his mind about letting us go. I must say, he didn't seem to miss my company."

Margaret leaned forward as she rocked the drowsy Camille. "But didn't you mention that he came to her christening?"

"Yes, that was strange," Emilie admitted. "We were all standing at the front of the church—David, Maria and I. I was about to give Camille to Pastor Fritz. Then suddenly, the door to the church flew open. The wind swept in—but the chill that fell over us seemed colder than the wind, even. I turned, and there he stood in the doorway. Everyone fell silent, even Pastor Fritz. Then he started up the aisle, and all we could hear were his boots pounding the floor. He got to us, and his face—"

"Yes, dear?" Margaret prompted, her eyes wide.

Emilie looked at Margaret sadly. "He never smiled. He just held out his arms, looking so solemn. I gave him Camille, and he handed her to the pastor."

Across the room, Margaret beamed as she tucked the blanket about Cammie's neck. "Oh, how romantic, dear! Doesn't that prove he cares for both of you?"

Emilie sighed. "I have given up on trying to guess his motives, Margaret."

"But from what you've told me, that was the first time he has left the plantation in five years."

"Aye," Emilie conceded. "Perhaps he cares for us a little—as he would for his other possessions. But he

442

didn't ask us to stay."

"Perhaps he'll come to Houston to ask you back," Margaret ventured. "He must miss the two of you greatly."

Emilie frowned, a faraway look in her eyes. "I think not, Margaret. Edgar's a lone wolf. His reasons for marrying me were—forgive my bluntness, dear friend, but his reasons were purely physical. They were also rather bizarre. You see, I look much like Olivia Rice Ashland."

"Yes, I know, dear," Margaret sympathized. "That hideous business with Olivia and her brother! David explained it to us at the funeral in Hempstead."

"Yes, it was good of David to take Aaron's body home to his family." Emilie grimaced, memories splintering her brain.

"There, dear, let's not discuss that scoundrel," Margaret soothed. "We must put our heads together and get you and Mr. Ashland back together. Despite what you say, I saw the look in his eyes at the *fiesta*. I'm sure he's in love with you."

"Margaret, he's not—"

"Hush, and listen to me," Margaret went on firmly as she rocked the sleeping babe. "Now, let's go back to what you said about his marrying you. Are you sure it was simply because you resemble Olivia?"

Sighing Emilie got up and walked to the window, pulling her shawl tightly about her as she gazed out at the midday bleariness, the muddy streets of Houston. "Yes. He pursued me from the moment I arrived at Brazos Bend. He even threatened me with ravishment if I did not marry him!"

"Oh, you poor dear!" Margaret exclaimed.

Emilie laughed dryly. "Within three days, I was

443

his bride. Surely his haste was due to the resemblance.'' Emilie turned to her friend, gritting her teeth as she continued. ''The cad even promised not to consummate the marriage until I was ready—then immediately broke his word!''

Margaret's eyes widened in her reddening face. ''How contemptible! You don't mean—'' her voice trailed off miserably as she stroked Cammie's tiny blonde head.

''Oh, he made his reasons for marrying me—'' she nodded toward the baby— ''quite clear from the outset.'' Noting Margaret's deepening blush, she went on apologetically, ''Forgive me if I've been indelicate, Margaret. But we've become such good friends, that I feel I can share these things with you.''

''Oh, of course, dear,'' Margaret assured her quickly.

For a moment, the two women fell silent, listening to the creakings of Granny's rocker and the deep breathing of little Camille.

Then Margaret giggled. ''Pardon me, Emilie, I'm a wicked girl for thinking this—but the entire situation has a ring of romance to it, does it not? I don't doubt Mr. Houston might have stooped to such shenanigans, had I refused his suit.''

Emilie laughed shortly. ''I doubt Mr. Houston would have thrown you in the river.''

Margaret's jaw dropped. ''He threw you—where, dear?''

''In the river,'' Emilie repeated grimly. ''Oh, in a sense I suppose I deserved it.'' She explained to Margaret the details of the episode with the pastor and Edgar.

When Emilie finished, Margaret expostulated, ''You did try him mightily, my dear—but it's a miracle you didn't drown!''

"Precisely," Emilie agreed. "That's why I can't live with him, never knowing what to expect. He has never communicated with me. All I know of him is his anger—and his lust. I just wish—"

"Yes, dear?"

Emilie shivered. "It's cold by this window," she muttered distractedly. She walked to the iron stove, held her hands out. "If only he would tell me what happened in the past, instead of turning livid every time I say a wrong word. If we could get everything out into the open, perhaps then there might be hope for us. I might be able to trust him."

"Ah," Margaret murmured, nodding thoughtfully as she rocked. "Then that is what you must do."

Emilie smiled dolefully. "It's useless, Margaret. He'll never confide in me."

"Then you must take the initiative, dear."

"How?"

Margaret's brown brows knitted in thought. After a moment, she snapped her fingers. "David lived with Edgar all those years, did he not?"

"Yes, but—"

"Then get *him* to tell you about Edgar's past!"

"But what would he know?"

"I'll wager he knows plenty," Margaret returned, smiling sagely. "David was *there*—he can't have been blind."

Emilie's eyes lit up. "You know, David once told me marriage can mean disaster between two people—that he'll never marry!"

Margaret nodded knowingly. "Aye, he must know a great deal." She leaned forward imploringly. "Didn't you mention earlier that he is also calling today?"

"Why, yes, his last letter did mention he would be in town—"

"Then you must interrogate him at the first opportunity," Margaret said firmly, "ruthlessly—if necessary."

"Oh, Margaret, must I? He is so very dear to me!"

"Of course you must—if you ever want to see Edgar again. Besides, it would do the young man good to discuss the situation with someone. He must be quite bitter, if he plans never to marry."

Emilie's face glowed with realization. "Margaret, you're right! It *is* time for the truth to be known— for everyone's sake!"

An hour later, while Margaret still rocked Camille, Emilie answered a knock at her door to find David Ashland on her porch, "Welcome, David!" she cried excitedly, hugging him.

"Greetings, my dear," he returned, kissing her. Grinning, his cheeks flushed from the cold, David entered the parlor. Spotting Margaret with the babe, he bowed. "Mrs. Houston! What a pleasure to see you again!"

Margaret smiled serenely and extended a beautifully shaped hand. "Likewise, Mr. Ashland."

David crossed to Margaret, stuffing his gloves in his pocket, shaking her hand. He glanced down at the tiny swaddled form in her arms. Stroking Camille's soft cheek with his index finger, he whispered, "Hello, little cousin! My, what a beauty you are!"

Emilie went to David, urging, "Give me your coat and go stand by the fire, David. You look half-frozen."

"Aye, the stove looks inviting," David agreed.

446

"But first, I must brave the cold again. I've something for you and the babe out in the buggy."

Pulling on his gloves, David hurried out the front door.

Margaret whispered to Emilie, "Dare we hope it's Edgar?"

Despite herself, Emilie smiled. "I think not, Margaret."

Margaret got to her feet and deposited the sleeping babe in Emilie's arms. "I'm going, dear. This is the perfect opportunity for you and David to have your talk." She took her cloak and bonnet from the peg near the door. "Mind you, interrogate him well, dear," she continued sternly, pulling her gloves from the pocket on her cloak. "Remember this—you and Mr. Ashland belong together. Sam and I have agreed upon it."

Emilie smiled, following Margaret to the door. "You're both such dears—but one can't saw sawdust, Margaret."

"Bosh!" Margaret Houston retorted briskly. "Now you find out from David what your husband's trouble is, then get things set right." She winked at Emilie. "Mr. Houston has indicated that he may intervene personally. You wouldn't want your marriage reestablished by presidential decree, now would you, dear?"

Emilie giggled. "Margaret, you're such a tease."

Margaret tied her bonnet, then quickly kissed Emilie on the cheek. "I can assure you, Emilie, Mr. Houston was not teasing."

She opened the door just as David appeared with what looked like a rocking bench. Margaret held the door open for him, then told them goodbye and departed.

David placed the bench near the iron stove.

"There," he beamed. "Happy Saint Valentine's Day, dear."

Holding Camille, Emilie crossed the room to gaze at the strange piece of furniture David had brought her. It was rather like a spindleback bench, with rocking treads. But half of the seat was also enclosed with spindles, in box fashion.

"What is it?" Emilie asked.

"It's a Mammy Rocker, of course," David said excitely. "It's the latest rage in motherhood, my dear." He took Emilie's arm. "You sit down here—and the baby goes in the cradle part."

Emilie sat down, as bid. "Let's see," David continued thoughtfully, "she'll need bedding." He crossed to the cradle in the corner and pulled out Cammie's mattress and pillow. "What a pretty heart-shaped pillow she has," he remarked as he returned and arranged the bedding next to Emilie. "Who embroidered her name?"

"Margaret Houston presented the pillow to us today," Emilie replied, watching him.

"There," he said, smoothing down the bedding, "all we need is the baby."

David took Cammie and placed her in the cradle part of the bench. "Oh, look—she's opening those precious blue eyes of hers! Good afternoon, little cousin! Now, Emilie, rock. Your baby goes to sleep, and you're free to do your knitting—or whatever it is you women do when your babies are sleeping."

Emilie giggled. "Thank you, David. It's quite clever."

David grinned. "It was in the window of the General Store. Couldn't resist. Only the best for my darling cousin." He extended a gloved finger to little Camille; the babe grasped the finger in a tiny fist and cooed up at David, grinning toothlessly.

"Oh, you sweetheart!" he breathed.

Emilie glanced up at David worriedly. "David, take off your coat and hat before you become overheated."

After kissing the babe, David complied, hanging his hat, scarf and greatcoat on the peg near the door. Then he crossed the room, sat down in Granny's rocker. "She'll sleep, now," he murmured, looking at the baby adoringly. "Have you—and she—been well?"

"Yes, thanks," Emilie replied, rocking. Her eyes swept David. He looked quite handsome in his black wool frock coat and matching trousers. His shirt front and cuffs were of ruffled linen; he wore a festive red bow tie. His blue eyes seemed even brighter than she remembered; his hair gleamed with blonde highlights.

"Your note was quite brief," she continued. "What brings you to Houston?"

"Business. Supplies for the spring planting. But mostly you."

"Me?"

"Yes, of course, dear. I worry about you here, alone."

"I'm not alone—I have Hallie and Jacob," Emilie put in defensively.

David glanced about the room. "Where are they?"

"I sent them shopping. They took Little Jacob with them."

"That's another matter I must discuss with you," David went on sternly. "Five people living in this tiny house—"

"It is *not* tiny!" Emilie cut in. "There are two large bedrooms—one for each family. We make out quite nicely, thank you."

David flushed. "Forgive me, Emilie. I didn't mean to sound harsh. But I'd be glad to buy you a larger house."

"I don't want a larger house. This is my home."

"Uncle wants you to have everything you desire. He worries about you so."

A glimmer of hope lit Emilie's eyes. "Did he say that—that he worries?"

"He didn't have to."

She shrugged. "I see."

An awkward silence fell between them. Then David cleared his throat and asked, "Did the bank inform you about the letter of credit I sent?"

"Yes. You've been quite generous. I don't think we'll need much money."

David's jaw tightened. "Now, my dear, I'm afraid I must be firm with you. The money in the accounts is for you to use. You're to lack for nothing, do you understand? You're to have every luxury until—"

"Until what, David?"

He frowned. "Until you come home to Uncle." He glanced about expansively. "Surely you don't expect to make this move permanent."

Emilie stopped rocking, her heart in her eyes as she gazed steadily at David. "Has he said anything of me? That he misses me—wants me back—anything?"

David's face twisted in pain. "No, dear."

He stood and walked to her, placing his hand over hers. "But it's written all over his face, Emilie. Come home, dear—he needs you. He's off riding his horse in the cold these days, when he's not drunk. He hardly utters a word to anyone."

Emilie felt her heart wrenching at his words. "I can't, David," she choked. "I don't trust him. I've the babe to think of now."

For a moment, they both gazed solemnly at Camille, who was now fast asleep, her small, round face peaceful as her mother rocked her.

David sighed resignedly. "Aye, you've a point, my dear." He walked back to Granny's rocker, sat down heavily. "Is there no hope of a reconciliation?"

Emilie searched David's face. He looked sad, vulnerable. Then she remembered Margaret Houston's suggestion. "David—there might be. Tell me about your uncle and Olivia."

Caught off guard, David sputtered, "W-what?"

"David, what did Olivia do to all of you? Your uncle is locked up in the past, Maria is desperately insecure, you have told me you'll never marry. And Aaron—" her voice caught, and she shivered.

David glanced at Emilie, his deep blue eyes sympathetic. "There, dear, let's not discuss that blackguard. You'll only cause yourself needless grief."

"But I must," Emilie whispered hoarsely, her eyes holding David's beseechingly. "Aaron told me that he—Olivia—David, is it true?"

David shook his head. "That you'll have to discuss with Uncle. I know no more than you."

"But your uncle will tell me nothing!" Emilie retorted. "Please, David, you must tell me everything you know of Olivia. If you care for your uncle at all—please, I beg you!"

Emilie looked at him intently, silent pleading in her eyes.

His face twisted in a play of tormented emotion. Then he sighed. "Ah, my dear, you do not make it easy for me, do you?"

The question was rhetorical, for he stood and walked to the window. Gazing out at the bleakness beyond, he whispered, "Perhaps, dear, it is best we lay Olivia to rest, once and for all."

Emilie stopped rocking. A chill swept through her. She felt her heart thudding as she gazed at David's black-clothed back.

"Olivia Ashland was one of the most fascinating women I've ever known. In many ways, she was the most wicked woman I've ever known. Yet she also possessed an unpretentious charm. It's easy to figure out why Uncle married her."

"But she ended up drowning," Emilie reminded him. "Why? Did she and your uncle quarrel over Aaron?"

David shrugged, his fingers tapping the window sill. "No," he replied. "As I told you, I know nothing of Olivia and Aaron. Actually, I knew little of Olivia's relationship with Uncle. I only know—what I know."

"Which is?" she prompted.

He turned to look at her, his face a study in torment mixed with fear. "Emilie, I beg you, let it go. What you want me to tell you could change the rest of your life—and mine. Please think, dear."

She did not think. She did not hesitate. "Tell me."

He frowned in resignation. "Very well, dear."

Slowly, he crossed the room, sinking into the rocker. Clutching the arms of the chair, he gazed off into space. "Olivia was—a flirt, a tease. She had a contagious smile, a very persuasive manner. She wasn't like you at all, Emilie."

He paused, shot Emilie a pleading glance, but she only nodded firmly. He sighed, running his hand through his hair. "I killed Olivia," he said dully.

"W-what?" Emilie sputtered, leaning forward in her chair.

"I killed her," he repeated woodenly. "I might as

well have tied her hands and thrown her in the river.''

''David, what are you saying? Olivia's death was an accident—''

''No!'' he cried bitterly, tears springing to his eyes. ''It was no accident. Uncle—when Uncle came home from San Jacinto, he found Olivia and me in bed together!''

Emilie's jaw dropped. She stared speechlessly at David's distraught face.

''It's true!'' he choked. ''I went to bed with my uncle's wife! Christ, Emilie, it was horrible! If you could have seen his face—it was all I could do to restrain him. I had to knock him over the head with a vase or he would have—he was going to kill Olivia!''

David broke down completely and began to sob, turning away and burying his face in his hands.

Emilie stood, steadied the rocking bench, then hurried to his side. She had never before heard a man weep, and the sound was piteous, wrenching her heart. Putting a hand on his shaking shoulder, she whispered lamely, ''David, I . . . David.''

He trembled with emotion, and she stood helplessly watching him. After a moment, he quieted, but he did not look up at her.

''So you knocked your uncle unconscious,'' Emilie murmured, ''and Olivia fled with the babes?''

He nodded.

''Then your uncle came to, chased them and—'' she paused, shivering.

Again, he nodded. No further details were necessary.

Emilie tried to digest the startling information David had just given her. ''How old were you then, David?''

"Sixteen."

"Sixteen!" she gasped. "And Olivia—oh, you poor dear!"

David looked up at her then, his eyes reddened, his face tortured. "Uncle never blamed me. He explained to me later that Olivia was the type who had to have a man, and that when he left for the war, she—she—"

"Seduced you?" Emilie supplied gently.

"Aye," he shuddered miserably. "God, Emilie, I wish Uncle *had* blamed me! I felt I should be punished. T'would be so much easier to accept his wrath than to watch his pain all these years!"

Emilie frowned, thinking of Edgar. "Aye, he must have suffered to have Olivia betray him with Aaron, then use you so heartlessly."

David stood, his eyes beseeching Emilie as he took her hand. "I hope you understand, now, how much my uncle needs you, Emilie. I was so hopeful for the two of you this summer. Uncle seemed—reborn. Then, after the *fiesta,* the two of you grew so estranged. Why?"

Emilie smiled sadly. "Why, David? Because of the past. Because Aaron Rice came, stirring up the dust of bitter memories. Oh, I can see it all so clearly now, David! Your uncle hates me—he has used me to punish Olivia! Don't you see there's no hope for our marriage? We can't alter the past—or change my face!"

"But Emilie, surely if you talk to Uncle—"

"No, it's over," she said resignedly. "I thank you for telling me, David. I'm sure it was painful for you, but now I know where I stand."

They stood gazing at each other, both close to tears. Emilie squeezed David's hand. "But don't let what happened with Olivia ruin your life, David.

None of it was your fault, do you hear? You did not kill Olivia—she killed herself. Now—go marry that Maria of yours and be happy."

David drew back, startled. "Oh, no, Emilie, I'll not marry," he told her vehemently. "Look how I've botched things—in both my uncle's marriages. No, I've done enough harm."

"Nonsense!" Emilie retorted.

"But Emilie," he argued, "even if I could forget what happened with Olivia, how can I live with what I did to you! I deserted you, left you at Uncle's mercy."

Emilie sighed. "That's not true, David. I realize, now, that had I truly hated him, wild horses could not have dragged me before the parson." She looked lovingly at her sleeping babe, then back to him. "Remember this, David Ashland. I do not regret a moment I spent with your uncle. And I—I'd give all my tomorrows for a single day in his arms." Her eyes filled with tears. "But that, I cannot have."

He put a hand on her shoulder. "Emilie, I—"

"Never mind me!" she choked. "Go to Maria—now—and tell her what you feel. She needs you desperately, David—I can't begin to tell you how much! It's too late for your uncle and me. But it's not too late for you. Tell Maria you love her. She loves you, too, you know."

"She does?" he asked in amazement.

"Yes—it's written all over her face! Are you blind?" She laughed weakly, remembering Sam Houston's words at the *fiesta*. "Yes, of course, you're blind—blind in love." She hurried to the door, took David's coat and hat. "Get your supplies and start home immediately, David," she urged. "You don't belong here."

"Very well, I'll go, dear," he said, dressing for the

cold. "But are you sure there's nothing you're in need of?"

She shook her head vigorously. "Go to her—now. Forget the past—and your pride. Don't make the same mistakes your uncle and I made."

He tied his scarf about his neck. "Any message for Uncle?" he asked hopefully.

She stood on tiptoe and kissed his cheek, then opened the door. "Goodbye, David."

Chapter Thirteen

March 14, 1842

David and Maria sat eating lunch in the dining room. Edgar stumbled in. He was unshaven, his eyes bleary. "Where the hell's the brandy?"

"Uncle, get a coat," David replied solicitously. "The room is chilly, and your shirt is open—"

"Hah!" Edgar snorted. "I've my brandy to keep me warm." He took the decanter from the sideboard and poured himself a generous glassful.

He sauntered back to the table, sat down. Pushing his chair back, he noisily crossed his boots on the table top, breaking a glass in the process. "Pray, continue with your lunch," he said with a crooked, sardonic smile.

"Señor Ashland, you should eat," Maria put in, her eyes widening.

Edgar waved her off. "I've all the nourishment I need in this bottle."

David and Maria exchanged worried glances. "Uncle, don't you think you should go a bit easy—it's just now midday—"

Edgar slammed down the decanter. "Don't dictate to me, boy! How much I imbibe is none of your

Goddamned business! Now—both of you—eat your food and quit carping!"

The two fell silent under his angry glare and began to pick at their chicken fricassee.

Presently, David looked up and sighed. "I fear Uncle's passed out again," he told Maria. "Daniel!"

The old servant hurried into the dining room. "Mister Ashland in'sposed agin?" he asked, scratching his wooly head.

Nodding, David removed the brandy snifter from Edgar's hand. The two men pulled him to his feet.

Edgar's eyes opened. "What the hell you doing?" he mumbled drunkenly.

"You're tired, Uncle," David told him firmly.

" 'Spose so," he grumbled, letting the two men help him out of the room.

As the threesome started up the stairs, Edgar whispered to David, almost shyly, "Tell me about her again—my daughter."

David's heart wrenched at his uncle's words. Every time Edgar got drunk—which was quite frequently, now—he asked of his daughter. "She's the most beautiful babe I've ever seen," he assured Edgar, as he always did.

"Aye, the most beautiful," Edgar agreed wistfully.

The three entered Edgar's bedroom. Once Edgar was deposited on the bed, David helped Daniel pull off his boots.

Edgar's eyes rolled toward a neat stack of letters on the bedside table. Gesturing unsteadily, he mumbled, "Going to burn those Goddamned letters from Houston's woman. Why does the wench torment me so? Emilie deserted me—why the hell

458

should I care how the girl spends her time?" His fist pounded the mattress. "Burn the letters, nephew!"

David took a step forward, staring flabbergasted at his wildeyed uncle. "But Uncle, I—"

"Don't you dare burn the letters!" Edgar contradicted hoarsely, jerking upright, shaking a fist at his nephew. He fell back, groaning, shutting his eyes. "Burn 'um myself, later."

David smiled, turning to leave. "Yes, Uncle."

"Wait, David," Edgar whispered, his eyes still closed. "Read to me—please."

Edgar's last remark was almost inaudible; David moved forward tentatively. "Which letter do you wish to hear this time, Uncle?"

"Doesn't matter—just read," he mumbled.

Sitting down upon the chair near the bed, David took the first envelope from the stack. Pulling out and unfolding the parchment, he cleared his throat and began, " 'Dear Mr. Ashland, Tiny Camille grows more beautiful each day, if that is possible. Your dear wife has regained her health, and is blooming like our lovely Texas wildflowers—"

Edgar's eyes flew open. "Damn the girl!" he growled.

His head fell to the side, and he began to snore.

"How is he?" Maria asked when David returned to the dining room.

Sitting down, David sighed. "He misses Emilie—and Camille."

Maria nodded solemnly. "So do I."

David glanced at her cajolingly. "Hey, where's that pretty smile of yours? We can't let Uncle's drinking throw us both into the doldrums."

"*Sí*, David—I try to be cheerful—for your sake.

But it's gotten so depressing here since Emilie and the *bebe* left.'' She blushed, lifting a delicate black brow. ''Why are you staring at me so, David?''

He smiled. ''I was just thinking of something Emilie said about you.''

''Yes?'' Maria asked apprehensively.

His eyes darkened. He stood, pulled her to her feet. ''My, that's a pretty dress you're wearing. Yellow really complements your hair and eyes. You say it's depressing here—come, dear, let's go for a ride about the countryside.''

She sighed, smiling. ''Oh, yes, David, let's leave this unhappy house for a while!''

Later, as the buggy bounced past rows of young cotton plants, Maria remarked, ''The air is delightfully cool today, *verdad?*'' Nodding toward the workers in the fields, she added, ''The slaves must find it pleasant to work.'' Suddenly, her eyes lit up. ''Oh, David—look at the prairie! The wildflowers are blooming!''

David smiled as he clucked to the team of matched grays. ''Shall we go have a look at my hillside?''

She nodded; David turned the team from the road, and they started across the bluebonnet-carpeted prairie. Soon, they entered the small Mexican settlement. Several of the *mexicanos* waved to them from their gardens or yards; chickens and pigs scurried out of the buggy's path.

Maria's eyes brightened. ''Shall we go say hello to Doña Elena?''

David shook his head gently. ''If you don't mind, my dear, I'd prefer being alone with you today.''

Maria's eyelids fluttered at his remark. ''Oh,'' she mumbled. ''Of course, David.''

Moments later, he stopped the buggy on the crest

of the hillside. He stepped to the ground, assisted Maria down. The two walked through an opening in the trees onto the vast green stage where the *fiesta* had been held.

They moved toward the center, holding hands. David stopped, held her hand tightly as he gazed down at her lovingly. "Do you remember—last October?" he whispered. "When you danced for me?"

She gazed up at him, her green eyes smiling beneath the cover of her yellow bonnet. "Oh, Davíd, how could I forget?"

"Davíd," he repeated. "I like it when you pronounce my name thus." He nodded toward the trees. "Do you remember—" he paused, smiled. Then he pulled her into his arms.

Her lips quivered as his mouth slowly descended upon hers. He kissed her gently, feeling his way. Her mouth yielded; her arms curled around his neck. Sighing heavily, he pulled her closer; his kiss deepened.

When they finally drew apart, both were breathless. After a moment of awkward silence, Maria asked almost worriedly, "Davíd, I must know—what is it Emilie said of me?"

He smiled a warm smile which lit his blue eyes. "She told me you're in love with me. Are you, dear?"

Maria flushed, biting her lip.

"Please, sweetheart, tell me," he coaxed.

She looked up at him slowly, adoration in her eyes. "*Sí*, Davíd, I love you," she whispered. "Do—do you love me?"

"Oh, my dear," he breathed, tears of joy in his eyes. "Yes, I love you! Yes!"

Her face lit up. "When did you know?"

"Well—I must have loved you for ages," he replied excitedly. "But I truly knew at the *fiesta.*"

"Me, too!" she gasped wonderingly. "Oh, Davíd, how I have dreamed of hearing those words from your lips. How I have—"

But he did not allow her to finish. He pulled her close, kissed her with a passion that startled and ignited them both.

Afterwards, he let out a whoop of joy. "She loves me! She loves me!" he shouted, grabbing her hand and pulling her, laughing, about the grassy clearing.

Once they slowed a bit, he told her breathlessly, "I'll build you a grand *hacienda*—here. We'll have dozens of children!"

"*Sí,* dozens," she laughed.

"We'll be married, of course," he added hastily.

"*Por supuesto,*" she agreed with mock gravity.

He squeezed her hand. "Thank heaven Emilie told me not to delay, to tell you of my feelings."

"She did? Then we both owe her a great debt, Davíd." Glancing about, she added, "We shall have a good life, *sí,* Davíd? Raising cattle—as my people have done for centuries! And we'll be so close to our *mexicano* friends." She nodded in the direction of the settlement. "I'm surprised we haven't seen any of our *amigos* from below—considering your loud declaration of your feelings, Davíd."

"Who would try to silence a man in love?" he quipped.

Suddenly, Maria smiled, her eyes sparkling dazzlingly. "Oh, Davíd—let's go tell Doña Elena and Don Lorenzo! I simply cannot wait another moment!"

David frowned. "I'd hoped we might tell Uncle

first. However—I do suppose the de la Peñas are family, also, aren't they, Maria?"

"Sí, mi amor."

Later, as Maria and David stood in the front hallway of Brazos Bend, hanging their outer clothing on hooks, they were surprised to see Edgar come tearing down the stairs.

He looked quite sober—clean-shaven, in a fresh suit. But his eyes were wild, and he held a letter tightly clutched in one hand.

"Another one!" he expostulated, shaking the envelope at them before he stuffed it in his breast pocket.

"You mean a letter arrived while we were gone, Uncle?"

"Yes! The circuit rider came an hour ago!" Edgar said agitatedly. Going to the hallway clothing rack, he grabbed his coat and riding crop.

David and Maria exchanged confused glances. "Well—what did Mrs. Houston, say, Uncle? And where are you going?"

Edgar scowled at David. "I'm going to Houston to get this matter straightened out—once and for all."

"You're going to Houston!" David and Maria exclaimed in unison.

"No, I'm going to hell to play poker with the devil!" Edgar shot back tensely, shaking on his coat. "Now—can you two addle-pated children keep the place standing while I'm gone?"

"Why—why of course, Uncle," David sputtered.

"Good." Edgar opened the door; a crisp breeze swept in.

"Uncle, before you go—" David said, grabbing

463

his arm.

"Yes?"

"I—I wanted to tell you—" David took a deep breath, "Maria and I plan to marry."

Edgar's features softened and he smiled. Shaking David's hand, he said, "About time, Nephew." He hurried to Maria, hugged her and kissed her cheek. "Congratulations, Maria. See my nephew behaves while I'm gone."

Leaving, Edgar called over his shoulder. "I must apologize that we cannot celebrate this joyous news until later."

David and Maria followed Edgar out onto the porch. "But Uncle, can't you tell us what the letter said, what you're planning to do?"

Edgar took Apollyon's reins from the stable boy and mounted the Arabian. He stared into space, a strange gleam in his eyes. "Only three days—I might make it, David, I just might." Looking down at the two of them, he whispered intensely, *"My* eyes. Can you believe it? *My* eyes! It simply cannot be borne, David!"

Uttering this strange remark, Edgar Ashland clenched his legs against Apollyon's sides, and the stallion raced off towards Houston.

David shook his head as he watched the man and horse disappear down the hillside. "Uncle's going to have a damn hard ride, if he isn't lucky enough to meet a steamboat somewhere down the line." He put his arm around Maria's waist. "Let's get inside, dear. You're shivering without your shawl."

As they reentered the front hallway, Maria asked, "What does your uncle mean by all this strange talk of eyes? I do not understand, Davíd."

David shrugged. "Perhaps my uncle finally looked into the mirror and saw the truth."

Chapter Fourteen

March 17, 1842

Emilie Ashland stood in her bedroom, smiling down at the cradles holding two peacefully sleeping babes. Leaning over, she covered both infants. Little Jacob looked like a small giant, with his stocky chocolate limbs and large head, especially in comparison to tiny Camille, who was delicately boned and featured, had smooth pink skin, a small head adorned with wispy blonde curls.

The babes slept beneath a window, bright light pouring in, making the room almost warm. Again, it would be a mild spring, Emilie decided. She gazed through the gingham-curtained window to the brightness outside—the muddy clearing which served as their back yard, the wilderness of trees beyond.

She felt her chest tighten as she thought of another year, another spring. Today was the first anniversary of her marriage to Edgar. She sighed. So much had happened, she seemed to have lived a lifetime in those brief months. And now—now she would never see him again. She bit her lip, a tear springing to her eye. By God, today she would not weep about him!

She had her daughter to consider!

As she started to leave the room, she caught her tearful reflection in the beveled mirror above the dresser. She fished through her pockets, drew out a handkerchief and dried her eyes. Returning the cloth to the pocket of her yellow gingham dress, she pulled her white wool shawl tightly about her. After smoothing down the gold curls cascading from the blue satin bow at the nape of her neck, she left the room.

Emilie returned to the parlor to find Hallie in one corner of the room, placing ironstone plates and silverware on a small, calico-clothed wooden table.

"Lil Jacob raisin' a fuss, Missus?"

Emilie smiled. "No, Hallie. He's fast asleep."

Emilie went to the rocking bench and took up her knitting.

"Might be nigh afternoon 'fore I'm through stirrin' that stew, Missus," Hallie called from across the room. "That chicken Jacob fetched me is tough as a boot."

Emilie shrugged as she worked the knitting needles. "Take your time, Hallie. I'm expecting Mrs. Houston this morning, anyway."

"Sure 'nuff, Missus? Ain't her man home right now?"

Emilie's brows knitted. "Yes, the note she sent yesterday did mention that Mr. Houston had just returned, rather suddenly, from Austin. But I suppose Mrs. Houston is calling because she knows today will be difficult for me."

Hallie nodded sympathetically as she opened the front door. "You call if'n you want tea, Missus."

Hallie went off to the kitchen, leaving Emilie in the lonely room, with only the creaking of the rocker to shield her from her painful memories. When the expected knock at the door came, she arose with great relief and anticipation.

Throwing open the door, she said cheerfully, "Well, good morning, Mar—"

She froze. Her husband stood on the front porch, holding a bouquet of wildflowers.

"Happy anniversary, sweetheart," he said.

She stared back at him. Words failed her; she was spellbound, mesmerized.

He smiled, and her heart fluttered. Never had he looked more handsome. He was dressed in a chocolate brown frock coat, fawn-colored trousers, and shiny black boots. He wore a pleated linen shirt and black string cravat. His hair gleamed with morning sunlight; his eyes glowed with a tender light.

After an eternity, he inquired gently, "Won't you ask me in, love?"

Slowly, Emilie's hand rose to her throat. "You—came," she breathed hoarsely.

"Yes, darling, I came."

Unsteadily, she moved back, holding the door open. "I—I never thought you would." After he entered, she closed the door, leaned against it for support.

He held out the flowers. "For you, love."

Emilie could not meet his gaze as she reached out and took the bouquet of bluebonnets and Indian paintbrushes. Their hands contacted briefly as the flowers were transferred, and his touch seemed to burn her. She walked off, hoping he could not see the trembling of her limbs, or hear the wild beating of her heart.

"They're lovely," she murmured, laying the bouquet gently on the calico-clothed table. She fingered the damp handkerchief wrapped about the flower stems, saw the embroidered initials, "M.H."

"Why, this is Margaret Houston's handkerchief!" she exclaimed.

"Aye," Edgar said, moving towards her. "I stayed with the Houstons last night."

"You—you did?" She turned to stare at him.

He smiled. "Margaret Houston is quite a letter writer, my dear. She's been providing me with all sorts of useful information about you—and our daughter."

"She *has?* I never knew—"

"No, of course you wouldn't. That noble lady is just the kind to perform miracles, without ever expecting recognition. God knows I never answered any of those beautiful letters—even threatened to burn them all on more than one occasion."

"But why?" Emilie blurted.

He moved closer. "Why? Because I missed you unbearably, my darling. And every letter was like a knife, twisting in my heart."

"You—you missed me?" Emilie choked, turning away to hide her tears.

But then Edgar's arms were around her, turning her. She buried her face against his shoulder, and felt as if she were melting into him.

"Margaret Houston told me some interesting things," Edgar continued hoarsely. His hand reached for her chin. "There, sweetheart, look at me. She said you have been miserable without me. At first, I simply could not believe it. But now, I must know—is it true?"

Emilie's mouth trembled as she met the searching, emotional gaze of her husband. She could not hold back her feelings when he looked at her so. "Y-yes," she whispered.

His eyes lit up. "She said—that you love me. Oh, it's so much more than I could ever hope for, but tell me—is it true, darling?"

Her pride seemed to evaporate with the heat of his gaze. "Yes!" she breathed ecstatically. "Yes—I love you! I—"

But she didn't have a chance to finish, as he kissed her passionately. Her arms curled about his neck; her senses ignited with the taste of him, the smell of him, the feel of him. All their feelings were poured into the moment, and they drew apart with the greatest reluctance.

"I love you, Emilie, God, how I love you!" Edgar whispered, running his hands through her hair. "I want you to come home with me—you and my daughter. Christ, I'm dying to hold my baby again!"

Emilie drew back, awed. "You mean you're not disappointed she's a girl? When I saw your face after she came—"

"Disappointed?" he laughed. "Love, after she came, I was heartsick about the way I had treated you. But the babe—why, the mite holds my heart in her wee hands!" He looked around in smiling anticipation. "Where is she?"

"She's sleeping."

He nodded. "Just as well. For I've a surprise to tell you about first. Do you remember when you told me you felt as if we never married?"

"Yes," she replied, her brow puckered.

He took her hand, caressed it. "Will you come with me to the church, now, to reaffirm our vows?"

Caught off guard, she sputtered. "I—well—"

"Let's have a new beginning, today, on our anniversary," he urged, looking down at her adoringly. "And we must hurry—everyone's waiting."

"What do you mean?" she gasped.

He chuckled. "Your minister and his wife are there, and Margaret Houston took the liberty of inviting most everyone in town.''

"Surely you're jesting!"

"No, darling, I've never been more serious. Everything is in readiness. All I need is you, my darling, if you'll have me. And our daughter.''

Emilie stared up at him, her heart overflowing. How easy it would be to go with him now! Yet fear also tugged at her heart—would things really be changed if she took him back, or would he retreat into his previous secretive, arrogant behavior?

"Edgar, I want to try again with you," she said sincerely, "but it frightens me. There's so much you've never told me. I just don't know if there's a chance for us, not if you'll never confide in me.''

Edgar pulled her close, kissed her hair. "I know, darling. I—I wanted to confide in you before, but I was afraid to trust you with my feelings. I always thought you wanted David, or Aaron. But now that I know you care for me, I'll do my best to change. It won't be easy, but I'll try.'' He continued impatiently, "But right now, sweet, I'm aching to see our daughter, and everyone is waiting—''

"Then let them wait," Emilie replied, shaking her head. She led him toward the settee. "First, we're going to talk about Olivia.''

Stiffly, he sat down beside her. "Darling, some things are best left—''

"No!" she cut in. Her voice trembled, but she plunged on, "I'll not live with secrets—with ghosts! If you can't be honest with me, then—'' her voice caught—"then I have no choice but to live apart from you, Edgar!''

His face fell. "Emilie, you can't mean—loving me as you say you do—''

"*Especially* loving you," she choked, "I can bear the torment no more.''

His dark eyes searched her face; his jaw tightened as he took her hand. Cautiously, he asked, "What is it you want to know?"

"About Olivia—all about her."

He sighed deeply, staring off, his eyes full of pain. For a long moment, she was sure he would tell her nothing—such was the struggle twisting his features. But finally, he spoke in a hoarse whisper. "Olivia was—an enigma. She was as spoiled, as carefree, as cruel as a child. She was. . . ." his voice trailed off.

"Did you love her?"

He looked back at Emilie, his eyes tortured. "Yes. I thought I did, at any rate. She possessed a certain charm, a seductiveness. Like a fool, I thought it was all for me." He laughed bitterly. "It was a disappointment, when we married, to find out she was—less than chaste, shall we say. But I accepted it like a gentleman, did not question her. The marriage was bearable for the first year, although she was headstrong and willful, and as you might imagine, we had our spats. Then Olivia found out she was with child—and it enraged her."

"But why?"

Edgar sighed. "Olivia was a child herself—and never grew up. She ranted at me, insisting her figure would be ruined, all her fun over. And she refused—" his jaw grew rigid—"refused to sleep with me. We got into one hell of a row, and that was when—" his voice froze, and he ran his hand through his hair distractedly.

"Yes?"

"That was when she told me about Aaron," he whispered.

Emilie's heart went out to her husband. "Darling, I'm so sorry. How—how did she become involved with her brother?"

"I didn't ask for particulars. However, I assume Aaron started the liaison, since Olivia told me they had been copulating together since she was thirteen."

Emilie shivered with revulsion. "How hideous! That man—was depraved!"

Edgar kissed the top of her head. "Easy, love—he's gone, now."

She clutched his hand tightly, nodded shakily. "So Olivia—told you about her and Aaron. Then what?"

"Then—everything I'd ever felt for her died. I couldn't stand the sight of her—to touch her."

"And things stayed that way?"

He laughed shortly. "They got worse. There was *Maria*."

"Maria? How does she fit into all of this?"

"Don't you know?"

Emilie shook her head, her face twisting in puzzlement.

Edgar got to his feet and paced off towards the window, his hands clenched at his sides. "I'd had thought you would have figured it out by now."

"What do you mean?"

Edgar turned to face Emilie, his drawn features revealing his inner struggles. "Maria is Olivia's daughter."

"What?" Emilie jerked to her feet, her face thunderstruck. "But what—how—"

"Haven't you ever wondered why Maria came to live at the plantation, why she was treated as a member of the family?"

Emilie shook her head in bewilderment.

Edgar crossed the room, taking Emilie's hands and pulling her down to sit beside him. Sighing heavily, he explained, "When Olivia was fourteen, and living with her family in Hempstead, she had an affair with

472

a *mexicano* named Ramero. A year later, Maria was born. Olivia's family paid off the father handsomely to disappear with the child.''

"Oh my God—poor Maria!" Emilie gasped. "You mean her father expected a bribe just to do his duty by her?"

Edgar nodded grimly. "Ramero was a ruthless fellow, which was precisely the reason he hung onto Maria. When the child was ten, and times got bad for him, he again sought out Olivia—at Brazos Bend. For almost a year, I did not know that he and Olivia were continuing the affair, while Ramero worked in our stable.''

Emilie slid her hand over Edgar's clenched fist. "How terrible for you. When did you find out about Maria?"

"I always rather wondered about the child, since Olivia took a fancy to her—at first. But as I told you, once Olivia became pregnant, something changed radically—it was almost as if she became demented. She turned on Maria, shrieking at the poor child when she came around. And, as I told you, that was when Olivia cut me off sexually, and informed me about Aaron. I assume she then cut off the affair with Ramero, too, for things soon came to a head.''

"Yes?" Emilie prompted.

"Ramero tried to blackmail Olivia about Maria, and Olivia called his bluff. She dragged Maria into my office—God, I'll never forget how terrified that pathetic child was! Then Olivia bragged, 'Meet my half-breed brat, Edgar!' ''

"How heartless!" Emilie choked.

Edgar nodded dismally. "Anyway, Ramero deserted the child after that, and we soon heard he was killed in Houston. I've my suspicions who did it, too.''

Emilie's eyes grew huge. "You mean Aaron?"

"Aye, according to the rumors circulating at the time, it was Rice who started the knife fight with Ramero. I suppose Aaron never forgot Olivia's affair with the man.''

"You know, considering Olivia's ways, it's a wonder she never had a child by Aaron," Emilie put in.

Edgar shrugged. "I'm not surprised. Rice wasn't much of a man.''

Emilie nodded. "Did Aaron ever show any interest in Maria?"

Edgar shook his head. "Luckily, Maria did not bear any real resemblance to Olivia, and I think Aaron deliberately forgot the child, since she was a painful reminder of his own inadequacies. Besides, Rice was barred from the plantation from the instant I found out about him and Olivia. I would have thrown Olivia out, too, had it not been for her pregnancy.''

"I'm sure it was hell for you. Tell me what happened after your sons were born. Did anything change?"

Edgar sighed, running a hand through his hair. "I made an attempt to be civil with Olivia—for the sake of the twins. Not that she cared. She ignored them from the start. But after a while—" he laughed bitterly— "she no longer ignored me.''

Emilie frowned. "What do you mean?"

"Soon after the babes were born, her lusts rekindled. She no longer had Ramero or Aaron, so she began to tease me, did her best to seduce me. I, however, still found her repugnant. My refusal enraged her, of course. One night she got drunk and dressed in a sluttish black dress, painting her face.

She told me, 'Let me whore for you, Edgar.' '' His fist pounded the settee. "God, I could have killed her that night!"

Emilie gasped. "Is that why you were so angry with me, that time when—"

Edgar nodded sadly. "Aye, I suppose 'tis the reason.'' His features tightened as he continued, "That was undoubtedly the worst fight Olivia and I ever had. I ended up dragging her upstairs and locking her in her room until she slept off her drunkenness. Luckily, I left for the constitutional convention the next day, and then the war began. When I returned. . . . Oh, God, sometimes I wish I'd never come back!''

Studying her husband's anguished face, Emilie said carefully, "David told me what happened when you arrived home."

Edgar's brows shot up. "He did?"

"Yes. But I want to hear it from you."

He breathed heavily. "I came home and found Olivia in bed with David." His hand gripped Emilie's. "Do you know she laughed at my rage? She said, 'What do you expect, Edgar? You've shirked your husbandly duties!' ''

"How cruel!"

"That was when I tried to kill her! David restrained me, knocking me out, giving Olivia just enough time to grab the babes and flee." His fist again pounded the settee, and his voice shook with emotion. "Christ, why did she take them? She never cared a whit for them! She did it to spite me!"

"So you pursued them?"

"Yes. Olivia never did learn to drive a carriage. The team was hysterical—it was raining, thundering—God, when I saw them fly over the bank—" he choked, then continued hoarsely, "I

475

dove in again and again, at one point nearly drowning myself when I got caught in some branches. Finally, I realized it was too late.''

She touched his arm. "I'm so sorry. I can't begin to imagine the torment you and David must have felt afterwards. And what of Maria? Wasn't she there while all of this happened?''

"Yes, she was in the house at the time. But if she heard or saw anything, she never let on." A vein jumped in Edgar's temple and he went on hoarsely, "You know, the hell of it is, I don't to this day know for sure whether or not the twins were actually mine.''

"Oh, my God—you mean because of Ramero? Oh, Edgar!" Emilie embraced her husband, tears of compassion brimming in her eyes. For the first time, she realized how grievously hurt Edgar had been by the events of the past. Wiping her tears with her sleeve, she asked, "Despite all, you loved your sons, didn't you?''

"Aye. I did.''

"I can see now why you shut yourself off after the drownings.''

"It was as if a curtain closed on my life," he concurred. "The guilt of losing the twins was excruciating. That, combined with the deaths of Charles and Amelia, the atrocities I'd seen during the war, drove me to the brink of madness. I sent David away to school—couldn't bear the sight of him, although I realized it wasn't his fault. Maria—I'm afraid I simply ignored the girl, God forgive me.''

"So five years passed—thus?''

He nodded.

"Then you married me.''

"Yes.''

"Why, Edgar?''

476

He smiled, reaching out to touch her cheek with his fingertips, his eyes a curious mixture of sadness and exultation. "Why? I think because I met the love of my life on a rainy hillside during the war, when I kissed the sweetest mouth in memory."

Emilie's jaw dropped. "You remembered?"

"Aye, love, how could I ever forget? You were so determined, so courageous there in Gonzales. And I've been dying to know—did *you* remember me?"

She nodded. "That's why I thought I hated you, at first."

He looked down at her, his heart in his eyes. "Will you ever forgive me for what I did to you during the war?"

She met his gaze evenly. "I forgave you—all—when I realized I loved you. But why *were* you so mean to me at Gonzales?"

"Well, love, I hardly had time to woo you, not with the Santannistas breathing down our throats. You were a trifle hysterical, as you may recall. And I suppose even young as you were, you reminded me somewhat of Olivia. And I hated Olivia."

Emilie's brow knitted. "Then you married me to punish Olivia?"

"Her memory might have influenced me," he conceded. "Perhaps part of me did want to punish her through you. Perhaps part of me wanted to relive the past, making it right this time." He drew her close, pressing his lips against her forehead. "But if you want to know the truth, sweetheart," he whispered, "I think the only thing that kept me alive during those five agonizing years was the memory of a proud, shivering waif who vowed one day to find me and seek her vengeance." His eyes glazed, he asked, "Have you received satisfaction, love?"

She drew back to look up at him, her eyes

brimming with wonder and love. "Not in full, m'lord," she murmured, a catch in her voice, "but I shall."

"How sweet shall be your revenge, love!" he breathed, pulling her closer and pressing his lips against her throat. "Speaking of which. . . ."

Despite her racing heart, Emilie suddenly stiffened at an unsettling thought. "But what about Avis?"

"Avis?" he repeated confusedly, drawing away to look at her.

"When she left, she told me the two of you were having an affair."

He scowled. "Why that old witch! We did have an affair, of sorts, but that was before you ever came. The first few years after the war, I couldn't bear the sight of any woman. When Avis came, she always did have eyes for me. I didn't find her appealing, however. But one night I got drunk—then woke up in bed with her. A brief affair followed, but I soon cut it off, infuriating her."

Yet Emilie frowned. "Tell me what happened the night before Avis left."

Edgar laughed mirthlessly. "She tried to seduce me, and I sent her packing."

"You did? She bragged to me that you went to bed with her that night!"

He leaned over and kissed her cheek. "Nay, my darling. You see, I knew I wanted only you. And you alone could arouse in me the feelings that were dead for so long."

Emilie blinked back tears at his words. "Avis admitted to me that she broke my mother's perfume bottle—out of jealousy."

"Aye, I surmised it was she. In fact, shortly after we discovered our bedroom in a shambles, I warned her that I would hold her personally responsible if there were further incidents.''

Emilie smiled wonderingly. ''And I thought you didn't care!'' She added, ''Maria told me you spoke with her, too, regarding the nursery. The day Camille was born, she admitted to me accidentally starting the fire.''

Edgar shook his head sadly. ''Poor Maria—the way I have neglected that girl has been criminal. But perhaps things can be righted—with your help. She misses you terribly, you know—she and Hallie have been repairing the nursery, and Maria has been training Peligra's filly as a present for the babe.'' Edgar snapped his fingers. ''Oh, I almost forgot— Maria and David plan to marry.''

''Oh, I'm so happy!'' Emilie exclaimed, clapping her hands. Then she frowned. ''But what of David? Did you ever tell him Maria was Olivia's child?''

''No. And I don't think Olivia told him, either. She aimed to seduce the boy, and I doubt she said anything which might have turned him against her. For that matter, as far as I know, Maria has no knowledge of David's affair with Olivia.''

''I see. Do you suppose David and Maria will admit the truth to each other?''

Edgar sighed. ''That must be their decision, Emilie. We'll simply have to hope that if the truth does come out, their love will be strong enough to survive the revelations.'' He leaned over and kissed her mouth. ''Ours has withstood the test, hasn't it, love?''

Emilie kissed him back, her eyes sparkling with adoration. ''Oh, yes, darling!'' But a final suspicion still nagged her, and she asked tremulously, ''Edgar, do I still remind you of Olivia?''

''Nay. You quit reminding me of Olivia shortly after you came to Brazos Bend. You are *you*—unique, the sweetest, the most loving, forgiving creature I've ever known.'' He brushed a curl from her forehead. ''I can't believe that after all I've done, you can say you love me. But I assure you, if you'll come with me to the church, now, there will be no cause for forgiveness—ever. You'll be my queen, love.''

She looked up at him. ''Does that mean we'll quit fighting?''

He chuckled. ''No. I'll always fight with you, just to have the pleasure of making up.'' His eyes grew serious. ''But will you come with me now, love? Will you trust me?''

Emilie nodded, her eyes filling with tears of joy. ''Aye. You've trusted me today, Edgar. And I'll trust you—with the rest of my life!''

Chapter Fifteen

March 17, 1842

Emilie and Edgar stood before Reverend Lundblad in the John Calvin Presbyterian Church. All Emilie's friends from the congregation were there—bonneted ladies in calico, men in Sunday suits, palmetto hats in their laps, children in starched homespuns.

On the front pew sat the Houstons—Margaret looking serene as ever, Sam smiling broadly. Next to them were Jacob and Hallie, holding the two infants.

As silver-haired Betta Lundblad banged out the last chords of "Blessed be the Tie that Binds," she smiled up at her black-robed husband, who began reading the marriage ritual.

Listening, the wildflowers in her hands, Emilie found her mind drifting to the last hour. She had hastily dressed in a beige, lace-trimmed gown, while Edgar had played with tiny Camille on the bed.

She smiled as she remembered the adoration in her husband's eyes when he was reunited with his daughter. To think she had felt a bit shy about dressing in front of him after all these months, only to discover that his eyes would not leave Camille! He

481

had kissed the babe again and again, causing Cammie to squeal gleefully. He had spoken incessantly of her beauty, her utter perfection.

When Emilie was about finished dressing, she had heard him chuckle, "And I've put my mark on her, after all."

Emilie remembered hurrying to the bed, asking what he meant. "The eyes," he had laughed. "She's going to have my eyes. Surely you must have noticed, for Margaret Houston told me in her last letter!"

Examining the infant closely, Emilie had laughed her own astonishment. "Why Edgar, you're right! Her eyes are filled with tiny brown flecks! Seeing her every day as I do, I hadn't noticed the change. Oh, she'll be beautiful—for I *do* love your eyes, Edgar!"

Emilie felt her face heating as she remembered what happened next—Edgar, laughing, pulling her onto the bed and kissing her until she was breathless. . . .

She felt her hand being squeezed, now, and turned, saw the tender amusement in Edgar's gaze as he winked at her. The rogue—he knew exactly what she was thinking!

Smiling serenely, Emilie turned her attention to Reverend Lundblad. This time, no one would have to prompt her. She would be ready, when the moment came, to say her vows and give her heart away.

"Esperanza assured me she was the most beautiful babe in all Houston—and may I now add, in all Texas as well!" Sam Houston exclaimed, gazing admiringly at tiny Camille Ashland, who was fast asleep in Margaret's arms.

As the foursome visited in the parlor of Granny's

house, Emilie stood, took cups of tea to the two men, who sat at the table.

"Thank you, my dear," Houston told her as he took his cup. Turning to Edgar, he continued, "Well, Ashland, now that your personal situation is resolved, will you tell your wife of the matter we discussed last night?"

Edgar Ashland pulled out the chair next to him. Taking Emilie's hand, he smiled and said, "Sit down, my dear."

Emilie sat down next to her husband, her eyes quizzical.

"Emilie, how would you like to live for a time in Washington?" Edgar asked.

Emilie's finely arched brows flew up as she looked from one man to the other.

Sam Houston leaned forward, lacing his fingers atop the table. "I hate to distress you, my dear, on this joyous anniversary day, but our republic is in grave danger." His eagle-like eyes glowing intently, he continued, "I'm afraid Santa Anna's army has again invaded us. A week ago, they captured San Antonio and Goliad."

"Good heavens!" Emilie gasped.

"Aye, it's quite distressing," Houston concurred solemnly. "I dispatched the army before I left the capital last week." He looked worriedly at his wife. "I'm only here to get Margaret packed—I'm putting her on a ship in Galveston tomorrow."

Emilie's gaze flew to Margaret, who sat in the rocker across the room from them. "Sam thought it best I go home to Mobile until the situation cools," Margaret whispered, stroking Cammie's back.

"I'm sure our brave boys will push the Mexicans back across the border," Houston hastily added, "but the fact is, we'll be facing the threat of Mexican raids until we have the protection statehood will afford us.''

"Sam wants me to lobby for him," Edgar put in, scrutinizing Emilie's face, as if to read her feelings.

"Edgar's the perfect candidate to get some action in Washington," Houston assured Emilie, "albeit it be secretly, until the slavery issue dies down and the time is ripe to resubmit out statehood petition.''

Edgar took Emilie's hand. "Obviously, Sam desperately needs help. But your needs—and the babe's—come first with me. What do you think, darling?''

Emilie looked at her husband adoringly. "I think I'm going to love Washington.''

"Amazing!" Edgar breathed, watching tiny Camille nurse at her mother's breast.

Emilie giggled. "That's the tenth time you've said 'Amazing!' in so many minutes! Tonight, there must be thousands of women around the world, nursing their babes as I am.''

Edgar stood next to the bed, unbuttoning his shirt. "Aye, but none of them are as special—or as beautiful—as *my* wife and *my* baby.''

Emilie smiled. "Oh, look, Edgar, she's fallen fast asleep!" she whispered. "Her tiny mouth is still open! Will you take her out to the parlor?''

Edgar frowned as he removed his shirt. "Will she be all right out there?''

Emilie nodded. "She and Little Jacob usually spend the night out there. They like each other's company.''

Edgar stepped forward, gently taking the blanket-wrapped babe from Emilie. He cradled Camille against his chest, leaned over and kissed her cheek. "Oh, little one, your skin is heaven! How would you like to go on very long journey—on a big ship?''

Watching Edgar leave the room with Camille, Emilie smiled as she buttoned her nightgown. She went to the dresser, started brushing her hair. The radiant, silky curls fell in soft waves about her face and shoulders.

Moments later, the hairbrush was taken from her hand, and she saw her husband's reflection in the mirror above her. Their eyes met as he gently ran the brush through her blonde tresses. "Your hair is spun gold, love," he whispered reverently.

He put the brush down. She turned, ran her hand over the muscles on his chest. His eyes darkened perceptibly.

"Should I leave the door open—for the babe?" he asked.

"No—close it. She has a healthy set of lungs."

He smiled, moved off and closed the door. As he began removing his trousers, Emilie felt herself trembling with expectation, like a nervous bride. In a sense, she was a bride, she decided, for their love had been truly affirmed for the first time, at the church today. She averted her gaze as he got into the bed, picking up the hairbrush again.

"So this is the bed you slept in as a virgin," he remarked.

"Aye—I must apologize—it's a small bed," she replied inanely.

"Nay, love, it's too large."

She dropped the hairbrush.

"Emilie, come here."

Her heart fluttering, she reached for the lamp.

"Please don't," he whispered.

She turned, eyeing him quizzically.

"Don't extinguish the lamp," he said, extending his hand towards her. "I want to feast my eyes on you."

"Yes, m'lord," she murmured. She moved toward him, a flush heating her body as she removed her nightgown and threw it on the floor. "Is this what you wanted? Shall I make love to you, sir?"

He groaned and pulled her down beside him on the bed, kissing her mouth, her eyes, her neck. "Oh, Christ, Emmie, you're beautiful!"

They devoured each other on the narrow bed. Edgar aroused every inch of his wife with his hands and mouth, while Emilie responded in kind, kissing him hungrily, running her tongue over his body. The moment came when Emilie was sure she would lose her mind if he did not take her, but he admonished, "Patience, love," as his lips slowly explored her most secret places, prolonging the glorious anticipation.

At last she could stand no more, and she perched above him, sighing in ecstasy as she took him deeply inside her. She paused to savor the exquisite rapture, the feel of him within her—where he belonged—after the long months of alienation.

Just that one moment would have been enough— to gaze into his eyes and see the love there, to be filled by him, filled to the core! She could have spent eternity that way!

But their passion soon demanded more, and they moved together towards fulfillment, his hands boldly caressing her body, her hair streaming in golden splendor about his face. Emilie left all inhibition behind, rolling her hips against his thrusting, making him cry out ecstatically, "Yes! Yes!"

Their movements grew wild with abandon as their lovemaking crested. When they arrived at the pinnacle, he moved upright, kissing her violently as he pulled her body downward, possessing her utterly.

He poured himself into her and she lost herself in him. They fell back, at peace, breathing endearments into each other's ears. . . .

Later, Emilie whispered, "What better beginning for a new life?"

"Aye," Edgar agreed. "And it's *only* the beginning, love, of a long, beautiful life, and a long, beautiful night!"

Epilogue

April 21, 1842

Emilie Ashland stood at the porthole, gazing at the ebony waters of the Brazos River. She, Edgar and Camille had been on the *Belle of the Republic* for three days, as the steamer journeyed downstream for Galveston. There, they would catch a ship bound for Washington, D.C.

The river looked peaceful tonight, at rest, Emilie noted. The malevolence she had once felt welling from its depths seemed gone now. Gone, like the nightmares—the visions of fire and water and demons—which haunted her no longer.

Emilie turned from the porthole and checked on her daughter. Camille was fast asleep in her cradle in the corner of the room, her lips fastened on a small fist.

Emilie kissed the babe, then went to the bed and pulled down the covers. She sat down and unbuttoned the front of her dress, thinking of the events of the past few weeks.

When they arrived home at Brazos Bend, they heard with relief the news that the Texan army had pushed the Mexicans back across the border. The weeks following contained a whirlwind of activities, as Emilie helped Maria prepare for her wedding with David.

Emilie remembered her reunion with Maria in the parlor of Brazos Bend, when she had surprised the Mexican girl by presenting her with a guitar she and Edgar had purchased in Houston.

"Oh, Emilie, you remembered that I want to learn to play *la guitara!*" Maria had exclaimed with tears in her eyes, as she hugged Emilie.

"I'm sure your *mexicano* friends will be delighted to teach you to play," Emilie replied, her own voice breaking.

It was an emotional moment for both women as Emilie told Maria, "Edgar explained to me about you and Olivia—everything. Oh, Maria, if only I had known!"

"I'm glad you know, Emilie. I have needed to share that with a friend."

Maria went on to explain how Olivia had befriended her when the girl first came to Brazos Bend, only to turn upon her later. "The señora was fickle," Maria explained. "She played with me for a time, as she would with a toy. But when she found out she was with child, she went *loco,* telling me Señor Edgar would cast me out when her *bebé* was born."

"No wonder you were always afraid of being turned away!" Emilie commiserated. "How you must have suffered then! Edgar told me what Olivia did—dragging you in to him and—"

"And calling me her half-breed brat," Maria finished bitterly. "It was not until that day that I found out she was actually my mother. Soon afterwards, she died, and I felt safer for a time. But when you came, Emilie, you reminded me of her, and all

489

the hatred boiled inside me again. You see, it was always her I really hated, never you. When I found out you were *encinta,* I was afraid—"

"Afraid history would repeat itself," Emilie supplied.

"Sí. In fact, the doll I mutilated was one Señora Olivia gave me years before. I wanted to frighten you away because I feared the child would take all Señor Edgar's attentions. I wanted his love—not as you think, but—"

"I understand. You wanted—and needed—a father. Maria, please remember that Edgar loves you as a daughter, and very much wants to make up for neglecting you before. His staying to himself all those years had nothing to do with you. It was—"

"Señora Olivia."

"Yes. Now you must forget the past, and dream only of your future happiness with David."

"David does not know of any of this," Maria had put in worriedly.

"Perhaps that's for the best. . . ."

Was it for the best? Emilie now wondered. Only time would tell. But if David and Maria's joyous wedding at Washington-on-the-Brazos were any indication, the two would share a very happy future. Even though a number of the townfolk declined to attend the mixed wedding, David and Maria hardly noticed, as they ecstatically repeated their vows before Pastor Fritz.

Before Edgar and Emilie left Washington-on-the-Brazos, Edgar instructed David in overseeing the plantation during their absence, since they might be gone a year or more. During the interim, David planned to begin building his *hacienda,* and to continue his cattle business, with Don Lorenzo's help.

Emilie got up from the bed and went to her trunk. Placing her carefully folded dress inside it, she took out a filmy nightgown. As the soft folds of batiste settled about her, she heard the door open, turned.

Her husband came in, grinning. "Miss me, darling?" he asked as he walked over, pulling her into his arms.

She looked up at his rakishly handsome face—the dark, devastating eyes, the straight, classic nose, the sensual mouth beneath the mustache. Would her breath always catch in her throat when she saw him? Would she ever believe he was truly hers? God, how she loved him!

She stood on tiptoe, kissed him. "Yes, I missed you." She wrinkled her nose. "You smell like tobacco and taste like brandy."

He chuckled. "I divested Captain Porter of a handsome sum at the card table this evening, love." His arms tightened about her. "Complaining?"

Her lower lip was petulant, but a smile tugged at the corners of her mouth. "Only that you were there—instead of here with me."

He grinned. "My apologies, sweet, but I've already refused the good captain for two nights in a row," He winked. "Besides, if I stayed here with you all the time, my poor daughter would starve."

Emilie giggled, curling her arms around his neck. "She's not starving, now—but I am."

She pulled his mouth down to hers, kissed him passionately, thrusting her tongue inside his mouth.

"Jesus!" he breathed. "What have I unleashed?" Gazing down at her lovingly, he asked, "Do you know what today is, love?"

"San Jacinto Day?"

He nodded, tucking her head beneath his chin as he stroked her long, silky hair. "I used to get roaring drunk this day each year—remembering the battle. But now I can cast aside my bitterness, knowing that hope was also born on that day, hope for the Texas I have come to love. I have neglected her shamefully in the past, as I have neglected you—''

Emilie drew back, her crystal blue eyes sparkling. "But now you shall serve Texas."

"Aye," he agreed gravely. "Now I have so much—because I have you!"

Suddenly, he swatted her soundly on the derriere. "Must you persist in wearing clothes to bed, woman?"

She laughed as his impatient hands gathered her nightgown, pulled it over her head. Her heart raced and she felt a flush spreading across her body.

He chuckled. "Will you always blush when I undress you, love?"

"Probably," she conceded.

He swept her off her feet, carried her to the bed. "That's what I love about you," he said as he laid her down. "You're half innocent maid, half fiery vixen."

She pulled up the sheet, looked up at him with breathless anticipation.

He gazed down at her with dark, adoring eyes as he unbuttoned his shirt. "How can I thank you for the new life you have given me?" he asked, his voice thick with emotion. "I feel—reborn."

She nodded. "So do I, darling."

He unbuckled his belt, a smile tugging at his lips. "And now, madam, I believe you promised me a son within the year, so we'd best be about it."

She giggled. "Do you have your heart set on a boy?"

"Of course!" he said with mock outrage. He glanced lovingly at Camille's cradle, then back to

Emilie. "Or a girl," he added, grinning.

He rubbed his jaw thoughtfully. "Come to think of it, another girl would be lovely. Then I'd have an excuse to make love to you all the more frequently and vigorously the next time!"

She looked up at him with a smile that came straight from her heart. "Will you ever need an excuse?"

"No!" he whispered vehemently, throwing back the sheet. "Never, my love!"

BESTSELLING ROMANCES BY JANELLE TAYLOR

THE BEST IN HISTORICAL ROMANCE

PASSION'S RAPTURE   (912, $3.50)
by Penelope Neri
Through a series of misfortunes, an English beauty becomes the
captive of the very man who ruined her life. By day she rages
against her imprisonment—but by night, she's in passion's thrall!

JASMINE PARADISE   (1170, $3.75)
by Penelope Neri
When Heath sets his eyes on the lovely Sarah, the beauty of the
tropics pales in comparison. And he's soon intoxicated with the
honeyed nectar of her full lips. Together, they explore the paradise
. . . of love.

SILKEN RAPTURE   (1172, $3.50)
by Cassie Edwards
Young, sultry Glenda was innocent of love when she met handsome Read deBaulieu. For two days they revelled in fiery desire
only to part—and then learn they were hopelessly bound in a web
of SILKEN RAPTURE.

FORBIDDEN EMBRACE   (1105, $3.50)
by Cassie Edwards
Serena was a Yankee nurse and Wesley was a Confederate soldier.
And Serena knew it was wrong—but Wesley was a master of temp-
tation. Tomorrow he would be gone and she would be left with
only memories of their FORBIDDEN EMBRACE.

PORTRAIT OF DESIRE   (1003, $3.50)
by Cassie Edwards
As Nicholas's brush stroked the lines of Jennifer's full, sensuous
mouth and the curves of her soft, feminine shape, he came to feel
that he was touching every part of her that he painted. Soon, lips
sought lips, heart sought heart, and they came together in a wild
storm of passion. . . .

*Available wherever paperbacks are sold, or order direct from the
Publisher. Send cover price plus 50¢ per copy for mailing and
handling to Zebra Books, 475 Park Avenue South, New York,
N.Y. 10016. DO NOT SEND CASH.*

EXCITING BESTSELLERS FROM ZEBRA

PASSION'S REIGN by Karen Harper   (1177, $3.95)

Golden-haired Mary Bullen was wealthy, lovely and refined—
and lusty King Henry VIII's prize gem! But her passion for the
handsome Lord William Stafford put her at odds with the
Royal Court. Mary and Stafford lived by a lovers' vow: one day
they would be ruled by only the crown of PASSION'S REIGN.

HEIRLOOM by Eleanora Brownleigh   (1200, $3.95)

The surge of desire Thea felt for Charles was powerful enough
to convince her that, even though they were strangers and
their marriage was a fake, fate was playing a most subtle trick
on them both: Were they on a mission for President Teddy
Roosevelt—or on a crusade to realize their own passionate
desire?

LOVESTONE by Deanna James   (1202, $3.50)

After just one night of torrid passion and tender need, the dark-
haired, rugged lord could not deny that Moira, with her
precious beauty, was born to be a princess. But how could he
grant her freedom when he himself was a prisoner of her love?

DEBORAH'S LEGACY by Stephen Marlowe   (1153, $3.75)

Deborah was young and innocent. Benton was worldly and
experienced. And while the world rumbled with the thunder of
battle, together they rose on a whirlwind of passion—daring
fate, fear and fury to keep them apart!

*Available wherever paperbacks are sold, or order direct from the
Publisher. Send cover price plus 50¢ per copy for mailing and
handling to Zebra Books, 475 Park Avenue South, New York,
N.Y. 10016 DO NOT SEND CASH.*